WOMEN ～～～ ～～ OF THE ～ ～～～ FUTURE:

The Female Main Character in Science Fiction

by
BETTY KING

The Scarecrow Press, Inc.
Metuchen, N.J., & London
1984

Library of Congress Cataloging in Publication Data

King, Betty, 1948-
    Women of the future.

    Bibliography: p.
    Includes indexes.
        1.   Science fiction, American--History and criticism--
Addresses, essays, lectures.   2.   Science fiction, Eng-
lish--History and criticism--Addresses, essays, lectures.
3.   Women in literature--Addresses, essays, lectures.
4.   Science fiction, American--Bibliography.   5.   Science
fiction, English--Bibliography.   6.   Women--Fiction--Bib-
liography.   I.   Title.
PS374. S35K44   1984   813'. 0876'09352042   83-20130
ISBN 0-8108-1664-4

CONTENTS

PREFACE

Science fiction has become an increasingly popular genre for fiction by and/or about women. Perhaps this is due, in part, to the fact that our present world cultures allow women so limited an opportunity for courage, bravery, strength, and command. Those qualities are still, for the most part, forbidden to women--except within the realm of a projected (future or alternative) universe: a remote future or galaxy where equality, even superiority is possible for women! In science fiction these whole women can be safely allowed full powers. There they can react with men who recognize them as equal, worth listening to, dependable, whole. There even men can be allowed to feel, to love, to cry. Science fiction is a door into a world in which men and women can be written about as whole beings, each with needs, each with shortcomings, each with strengths.

However, science fiction (sf) has not always presented whole men and women. In fact, it is still debated whether it really achieves that goal now. Regardless, what becomes obvious when scanning a variety of sf works from the nineteenth and twentieth centuries is that a gradual evolution has taken place from a time when men were most frequently presented as logical, dependable, strong, serious and protective, and women, when allowed in the story at all, were the perfect foil: emotional, unreliable, weak, frivolous, and in need of protection.

Today, due to this gradual evolution in science fiction writing, there are many female characters who portray complete, well-rounded humans. The key now seems to be that there are as many options as there are women. Science fiction, more than any other medium, points out by its sheer vastness of diversity, that women have as many choices, as many possibilities of personal success, as many directions of interest as there are women. Each of us, men included, would benefit by synthesizing our own role models. Science fiction, as it is today, can help us piece together a composite of attractive characteristics in the creation of our own "most wonderful person in the world"--ourselves.

It is part of my purpose here to set down at least some of this evolution, to capture in synopsis form the maturing of women in sf into whole humans, into three-dimensional characters. (Ironically, as an offshoot of this process, men characters usually become whole beings also.) The primary aim of this book, however, is that it be used both as a pedagogical tool--a reference book tailored for use by teachers--and as a guide to readers of sf in their efforts to locate characters about whom they want to read. In keeping with this aim and to ensure reasonably easy access to the works listed here, I have only included sf works that are or have been available in book form: novels plus collections and anthologies of short stories and novellas.

My motive in writing this book is quite selfish in its origin. When I was avidly searching for books and stories with women main characters, I realized that there was no resource available that would be of help to me in my search. Often after I had purchased a book, I would discover that the character, though a main character by definition, was subservient, fearful, easily led or seduced, and generally speaking not a character I was interested in reading about. When rape occurred, it was often portrayed as a male fantasy fulfillment rather than as the act of violence it is in reality. I was searching for female role models and was not at all interested in male sexual fantasies. My reading of books with risk-taking, adventure-seeking women characters was often unhappily punctuated with a work about a character I couldn't possibly respect, much less wish to emulate. I gradually came to realize that I could not be the only person floundering around in the sf section of bookstores in search of women characters I could actually admire. That realization led to the idea for this reference book.

This self-selection tool, in spite of being limited to works of sf available in bookstores and libraries, will allow the reader to gain some perspective on women in sf. If, in the process, we should discover a much-needed role model or two, let us be grateful that at least in sf women are now allowed full expression.

I have tried to be as accurate as possible in my

research; however, I would appreciate being corrected on any faulty information. Also, as women sf authors and the evolution of the woman character in sf are of continuing interest to me, I would be most grateful to anyone who has additional authors and titles for me to "discover." I don't claim to be an expert--not yet anyway! So please keep me informed and educated.

And happy reading!

ACKNOWLEDGMENTS

I owe thanks to many people:

to Jeanne Graybill-Molineaux and Jerri O'Neil for helping me care about who I am--a woman.

to Dan Cogburn, Diana Harryman, Myra Grzebyk, Pat Ancinec, and Shari Sitko for listening to my ideas and for encouraging me.

to James E. Miles for encouragement when I needed it the most.

to Gary Kuris for his invaluable editorial hints and suggestions which made everything fall into place.

to Tony Cannon, Rickey Sheppard, Gary Michael Suiter, Melody Natcher and Martha Jo Lyne, for their encouragement during the grind of the last six months of writing.

and most of all to my parents, Frank and Lucile King, for their support and encouragement during one of the most exciting and challenging times of my life.

INTRODUCTION

Debate still prevails on what the first science fiction (sf) book actually was. Part of this debate stems from a very loose definition of what criteria a story must meet to be called sf. This debate has been well ventilated in other books and will not be seriously discussed here. As Peter Nicholls wrote under "History of SF" in The Science Fiction Encyclopedia, "It would be relatively simple to recount the history of sf if we could say with conviction exactly what sf was, but we cannot...." He added, "The entire history of literary genres shows that the more accurate the labelling procedure becomes, the tighter the straitjacket so produced, and the greater the likelihood that rigour will bring about stasis and final decay, with writers producing only increasingly feeble imitations of what has gone before."

Seen in this light, the unsuccessful labeling of the genre has indeed been fortunate for sf; however, it has made tracing the history of sf next to impossible. Some trace sf back to The Republic of Plato, or to Thomas More's Utopia. Others trace it back to Mary Shelley's Frankenstein, and at least one, notably Carl Sagan in Cosmos (New York: Random House, 1980), names Johannes Kepler's Somnium as "one of the first works of science fiction." Even Leonardo da Vinci left notes for a short sf novel. Those notes have been compiled into a book, The Deluge, which has been "edited" by Robert Payne (New York: Lion Books, 1954).

Most sources tend to name Mary Shelley as the mother or pioneer of sf and H. G. Wells as the father or settler. The subject of this book, however, is not who gave birth to the genre of sf or what the first book or story was. The subject of this volume is women characters in sf. Though I do not pretend in this book to draw specific conclusions about the changes in the women main characters in sf, the reader

will probably gain, along the way, a sense of the development and maturation of the female character in sf from a
one-dimensional stick figure included as an afterthought or
as a reward for the hero, to a three-dimensional, thinking,
feeling, action-oriented individual who is the main character of the story.

Women characters in sf before the 1900s were minor
ones, "a compulsory appendage" as the Swedish author Sam
J. Lundwall calls them in his book Science Fiction: What
It's All About. (First published in Sweden in 1969, this book
was published in English in 1971 by Ace Books.) Women
were typically portrayed as helpless, weak, easily frightened,
and angelic; or, in contrast, they were witch-like, mothering
or child-like, indecisive or sly and manipulative, coy, and
never, never had sexual attractions or desires of their own.
Women were portrayed as lacking in that adventuresome
spirit or professionalism that was needed in a sf hero. Lundwall once more hits home when he writes, "The classic function of the woman, as depicted in gaudy colors on the covers
of the pulp magazines, was to follow the hero as a kind of
reverentially listening Dr. Watson." Most were incidental to
the story, there to be saved, damned, or married as a reward or punishment, or as a contrast to the fearless adventurous male hero.

Lundwall devotes a good portion of one chapter to the
subject of woman's place in sf. He begins, "Science fiction
is on the whole a very progressive literature when it comes
to freedom and equality, but there are things in the field
that can make even the most narrow-minded prelate look like
a veritable light-bearer. Foremost among these dark spots
stands Woman." He adds, "In a world where women at last
are beginning to be recognized as human beings, science fiction still clings to the views of the last century. If a daring
member of one of the current women's liberation movements
stepped out into the men's world of the future, she'd probably
be shot on sight." Certainly not a very pretty picture of sf,
but thankfully in the years since that was written, sf has
taken enormous strides not only in updating its female characters, but also in projecting future female heroes. It is
probable that this is due in part to the increase in female
sf writers over the years.

Before 1900, almost all sf writers, except for Mary
Shelley, were male and wrote exclusively from a male viewpoint. It wasn't until the twentieth century that an increasing

number of women began to get their sf published.   Even then, many used male pseudonyms and wrote from a male point of view.   Andre Norton (Alice Mary Norton, now legally Andre Alice Norton) and James Tiptree, Jr. (Alice Sheldon) are two of the more widely known female sf authors who use male pen names.   Some used initials, like C(atherine) L(ucille) Moore.

However they managed to become published, women were more or less forced to write from a male point of view. When Tiptree chose to occasionally write about a female main character, suspicion began to grow about the sex of the author.   In one humorous preface, Roger Silverberg says of James Tiptree, Jr., "It has been suggested that Tiptree is female, a theory that I find absurd, for there is to me something ineluctably masculine about Tiptree's writing.   I don't think the novels of Jane Austen could have been written by a man nor the stories of Ernest Hemingway by a woman, and in the same way I believe the author of the James Tiptree stories is male." In a later preface to the same book, Silverberg, after discovering that Tiptree was a woman, maturely admitted his mistake and wrote, "She fooled me beautifully, along with everyone else, and called into question the entire notion of what is 'masculine' or 'feminine' in fiction" (from the introduction to James Tiptree's Warm Worlds and Otherwise, Ballantine Books, 1975).

Much of the prejudice against female sf authors and main characters has dissipated.   A fact not to be denied is that sf is still predominately written by male authors and about male heroes; however, an ever-increasing number of female writers and main characters may soon turn that tide. In addition, male writers of sf are writing about women characters more than ever before, and many take pride in their portrayal of their female characters.

Along with a gradual increase in the number of female heroes has come a new sexual openness and exploration in sf. Lundwall, writing about sexuality in sf in Science Fiction: What It's All About, rightfully lambastes the United States for "its dread of sexuality."   He claims that "most science fiction is written in the U.S.A., and the U.S.A. is perhaps the most puritanical country in the world."   But fortunately for women, men, and sf as a whole, that is changing gradually.   More and more female heroes are appearing, and many are sexually active.   The greater numbers of female authors being published (as well as some male authors) are

fearlessly providing readers with heterosexual, homosexual,
and bisexual female heroes, presented in a non-pornographic,
non-exploitive fashion and with dignity. Publishers are beginning to recognize that most sf readers do not object to
sex in their sf. It would seem that, at long last, sf is growing up.

Perhaps the increase in the number of female protagonists came about as it became more obvious that there
was a greater following of female readers, or because women
have entered more and more diverse and professional career
fields, or because more women were writing sf and being
published. Whatever the cause, female main characters are
increasing in number and in their spirit of adventure--quite
a change from the beginnings of sf.

Although there are some sf writers who still insist on
viewing women in a traditional, stereotypical manner, there
are many writers now being published who are more fully
exploring the possibilities of the female human experience
through the realm of the sf genre. Sf has always been the
ideal genre for this exploration because of the experimental
and speculative nature of its approach, but this exploration
has, in the past, been directed primarily towards space,
other life forms, telepathy, and other dimensions rather than
the exploration of the human potential.

In her article "What Can a Heroine Do? or Why Women
Can't Write" (in Images of Women in Fiction--Feminist Perspectives, ed. by Susan Koppelman Cornillon, Bowling Green
University Popular Press, Bowling Green, OH), Joanna Russ
writes that sf is one of the very few genres in which women
characters can be portrayed as whole people, free of myths
surrounding gender roles. Of fiction as a whole, Russ writes,
"What myths, what plots, what actions are available to a female protagonist? Very few." Of sf, she writes, "The
myths of science fiction run along the lines of exploring a
new world conceptually (not necessarily physically), creating
needed physical or social machinery, assessing the conse-
quences of technological or other changes, and so on. These
are not stories about men qua Man and women qua Woman;
they are myths of human intelligence and human adaptability."

It is my belief that the potential freedom sf has from
gender role myths, as Russ calls them, is precisely the reason why sf is the ideal genre for women to explore new self-
concepts, to expand their view in literature of women as

"human" first and "female" second, to create much-needed
composite models of whole women with characteristics that
they can admire and emulate.   It is also my belief that sf
writers are finally accepting the challenge to ignore the gender role myths of which Russ wrote, and to strike out into
uncharted territory--the psychological and the physical potential of the female of the human species.

At last, writers of science fiction are allowing the
female of the human species to explore the full heights and
depths of her potential.   No longer are her portrayals rele-
gated to a narrow band within which she is seen only as she
relates to man, in which she must be mother, possessed object, or slut (if allowed sexuality) or witch, amazon, or queen
(if cold and unyielding to men).   Women characters in sf are
now often given the opportunity to exist outside the orb of a
man's existence and frequently are recognized as having the
right to exist for their own sakes, thinking and functioning
independently, having adventures and responsibilities, making
decisions that not only affect themselves, but change the
world.

Some have expressed the opinion that sf may die out,
perhaps because they think everything has been said that can
be said by sf in at least a dozen ways, or perhaps because
book publications and sales have been dropping for several
years now.   (It should be kept in mind, though, that overall,
the number of sf book publications has tripled in the last
decade!)   In my opinion, however, sf is merely growing into
a new era, as has happened in the past.   Sf today has all
the earmarks of evolving into a fictional form which explores
both the female and the male human potential.   If we are to
mature as a species into responsible, farsighted planners for
the future and protectors of our world, such an exploration
will not only be helpful, but necessary.

The purpose of this book is to provide readers of sf
with a self-selection guide in their search for works with
women main characters (usually protagonists) and to offer
teachers a pedagogical tool for women's studies, sf studies,
or other types of classes in which the inclusion of women
main characters in sf is desirable.   A side benefit of this
work may well be that readers of sf can gain from this volume some perspective on the evolution of the woman character
in sf.   Readers should keep in mind, however, that the exclusion from this book of works appearing to date only in sf
magazine form makes this volume less than comprehensive

and makes it inappropriate for use by sf researchers desiring to derive statistical data from it.   For the same reason,
the index of characteristics should not be used for drawing
specific all-inclusive conclusions about women characters in
sf for statistical data; the index is provided as an aid to people desiring to read about a particular type of character (for
example, a 30- to 40-year-old woman character with black
hair and a scarred face who is a spaceship pilot).   Because
this work is a tool and not a comprehensive compilation, no
accurate conclusions could be drawn about all sf with women
main characters based on this book or its index of characteristics.

     The first chapter of this book covers the period be-
tween 1818 (the date of the first publication of Mary Shelley's
Frankenstein) through 1929.   The approach in that chapter is
dissimilar to those that follow in that it is not structured to
reflect physical or mental/emotional characteristics as are
the subsequent chapters, but to historically trace women main,
secondary and minor characters in sf through a period of
gradual change.   The more relaxed structure of the first
chapter is used to facilitate the description of works in which
women characters played roles varying in importance.   This
inclusion of secondary and minor characters is necessary in
order to explore the position female characters have held in
sf through the years.   Subsequent chapters cover a decade
each, starting with the 1930s.   (The exception is the 1980s
chapter, which includes only three years.)   In these later
chapters, I have attempted to include only works with women
protagonists, or main characters.   Each of these chapters
ends with an additional reading list of works with women main
characters.

     The aim here is to provide, in one volume, a more
complete listing of sf with women as principal characters
than has been available to date.   George Fergus in "A Check-
list of SF Novels with Female Protagonists" (Extrapolation,
Vol. 18, No. 1, December 1976) provided readers searching
for women characters in sf with a starting place.   His check-
list contained a total of sixty-four brief annotations, a figure
which now seems small when considering the dramatic increase of works fitting that description since 1976.   In addition, Fergus considered in his list only novels.   Collections
and anthologies of short stories, novellas, and novelettes
containing women main characters were not considered.   As
these forms are frequently more popular, both with teachers
and sf readers, the compilation of stories, novellas, and

novelettes provided here should prove useful and offer readers a more accurate perspective on women main characters in sf than could the perusal of just novels.

For the purposes of this book I have defined main, secondary, and minor characters as follows:

> Main Character: The story begins, continues, and ends with the words and actions (but not necessarily the thoughts) of this character. (Note that this character might not be the viewpoint character or narrator.)

> Secondary Character: The actions and words of this character are not the main focus of the book, although some character in this position is necessary.

> Minor Character: This character appears briefly or intermittently and is expendable in the story.

This definition of main character makes allowances for sf in which two or more characters are present and active throughout the work, but in which the woman character is not the viewpoint character. Secondary and minor characters are rarely mentioned outside of the first chapter.

It must be kept in mind while reading the bulk of this book that most of the main characters are not female heroes, but heroines. A main character is not synonymous with a heroic character. For our purposes here, "hero," as defined in Webster's New Collegiate Dictionary, means "one that shows great courage," and/or "an illustrious warrior." (Unfortunately, even "warrior" is sexist, denoting the male soldier only; however, here I intend it to be used for female soldiers also.) My decision to use the word "hero" when referring to some of the female protagonists in sf hinged on the fact that the word "heroine" describes a woman character who is only in the work to be an assistant to a hero, there to be won and/or saved by him. The connotation of the word "heroine" in literature has become loaded with the message that the character is never independent of male control or influence and is quite often merely a distant secondary or minor character. At her worst, the heroine is merely an object, a reward to the hero, and because she plays the admiring audience of the male hero, she has no real part in the action at all.

I am not alone in differentiating between "hero" and "heroine" when referring to women characters. Susan Koppelman Cornillon, in her introduction to Images of Women in Fiction--Feminist Perspectives, makes clear distinctions between "The Woman as Hero" and "The Woman as Heroine." (In fact, these titles constitute two of the four divisions of her book, the other two titles being "The Invisible Woman" and "Feminist Aesthetics.") Science fiction is a literature in which a woman character can be allowed the alternative of independent action and thought, where she has a chance to be heroic without leaning on a male character; however, that isn't always the way she is portrayed. Because of that, some distinction between hero and heroine is necessary.

Deciding which fiction to include or exclude on the basis of whether it actually qualifies as sf has been a major chore. The term "science fiction" will not be formally defined here. That task has been tackled at length and with varying results by almost everyone who has ever written about sf. (For 68 definitions of sf, see Roger C. Schlobin's "Definitions of Science Fiction and Fantasy" in The Science Fiction Reference Book, ed. by Marshall B. Tymn, Starmont House, 1981.) One definition which is particularly interesting is the one given by Alice Laurance in the preface to Cassandra Rising (Doubleday, 1978). There she distinguishes sf as "fiction which takes place elsewhere, elsewhen or elsehow." However, what criteria a work must meet to be called sf will not be explored here. Although it is agreed upon by many writers and readers of sf and fantasy that publishers frequently market these genres under the wrong category, sf will be defined in this book as any work which is marketed as sf by the publisher. In the case of older works that were not marketed as sf at the time, I have loosely defined sf as a work dealing with any of the following: a future time; space or time travel; or speculation on science, scientists, or scientific discoveries. An addition to these definitions is that any work which is considered sf by two or more of the reference sources listed in the Bibliography at the end of this book will also be considered to be sf here.

Along with the sf works, some few sword-and-sorcery sf (usually marketed as fantasy) have been included in some chapters, primarily because of their singularly powerful impact on sf readers. For example, the sword-and-sorcery sf of C. L. Moore, who was one of the first writers to introduce readers to amazon-type female main characters (Jirel of Joiry), preceded the introduction of the bulk of other ad-

venture-seeking women main characters in sf. Though the
amazons cannot usually be considered the average woman
dealing with average problems, the popularity of the use of
the female main character in sword-and-sorcery sf continues
today. Some feel that the amazons are the antithesis of real
heroes and that they are just women trying to be men in
strength, in their ability to coldly kill and fight skillfully,
and in their adventuresome approach to life. This can be
disputed, however, by reading about the amazons in all their
variety as presented in editor Jessica Amanda Salmonson's
Amazons! and Amazons II (Daw Books, 1979 and 1982 respectively). The characters contained in the stories in these
two books are not stereotypical of the amazon image gained
over the years, and the anthologies are delightful reading.
Salmonson's own sword-and-sorcery hero, Tomoe Gozen, is
a fascinating Oriental warrior. (Tomoe Gozen, Ace Books,
1981, and The Golden Naginata, Ace Books, 1982, are the
first two in the series.) Appendix C lists a number of works
containing amazon women and can be found at the end of this
book.

As the purpose of this work is to provide readers
with synopses and reading lists of books that are easily ac-
cessible in libraries and book stores, works contained only
in sf magazine form have been excluded here. This decision
was made to ensure that readers could easily locate the items
listed. Because sf magazines are not as easy to locate as
books and are generally unavailable in school and public libraries, fiction contained only in magazine form has been
excluded from this book.

I have been told that the decision to exclude works
that are available only in sf magazine form performs a great
disservice to researchers in the field since that exclusion
implies that the magazines and their fiction don't exist. I
don't deny the existence of sf magazines, or the valuable impact they have had and continue to have in their publication
of stories with women main characters. On the contrary,
sf magazines remain at the forefront--far ahead of the novel
trade--in their frequent inclusion of women main characters!
I would very much like to see someone compile a comprehensive reading list of stories published in sf magazines with
women main characters; however, if and when that is done,
the final product will not be a self-selection aid or a pedagogical tool as this book is, but a reference tool for researchers.

The point here is that this book is not a comprehensive resource for researchers but a tool for teachers and other people interested in works that are available in the form most readily and easily available--books.   For that reason, only novels, novellas (in Ace Double form, for example), novelettes, and anthologies and collections of stories in book form have been included in this work.   This will ensure the reader of at least the possibility of finding an older work, perhaps in a library or on an interlibrary loan.   Old copies of sf magazines, on the other hand, are more difficult for anyone but a collector (willing to pay collector prices) to obtain and are impractical as a teaching resource.

Original publication data and most current publication data have been included to aid the reader in locating the work.   Interim publication data have been excluded except in the following cases:

    editions with color plates

    editions containing the work in substantially different form (story-length work becoming a novel-length work, for example) or retitled for that edition.

    two or more books currently available which contain the story

    first publication of a story in book form as well as most current.

Readers who desire to research all publication data on the works included here may consult the Bibliography at the end of this book for index works.

It is not the purpose of this book to form a definitive history of women characters in science fiction or to analyze the changes in the types of characters portrayed in sf.   Neither is the purpose of this book to list just the feminist female main characters.   A side benefit of this work, of course, is that feminist main characters are included; however, I have not defined what constitutes a feminist female hero and do not attempt to separate feminist sf from non-feminist sf.

That a sf work has a female main character does not necessarily mean that the work is feminist literature.   Some few readers may disagree and say that any sf work having a female protagonist is feminist literature.   Other readers may feel that even the most seemingly independent, adventurous female main character may not be truly a feminist in her words and actions. It is not my intention to define what constitutes a feminist female character or a feminist author. In my opinion, based on my own view of what constitutes a feminist character, a number of the sf works written about in this book have main characters who are feminists, but certainly not all of them, and in fact, not even nearly half. The works of the 1970s and 1980s quite naturally have a higher percentage of feminist characters probably due to the increasing number of feminist authors entering the sf field; however, sf has by no means matured sufficiently in its treatment of female characters that all readers can agree that sf is feminist in its philosophy. In spite of this, sf remains one of the best, if not the best, type of literature for feminist fiction.

Although I have attempted to be objective in my writing about the works in this volume, there are probably lapses in my objectivity. Perceiving oneself as being objective is a subjective process in and of itself and therefore not foolproof. Whether or not any particular work portrays woman in a gender-free manner must ultimately be judged by the reader, and that too will be, by necessity, a subjective judgment. Nonetheless, it is my hope that this volume's annotations are of assistance in choosing which works to read. At the very least, this book should be of value in providing readers a heretofore unavailable listing of both short and long sf works containing women main characters.

CHAPTER 1: HISTORICAL PERSPECTIVE--
1818 THROUGH 1929

Within this chapter, which covers sf until 1930, I will briefly
describe the works of some of the authors who first brought
the female character, although mostly in secondary and minor
parts, into sf. The works included here are not, by any
means, all of the sf which has women characters. To fully
explore the role of every female character in sf prior to
1930 would require considerably more space then a single
chapter allows. This chapter, at best, highlights the sf
works that have been either the most influential and widely
read in sf as a whole, or worthy of note here because the
work has a woman main character, a situation which was
unusual at the time. Usually one of these criteria is met
at a time. Generally speaking, if a sf book was widely read,
it had either no women characters or women in only minor
or, at best, secondary character roles. If a sf book had a
woman main character, it was not widely read or, at least,
did not remain popular into our own time.

    Frankenstein; or, The Modern Prometheus (London:
Lackington, Hughes, Harding, Mavor & Jones, 1818) falls
into the category of being widely read and is a book in which
women held only secondary or minor character roles. Elizabeth, Justine, and Margaret are all secondary or minor
characters in Mary Shelley's Frankenstein. Margaret, never
to write or speak in the book, is the sister of the narrator.
She is the person to whom Robert Walton writes in the book,
the person to whom he tells the story. Justine, a servant
in the Frankenstein household, is introduced briefly after being wrongly accused of killing young William Frankenstein, a
crime belonging to the monster, but for which she is found
guilty and executed. Elizabeth Lavenza holds the major female role in the book as Victor Frankenstein's stepsister and
betrothed. It is she who briefly brightens his guilt-ridden

1

life, who marries him because she loves him, and who is
also killed by the monster in his act of revenge against his
creator.   In this book the women are either passive receivers
of information (Margaret) or killed to enlarge Victor Frankenstein's horror at his own creation.   In the latter cases, the
two women in their secondary character roles are used as
tools to increase the impact of the story.   Frankenstein's
horror at himself because of his creation is certainly deeply
dramatized by the killing of the innocent, helpless women so
close to his heart.

In the case of one of Mary Shelley's lesser known
works, The Last Man, published in February of 1826 (London: H. Colburn, and currently in print at The University
of Nebraska Press, Lincoln), is entirely different from
Frankenstein in the importance of the women characters.
Also unlike Frankenstein, this work met with instant critical
contempt[1]* and apparently virtually disappeared from sight
into relative obscurity.   The work, set between A.D. 2073
and 2097, has two strong secondary women characters, one
of whom is narrator Lionel Verney's sister and the other
Lionel's love interest who eventually becomes his wife.

Perdita, Lionel's sister, marries the ill-fated Raymond.   She is intelligent, "sincere, generous, and reasonable," and has understanding which is "clear and comprehensive" and a "vivid" imagination.   She is selfless, thinks "constantly of others," and strives "to take from those around
her a sense of inferiority; a feeling which never crosses her
mind."   If Perdita can be said to have a fault, it is her
overwhelming and all-consuming love and adoration of Raymond, whom she sees as "a superior being."   It is this passion which drives her away from him when she finds he has
been seeing another woman and which ultimately causes her
to drown herself in the ocean when Raymond dies.

Lionel's love interest, Idris, runs away with him when
she discovers that her mother, the ex-queen as she is called,
plans to force an unwanted marriage on her.   Idris is described as "gentle and good," "peculiarly frank, soft, and
affectionate," and sweet tempered.   She is "firm and resolute
on any point that touched her heart," yet is "yielding to those
she loved."   Idris, who is an "affectionate wife, sister and
friend," approaches motherhood not as a "pastime," but as

*Notes to Chapter 1 can be found on page 36.

"a passion. " It is this passion for her children which drains
her near the story's conclusion. Her concerned worry for
them during the totally devastating plague eventually makes
her consumptive, filled with "gloomy prognostications, care,
and agonizing dread"; her death is not caused by the plague,
but by poor health due to extended worry combined with severe cold。

The lives of both Perdita and Idris revolve totally
around their respective spouses and only to a slightly lesser
degree do their spouses' lives revolve around them.   (Perdita does, at one point, desire a "career" in order to be
happy without Raymond.) They are a close-knit group, ro-
manticized and idealized. It is the destruction of these idyllic
relationships which heightens the final sense of isolation felt
by Lionel.

Associate editor John Clute wrote in The Science Fiction Encyclopedia (ed. by Peter Nicholls, New York: Doubleday, 1979) that the narrator of The Last Man was "rather
like her (Mary's) husband"; however, Hugh J. Luke, Jr。 in
his introduction to The Last Man (mentioned in note 6) claims
that it is Adrian, Earl of Windsor who is most like her husband, Percy Bysshe Shelley.   Luke continues that other "frag-
mentary" portraits of Percy Bysshe Shelley can be found in
Idris and the astronomer Merrival. Luke suggests that narrator Lionel is a character "based on Mary's own life. " During the time Mary wrote The Last Man, she was suffering
grief from the death of her husband and was feeling very isolated and friendless according to her journal. Like Mary,
Lionel, orphaned as a child and finding companionship in his
adult life, ultimately suffered the loss of his "beloved companions" and is completely "alone" in the world, not only
psychologically, as was Mary, but physically as well. (Luke's
introduction to The Last Man is well worth the time spent
reading it for those wishing to obtain scholarly insight into
Mary Shelley's work, as well as psychological insight into
her motivation in writing The Last Man.)

In 1871, shortly before his death, Edward George Earle
Bulwer-Lytton gave the world, at first anonymously, The
Coming Race or The New Utopia (Edinburgh and London: W.
Blackwood and sons, and currently available from Woodbridge
Press, Santa Barbara, CA).   This novel is about a human
civilization living underground for "many thousands of years, "
since "before the time of Noah, " in which the women are con-
sidered the more physically powerful and the natural rulers.

In this utopia, the narrator of the story unwittingly attracts
the attentions and affections of Zee, a single woman who is
an "authority" on the parasitic insect which dwells in the
hairs of a tiger's paws.   Zee is called by the narrator
"perhaps the wisest and the strongest" in her community;
however, she is also "by common repute, the gentlest, and
she was certainly the most popularly beloved."   She has a
face which is "grand" and "faultless," and an expression due
to her studies, which was somewhat "stern when in repose."

        The women in this civilization are taller than the men,
and have "countenances" that "were devoid of the softness and
timidity of expression which give charm to the face of women
as seen on the earth above."   Because of their greater height
and their "embedded sinews and muscles as handy as those
of the other sex," the women there can protect themselves
from male aggression and claim the right to choose the mate
of their choice and to be the suitor in the courtship.   Zee,
as is her right in her world, openly expresses her feelings
for the narrator which he, rather comically and frantically,
tries to forestall.   Zee is hurt but remains the gentle protec-
tor and giver of aid, and sneaks the narrator to safety--back
to his world.   Ironically, the narrator, after regaining his
world, comes close to regretting having left Zee.

        Zee is an unusual character for that time period.
She is physically, mentally, and emotionally strong, yet is
gentle and caring, open and giving.   She is the embodiment
of a combination of qualities almost exclusively attributed to
the male sex at that time and can easily be called an early
hero because she does save the narrator from death in her
world and helps him escape.   The narrator expresses at one
point his unwillingness to argue with a seven-foot-tall woman,
on the basis that arguing even with "any ordinary female" is
"useless."   In spite of this aversion, at the story's conclusion, the narrator's wonderment at his refusal of Zee's love
leaves the reader with the impression that the narrator (and
possibly Bulwer-Lytton as well) found the ways of Zee and
her people admirable, even preferable to the disappointments
"in matters connected with household love and domestic life"
he experienced among his own people.   Most certainly the
narrator thinks that Zee's civilization is stronger than his,
and expects her people to destroy his civilization one day,
as their legend predicts will occur.

        Though not called amazons, the women of that world
are an early sf prototype of the amazon women that became

so popular with sf writers and readers alike in later years;
however, unlike many of the amazon stories to follow in
which the women are cruel, oppressive, and hateful to men,
these women love and pursue the men of their world and do
not use their greater strength and influence to force their
men into slavery or subservience. Bulwer-Lytton gives sensitive and sympathetic treatment to his women characters who,
though not yet warlike in behavior, are in size and strength
truly amazon women.

Although he sees the lives of Zee and her people as
ideal and happy, Bulwer-Lytton does not try to impose this
utopia upon his own peers. He writes that he sees Zee's
people as "a distinct species with which it was impossible
that any community in the upper world could amalgamate."
This makes the utopia unattainable and fosters speculation
on what type of people humans might have become under a
different set of circumstances.

Another utopia in which the inhabitants live in a world
beneath the Earth, originally serialized in four installments
in the Cincinnati Commercial in 1880-81, was Mizora: A
Prophecy (printed in 1975 in book form by Gregg Press,
Boston, MA), a work which is strongly feminist in its content. Although the series, published in book form by G. W.
Dillingham in 1890 (New York) was supposedly written by the
narrator, Princess Vera Zarovitch, the copyright was in the
name of Mary E. Bradley, and the work has been attributed
to Mary E. Bradley Lane by the Library of Congress. Little
else is known about the author. The Preface to the 1890 book
contains a letter by Murat Halstead, who wrote that the author "kept herself in concealment so closely that even her
husband did not know that she was the writer who was making this stir in our limited literary world." He also wrote
that she was a "shade indifferent on the subject" of publishing the series in book form.

Princess Vera Zarovitch, a 5'5" dark-haired Russian-
born woman who was "born to a family of nobility, wealth
and political power," describes herself as having a "hardy
constitution" and "strong nerves." When in her early twenties, she unwisely expresses her political views to a Russian
soldier who has just killed a friend from Poland. She is
arrested, tried, and condemned to the mines of Siberia for
life, which separates her from her husband and newborn
child. Vera bravely escapes and plans to flee to France,
but is only able to get passage on a northbound whaling ves-

sel which becomes shipwrecked, leaving her alone among the
"Equimaux." When she feels "a strong desire to sail" across
an open sea, she sets off alone and is eventually sucked down
a whirlpool into the land of Mizora, an all-female world beneath the Earth containing only thick-waisted, blonde-haired
women. (The Mizora women "considered a large waist a
mark of beauty, as it gave a greater capacity of lung power.")
One of Vera's first questions, which she refrains from asking the inhabitants of Mizora until late in her stay, is where
the men of their world are. When it is finally discovered
that in Vera's world there are men, and that, in fact, Vera
is married to one and has a son, the response is, at first,
one of "loathing and abhorrence," then one of compassion.
Their science, all important in Mizora, holds the "Secret of
Life," allowing their work on the "germ of all Life"; this
scientific process keeps Mizora supplied with beautiful blonde
babies, thus eliminating the need for men.

When Vera finally asks about the whereabouts of the
men in Mizora, she is told by the Preceptress that men became extinct three thousand years before. At that time men
ruled and women were beasts of burden and considered in-
ferior. When a dissolution of the government occurred,
women organized to protect themselves from lawlessness,
and developed into a military power of their own, eventually
forming a government themselves. The constitution they ap-
proved excluded men from "all affairs and privileges for a
period of one hundred years." Educational institutions, and,
in particular, science opened to women, and women discovered the "Secret of Life." Meanwhile, the constitution was
amended, men were given "an equal share of the ballot" and
the old practices began all over again. "The women looked
forward to their former subjugation as only a matter of time,
and bitterly regretted their inability to prevent it. But at the
crisis, a prominent scientist proposed to let the race [men]
die out." The resulting world was one of all women, and
all blonde and fair because "The elements of evil belong to
the dark race," Vera was told. Vera doesn't swallow many
of the precepts put forth by the Mizora inhabitants, including
the equating of the dark race with evil and the denial of a
"Deity" and an afterlife.

In spite of Vera's dislike of some of the ideas the
Mizora people hold, she could not deny that their society was
more advanced than her own. Mizora is a land without crime,
with unlocked doors and honest merchants. Education is free
as the development of the mind is emphasized there. The

aristocracy of Mizora is composed of those with the most
highly developed minds, and teachers, as the developers of
those minds, receive the highest salaries and are held in
the highest respect. In Mizora, science is the all-important
pursuit, providing the inhabitants with bread from limestone
and marble (they are all vegetarians, by the way), rain from
electricity in the air, and a multitude of inventions which an-
ticipate inventions still not fully realized in our world a hundred years after the publication of the series. The Mizora
people have a hologram-like projection which enables a speaker
to give a talk from her home and yet appear in three-
dimensions on many stages at once. They have a communication device which sends the image of the speaker as well
as the voice. Elastic glass, which sounds much like plastic,
is used in many things including cooking utensils, pipes, and
fabrics. Machines do the heavy work, including the scrubbing
of the kitchen, which is performed by a machine equipped
with brushes and sponges. Mizora people also have private
vehicles propelled by compressed air, by electricity, and by
a power "acted upon by light," which sounds very much like
a solar-powered vehicle. They use water, separated into its
two gaseous forms to provide "an economical fuel." (It is
remarkable that Mary E. Bradley Lane anticipated the experimentation on all of these inventions.)

Vera, in the midst of all this scientific wonder, con-
tinually embarrasses herself with such questions as, "Where
is your other parent?" and "Where do you perform your religious rites and ceremonies?" She is treated, nonetheless,
with patience and compassion, and stays in Mizora for a total
of fifteen years, during which time she never seems to stop
thinking things like "It would be a paradise for man." Her
friend during these fifteen years, Wauna, is the daughter of
the highly respected Preceptress of the National College, who
tries, along with her mother, to educate Vera on the importance of education. Vera is told by the Preceptress, "Uni-
versal education is the great destroyer of castes. It is the
conqueror of poverty and the foundation of patriotism." When
Vera decides she must return to her world with "some of the
noble lessons and doctrines" of Mizora, she decides to take
a Mizora woman with her. Vera persuades Wauna to go
with her, which turns out to be quite fatal to her due to
"homesickness, and coarse diet and savage surroundings"
found in the far north. The men in Vera's world appreciated
Wauna only for her beauty. "The lofty ideal of humanity that
she represented was smiled at or gently ignored." Wauna's
death is deeply regretted by Vera. As Vera's husband and

child had died, she is left alone in her own world, "Childless, homeless and friendless,. in poverty and obscurity. "
After a book filled with utopian ideals, Vera's last words to
the reader are "Life is a tragedy even under the most favor-
able conditions. " Like the narrator of Bulwer-Lytton's The
Coming Race or the New Utopia, Vera is left somewhat
haunted by her experiences when she returns to her world.
She tells the reader that "the world's fame can never warm
a heart already dead to happiness; but out of the agony of
one human life, may come a lesson for many. " Vera's desire for obscurity seems to have been merely a reflection of
Mary E. Bradley Lane's own desire for anonymity, but Mizora's "lesson" remains even today.

     Mary E. Bradley Lane's longing for a utopian world
run by women--a world in which women are given every opportunity for education and career advancement--was certainly
not shared by many other writers.   Published anonymously in
1882, The Revolt of Man (Edinburgh and London: W. Blackwood, 1882, and London: Chatto & Windus, 1896) tells the
story of men who take over the control of the government,
industry, and arts from women who have been in charge of
those areas for over a hundred years.   Walter Besant, in
later editions of the book, claimed authorship of it, and wrote
in the preface of the 1896 edition of the book that "two la-
dies" advised him during the writing of the book (on his summer vacation) to make the revolt of man a "bloodless" one.

     In The Revolt of Man, women are raised to run the
government and businesses, and the men stay home with the
children and marry whoever asks them, usually older, financially established women who can afford to support them.
The book introduces two main women characters: the notable
elderly Professor Dorothy Ingleby of the University of Cambridge and Constance, Countess of Carlyon, a 20-year-old of
considerable influence.   The distinguished and respected Professor Ingleby, unlike other women of her era, secretly holds
her husband as lord of the family and teaches her two daughters, Faith and Grace, that men are superior.   If not for
Professor Ingleby's lengthy, coercive, and covert training of
Edward Chester, who at the end of the book becomes King of
England, he would never have been psychologically prepared
to be a dominant rather than a submissive individual.   In
other words, a woman was the primary influence in molding
young Edward for dominance over women.

     Once Professor Ingleby informs Edward of the plot to

put men in control once more, she helps him with his speeches and tells him that men "are all alike unhappy, and they know not why. It is because the natural order has been reversed; the sex which should command and create is compelled to work in blind obedience." She tells Edward that women are incapable of creating, and that "at no time has any woman enriched the world with a new idea, a new truth, a new discovery, a new invention." Musical composition is also tacked onto this list of things Professor Ingleby tells Edward that women are incapable of doing. Professor Ingleby claims that the "highest function" of her sex is to "cheer and comfort" men, and that women have failed in their rule because they cannot expand knowledge, only "receive" it. Divine Woman must be overthrown, says Besant, and Divine Man put in her place.

There is, of course, a little romance in the novel. Constance is in love with her cousin Edward Chester, and he with her. Professor Ingleby conspires to unite the two, but first puts Edward under the tutelage of her husband, who tells Edward that he will be the King of England after the successful revolt of man. Constance is fearful for Edward's life, but after seeing that Edward is determined to lead this revolt of men, "She was conquered; Man was stronger than Woman." Professor Ingleby comforts Constance as Edward prepares for battle by telling her, "We shall take our own place--we shall be the housewives; we shall be loving and faithful servants to men, and they will be our servants in return. Love knows no mastery. Yet man must rule outside the house." Constance's response is merely "Oh!" Constance, at Edward's bidding, symbolically buckles his sword on him just before combat, thus, in effect, giving him his phallus, or his manhood, so to speak.

The revolution was bloodless, because some women of "wit" frightened the defenders of women's rule by telling them they were vastly outnumbered by the army of rebels. Besant states that "No woman was insulted" in the male take-over, and that the cheering victory crowd was composed primarily of women. At least Besant recognized that older women would feel nothing but "blind hatred" because of the change in power. He wrote that some middle-aged women who were professionals received "compensation" and were allowed to "practice in their own houses." Besant assumed that the young women, though, would adjust quickly to the change in power. He wrote that no longer did they have to study or accept responsibility, or worry about a profession.

They had "unlimited time to look after dress and matters of
real importance." (What those "matters of real importance"
might happen to be was never explained in the book.) Besant
wrote that young women resurrected "that sweet feminine gift
of coquetry" and "There was laughter once more in the land."
Constance all but physically grovels before Edward, the new
King of England, and vows to be his "most faithful subject."
She tells him, "There is the Perfect Woman; but she lives
in the shadow of the Divine Man." Of the rule of women,
Constance tells Edward, "It is as if the foot of woman destroyed the flowers which spring up beneath the foot of man."

The Revolt of Man is a political statement against suffrage and equal rights for women, and for male supremacy.
Because of that, the two main women characters, though portrayed as intelligent and influential, accept the new male supremacy and willingly relinquish their power. No hint is
given by Besant that they might be dissatisfied at having their
power and influence so abruptly taken from them. Their activities after the revolt are not discussed, and the reader
must assume that Besant envisions them, along with all other
women, contentedly retiring to their homes. Of course, Constance, as Queen of England, gives up less power than most,
but, after all, there is only one queen.

From a psychological point of view, the conclusion of
The Revolt of Man is unlikely. People with power and influence are rarely willing to relinquish their power readily to
others. The believability, both of the book and of the women
main characters, is affected by Besant's doubtful premise
that women would, en masse, gratefully become subservient
to men (trained to be submissive) after having been raised
to be decision-makers, professionals, breadwinners, and
policy-setters. In The Revolt of Man, Besant adhered to the
highly debated concept that basic male/female "instinct" (ag-
gression/submission) will always be stronger than any amount
of training or societal expectations to the contrary. The an-
thropological studies of various cultures done by Margaret
Mead are, in themselves, sufficient to disprove this premise;
nevertheless, this debate remains popular even today.[2]

Another book dealing with the subject of women's superiority and suffrage is The Gay Rebellion (c. 1913), a collection of related stories by Robert W. Chambers. He treats
the subject in a humorous, lighthearted manner, but nonetheless marries off all of the rebellious women and sends them
to their homes to forget their foolish thoughts of equality.

At least in his preface, he warns prospective readers that this book should be read by "old-fashioned young people only." The Gay Rebellion is more of a satirical fantasy than a true sf work.

On the other side of the coin were writers who would have preferred, if at all possible, to entirely exclude women from the world--or at least from the world of their fiction. For example, H(enry) Rider Haggard published several books in the 1800s: King Solomon's Mines (New York: Cassell, 1885), Allan Quatermain (London: Longmans, Green, 1887), and She (New York: Harper & Brothers, 1886), to name three, all of which are still available from several publishers. King Solomon's Mines is notable (in regard to the subject of women characters in sf) for its open statement that no women of any importance were in the book. In this book, narrator Allan Quatermain (Haggard's most frequently used character) lists four reasons why he is writing the book. "Fourth reason and last: Because I am going to tell the strangest story that I know of. It may seem a queer thing to say that, especially considering that there is no woman in it--except Foulata. Stop, though! There is Gagaoola, if she was a woman and not a fiend. But she was a hundred at least, and therefore not marriageable, so I don't count her. At any rate, I can safely say that there is not a petticoat [Haggard's emphasis] in the whole history." There, in a single paragraph, Haggard equates women with strange stories, names one of the two women in the work as a fiend, and states that if a woman is "not marriageable," or worth male consideration, she doesn't count as a woman.

Allan Quatermain, the main character in King Solomon's Mines, had an entire book named after him the following year. Allan Quatermain, a book filled with Allan's adventures in Africa, has a couple of secondary women characters. Flossie MacKenzie, the most notable of the two, is a child to whom Allan grows very attached. Flossie goes to pick a lily for Allan and is captured by the Masai. In a note to her parents, she says she will kill herself before allowing the Masai to kill her, and that Allan Quatermain should not, under any circumstances, exchange himself for her to free her. He considers her "a brave little girl" and vows to save her. When Flossie is saved and safe once more, she becomes upset at having had to kill someone. Says Allan, "It struck me as an odd thing that a girl who could find the nerve to shoot a huge black ruffian rushing to kill her with a spear should have been so affected at the thought afterwards; but it is,

after all, characteristic of the sex." Allan gives Flossie,
at their parting, some "old-fashioned advice": "Be unselfish,
and whenever you can, give a helping hand to others--for the
world is full of suffering, my dear, and to alleviate it is the
noblest end that we can set before us. If you do that you
will become a sweet and God-fearing woman and make many
people's lives a little brighter, then you will not have lived,
as many of your sex do, in vain." Allan obviously doesn't
have an abundance of respect for the female sex.

The two women in She are opposites. Ustane is called
"a remarkable young person," being of a race in which "the
weaker sex has established its rights." Though the "women
among the Amahagger are not only upon terms of perfect
equality with men, but are not held to them by any binding
ties," the men periodically kill off the older women to keep
them in line. The character She--also called She-who-must-
be-obeyed and Ayesha--is Queen of the Amahagger, is two
thousand years old, and "can see without eyes and hear without ears." She is just the opposite of Ustane's kind, loving,
caring nature. Ayesha was "evil," but was also "the wisest,
loveliest, proudest creature ... in the whole universe. She
had been wicked, too, in her way; but, alas! Such is the
frailty of the human heart, her wickedness had not detracted
from her charm ... there was nothing mean or small about
Ayesha." Or, at least, so thought the narrator.

Haggard evidently had a very real phobia about women.
Even in the beginnings of She, when the narrator Holly becomes young Leo's caretaker, he states, "I would have no
woman to lord it over me about the child, and steal his affections from me." Haggard consistently belittles women and
avoids them as much a possible in his writing. His most
admirable and beautiful woman character, Ayesha, is called
"evil." Ustane, who is kind and loving, is killed by Ayesha,
but even had she lived, she looked forward to being killed
later in life by the men of her culture to keep the younger
women in line. Allan instructs the child Flossie, supposedly
in order to keep her from living in vain, as he believes most
of her sex do. Women have a place in Haggard's work, but
that place is always carefully defined, enclosed, and controlled
by him.

A work similar to H. Rider Haggard's adventure sto-
ries, in particular She, is Mabel Fuller Blodgett's At the
Queen's Mercy (Boston, New York, and London: Lamson,
Wolffe, 1897). An adventurer in Africa, John Dering, the

large, forever-womanless male narrator, learns to love the
"Childlike, lovable, gentle then fierce, treacherous, and oh
so unspeakably cruel" Lah, the Queen of the people of the
Walled City. Like Ayesha (She-who-must-be-obeyed), Lah
is not only beautiful beyond words, but also cruel.

A book by Florence Carpenter Dieudonné with a mis-
leading title, Rondah; or Thirty-Three Years in a Star (Philadelphia: T. B. Peterson & Brothers, 1887), would have logically been about Rondah, the woman character called the
"heroine" in the brief advertisement on the title page. Not
so. Rondah, though she is the character who supposedly performs relatively heroically at the book's conclusion, is absent
from the action in the story for nearly half of the book. When
she does finally make an appearance in the novel, she names
the meteor to which she has been transported, marries Regan
(a man she loves although she hasn't seen him for 33 years),
is stolen away from her husband to spend a long winter reading in isolation, and refuses to go to Jupiter to save the souls
there because of her love for Regan. In other words, Rondah
does little that can be considered heroic. She does correct
a wrong done by Regan by saving some winged people he had
tried to kill; however, for the most part, she is remarkably
unheroic and is, in fact, rather weak as a character.

Edward Bellamy, in his book Looking Backward: AD
2000-1887 (Boston: Ticknor, 1888, and now available from
several sources), created a secondary character remarkable
for his time. She is Edith Leete, a resident of Boston in
the year 2000. She is frank, open, free to express her opinions and her love. She is generally less fettered by the social restraints of the 1800s than most any other female character written about at that time. She is still introduced,
however, as the daughter of a doctor, a common method of
getting a woman into a book at that time.

The main character, Julian West, sleeps under hypnotic
trance, from 1887 until the year 2000. Then he is discovered
in an underground room and is cared for by Dr. and Mrs.
Leete and their daughter Edith. Intended as a portrayal of
a utopian society, the book consists primarily of dialogue
between Julian and his concerned hosts, and little action takes
place. Edith, the great-granddaughter of the Edith to whom
Julian was betrothed, falls in love with the main character
and he with her.

Because Bellamy envisioned future women differently

from the way they were presented in his time, Edith Leete
is an interesting character. Bellamy wrote that in the year
2000, women had their own careers, were financially independent of men (as the world was socialistic), and were therefore free to express love. Says Dr. Leete to Julian, "When
for a woman to proffer her love to a man was in effect to
invite him to assume the burden of her support, it is easy
to see that pride and delicacy might well have checked the
promptings of the heart."

Edith openly takes Julian's hands in sympathy with his
misery and confusion, and cries with him when he is at the
depth of despair. (Here a man is allowed to cry, a fact
quite unusual for both the genre and the time.) Julian says
of her, "I had been struck with the air of serene frankness
and ingenuous directness, more like that of a noble and innocent boy than any girl I had ever known, which characterized
her." Julian also says of her, "Feminine softness and delicacy were in this lovely creature deliciously combined with
an appearance of health and abounding physical vitality too
often lacking in the maidens with whom alone I could compare
her."

However, in spite of the claims of Bellamy regarding
his utopian society, Edith is not a twentieth-century type of
secondary character. She is given to attacks of blushing and
often her eyes fall before Julian's. In spite of her otherwise
open ways, she forces her father not to tell Julian that she
is Edith's great-granddaughter until Julian confesses his love
for her. Then she refuses his kisses until he is told of her
heritage. "You must not touch me again till you know who
I am," she tells him. It seems that "she used to tell her
parents she would never marry till she found a lover like
Julian West." She is a romantic, and believes herself to
be the reincarnation of Julian's old love, Edith Bartlett. She
would seem more at home in a modern romance or gothic
than she would in modern sf.

In addition, it would not be a totally ideal society for
some women since "the higher positions in the feminine army
of industry are entrusted only to women who have been both
wives and mothers, as they alone fully represent their sex."
An unfortunate situation for single or childless women who
desire to advance in their careers! Sam Lundwall calls the
women in the book "walking and talking wombs," but does
concede that the book was "an important literary event." For
the most part, the book is a landmark in the presentation of
women.

A second book by Bellamy in which Edith, Julian, and her father appear is Equality (New York: D. Appleton, 1897, and currently available from several sources).   In this book, Bellamy used the story presented in Looking Backward: AD 2000-1887--which was very successful--as a vehicle by which he could more fully express his philosophical viewpoints. Almost predictably, his success with this second work was not as great.

Bellamy was not alone in his belief that careers should be balanced with a rich personal life--with love.   The woman main character in Mary (Platt) Parmele's Answered in the Negative (New York: Parmele & Chaffee, 1892) is an artist who has been studying "abroad."   Margery Middleton gives up her artistic "aims and ambitions" to marry the ambitious Bruno Middleton, who is obsessed with perfecting his technique of "Astronomical photography."   Bruno sees Margery as very bright in that she can understand his esoteric discussions and tells her that she must have been made of "the material intended for half-dozen women."   He finds her a fascinating "highly-organized soul."   Even though Bruno and Margery are newlyweds, Bruno is so totally absorbed in his work that Margery is left alone for long periods of time. Although she is lonely, Margery is passionately enthusiastic about his aims and takes upon herself the study of scientific books because of his work.   She is quietly patient with Bruno although she hates their separation.   As he grows closer to the successful conclusion of his work, he moves into his laboratory entirely, leaving Margery alone with the servants. When he receives a note from one of the servants, he pockets it absently and continues to work on taking a clear picture of Mars which shows that planet to be inhabited.   When he finally goes home, Margery has died, leaving him with a brand new baby girl.   Margery, even to her end, doesn't want to be a bother to Bruno or to interrupt his work.   Bruno is so physically worn down that when he learns that Margery is dead, he has a mental breakdown from which it takes him two years to recover.

The book is, in essence, a warning to people who go to extremes in either work or love.   In this case, Bruno was so totally absorbed in his work that his personal life suffered.   Bruno became completely devoted to his work to the exclusion of all else.   Margery, on the other hand, gave up her career goals entirely and became completely devoted to Bruno and his work.   Neither extreme works.

Margery is a character with intelligence, artistic talent, and devotion to Bruno and pride in his work. Her attributes make her loss to Bruno seem even greater than they might have had she been less his equal in intelligence and enthusiasm.

A more popularly known author than Mary Parmele was H(erbert) G(eorge) Wells, a British writer whose five sf novels written prior to 1900 are well known even today: The Time Machine (New York: H. Holt, 1895), The Island of Dr. Moreau (London: W. Heinemann, 1896), The Invisible Man (New York and London: Harper & Brothers, 1897), The War of the Worlds (London: W. Heinemann, 1898), and When the Sleeper Wakes (New York and London: Harper & Brothers, 1899). (All but When the Sleeper Wakes are available from several publishers. When the Sleeper Wakes is available under the title Three Prophetic Novels from Peter Smith Publisher, Magnolia, MA.) Wells' later work tended to be loaded with messages for the reader, but his novels prior to 1900 were very entertaining stories. His treatment of the female characters, however, was not always the best.

The Time Machine, narrated by the guest of the Time Traveller (as he is called throughout the book), is about a future utopia gone awry. The Eloi and the Morlocks, once from the same branch of the family tree, are now vastly different: the Morlocks, living underground, are cannibals, preying on the Eloi; the Eloi are frail and fair, like butterflies or "Dresden-china" types. The Time Traveller rescues an Eloi female who is drowning before the eyes of her peers and receiving no assistance. Weena, as she calls herself, is extremely grateful, to the point of almost canine devotion to him. Although he tells himself he hadn't come into the future to carry on a "miniature flirtation," he is nonetheless comforted by her company. Weena, like all the Eloi, is frail and fearful and has little in the way of native intelligence. The Time Traveller says she is "exactly like a child" and is a "little doll of a creature." He even considers bringing her back to his time, but she dies before he returns. Because of the narrative structure of this book, no one, including Weena, speaks actual words except what the narrator himself actually hears in the Time Traveller's home. But at least the book has a real, honest-to-goodness female secondary character, which is more than can be said for Wells' second sf book, The Island of Dr. Moreau.

The Island of Dr. Moreau, in spite of the appearance

of Maria in the film version, doesn't have a female character of any type who is named.   There is a vague reference or two to females of various descriptions, such as "a Swine Woman" and "a vixen and bear, whom I hated from the beginning." In another reference to females he writes, "these weird creatures--the females I mean--had in the earlier days of my stay an instinctive sense of their own repulsive clumsiness, and displayed in consequence a more than human regard for the decencies and decorum of external costume." In other words, they kept themselves covered.

In the first portion of The Invisible Man, Wells does manage to squeeze in a few minor female characters: a housekeeper and her helper, and Mrs. Bunting, Rev. Bunting's wife.   Mrs. Hall, the housekeeper, is portrayed as an overly curious woman (one might say a nosey busybody).   She attempts to find out the reason for the Invisible Man's bandages by telling him of her sister's son who had an accident with a scythe, and rambles on until he abruptly terminates the conversation.   She is appalled, thinks him quite rude, and is irritated by his manner.   Naturally she takes it out on Millie, her helper.   The Invisible Man finally "explains" to Mrs. Hall that he's had an accident, and cuts off further questioning.   But she is still overwhelmingly curious, and faints when she finds out he's invisible.   Mrs. Bunting, the Reverend's wife, responds as her husband does to the theft of their money by the Invisible Man: with abundant "marvelling." She and her husband are described as "a quaintly-costumed little couple." Millie has no speaking part at all.

The situation is little different in The War of the Worlds.   Told from a first-person male point of view, the only female characters in the book are "my wife," and Mrs. Elphinstone and her sister-in-law, Miss Elphinstone.   All could really be considered minor characters.   The only character that could be called secondary is the brother of the main character.   In one of the few times that the "wife" appears, she and the main character take a moonlit walk together and he explains the "Signs of the Zodiac" to her.   The second time the reader hears of the wife, she greets the news of the men from Mars by knitting her brows and turning white.   The third time, the main character and his wife have tea together and he drags her out of the book and unceremoniously dumps her safely with relatives, thus removing her from further action until they are reunited at the book's end.

Mrs. Elphinstone spends most of her brief exposure

in the book dressed in white and crying and screaming at one
thing or another. Her sister-in-law, Miss Elphinstone, is
more self-contained. She is a slender dark figure, with
some spunk and fight left in her. She strikes out at an attacker with a whip and "very pluckily" returns to help her
rescuer when he is attacked. She doesn't hesitate to use a
gun on the attackers, but turns it over to the main character's brother when the attack is over. (And yes, both Elphinstone women are related to a surgeon.) Miss Elphinstone
also has a second opportunity to prove "her quality" when
they get stuck in a "torrent of people" and have to force
their way back out, once more with the help of a revolver.
None of the female characters, however, could be said to
have important roles in this book.

By the time When the Sleeper Wakes was published,
Wells had begun to place a strong message into his novels.
In this novel, Wells wrote of a future world filled with slavery and oppression. The Salvation Army (which had replaced
workhouses) was bought by the Labour Company, and more
than a third of the people wore the blue canvas clothing of
the Company. Graham, the male main character, wakes into
this world after a 200-year sleep (shades of Bellamy's Looking Backward, 1888, which is noted early in the book) to find
that it is he who owns half the world (thanks to the miracles
of compound interest!). And by owning it, he rules it. Unfortunately, since Ostrog has been ruling it for him, he has
a lot to lose by Graham's awakening and fights to maintain
control.

This anti-utopia at least has a female secondary character who is concerned and responsible, intelligent and thinking, compassionate and mature. She is Helen Wotton, the
niece of Ostrog, who is reported by another to know "a great
many serious things. She is one of the most serious persons
alive." Helen, alone, risks Ostrog's wrath by telling Graham
the true situation and what he must do to help the people.
Her dialogue with Graham is full of "resolution" and "her voice
clear and strong." She fires him with her speech, then he
agrees to do as she says, to rule, on one condition--"That
you will help me." Her response, totally out of character
for the strong individual she has heretofore portrayed, is,
"I!--a girl!" And then "she stood before him, beautiful,
worshipful, and her enthusiasm and the greatness of their
theme was like a great gulf fixed between them. To touch
her, to clasp her hand, was a thing beyond hope." Except
for this affected half page, Helen is a strong, confident, and
perceptive secondary character.

Wells did not allow women to hold main character
roles in these five books. A casual reader might even interpret this to mean that Wells was firmly convinced that
women had their place and should stay in it.   But, in reality,
Wells was merely following the sf standards of his time.
Says Sam Lundwall, "Even a progressive writer like H. G.
Wells, who had firm opinions regarding woman's right to
personal and sexual freedom, kept his sf writing free of any
ideas to this end.   The debate around women's liberation was
reserved for novels like Ann Veronica."[3] However, it remains a fact that women characters in sf by Wells were destined to be secondary and minor characters.

About this time, sf began to emerge which contained
couples--a man and a woman--as main characters.   Charles
H. Palmer's "Citizen 505," published initially in The Argosy
in December of 1896 (later in Science Fiction by Gaslight,
ed. by Sam Moskowitz, World Publishing, 1968, and Hyperion
Press, 1974), is about a man and a woman in the twenty-third
century when cities have been replaced by townships according
to the theories of Chauvel.   Existing on the prior site of New
York City, Township No. 1 is a place where everyone can
experience the beauty of fields, fresh air, woods and water
unobstructed by the tall buildings, noise, and "tiers of walks
and electric railroads" which filled New York in the past.
Alora Swift, unlike her friend Eric Holt, claims to be happy
to live in such an ideal world, and yet she, too, is worried
about who the Marriage Bureau will choose as her mate.
Aloud, Alora chides Eric for his doubt and lack of faith in
their marriage system, telling him that romance was a disease and that the romantic image of love was almost invar-
iably shattered by marriage.   She claims to have faith in the
Bureau, but becomes "unnerved and utterly helpless" when
she learns that the Bureau has chosen a mate for her, and
later becomes angry and dissolves into tears when she discovers the choice is Citizen 504, Lemuel Phelps.   Alora refuses to see Eric at first, but eventually he corners her and
suggests they run away together by ship, a suggestion to
which Alora agrees; however, before they leave, Alora finds
her volume of "Life of Chauvel," and decides she cannot be
"untrue" to Chauvel's beliefs.   Shortly after the steamer
leaves without them, a letter arrives from the Bureau which
informs Alora that due to "a clerical error," Citizen 504 was
mistakenly named as her mate, when in reality Citizen 405--
none other than Eric Holt--is her mate-to-be.

Alora seems comfortable spouting beliefs which she

has been taught all her life, unlike Eric who has the courage
to dissent. Alora, the story concludes, is a big help to Eric
after their marriage in his efforts to change the marriage
system, especially after it was proven that the system was
not Chauvel's idea at all. On the other hand, if Alora had
actually left with Eric, the system might have never been
challenged. Her refusal to drop conventionality resulted in
possible change in the system for couples yet to be married,
in spite of the fact that, ironically, that system united her
with Eric. Though not heroic, she does have the courage
of her convictions, even if it means a lifetime of living with
a man for whom she doesn't care.

        Another sf work with a couple as main characters is
George Chetwynd Griffith's A Honeymoon in Space (London:
C. Arthur Pearson, 1901, and currently available from Ayer
Co., Salem, NH), which first appeared in story length ("Stories of Other Worlds," Pearson's Magazine in 1890). Griffith's novel is about a young couple's discovery of life on
various planets in the solar system while on their honeymoon
--the first such voyage in space. Young American Lilla Zaidie Rennick, with "gold-brown" hair, "violet-blue" eyes, fair
skin, and eyebrows which are "perhaps just a trifle heavy,"
is on her way by oceangoing ship to be married to the Marquis of Byfleet in London when her previous romantic interest,
the British Lord Rollo Lenox Smeaton Aubrey, Earl of Redgrave, swoops down in his unique--in fact, unheard of--"air-
car" (space ship) and whisks her away to marry him. This
takes place, of course, much to the initial disapproval of
chaperon Mrs. Van Stuyler, who finally yields to the inevitable. Zaidie and Lenox met when he was working with her
father, an inventor who was trying to create the space ship
that Lenox now flies. After the death of Zaidie's father,
Lenox continued the work and completed the ship. He is now
ready to marry Zaidie, and to bring peace to the world with
the threat of rapid retaliation using just such a vehicle, a
tactic which, at least in this story, succeeds in bringing
world peace. Zaidie and Lenox, after succeeding at bringing
world peace with the mere existence of the space ship, decide to take a "two thousand million"-mile honeymoon voyage
in space, accompanied by Lord Redgrave's faithful family
servant, Andrew Murgatroyd.

        During the trip Zaidie, Lenox, and Murgatroyd visit
the Moon, Mars, Venus, Calisto, Ganymede, Jupiter, and
Saturn and discover life, in one form or another (but usually
intelligent), at almost every stop. When necessary, they use

some sort of "breathing dress" with "telephonic" receivers and transmitters in the "head-dresses." In spite of, or perhaps because of, their various peculiar experiences, Zaidie finally gets homesick for Earth, and they return there with barely enough fuel to make it. As a character, Zaidie has presence of mind (or lack of it) to sing "The Swanee River" and "Home, Sweet Home" in order to communicate to the angel-like intelligent life on snow-covered Venus and to kill a life form on Mars which was attacking her; however, although Zaidie defies the carefully prearranged marriage to the Marquis of Byfleet and though she is said to have "a very proper spirit of her own," she faints when under stress, is "a wise wife who commands by obeying," and is, generally speaking, not heroic by nature, preferring that husband Lenox take that role.

The entire trip is joyful, an exploring game for newly-weds, plus servant, during which they meet both very pleasant and very unpleasant intelligent life from other worlds. The book's tone is light and fun, full of banter between the couple as they travel and of polite responses from the servant, who always maintains strict British decorum. Zaidie, who becomes Countess of Redgrave when she marries Lenox, has little need to perform heroically. She simply enjoys the trip without responsibility.

Still another sf work with a couple as main characters was published in June 1906 by The Argosy. "Finis" is a short story by Frank Lillie Pollack about a man and a woman sharing the last dawn of Earth together. (This story was reprinted in Horror Omnibus, W. H. Allen, 1965, compiled by Kurt Singer, under the title "The Last Dawn"; it was also in Science Fiction by Gaslight, ed. by Sam Moskowitz, World Publishing, Cleveland, OH, 1968, and Hyperion Press, Westport, CT, 1974.)

The story, set in the late twentieth century, chronicles the arrival of a new sun on Earth, a sun which will quickly destroy the Earth because of the intensity of its heat. The two main characters, Miss Alice Wardour and Assistant Professor Eastwood, watch the coming disaster from a relatively safe vantage point, the fireproof physics building at Columbia University. Alice, who works at the Art Student's League, is "painfully shy," and "plain," but has "ethereally brilliant hair that burned like pale flame." Eastwood assumes she probably has "brains" because he has "seen her reading some extremely 'deep' books"; however, she has "no amusements,

few interests. " Their vigil in the physics building is paral-
leled on the city's streets by throngs of eager people--people
who are eager only until they are killed in the first wave of
the new sun's destruction. As Alice and Eastwood wait
through the night, Alice speculates with "intellectual initiative"
and "an assumption of authority" that they are quite possibly
the last people in New York, or even in "America." Just
before the new sun rises on its second, and certain to be
fatal day, Alice surprises Eastwood by throwing her arms
around him and asking him to kiss her. He falsely assumes
she is afraid and in need of comfort and tells her to "try to
face it bravely. " Alice shares with him that she is not afraid
of death, but that she has "never lived," and "never been
happy. " She tells Eastwood, "I have always been timid and
wretched and afraid--afraid to speak--and I've almost wished
for suffering and misery or anything rather than to be stupid
and dumb and dead, the way I've always been. " The reader
can conclude that Alice was asking for a sexual encounter
from Eastwood because following the kiss is a double space,
and the sentence "The twilight was gone before they knew it. "
Alice's new courage and peace glow through her eyes, "shining with an unearthly softness and brilliancy," as she turns
to meet her fate.

This story handles the theme of a man and a woman,
alone together and facing death, with a sophistication unusual
in sf during that time. Alice, though timid and inexperienced,
summons the courage to face life before her death and boldly
makes her desires known to Eastwood. In addition, she is
intelligent and not afraid to show it. Alice is a character
who is unusual for her time.

Another story about human destruction on a massive
scale, "The Machine Stops" (Oxford and Cambridge Review,
Michaelmas Term, 1909, Volume 8), by E(dward) M(organ)
Forster, is a novella which has a woman main character,
Vashti, who lives underground with what she assumes is the
rest of humanity under the protection of the Machine. The
Machine cleans the air, furnishes food and bed, provides
communication with other people by audio-visual means of
some sort, and makes human work obsolete. The Machine
is also worshiped. Vashti is content in this environment,
listening to music and occasionally delivering lectures on
music history from the comfort of her own apartment. Naturally she is disturbed to hear from her son, Kuno, that he
wants to see her in person--something which is rarely done
anymore. At first, Vashti refuses, but eventually she agrees

to leave her home in the southern hemisphere and to seek out
her son in the northern hemisphere by means of an "air-
ship." When she sees him, she is told a strange story about
his finding a way to the Earth's surface where he not only
breathed without mechanical assistance but saw another human being. Certain that her son has gone mad, Vashti leaves
him. Years after their meeting, she receives another call
from Kuno during which he tells her simply, "The Machine
stops." She laughs at him but gradually begins to notice that
the Mending Apparatus is not keeping up with the demands
placed on it by the populace. Music was not played properly
by the Machine, but that was minor compared to the day when
the beds failed to appear when summoned from the Machine.
Things went from bad to worse after that until foul air and
dim lights seemed unimportant next to the fact that the Eutha-
nasia mechanism had failed, a failure which brought humanity
pain for the first time in many years. When the steady hum
of the Machine--a hum that had always existed--suddenly
stops, Vashti panics. The tunnel outside her apartment is
filled, as in her worst nightmares, with people also in a
state of panic. She and her son are reunited briefly just
before the entire underground structure is destroyed by an
air-ship which is out of control. He tells her once more
of the people on the Earth's surface, the people waiting for
the Machine to stop, waiting to claim the earth for their own.
She fears that someday someone else will turn the Machine
back on, but he insists that humanity has learned its lesson.

Forster's story is a vehicle for a dystopian message
--nothing more, nothing less. Even Vashti, as the main
character, is incidental to the story, there only to present
the message in the most succinct form. (This story was
published in The Eternal Moment and Other Stories, Harcourt,
Brace, Jovanovich, New York, 1928; in The Science Fiction
Hall of Fame, Volume IIB, Doubleday, New York, 1973, and
Avon Books, New York, 1974; and in James Gunn's The Road
to Science Fiction #2, New American Library, New York,
1979.)

Dormant, by Edith Nesbit (Bland), a revive-the-dead
novel somewhat reminiscent of (though considerably less tragic
than) Mary Shelley's Frankenstein, was published in 1911
by Methuen in London. The female protagonist, Rose Royal,
a "strong self-reliant" woman, has turned down all her male
suitors, but is attracted to a man with whom she has been
"chums for ages," Anthony (Tony) Drelincourt. (It is suggested that perhaps she is attracted to Tony because he wasn't

among her suitors.) Tony is a physiologist who has been
fascinated for many years with bringing dead animals back
to life, a fascination he has inherited from his uncle. By
coincidence, Rose discovers a volume in a secondhand-book
store which was the property of Tony's uncle and buys it for
Tony's birthday gift. In it Tony's uncle had written the secrets of life, secrets very similar to the ones Tony has already discovered. When Tony inherits a great deal of money,
he and Rose decide to marry.

Prior to marriage, they visit Tony's aunt Lady Cecily
Blair, who tells them of Eugenia, the woman who disappeared
fifty years before just prior to the date she was to marry
Tony's uncle. While visiting Lady Blair, Tony discovers the
body of Eugenia and sets about reviving it with his new "discovery." Eugenia, small and frail, is understandably dis-
oriented when she is awakened from a fifty-year death and
believes Tony, who bears a strong resemblance to his dead
uncle, to be her lover. Tony, who has fallen in love with
her, cannot bring himself to tell her that he is to marry
Rose and decides to marry Eugenia instead. It is Lady Blair,
the only person who knew Eugenia in 1866, who tells Eugenia
what year it now is, horrifying Eugenia with the knowledge
that she has been in a death-like sleep for fifty years.

Rose takes the news of Tony's new love extremely well,
and refuses to add to his guilt or pain by accusing him of
being unfaithful. She even tries to ease his guilt by telling
him that she could not have married him once he had made
his discovery about the "Elixir of Life." The book's conclusion brings the end of Tony and Eugenia as well, and the
paralysis of Lady Blair as she watches them die. The reader
is left with the implication that Rose will marry Tony's good
friend William Bats, a minor character in the novel who de-
ciphers the notes of Tony's uncle. A thoroughly decent human being, Bats deservedly inherits Tony's fortune, and evidently the affections of Rose.

Like Frankenstein, Dormant contains a warning about
the misuse of science in its efforts to bring the dead to life.
Unlike Frankenstein, Dormant has a strong female character
who does not pay with her life for her love of the meddling
scientist. Rose survives. In Dormant, it is the scientist
who dies.

Returning to the couple-as-main-characters motif,
there surfaced a novel (first run in 1912 in Cavalier Magazine)

by George Allan England entitled Darkness and Dawn (currently available from Hyperion Press, Westport, CT). Two sequels, entitled Beyond the Great Oblivion and The Afterglow, were run in Cavalier the following year. (In the Avalon Book editions of the 1960s, the three stories were made into five by the division of Beyond the Great Oblivion into a second volume, The People of the Abyss, and by the division of The Afterglow into Out of the Abyss and The Afterglow.) Darkness and Dawn, with its two characters Beatrice Kendrick and Allan Stern, is a last-woman-and-last-man plot in which an early twentieth-century stenographer and her employer, both of whom work in the Metropolitan Tower in New York City, fall asleep on the job, so to speak, and awaken approximately 800 years later in a world seemingly devoid of other human beings. (No answer is given about what happened to kill all of the population.) Their challenge is to find a way to survive in the overgrown forest which now fills the city's streets.

Much conflicting information is given about Beatrice. At one point, she is a "strong woman, eager-eyed and brave." At another, she is "grief and terror" stricken, and at still another point, she is "barbarous," and "seductive." She cries like a "frightened child," but "addressed herself eagerly to the fascinating task of making a real home" for them. She also sews their clothes out of furs, and is a "good cook." On the other hand, Beatrice kills a deer for food, and then tells Allan, "I'm not a child. I'm your equal now." Except for occasional displays of independence and strength of character, Beatrice's primary purpose in the book is to cling to Allan and to provide him with a motivation to survive. Early in the book, Allan promises himself to "find a way to smooth her path, to be a strength and refuge for her." Near the book's conclusion Beatrice tells Allan, "I trust you in everything. I'm in your hands. Lead me." Allan does his best because, after all, his reward at the novel's end for all his brave efforts is her willingness to be his mate, which he has wanted almost since their awakening. Typically for the time, the book ends with their first passionate kiss.

Beatrice is not a hero, but is used in the work as the only person left for whom Allan, as a hero, can be heroic. The two other books in the series follow Beatrice and Allan on further adventures and explorations, but little changes for Beatrice. Adoring mate to the end, Beatrice, now a mother, tells Allan as they survey the results of their hard work, "And but for you, ... none of all this could ever possibly have been."

Another sf work in which the human population is quite
suddenly reduced and the survivors must work to build a new
world is J(ohn) D(avys) Beresford's Goslings (London: William Heinemann, 1913), which portrayed a plague-devastated
world in which the vast majority of the survivors are women.
(Somewhat appropriately, the book was titled A World of
Women when it was published by The Macaulay Company in
New York.) Brian Stableford (in The Science Fiction Encyclopedia's entry for Beresford) calls the work "the first attempt to depict an all-female society which treats the issue
seriously and with a degree of sympathy. "   Though the book
does not contain one character, male or female, who can,
by this writer's definition, be called a main character, it
does contain several survivors who pave the way for the future.

Blanche Gosling, pampered and cared for in a male-
dominated world, accepts the challenge of survival in the
female-dominated world.   At the book's beginning, the most
important thing in her life seems to be how far the money
her father gives her will go towards clothing her in the latest
fashions she finds in London.   When the plague takes nearly
all of the male population, Blanche gradually takes the leadership position with her mother and her sister Millie.   Blanche
learns to perceive herself as more intelligent than the others
and to pride herself "on her powers of descrimination. "
When she meets Aunt May, a published writer and now the
provider for four other women, Blanche is inspired by her
strength and emulates her.   She sees the individuality of
people in a more pronounced way and sees everyone as having less restraint and as being more natural in the world
without men.   Blanche awakens the morning after her encounter with Aunt May with a joyful sense of purpose and finds
that the survivors need her intelligence because it "was of
a somewhat more masculine quality in some respects than
of the average woman. "   Blanche is needed and useful in a
world of women and settles with her mother and Millie in the
Marlow community.

Mrs. Gosling and Millie, on the other hand, are fully
at a loss without men.   Mrs. Gosling loses touch with reality at some point in the novel and never fully regains it to
the reader's knowledge.   She is said to be "too specialized"
as a homemaker living in the city to be flexible in this new
situation and is likened to "some great larva dug up from
its refuse heap--confused and feeble in this new strange
place of light and air. "

Millie, as Aunt May predicted to Blanche, seeks out one of the few remaining men "over the hill" and returns to Marlow only when she can stand the taunts of envious women no longer. Her return triggers a reaction of old morality and religious fervor which results not in her expulsion, but the expulsion of thirty-nine Jenkynites, as they are called, who disapprove of her. Millie's friendly acceptance by the remainder of Marlow is in no way lessened by her pregnancy.

Lady Eileen Ferrar, who calls herself Eileen of Marlow because there is no other Eileen there, enters the book quite late, but is the epitome of the new woman. It is Eileen who recruits Jasper Thrale as "chief mechanic" of the Marlow community of just under one thousand women. Jasper, who enters the book quite early with insightful warnings for the public about the plague, has a distinct aversion to relationships with women (or with men, for that matter), and settles into the Marlow community without incident after first insulting a number of female pursuers. Eileen, a hearty soul, tells Jasper right off, "Men are so jolly good at machinery. We shouldn't miss them much if it weren't for that." Eileen is independent, a hard worker who doesn't mind getting dirty while running the mill for Marlow. Jasper is disturbed to find himself attracted to Eileen and pushes those fears to the background while working by her side "as two men might have worked." Eventually, however, the attraction they feel for one another once more comes to the forefront, and they admit their feelings. Eileen is happy at the admission of mutual affection and tells Jasper, "Now we can be two jolly, clean human beings who understand each other, can't we? And we shall be such ripping good friends always; quite open and honest with each other." Jasper claims he has an excuse for never having found love. "I didn't know, because there was no woman like you to teach me. All the women I've known have been secretive and sly. They've fouled love for me by making it seem a hidden, disreputable thing. Oh! we shall be ripping good friends, little Eileen--magnificent friends." Eileen, with her usual intelligent insight, tells Jasper, "We'd never have understood each other so well if we hadn't worked together on the same job," and adds, "That and there being no footle about marriage."

Eileen is by far the character who is most successful in her transition into a world in which women share "Equality," as she calls it. When 1200 men arrive on a ship, she tells Jasper that she is sure the world had learned to avoid "class distinctions and sex distinctions, and things like that."

She also expresses that she believes the continued obsolescence of marriage would help to keep equality a reality. She
tells Jasper that "social conditions will be so different now
that there won't be any more marriage. Marriage was a
man's prerogative; he wanted to keep his woman to himself,
and keep his property for his children. It never really protected women, and anyway they were capable of protecting
themselves if they'd been given a chance." Better wages for
women and childcare as "everybody's business" are mentioned
as social changes by Eileen. Of all the characters in Goslings, Eileen is Beresford's best representation of the future
woman, the one who will survive with or without men.

        As a matter of interest, George Gosling, Mrs. Gos-
ling's spouse and father of Blanche and Millie, disappears
somewhere in the book after successfully surviving the plague.
George, it seems, took "a fancy" to a young woman on a
farm near where he had moved his family and decided to go
visit one day and not go home to his nagging wife and dependent daughters. Mrs. Gosling and her daughters never learned
of his whereabouts and assumed that he, too, had died of the
plague. Many of the surviving men took it upon themselves
to share themselves, so to speak, with as many women as
possible. Millie's affair was with one such man, and the
reader can't help but wonder if George followed a path similar to his.

        The year 1914 brought Angel Island (New York: Henry
Holt; reprinted by Ayer, Salem, NH, 1978) by Inez Haynes
Gillmore (Irwin), also a novel about a fresh start in struc-
turing society. It is the story of five lonely shipwrecked
men on an island and the five "air-women" or "angels" whom
they discover there. After barely surviving the shipwreck,
the men are surprised to see angels in the sky. The five
air-women--Clara, Chiquita, Lulu, Peachy, and Julia--are
the scion of a winged race who decided to fly north to their
freedom, "free from earth-ties--five incorruptible air-women,"
as Julia puts it. Julia is the leader of the group of women,
emotionally stronger than the rest and a thinker with much
insight into the relationships that develop between the men
and the air-women. It is her leadership which eventually
forces a change upon the men.

        When the men realize that the angels are women, each
man responds in his own unique way. Pete Murphy declares
that the air-women are "neither birds nor women" and feels
that the men have as their duty "to fall down and worship

them." Billy Fairfax claims they are women and, as such, deserve to be cherished and protected. Honey Smith insists the air-women are "girls" who need men to "josh and jolly them, to buy them taxicabs, theater-tickets, late suppers, candy, and flowers." Ralph Addington, "an offensive type of libertine," contemptuously tells the men, "They're females.... Our duty is to tame, subjugate, infatuate, and control them." Frank Merrill, the scholarly type in the group, chooses to look on the air-women as "an entirely new race of beings, requiring new laws."

In spite of their differences of opinion, the men create a plan to lure the air-women to earth and capture them in the men's newly built Clubhouse. It is there that the men tie the air-women to the walls and cut off their wings. As the women cannot walk, they have no mobility at all at that point and are, in every sense, prisoners. Ironically, after the men have cut off the air-women's wings, Billy is unable to understand why the men are having such a difficult time winning the women's trust. He tells his friends, "But what I can't understand ... is that they don't realize instantly that we wouldn't hurt them for anything--that that's a thing a fellow couldn't do."

Eventually the air-women learn the men's language, and marry the men, and then, of course, babies arrive on the scene--Angela, Honey-Boy, Peterkin, Junior, and Billy-Boy. After the air-women are captured and their wings are clipped, literally as well as figuratively, they find the men growing less and less attentive and interested in them. The men are bored by life on the island. Julia realizes that boredom is their enemy and suggests a project to Billy--to build a "New Camp." Unfortunately, what Julia doesn't predict is that the men will not take the women with them to help, but instead will leave the women at home while they go off each day to work by themselves. Julia realizes finally that the "Bond of Work" is stronger than the "Bond of Sex" and that the men are growing closer at the expense of their relationships with their women. In addition, the men refuse to let the air-women grow their wings back in and tell the women that when Angela (the only child with wings) reaches maturity, her wings will also be cut off. Julia, at this news, takes a stand and leads the air-women in revolt against the tyranny, teaching the other air-women how to walk and persuading them to leave their husbands until the issue surrounding the flight of Angela and of any other future children with wings can be resolved. The threat--that the women will leave

the men permanently isolated on the island with no female
companionship--produces rage in the men, who hunt the
women in the woods like game.   The women grow their wings
to make their escape from Angel Island possible, thus providing the men with the very real fear of their loss.   As a
consequence, the revolt is a successful one, and the right to
fly is secured for the offspring.   Of particular note is the
fact that Julia doesn't marry Billy, the man she loves, until
the book's end--until she has secured the right to fly for the
children.   As Julia has her wings at the end of the story, it
is also likely that she and the other women regained their
own right to fly as well.   Julia dies, leaving Billy a new son
who has wings.

There is some discussion among the women in the
book about thinking versus feeling.   All of the women but
Julia see themselves as feelers, not thinkers.   Julia is recognized as the thinker of the group, the one the men enjoy
talking to.   Lulu tells the women, "I hate to think."   Chiquita announces, "I never think."   Peachy tells the women
that she refuses to think: "I won't think.... I feel. That's
the way to live."   Clara is proud to tell the women, "I don't
have to think.... I've something better than thought--instinct
and intuition."   Peachy tells the women, "We don't have to
think any more than we have to walk; for we are air-creatures.
And air-creatures only fly and feel.   We are superior to them
[the men]."   It is this misconception of superiority that Julia
corrects.   She is a strong woman character who teaches the
women to walk and to think, and who leads them in their rebellion.

Not every sf writer, however, was intrigued by the
theme of building a new world or creating a new social structure.   Edgar Rice Burroughs, for example, was much more
interested in telling an exciting story and holding reader attention.   One of the ways he accomplished that goal was to
make his female characters sexually alluring.   His women
characters were constantly placed in the path of sexual assault.

Burroughs wrote between the years of 1912 and 1950
and is "universally acknowledged as the grand-daddy of American science fiction."[4]   He was a tremendously prolific author, writing more than 60 books in that period.   He was an
author who included a great number of women characters in
his books, though for the most part they are secondary to the
hero and included for a purpose.   Unfortunately, most if not

all of the women were included primarily for the excitement
they produced for the male readership. To quote Science
Fiction: History-Science-Vision, "One critic has counted
seventy-six threatened rapes in ERB's output for four years
(1912-15), without a single consummation. The women in
these tales are tantalizing and scantily clad. They are threatened by hideous monsters out of fairy tales and the Arabian
Nights, and protected by muscular heroes who also long to
possess them, but respect their virtue utterly."[5]

     Passion runs especially high in his books with women
main characters or women characters sharing that role. For
example, Thuvia, Maid of Mars (All-Story Weekly, April 1916;
currently available in Three Martian Novels from both Peter
Smith Publisher, Magnolia, MA, and Dover, New York) has
a female main character who must almost constantly fight off
sexual assault using her metal armlets as weapons. In spite
of her frequent battles with her assailants, the princess Thuvia usually manages somehow to maintain her haughty, scorn-
ful manner towards men. She is a bitch who falls in love.

     In The Cave Girl (1913-1917 in All-Story Weekly, and
in book form from Ace Books, 1975), on the other hand,
Nadara is a cave princess who innocently bounds through the
novel naked except for a skin around her waist. Nadara tells
Waldo, the hero, "My people take their mates as they will."
However, Waldo Emerson Smith-Jones refuses to give rein
to his passion for "the lovable little pagan" until their marriage, which, of course, occurs on the last page of the novel.
That is also when the reader discovers that Nadara's mother
was actually a countess (the royalty motif once more). Nadara plays a wide-eyed innocent who feels "reverent adoration" for sickly, weakling Waldo Emerson, who is prone to
cold sweats of fear. In spite of this weak male main character, who is so ill from a cough that his doctor predicts a
wasting death, Nadara turns to him for strength. At one
point Burroughs wrote, "The girl drew quite close to Waldo
in the instinctive plea for protection that belongs to her sex."
Nadara is no hero, but is there to give the sickly weakling
Waldo a chance to get well and grow strong and brave under
the adoring eyes of a weak, helpless female. And, of course,
it works. Nadara, the willing, compliant female, is an extreme contrast to Thuvia, the haughty bitch, but both are
used as tools to excite the reader.

     In direct contrast to Burroughs' women characters is
the woman main character in Gertrude Atherton's Black Oxen

(New York: Boni and Liveright, 1923, and available currently
from Folcroft Library Editions, Folcroft, PA).   The main
woman character in this work is the brilliant, "well-informed,"
intellectual, arrogant, self-assured, worldly-wise, sophisticated Countess Marie Zattiany, a woman who is aged 58,
though due to some sort of X-ray treatment appears to be
in her early thirties.   This "damnably clever" woman arrives in New York from Europe and attends plays, where she
attracts the attention of Lee Clavering, a promising play re-
viewer in his mid-thirties.   The mutual attraction develops
into a love relationship, which forces Marie, known in her
unmarried youth as Mary Ogden, to tell Lee the truth about
her age and her life story.   The revelation, though it shakes
him, does not deter him from seeking to marry her, which
pleases Marie greatly.   All goes well until a gentleman of her
own age, Prince Moritz Hohenhauer, tells her how foolish
she would be to marry merely for love.   He points out that
she cannot return to a time when she was not disillusioned.
"You, your ego, your mind, your self, are no younger than
your fifty-eight hard-lived years."   Marie, in her wisdom,
realizes he is right, and refuses to marry Lee.   She chooses
the position of power and influence which Hohenhauer offers
instead of the love offered by Lee.

        Marie Zattiany, though she attracted Lee Clavering
with her youthful appearance, cannot keep her years of experience from her facial expressions.   Lee notices "... that
look of ancient wisdom, disillusioned and contemptuous, [which]
came into her eyes," and doesn't understand why he is at once
attracted by her, yet unable to touch her.   "But she radiated
power, and that chin could not melt."   When Marie finally
tells Lee of the X-ray treatments and of her life, she tells
him she doesn't regret any of her experience, her love li-
aisons, but regrets the "weight of memories, the complete-
ness of disillusion, the slaying of mental youth--which cannot
survive brutal facts."   Reflecting on her "lover phase," she
says, "I believe that my education would not be complete
without that experience--mine, understand.   I am not speaking for women of other temperaments, opportunities, of less
intellect, of humbler character, weaker will...."   Of the
termination of this phase of her life, she says, "Men are
gross and ridiculous creatures in the main, and aside from
my personal disappointments, I thought it was time for that
chapter of my life to finish."   She summed herself up by
calling herself an "intellectual siren" who is motivated by
"curiosity, love of adventure, ennui...."   Marie's experience
and sophistication were highly unusual for a sf character in

1929. Her motives and desires are complex and believable--
three-dimensional.

         The depth and three-dimensionality of Gertrude Ather-
ton's main character in Black Oxen serve as a sharp contrast
to the shallowness and superficiality of E(dward) E(lmer)
"Doc" Smith's women characters in The Skylark of Space.
"Doc" Smith was a writer of sf who scattered women characters throughout his books. The women were not main characters; however, there were frequently women secondary
characters. John Clute (in The Science Fiction Encyclopedia's
entry for Smith) writes that "the chummy idiocy of the women"
is consistent in the Skylark series and that in the Lensman
series, "awfulness of its female characters" does not prevent the series from being popular even today. Such is the
case in The Skylark of Space (Amazing Stories, August 1928,
and currently available from Garland, New York), the initial
book in the Skylark series which he wrote with Mrs. Lee
Hawkins Garby.

         Dorothy Vaneman, Richard Seaton's fiancée and a sec-
ondary character in the book, is a "Doctor of Music and an
accomplished violinist" and has the "plenty of guts" necessary
to be among the first people in space. She and Dick along
with Margaret Spencer and Martin Crane--plus the wicked
Blackie DuQuesne--take a nine-week voyage out of the Milky
Way galaxy and struggle to find copper for the space drive
in order to get back to Earth. During their adventures,
Dorothy, "scared blue half the time," falls like Margaret
into "a ghastly purple funk." Since both couples need someone to lean on, and Dorothy insists that she's "scared to
death to go to bed," especially alone, the solution, forced
under Dick's nose by his fiancée, is a double wedding on the
planet where they have stopped briefly. Dorothy, who has
total faith in Dick's abilities, is a great admirer of Margaret,
and is admired in turn by Dick, who at one point says, "What
a girl!" Perhaps "chummy idiocy" is a bit strong, but certainly a mutual admiration society, which isn't completely
justifiable, does seem to exist.

         Another woman character brave enough to go into space
was the main character of Thea Von Harbou's book The Rocket
to the Moon (first published as a serial in Berlin Woche, No-
vember 3-December 8, 1928, under the title of Die Frau im
Mond, "The Woman in the Moon"; published in English by
World Wide Publishing, New York, 1930; reprinted by Gregg
Press, Boston, 1977). The book has also been published in

English under the title of The Girl in the Moon. In spite of
the title, the "girl" or "woman" Friede Velten is a secondary
character. For the most part, the story follows the actions
of Wolf Helius, who is in love with Friede and who plans and
executes a trip to the moon. Friede, nonetheless, is a strong
woman character, both in her physical appearance and in her
personality. She has a "golden mane" of hair, an "out-of-
door complexion," and "beautiful eyes, like aquamarines."
She is called an "Amazon" by her fiancé, Hans Windegger,
Helius' very close friend and his rival for Friede's affections.
She has "strong, energetic little hands" and a "lovely, frank
young face." She is strong-willed, insistent once her mind
is made up, and courageous in the way she faces new and
dangerous situations. As it turns out, she is adventurous
enough to stay on the moon in spite of her opportunity to return to Earth.

     At the book's beginning, Helius is silently heart-broken
over Friede's engagement to his friend Hans and decides to
go to the moon in his newly-built "Space-Ship." He asks
Professor Manfeldt, who has longed to travel to the moon to
search for gold, to go also; however, very soon the number
of passengers planned upon has tripled. Walt Turner, a first-
rate scoundrel, threatens his way onto the passenger list.
Friede and Hans insist upon going as well, and a boy stows
away, making the total number of passengers six. Friede,
the only female on board, performs the task of preparing
meals in an "obedient and cheerful" manner. It is Friede
who discovers the 12-year-old stowaway, Gustav, but it is
Helius who becomes the boy's idol. Considering the tension
the group feels with the unwelcome presence of Walt Turner,
the trip to the moon is a calm, uneventful one. Helius finds
oxygen and water on the dark side of the moon and lands the
ship. Professor Manfeldt, who becomes demented, finds the
gold he has longed for. Hans, who hates the moon and wants
to return to Earth, can't understand Friede's enjoyment of
the moon or her desire to stay there.

     The devious Walt Turner, disguised as Helius, plans
to steal the Space-Ship and to return to Earth with Helius'
identity. Before he can execute his plan, Helius attacks him
to prevent him from harming Friede. In the struggle, Turner
shoots part of the oxygen supply, making the return to Earth
impossible for three of the party. As Professor Manfeldt refuses to leave his moon of gold, and Turner dies in his
struggle with Helius, there are only four people who are considering the trip; hence, Helius sneakily drugs the dinner

wine and magnanimously fires Hans, Friede, and Gustav off
towards Earth. What Helius doesn't expect is Friede's insight into his plan and her stealth until the ship is gone. She
has outsmarted him and plans to stay on the moon with him
until the time (if ever) when the ship can be outfitted for return on a rescue mission. An interesting note is that Friede
also suggested that she and Hans stay on the moon. Naturally,
Hans refuses since he hates the moon. The reader is left
wondering if this is her final test of Hans' courage (for she
has been disappointed by his actions several times before),
or if she just wants to stay on the moon, whoever her companion will be. Whatever her real reason for staying, Friede,
in spite of her status as a secondary character, is courageous
and adventurous in her determination to remain in such a
strange and isolated environment.

The year 1929 brought the novel The Princess of the
Atom by Ray(mond) (King) Cummings. (It was published originally by Avon; reprinted by Avon Books, 1950, and by Board-
man, London, 1951.) Though the narrator is Frank Ferrule,
the story's focus is Dianne Ferrule, who is a princess from
an "infinitely small" world called Mita, originally located in
an atom inside a rock on Bird's Nest Island on the coast of
New England. Frank's father and mother find Dianne on the
island, human-baby size, when she is approximately a year
old and adopt her as their own. She is "blue-eyed" and
"flaxen-haired," and has hair which "grew down at the center
of her forehead in a queer little peak" and a "crescent-moon
scar" on her forehead. When she is 16 years old, she disappears while she, Frank, and his brother Drake are swim-
ming. It is then that Frank and Drake are told by their father that Dianne is not their sister, but a "foundling." Five
years later, Dianne reappears with the aid of a growing and
shrinking drug, explaining to her foster father and brothers
that she is the princess of this diminutive world called Mita
and is in need of their help to defeat Togaro, who plans to
conquer not only her world, but the entire Earth as well.
Naturally they agree to assist her.

Frank, in the midst of his assistance, begins to see
Dianne not as his sister, not as a princess, but as "just an
apprehensive, frightened little girl." His attraction to Dianne
is obvious and fortunately for Frank, Dianne is attracted to
him, too. Togaro, however, also wants Dianne and captures
her, keeping her with his troops as they prepare to attack
Earth. It is Dianne who launches her own personal attack
against Togaro once they have achieved giant size, an action

which forces Frank to fight Togaro to the death.   Naturally,
Frank and Dianne (as well as Drake and Dianne's servant
Ahlma) marry at the book's conclusion.

There is much shrinking and growing of the characters
in the novel, a factor which gives the fights and escapes an
interesting variety and uniqueness. Descriptions of the physical sensations and changing landscapes viewed in the process
of growing and shrinking (and of the pitted quality of seemingly the smoothest surface as the characters shrink in size)
fill the book and set the stage for the action.

Dianne, even as a main character, is never fully developed into a three-dimensional one.   Though she is the
focus of the book, her actions are usually kept in the background.   Primarily she offers the foster father and brothers
motivation for their involvement in the affairs of Mita.   She
does, at one point, manage to hold her hand over Togaro's
mouth for a moment, an act which gives Frank the chance
to reach him and knock him out before Togaro's men can
capture them.   Also, her blatant refusal to stay in hiding
at the story's conclusion and her determination to reach Togaro and stop him even if she must go alone provide Frank
with the final motivation he needs to confront and kill Togaro.
However, she does land the first blow, so to speak, when
she grabs Togaro and trips him, and later in the same
struggle she tosses a rock at Togaro which hits his shoulder,
but doesn't hurt him.   For the most part, though, Dianne
accepts help and stays out of the way of the fighting.

NOTES

1. In the 1965 University of Nebraska Press edition of The
    Last Man, Hugh J. Luke, Jr. quotes reviewers of the
    work who wrote that the book was " 'an elaborate piece
    of gloomy folly' " and " 'the product of a diseased imag-
    ination and a polluted taste.' "

2. Margaret Mead, Sex and Temperament (1935) and Male
    and Female (1949).

3. Science Fiction: What It's All About (New York: Ace
    Books, 1971), p. 148.

4. Baird Searles, Martin Last, Beth Meacham, and Michael
    Franklin, A Reader's Guide to Science Fiction (New York:
    Avon Books, 1979), p. 31.

5. Robert Scholes and Eric S. Rabkin, Science Fiction:
    History-Science-Vision (New York: Oxford University
    Press, 1977), p. 12.

The decade of the 1930s was the era of the popularity of the
pulp magazine in the United States. Hugo Gernsback, as
founder of Amazing Stories and Wonder Stories, not only directed the path of sf during the crucial early period of its
growth, but also encouraged readers and writers of sf to
correspond through his magazine Wonder Stories.   The result of the enthusiastic communication between readers was
the creation of sf fandom, and, subsequently, fanzines.
("Fanzine" is defined in The Science Fiction Encyclopedia as
"A term describing an amateur magazine produced by sf
fans. ") Said to be "the schools and play grounds for develop-
ing writers and editors" (Robert Scholes and Eric S. Rabkin
in Science Fiction: History-Science-Vision), the fanzines (as
well as fandom as a whole) continue to flourish today.   So
influential was Hugo Gernsback during this critical time of
growth in the sf field that the Science Fiction Achievement
Awards are also called Hugo Awards in his honor.

However, it wasn't Hugo Gernsback who broke ground
in permitting or encouraging writers of sf to write about
women characters.   Astounding Stories, edited by F. Orlin
Tremaine, and Thrilling Wonder Stories, edited by Mort Wei-
singer, were the ground-breakers in this area.   Although
Stanley G. Weinbaum's first story, "A Martian Odyssey,"
appeared in Wonder Stories, the larger proportion of his fiction appeared in Astounding Stories.   In the mid-thirties,
Weinbaum was a tremendously important writer of stories
with strong women characters.   Sam Moskowitz, in his introduction to A Martian Odyssey and Other Science Fiction
Tales (Westport, CT: Hyperion Press, 1974), attributes
Weinbaum's abundance of strong women characters to "his
subconscious wish to meet a woman who was his intellectual
equal. " It might be more accurate to say that Weinbaum
wished to meet a woman who was willing to admit she was

his intellectual equal. Certainly such women existed in the
1920s and 1930s, although it was difficult for women of intelligence to find the educational and career opportunities
open to men. Increased opportunities for women to get education and a gradual societal acceptance of women with intelligence have made a difference in the willingness of women
to recognize and admit their intelligence, which would have
probably made Weinbaum happy.

Arthur K. Barnes' contribution to women characters
in sf should also be mentioned. Interplanetary hunter Gerry
Carlyle and her male subordinate (and later fiancé) sought
and found a variety of life forms in our solar system and,
to paraphrase her nickname, brought them back alive. Thrilling Wonder Stories once more brought readers stories about
strong women characters.

Weird Tales introduced C. L. Moore's famous warrior Jirel of Joiry in 1934 and continued to furnish readers
with periodic stories about the passionate, fighting redhead
throughout the 1930s.

Aside\from the works of Barnes, Weinbaum, and Moore,
sf in the 1930s contained few women heroes. Unfortunately,
this situation was to get worse before it got better.

* BARNES, ARTHUR K. "Hothouse Planet," in Thrilling
       Wonder Stories, Oct. 1937; also in Startling Stories
       Sept. 1949; retitled "Venus," in Interplanetary Hunter.
       Hicksville, NY: Gnome Press, 1956; rpt. New York:
       Ace Books, 1972.

Main Character: Gerry Carlyle, nicknamed Catch-
'em-alive Carlyle.
       Physical Characteristics: Is beautiful with "spun-
gold hair, intelligence lighting dark eyes, a hint of passion
and temper in the curve of mouth and arch of nostrils"; is
an "interplanetary hunter" and explorer, "a woman of action"
and the "sole leader" of the hunting party on Venus.
       Mental/Emotional Characteristics: At first, Tommy
Strike considers her "an arrogant female," "wilful," "selfish," and aggressive, with a "terrific sense of her own importance"; then Strike sees her as "one instant so warm and
friendly, the next imperious and dominating," and "arrogant
and cocksure"; he perceives her as "a woman walking in a
man's world," purposely emotionless--"the most pathetic of

beings--a woman who dared not be a woman"; she considers
herself "man enough to face anything" and is proud of her
accomplishments and the recognition given to her; is determined to succeed.

Story Particulars: Tommy Strike, Venusian trader,
has been instructed to assist interplanetary hunter Gerry
Carlyle on his search for animals to capture to take to the
Interplanetary Zoo in London.   What Tommy doesn't know is
that "Catch-'em-alive" Carlyle is a woman.   When she arrives on Venus in her famous expeditionary ship, The Ark,
Tommy is dumbfounded and immediately insults her by blurt-
ing out his feeling that her work is "more like a man's job."
Gerry informs him that she is the best hunter in the business
and that she is "man enough to face anything this planet has
to offer."

As they become acquainted, Tommy sees Gerry as
"wilful," arrogant, and aggressive, and decides he doesn't
like her.   On the first hunting trip, Gerry loses one of her
men to a monster called a whip.   She, remaining cool and
in command, appears to be unaffected by the death of her
assistant until Tommy notices the unshed tears in her eyes.
Tommy begins to pity her and sees her as the "most pathetic of beings--a woman who dared not be a woman."
Gerry, "a woman walking in a man's world, speaking man's
language, using man's tools," continues her hunt, gradually
filling The Ark with live Venusian animals; however, one animal, the Murri, eludes her, and Tommy veils from her information about the difficulties she will have capturing and
saving the monkey-like creatures.   This withholding of information irritates Gerry, but doesn't alter her plan to take
several Murris back with her to London.   After the successful capture of two Murris, Gerry is at first disturbed and
then distraught over the Murris' refusal to eat.   She sends
a work party out to take the one tree they need to survive,
horrifying Tommy.   As she and Tommy rush to stop the
work party, they and the workers are drugged by gases the
Murris make from a native plant, and Gerry is captured by
them.   Tommy plays the hero and rescues her, taking a kiss
as a reward.   Tommy, in later stories, is Gerry's second-
in-command, the Captain of The Ark, and their romance
progresses through their engagement and a number of hunts.

A paradox exists in the portrayal of Gerry in this
first story of her adventures.   She is viewed as pathetic yet
"incredible"; as "wilful" and aggressive, yet an excellent
commander; as having a "terrific sense of her own importance," yet lauded as the best interplanetary hunter in existence.   When she feels pity for the Murris as the male hunter

before her had, Tommy sees her as a "bewildered girl, needing a man's comfort but not knowing how to get it." In later
stories, Gerry is allowed to be the heroic character the reader
glimpses in the first story without the accompanying criticism
from Tommy.

★   BEYNON, JOHN (John Wyndham Parkes Lucas Beynon
      Harris). The Secret People. Serialized in Passing
      Show, July-Sept. 1935; rpt. London: George Newnes,
      1935; rpt. New York: Fawcett World Library, 1973.

      Main Character: Margaret Lawn.
      Physical Characteristics: Has "deep red curls," and
"slender, sun-browned hands"; her face has "a tinge of golden
brown"; has "hazel eyes" and "perfectly genuine dark lashes."
      Mental/Emotional Characteristics: Knows "her own
mind," and dislikes "elementary tricks"; is spirited with a
willingness to have adventures; is emotionally "a brick"; refuses to allow Mark to act like a he-man and hide fearful information from her; is told she has guts by her torturer, but,
like all people, has her breaking point.
      Story Particulars: In September 1964 (i.e., 29 years
in the future) Mark discovers Margaret Lawn in Algiers while
on a one-night rest on a trip in his rocket plane, the Sun
Bird. Margaret is strongly attracted to him and agrees to
go for a flight to see the New Sea that France has created
in the Sahara Desert. On their return, an explosion occurs
on the plane, followed by their rapid descent into the sea,
and a wild adventure. The plane cabin, fortunately, is water-
tight, and they float, sans wings, to an island recently created
by the sea. There they find a cat which they name Bast and
decide it would be better to sail the Sun Bird to possible
safety than to stay and starve.
      On their makeshift-boat ride, the cabin, occupants
inside, is sucked down a whirlpool to a subterranean cavern
which is filling with water from the flooded desert. There
they discover giant mushrooms and pygmies, seemingly right
out of fairy tales. And as in fairy tales, nothing goes as
expected. Attracted to the cat because they worship animal
deities, the pygmies rush the couple and at this point Margaret and Mark become separated. Mark, beaten senseless
because he fires a gun at them, discovers that the pygmies
keep all people who see them as prisoners to prevent information about their race from getting out.
      After Mark recovers from his beating, he and a group
of prisoners create a plan of escape, keeping in mind that the

caves are filling with water from the New Sea.   Unfortunately,
part of the plan includes fighting and killing pygmies which,
now, Mark doesn't relish.   Margaret, who has become the
honored chief attendant to the cat-goddess she has brought
in her arms to the pygmies, fares much better than Mark.
Her duty is to take the cat to the cavern of worship when
ordered where the pygmies assemble and pray to it.   Carm,
a dignified pygmy who befriends Margaret, tells her that Mark
is alive, though still weak from the beating the pygmies gave
him.

        A prisoner hears of the Sun Bird from Mark and be-
trays his fellow prisoners by telling the pygmies of an escape
tunnel they are digging in exchange for free access to the
pygmies' caverns.   This prisoner, Miguel, with his newly-
traded access to the caverns, approaches Margaret to get
the location of the Sun Bird from her so he can escape.   She
carefully considers telling him and wisely decides not to, sus-
pecting he can not be trusted to send help once he's reached
safety.   He is furious and ends up capturing and torturing
her to her breaking point.   It is surprising to Miguel that
Margaret has so much "guts," but his admiration doesn't
keep him from continuing the torture--stone knives under the
fingernails and threats of additional torture--until she breaks.
Sobbing in agony, she agrees to take him to the Sun Bird.
Following her directions, he carries her to the plane-boat,
only to find that Mark and three other prisoners are near the
ship, too.   Naturally, a scuffle ensues and Miguel is killed.

        The reunion of Mark and Margaret is a warm one,
and a happy ending follows for the five escapees.   Margaret,
much to Mark's shock, feels sorry for her torturer.   This
novel was written about characters with bold sophistication,
who frequently use "darling" and "dear" in their vocabulary,
and who aren't afraid of a few adventures.

*   BOND, NELSON.   "The Priestess Who Rebelled," in
        Amazing Stories, Oct. 1939; retitled "Pilgrimage," in
        Isaac Asimov Presents the Great Science Fiction Sto-
        ries, Volume I, 1939.   Ed. Isaac Asimov and Martin
        H. Greenberg.   New York: Daw Books, 1979.

    Main Character: Meg.
    Physical Characteristics: Ages from 12 to 17 years
old in the story; has long, firm legs and a supple body
"bronzed by sunlight except where her doeskin breech-cloth
kept the skin white"; has hair which would "have trailed the
earth, but she wore it piled upon her head"; is beautiful; has

skin of "golden-brown" and "high, firm breasts"; is strong
enough to make a long journey on horseback and on foot.

Mental/Emotional Characteristics: Is only 12 when
she decides she wants to be the Jinnia Clan's next Mother
(clan leader); is bright enough to learn to write and deal with
multiplication and division; is highly motivated by her passions and angers easily.

Story Particulars: It is an unnamed but long time
since the war which started in 1960--the war which lasted for
"many years" and occurred "across the sea"; the war that
women finally grew tired of and ended by refusing to send
further supplies and ammunition to the men. Now remaining
in the United States are scattered Clans, ruled by and con-
sisting mostly of women who are warriors, mothers, and
workers. Men, few in number, are counted in the record
books of the Clan Mothers with the cattle and horses.

When Meg reaches her 12th year in the Jinnia Clan,
she decides she wants to be a Clan Mother and, after being
accepted by the current Clan Mother as a trainee, sets to
work learning to read, write, multiply, and divide, and to
recite the strange rites and rituals of the Clan, such as the
Sacred Song, "O, Sakan! you see by Tedhi on his early
Light--."

Meg grows into a beautiful young woman, though as
the vanity-god was dead, she was unaware of her beauty.
At age 17, Meg the Priestess is sent off on a pilgrimage by
the Clan Mother to see the Place of the Gods and is told by
the Clan Mother that the "final secret which the clan must
not know" will be told to her on her return.

On her horseback journey, Meg is attacked twice by
Wild Ones, men not of a clan. The first time, she kills her
attacker, but the second time, she is rescued by a Hairless
One, a "Man-thing" who calls himself Daiv, He-who-would-
learn. Meg is surprised by his openness and willingness to
share information, and she enjoys his company on her journey, in spite of his various insults. When Daiv finds her
horse has run away, he spits out, "You women! ... Bah!
You do not know how to train a horse." When he proceeds
to ask her to stay with him and become his mate, she is af-
fronted, a reaction which amuses him. Daiv introduces her
to "the touching-of-mouths," which he says "is the right of
the Man with his mate."

Daiv also horrifies her with the notions that the gods
are Men, not Women as she has been raised to believe, and
that a war "between the sexes" followed the war of 1960.
Women, he told her, refused to take their men back and thus
the Clans and the "Wild Ones of the forest" were divided.

Daiv also tells her that he is from Kirki, one of the few
places which does not have a matriarchy. Naturally, Meg
thinks he is insane; however, when she sees only male gods
at the Place of the Gods (Mt. Rushmore), she realizes that
he is telling the truth--men were the rulers and the gods.
The matriarchal Clan life, Meg decides, is "artificial" and
the result of "an ill-conceived vengeance." Believing that her
clan and all clans are destined to die out because of their
"cold and loveless courses," and tempted by both her passions and Daiv's request that she be his mate, Meg leaps at
the remnant of a prayer, "shall not perish from the earth,
but have everlasting Life ... " and decides to do her part to
propagate the species.
     There are two additional stories in this series: "The
Judging of the Priestess" (Fantastic Adventures, April 1940)
and "Magic City" (Astounding Science-Fiction, February 1941).

* CROSS, VICTORIA (Vivian Cory). Martha Brown, M.P.,
     A Girl of To-Morrow. London: T. Werner Laurie,
     1935.

     Main Character: Martha ("Marte") Brown.
     Physical Characteristics: Is a "lithe, active figure";
is "a magnificent specimen of bronzed womanhood"; has blue
eyes which are "clear and bright"; smokes a pipe; has "fine
legs, slight waist and broad shoulders"; has "shiny, vigorous-
looking hair" which is "chestnut" brown; has a "round, smil-
ing face," "great intelligent eyes," and a "soft voice"; is
aged 35; is beautiful; wears clothes, as do all the women in
England at that time, that were considered masculine in the
twentieth century.
     Mental/Emotional Characteristics: Has "never-failing
good spirits"; is considered "a leading woman of her time";
makes "fiery speeches," and has "unshakable logic"; is a
"self-made woman"; is a "bank director, a member of Parliament, a well-known author, and in possession of an income
from investments"; is "not easily frightened" and is "ready to
meet a man's desires"; works with "ardour and vigour"; is
"rich, brilliant, famous."
     Story Particulars: Set sometime in the thirtieth cen-
tury, this novel chronicles the change in Martha Brown, a
member of Parliament in England, from a woman secure,
successful and happy in her life to a woman who has thrown
away an opportunity to be Prime Minister of England for an
American man she has just met. Men in England at this time
were effeminate and small in stature, and dressed in skirts,

lace, and stockings. The women were stronger, self-
confident, and in control, and wore pants and jackets, or
suits on more formal occasions.

Though some social reform is mentioned, giving the
work the flavor of a utopia novel, for the bulk of the book,
Martha, happily in charge of her life, travels from place to
place, much as a well-to-do man of the twentieth century
might have done, visiting with her four husbands, each of
whom is completely different from the others. Her main
husband, James Brown, is intuitive, emotional, and dependent and keeps the three children she has borne for him in
the Manor House in the country. She visits him as little as
possible, primarily because he irritates her with his inces-
sant need for her. Carlo Matteo, her Italian lover/husband
who lives in Newquay, keeps a child of theirs and paints pictures. Cyril, ten years her junior, is the happy and frivolous husband who always makes "his gay society" available
to her. With him, she feels "no jar, no discord," probably
because he places no serious demands upon her and occasionally has a superficial fling himself. Gerald Kingsley, wealthy
and important in his own right as a play Censor for the Queen,
is thirty years her senior. He is the dearest of her loves
as well as the first.

In the midst of all of this male affection, Martha became a successful playwright quite early in life and later, a
bank director and a member of Parliament. She is well
known for her reforms in the prison system in England and
is admired in America as well. She is so popular that she
is in line for the position of Prime Minister when Bruce
Campbell Campbell (sic), a virile American, enters her yard
and her life, and shakes her secure, content life to its very
core. He dresses as she does, wears a moustache, and can
do things like "building a house, felling a tree, sawing up
lumber, riding wild horses ..." which Martha finds utterly
fascinating and attractive about him. He refuses to share
her, but offers her his love if she will leave her four husbands for him. He tells her she is needed in America, that
there she can bring about great changes. He also tells her
he doesn't break horses as some people do, but charges
them with the electricity of his love, so to speak, until they
want to do what he wants them to do. Martha has never felt
this type of love before and must make her decision about
him in the face of being offered the position of Prime Minister. When she asks him why she should sacrifice everything for him, he responds, "For pleasure, for joy, for
life!" Whatever her reasons, Martha, the "Girl of To-
Morrow," flees England with Bruce for America, leaving

her four husbands and her four children to collect support
allotments from her wealth.

The reader is left to guess at the success or failure
of this new liaison. Cross's emphasis, at this point, is not
upon character development, but on her belief that there is
a need for complete involvement of both sexes in the emotion
of love. Cross takes the twentieth-century male social norm
of behavior, gives it to the female portion of the thirtieth-
century society, and then proceeds to imply that neither way
is truly fulfilling or satisfying for either sex. Her implication is that only a sacrificing, all-encompassing type of love,
shared by both partners, can be called love at all.

* DEL REY, LESTER.   "Helen O'Loy," in Astounding
    Science-Fiction, Dec. 1938; in The Science Fiction
    Hall of Fame, Volume I.   Ed. Robert Silverberg.
    New York: Doubleday, 1970; rpt. New York: Avon
    Books, 1971.

Main Character: Helen O'Loy.
Physical Characteristics: Is a robot "in spun plastics
and metals" (android), "the plastic and rubberite face was
designed for flexibility to express emotions"; has "tear glands
and taste buds"; is "beautiful, a dream."
Mental/Emotional Characteristics: Cries when she
thinks Dave doesn't like her; loves Dave; is a good cook, a
good companion, and a good homemaker.
Story Particulars: Phil, a doctor, and Dave, a robot
specialist, are friends and roommates with a problem: their
housemaid mech (robot) is impossible. So when they order
a new robot, they ask that a special one be built "with a full
range of memory coils." The result is Helen O'Loy (a cross
between "Helen of Troy" and "Alloy"), a beautiful robot with
a human appearance that (who?) steals both their hearts away.
Unfortunately, Phil is called away on business before
she is activated and Dave decides to activate the robot and
leaves her watching a travelogue on the stereovisor. After
the travelogue plays, the stereovisor switches automatically
to the serials. Helen O'Loy, after carefully studying love
stories (soap operas) all day, learns how to fawn and coo,
and throwing her strong arms around Dave when he returns
home, declares her love and passion for him. Although Dave
lectures her about her behavior for three hours, Helen still
insists that she loves him. Dave reacts to her insistence
by drinking heavily and avoiding Helen. By the time Phil
returns home, the matter has become serious. Dave is near

exhaustion from no food (he refuses to eat with Helen, so
doesn't eat) and stress.   The solution to the problem is
simple: Helen makes a wonderful homemaker and a loving
wife.

Peter Nicholls has written of this story that it is a
"classic of sexist sf" and is "one of the most unconsciously
disgusting stories in the genre, in which a ROBOT woman
is the perfect helpmate, a state of which the narrator senti-
mentally approves ..." (The Science Fiction Encyclopedia, ed.
by Peter Nicholls, Doubleday, Garden City, NY, 1979, p.
661).   By no stretch of the imagination can Helen be called
a three-dimensional character.   (See the 1980s chapter for a
synopsis of Tanith Lee's The Silver Metal Lover, a novel in
which a male android is loved by a woman.)

* ERTZ, SUSAN.   Woman Alive.   London: Hodder &
     Stoughton, 1935; rpt. New York: D. Appleton-Century,
     1936.

Secondary Character: Stella Morrow (doesn't enter the
story until a third of the way into the book, but is the focus
of the book from then on).
Physical Characteristics: Is young; is not beautiful
but has "irregular" features with full lips, a nose which is
"short and blunt," and eyes which are "small and deeply set";
has a "full and intelligent forehead and a firm and slightly
prognathous jaw"; is 5'6" tall and weighs about "nine and a
half stone"; has strong wrists and ankles and clear skin; has
"very light brown" hair which tends to "curl about the forehead"; has "scarcely any eyebrows at all," "strong teeth"
and small blue eyes behind thick eyelids; is considered by
Dr. Selwyn to be "Very Saxon"; has "broad hips, full bosom
and calm looks" and according to Dr. Selwyn "was born to
be the mother of many children."
Mental/Emotional Characteristics: Is strong-willed
and a pessimist; has "sense and intelligence"; is shrewd and
has common sense; has an "orderly mind"; is totally and ab-
solutely opposed to war and violence; according to Dr. Selwyn,
has "strong character and sound views."
Story Particulars: Although she doesn't enter the story
until a third of the way into the book, Stella Morrow, as the
only woman who survives the plague of 1985, is the focus of
the book from that point forward.   The story is told in first
person by Dr. Selwyn, who in 1935 requested to see his own
life fifty years in the future from Ugolino Spero, famous for
his ability to go into a trance and allow those near to him to

have very real flashes of other places. Spero grants this
wish, sending Dr. Selwyn forward in time to 1985 where the
good doctor, then a very old man, discovers that all the
women in the world but one have died of a plague. Dr. Selwyn finds the one survivor, Stella Morrow, and contacts the
Prime Minister of England, thus starting her on a road of a
very public life, filled with pressures from all sides for her
to marry and start future generations.

Though she refuses any title, Stella is installed, for
safety's sake, at the Palace of the deceased Queen of England,
Stella graciously receives guests from all over the world and
listens to scientists, artists, and musicians argue at her
table. The plan of the world is to find Stella a husband and
start raising daughters; however, Stella wants nothing to do
with that plan as she had previously fallen in love and had
been rejected when her lover grew famous. She sees the
male of the human species as a "fighting animal," violent
and self-destructive, and feels that the human species should
die out completely. She blames women, herself included,
for not uniting against war and against the romantic notions
of men. In one of Stella's many talks to the public, she
says, "... romantic people are nearly always bloody-minded.
That's the reverse side of the picture. If you're romantic,
you like the idea of war and killing. Why, heaven knows."

The world's reaction to her refusal to marry requires
all of her diplomacy to avert war. In essence she promises
one of her daughters (not yet conceived or even seriously
considered) to a foreign government to ensure the continued
bloodline of that nation, with the stipulation that the male
child will be raised by her in the Palace. She eventually
yields and decides to marry Alan, one of the first men she
sees after the plague. Alan is "lovable and endearing" and
has been wise enough not to pressure her. Even on her wedding day, Stella cries out to the men who have fanatically
watched the ceremony, "Oh, you strange creatures! ... So
careless of life and of the world, so eager for it to continue!
Who can understand you?"

When Dr. Selwyn suddenly and unexpectedly returns
to 1935, Spero is dead; however, Dr. Selwyn locates Stella's
grandparents and knows his experience was--or will be--real.
Stella is a country woman with a world of common sense
and a healthy pessimism derived from her own insight and
experience and from her excellent educational background.
Though she enters the story far into the book, Stella is the
star of this saga, and it is hers to tell. As the last woman
alive, she embodies the collective opinions and insights of
all women. Her words and actions are the focus, the pivotal
point for the future in this world.

* MOORE, C(ATHERINE) L(UCILLE). "Black God's Kiss,"
   in Weird Tales, Oct. 1934; in Shambleau and Others.
   Hicksville, NY: Gnome Press, 1953; in Black God's
   Shadow. West Kingston, RI: Donald M. Grant, 1977
   (with color plates); rpt. as Jirel of Joiry. New York:
   Ace Books, 1982.

Main Character: Jirel of Joiry.
Physical Characteristics: Has short, "wild red hair"
and "wild lion-yellow eyes"; is "as tall as most men, and as
savage as the wildest of them"; has a face which has "a biting, sword-edge beauty as keen as the flash of blades"; uses
both a dagger and a "long two-handed sword"; is physically
as "strong as many men."

Mental/Emotional Characteristics: Is a proud warrior
and curses freely; hates with a "blaze" of passion and frequently flares into "a haze of red anger"; is "not innocent
in the ways of light loving" but refuses to be any man's
"fancy, for a night or two"; is a fiercely resolute, determined, vengeful person; is intelligent and wary; does not
recognize the "heady violence" of love when she feels it.

Story Particulars: The Jirel of Joiry stories are
considered sword-and-sorcery fantasy rather than sf, but
one is included in this volume both because of the strong
character portrayed and because of the classic nature of the
series. Jirel is a volatile, vengeful warrior, the commander
of Joiry, the strongest fortress in the kingdom. In this story,
dressed in helmet, mail, and "greaves of some forgotten le-
gionary, relic of the not long past days when Rome still ruled
the world," she wields her dagger and sword powerfully when
her fortress is attacked, but she and her fortress are conquered by Guillaume, a man who forces his kiss on her.

Though she is not unfamiliar with "the ways of light
loving," she curses furiously at his insolence in forcing a
kiss on her and vows vengeance on him. She travels down
through the dungeons to a secret cave "into hell," where she
seeks a weapon from the devil to destroy her conqueror. It
is only her strength of purpose and her will which keeps her
from fleeing from the horrible land she finds beneath the
dungeon. There she finds her weapon--a kiss bearing a seed
of "something alien beyond any words." When she returns to
the surface, Guillaume waits for her and welcomes the kiss,
a kiss of death. It is only as he lies dead at Jirel's feet
that she realizes the "heady violence" she felt when she
thought of him was not hate, but love.

There are a total of six Jirel of Joiry stories. In
the second, "Black God's Shadow," Jirel's torment over the

death of Guillaume is resolved when she once more goes beneath the dungeons to free his soul from hell.

★ QUICK, DOROTHY. Strange Awakening. New York:
       House of Field, 1938.

       Main Character: Iva.
       Physical Characteristics: Is very beautiful; has "big
blue eyes" with "heavy black lashes" and short hair that falls
in "golden curls about her forehead."
       Mental/Emotional Characteristics: Is "quite fancy-
free" and "enjoyed everything"; is "remarkably fatalistic" in
her "view of things"; blushes rather frequently.
       Story Particulars: Iva, a young Earth woman who is
insomniac one evening, is looking out her bedroom window
and finds herself suddenly in "a blaze of light." She finds
herself subsequently transported from a Long Island village
to Venus where she meets and falls in love with the ruler of
the Blue Land, Ota. He gives her a language tablet of wisdom so that they may communicate and a belt which is worn
because it is supposed to preserve life there. Iva blushes to
learn that in the act of donning the belt she has become the
wife of Ota and is under his protection from his father, the
Great Mind, who transported her there and wants her for his
own. Iva, who loves Ota, is reassured that the feeling is
mutual, and that Ota will do everything in his power to keep
her for himself.
       Before Ota and Iva can be married, Efa, a mad ser-
vant, kidnaps Iva for herself. Iva manages to escape only
to fall into the hands of the Messenger of the Great Mind.
It is from the Messenger that she learns that the people on
Venus are amphibian. The attack of the dragon as they travel
gives Iva her chance to escape, an escape which is thwarted
by the men of the Great Mind who find her in the woods and
take her to him. When she meets the Great Mind, she is
surprised to learn that he is very handsome but also very
cold, arrogant and merciless. Iva's virginity is saved from
the Great Mind's passionate advances when Ota and his men
storm the city of the Great Mind and rescue her.
       Iva spends a lot of time in this novel blushing and es-
caping from the frying pan into the proverbial fire. Her trust
in Ota is instant upon their meeting, and she never doubts the
appropriateness of that response. At the book's conclusion,
she is most happy to retreat to Ota's Blue Land and be his
wife.

★   TAINE, JOHN (Eric Temple Bell). "The Ultimate Cata-
      lyst," in Thrilling Wonder Stories, June 1939; in
      Startling Stories, Nov. 1949; in My Best Science Fic-
      tion Story. Ed. Leo Margulies and Oscar J. Friend.
      New York: Pocket Books, 1954.

      Main Character: Consuelo Beetle (almost named Bug-
lette by her father, a name which he occasionally calls her).
      Physical Characteristics: No physical description
given except that she is half Portuguese.
      Mental/Emotional Characteristics: Is a scientist, spe-
cifically a "biological chemist"; is fascinated by her father's
work and "each new creation of his filled her with childlike
wonderment and joy"; pursues knowledge even if it is distaste-
ful; keeps her head in an emergency; has intelligence, stability, and sound thinking and judgment.
      Story Particulars: Emperor Kadir is the last of the
dictators on Earth, quarantined in Amazonia with his band of
invaders. Only the American biochemist Dr. Beetle and his
daughter, Consuelo Beetle, remained when everyone else fled
two years before. Meat-eaters in an area where no meat is
available, Kadir and his people crave meat, a craving to which
Dr. Beetle caters. He grows what he calls greenbeefo fruit,
injects it with snake blood unbeknownst to Kadir, and feeds
it to the gullible, bloodthirsty invaders with the falsehood that
he has found a way to turn chlorophyll into "haemoglobin."
      Consuelo, a biochemist and her father's lab assistant,
helps Dr. Beetle care for the greenhouse plants and seriously
doubts anyone's ability to produce a plant filled with hemo-
globin. When he tells her the truth, that he had injected
snake blood into the fruit, she is at first curious, then concerned over her father's motives. She has been adding "the
exact amount of chloride of gold which he prescribed" to the
hydroponic solutions without knowing why, and realizes that
her father has a plan to rid the world of Kadir, though she
is unable to divine what it is.
      Each day Dr. Beetle takes a satchel with a snake in-
side into the jungle at 10 a.m., and returns at 11 a.m. One
morning while he is gone, Kadir tries to force Consuelo to
admit that Dr. Beetle injects snake blood into the fruit. During the disagreement that follows, Dr. Beetle arrives and
promptly forgets about the contents of his bag in his successful effort to convince Kadir that the fruit is legitimate and
contains no snake blood. Felipe, the Portuguese foreman of
the native workers, brings Consuelo the bag later and shows
her the fungus-like contents which he watched change from a
snake. As Consuelo has just seen similar fungi in the jungle,

rooted but yet moving against their roots, she suspects that
her father is somehow connected to this intrigue. She instructs Felipe to dispose of the bag's contents and to tell no
one; however, her suspicions about her father's activities are
heightened, quite justifiably, and she vows that he must be
stopped. Unfortunately, she is too late. The following day,
her father delivers his feast to the invaders and partakes of
it himself, horrifying Consuelo with the results.

Consuelo's deductions about her father's activities, her
willingness to doubt his previously-unshakable good-hearted
image, and her presence of mind during the story's final,
horrible conclusion reveal intelligence, stability, sound thinking, and judgment, and considerable self-control in an insane
situation. She may have entered the story as the daughter of
a scientist, but she is also a biochemist in her own right,
and on close examination, Consuelo emerges as a reasonable
and quite plausible character. None of the characters are
truly three-dimensional, but of all the characters portrayed,
she is the most sane. This reader would like to have seen
more written about this character.

★ WEINBAUM, STANLEY G.   "Dawn of Flame," in Thrill-
     ing Wonder Stories, June 1939; in Fantastic Story
     Magazine, Spring 1952; in The Black Flame.   Reading,
     PA: Fantasy Press, 1948; rpt. Mattituck, NY: Am-
     ereon, 1976.

Main Character: Margaret Smith; called Black Margot,
Margaret, Princess of the Empire, the Princess Margaret,
and (by those who love her) Margaret the Divine; in the past,
was called Princess Peggy and the Maid of Orleans; in the
future will be called Margaret of Urbs.
    Physical Characteristics: Is "slim," beautiful and
appears to be between 18 and 25 years old although is much
older; has "icy green eyes" and "a flaming black mop of hair,
so black that it glinted blue"; has Spanish blood and olive
skin; rides a horse gracefully and is as strong as most men;
has a beauty which is "sultry ... with a hint of sullenness in
it"; has a perfect, mocking mouth and a voice "low and liquid, yet cold"; will live three times as long as a normal human, because of her status as an Immortal.
    Mental/Emotional Characteristics: Is called "heart-
less, ruthless, and pitiless"; is considered "a witch" with
her powers; is a brave warrior; says that "fighting, killing,
danger, and love" are all that keep her "breathing"; is unhappy in her lonely and loveless life; is "the most brilliant

woman of all that brilliant age, and one of the most brilliant
of any age"; does not break her word; admires and loves a
man of "slow strength, ... stubborn honesty, and ... courage."

Story Particulars: Three centuries after a late twentieth-century war fought with diseases and ended by the on-
slaught of the Grey Death, the worst plague since the four-
teenth-century Black Death, the human species still struggles
to reestablish civilization. John Holland, a century before
the story takes place, wanted desperately to study and learn,
so he founded a library from the remains of the books of the
twentieth century. Gradually others joined him and, at least
in N'Orleans, power for lights and machinery was created
from atomic energy. This event attracted the attention of
Martin Sair, and brother and sister, Joaquin and Margaret
Smith. Sair, a genius, learned how to make people "immortal" at the cost of their reproductive abilities. Margaret
Smith, now called Princess Margaret, but most popularly
called Black Margot, is one of the Immortals, a warrior
with her brother, Joaquin. Together they march with their
army, conquering villages, overturning local rule, and estab-
lishing their own government, centered in N'Orleans.

Black Margot, known to be a ruthless, proud, courageous warrior, is also lonely, a fact which is less well known.
Into this drama steps Hull Tarvish, a strong mountain man
from "Ozarky," who is traveling out to see the world. On
his way, Hull falls in love with Vail Ormiston, the daughter
of the eldarch, the leader and a property owner in that area.
Naturally, he has the opportunity to become a hero by pitting
his sole powers against the Smith army. Black Margot, impressed by the nerve of a solitary attacker, spares his life
in spite of his refusal to pledge loyalty to her. He is over-
whelmed by her beauty, and she, with her brilliant mind,
questions and taunts him, finally forcing him to admit that
he loves her in spite of his love for Vail. Black Margot,
realizing he would be happier with Vail, leaves him with her,
an act of kindness which leaves her lonely, and rides off into
war once more with her brother at her side.

In the sequel, "The Black Flame," she is Margaret
of Urbs, which is the world capital, and finds a cure for
her loneliness.

* WEINBAUM, STANLEY G. "Flight on Titan," in Astound-
       ing Stories, Jan. 1935; in The Red Peri. Reading,
       PA: Fantasy Press, 1952; in A Martian Odyssey and
       Other Science Fiction Tales. Westport, CT: Hyperion
       Press, 1974.

Main Character: Diane (Di) Vick.
Physical Characteristics: Has brown eyes; is young;
was born in Canada.
Mental/Emotional Characteristics: Is cheerful, determined, brave, courageous, and loyal.
Story Particulars: In 2142, Diane and Tim Vick, suffering financially as most people are from the "collapse of the
Planetary Trading Corporation" and "the resultant depression,"
decide to risk their lives to get wealthy by going to Titan, a
moon of Saturn, and finding some of the nearly priceless
flame-orchids, a gem much in demand on Earth. They knew
Titan would be cold, but grew quickly tired of the eighty-
below-zero temperatures which they would have to bear for
a year. Somehow, though, the six flame-orchids the natives
had brought them in exchange for "little mirrors, knives,
beads, matches and nondescript trinkets" made the cold worth
it. What they hadn't really expected, in spite of the warning
system they had installed, was that their shack would be buried by the shifting cliff sheltering their Titan home. The unexpected happens, and Diane and Tim find themselves walking
against a deadline to reach Nivia, the City of Snow, one hundred miles away, before the powerful winds shift from their
back to their front.

In the bitter cold and high winds, the couple courageously struggle to survive, fighting hopelessness frequently.
They find shelter and rest along the way in the domes of the
ice-ants where the temperatures rise to above forty degrees.
The ice-ants, attracted to Diane's leather neck pouch which
contains the flame-orchids, roll the gems down a hole, leaving the couple only one. They are understandably disappointed, but continue to struggle towards Nivia. As they
near the tall Mountains of the Damned, the domes become
smaller--too small for a person to get inside. They find
"curious caves in the ice" in the mountains and take shelter
there, only to find an ugly "threadworm" which tries to put
them to sleep. Diane saves them by insisting that they are
asleep, thus waking Tim in time for him to shoot the creature.

After Diane falls asleep in the relative safety of the
cave, Tim discovers the one remaining flame-orchid is
cracked and therefore worthless. In anger, he pulverizes
the gem and sleeps in exhaustion. When they wake, the gem
crystals have grown into fifty to one hundred flame-orchids,
which they quickly gather. If they make it to Nivia, they
realize, they will be rich. The last hours of the struggle
to conquer the Mountains of the Damned, Tim climbs alone,
dragging the exhausted, unconscious Diane (who has a concus-

sion) after him by one arm. Diane, Tim realizes, is "loyal"
and "courageous." It is their partnership which makes their
survival possible.

* WEINBAUM, STANLEY G. "Parasite Planet," in Astound-
        ing Stories, Feb. 1935; in A Martian Odyssey and
        Others. Reading, PA: Fantasy Press, 1949; in A
        Martian Odyssey and Other Science Fiction Tales.
        Westport, CT: Hyperion Press, 1974.

   Main Character: Patricia (Pat) Burlingame.
   Physical Characteristics: Has "cool gray eyes," a
lovely face, brown hair, a "dainty nose," and bronzed limbs;
is tireless, agile, and graceful; is the first human child born
on Venus, of British stock, and 22 years old.
   Mental/Emotional Characteristics: Is a biologist; is
confident, and adventurous; Ham sees her as "an arrogant,
vicious, self-centered devil," and "cool as crystal, and as
unfriendly" at first, and then sees her as "courageous."
   Story Particulars: Pat Burlingame, biologist daughter
of explorer Patrick Burlingame, is on an expedition financed
by the British Royal Society in the Hotlands of the 500-mile-
wide strip of habitable zone on Venus. There she is identi-
fying and classifying Hotland flora and fauna. When an American man, Hamilton ("Ham") Hammond, forces his way into
her shelter, Pat is justifiably angry, but fate, in the form
of an enormous doughpot devouring her home, forces the two
together on a journey across the Hotlands to Cool Country.
   Their initially hostile meeting becomes a battle of
words. She calls him an "American poacher" and he calls
her a "cool devil." The battle continues as she supposedly
slits his collection bag which holds his hard-won spore pods
from the Venusian plant xixtchil, worth a great deal of money,
on the grounds that he poached them from British territory.
Ham stomps off, furious with her, but when Pat turns south
towards the dangerous Mountains of Eternity, he discovers
he cannot allow her to walk to her death.
   On their joint travels, each saves the other's life,
making it obvious that alone, neither would have survived.
Sliding on mudshoes on boiling swamps and being attacked
by a false Friendly tree and the triops noctivivans (three-
eyed flying creatures living on the dark side of Venus) punc-
tuate their dangerous trip. At the story's end, Ham finds out
that Pat had not disposed of his spore pods and a solid relationship is in the making.
   This story was the one in which Pat and Ham meet.

These characters were also featured in two additional stories,
"The Lotus Eaters" (in Astounding Stories, April 1935)
and in The Best of Stanley G. Weinbaum, Ballantine Books,
1974) and "The Planet of Doubt" (in Astounding Stories,
October 1935).   All three stories are printed in A Martian
Odyssey and Other Science Fiction Tales (Westport, CT: Hyperion Press, 1974).   This book, in fact, contains the complete short stories of Stanley Weinbaum.

★   WEINBAUM, STANLEY G.   "Redemption Cairn," in As-
      tounding Stories, March 1936; in The Red Peri.   Read-
      ing, PA: Fantasy Press, 1952; in A Martian Odyssey
      and Other Science Fiction Tales.   Westport, CT: Hy-
      perion Press, 1974.

      Main Character: Claire Avery (although she doesn't
appear until several pages into the story, she is a main character).
      Physical Characteristics: Has "cobalt-blue eyes," and
hair the color of "metallic gold"; is pretty; weighs about 100
pounds.
      Mental/Emotional Characteristics: Has "brass nerves"
according to Jack Sands; is determined; takes chances as a
pilot to earn money in order to save the family home; is
called the Golden Flash because of her reputation as a pilot;
hates taking the gambles with her life that she must in order
to earn lots of money; makes money endorsing products on
the basis of her name, gained by performing dare-devil stunts.
      Story Particulars: In the year 2110, space travel is
common and good pilots are in great demand.   When washed-
out ex-pilot Jack Sands is hired for a piloting job and given
his pilot's license once more, Claire Avery, also popularly
known as the Golden Flash, is assigned as co-pilot against
his wishes.   Her reputation as a wealthy, thrill-seeking,
dare-devil pilot doesn't comfort Jack Sands in the least.   The
fact that she is the only woman to have her name put on the
Curry cup, this year's winner of the Apogee race, is no relief either, because Sands claims she gambled on her braking
orbit on her return and was lucky.
      Sands, already prejudiced against her, forces Claire
to relinquish control on her take-off from earth and taunts
her on her landing on Europa, a moon of Jupiter, rattling
her confidence to the degree that she turns the controls over
to him.   An uneasy truce is called on Europa when she takes
the initiative and apologizes for her attitude towards him and
admits to being a "rotten pilot" (which later she proves not
to be).

The purpose of the trip to Europa, supposedly an exploring expedition, was actually to recover a lost chemical formula left by a now-deceased scientist--a scientist killed in the last landing Sands made prior to the revoking of his pilot's license. And Kratska, his co-pilot on that flight, now in disguise, has returned with them to find that formula. Claire and Jack struggle to survive Kratska's attempts to murder them, and Claire saves the day (and their lives) with her piloting ability.

The reader may sense a tongue-in-cheek attitude toward the prejudices of Jack Sands. The story, written in first person from Sands' point of view, at first presents Claire as a contemptible, rich, dare-devil pilot with little piloting know-how or ability. ("She was worse than I'd dreamed," says Jack.) But the story's end shows her to be a capable pilot, even on a shift of fifty hours. Jack says of her landing, "We came down without a roll, and landed like a canary feather. But I hadn't a thing to do with it; I was so weak I couldn't even move the U-bar, but she didn't know that. Confidence was all she needed; she had the makings of a damn good pilot. Yeah; I've proved that." Jack's initial doubt in her skill and his certainty that he'd made all the difference in her ability to land when she proves to be quite capable as a pilot make Jack charmingly human. His awkwardly large pilot's ego also suggests to the reader that Claire is perhaps even more capable as a pilot than Jack is ever willing to admit.

* WEINBAUM, STANLEY G. "The Red Peri," in Astounding Stories, Nov. 1935; in The Red Peri. Reading, PA: Fantasy Press, 1952; in A Martian Odyssey and Other Science Fiction Tales. Westport, CT: Hyperion Press, 1974; in Gosh! Wow! (Sense of Wonder) Science Fiction. Ed. Forrest J Ackerman. New York: Bantam Books, 1982.

Main Character: Red Peri Maclane (Peri is "the Persian word for imp or elf").

Physical Characteristics: Has red hair "between copper and mahogany"; has "bright green" eyes and pale skin; is a pirate and thought to be a man until Frank Keene sees her on Pluto; appears to be 17 years old, but is actually 19; is "slim, curved, firm" and has a "litheness and sturdiness to her limbs"; is an "exquisite and fantastic beauty."

Mental/Emotional Characteristics: Steals from spaceships and will kill if necessary; is called "ruthless and ar-

rogant and proud" and "utterly heartless and indifferent"; all
of her men followers worship her and "half of them love
her"; is not afraid of anything; is "self-sufficient" and "mocking"; has "courage" and "nerves of steel"; enjoys "a deliber-
ate taunt"; finds she can love and take chances in the name
of that love, but chooses a lonely freedom over a loving imprisonment.

   Story Particulars: A notorious space pirate, the Red
Peri, with a ship by the same name, raids only ships of Interplanetary, a large and double-dealing corporation. Frank
Keene, a radiation engineer, is aboard a vessel which the
Red Peri robs and sees beneath the space suit a head of red
hair; but it isn't until Keene goes on a Smithsonian expedition
with Solomon Nestor to study cosmic rays in outer space that
he discovers that the hideout of the pirate is Pluto.

   Keene and Nestor land on Pluto to make repairs on
their ship, setting down, by a remarkable coincidence, in the
valley that the Red Peri calls home. When Keene and Nestor
are captured and taken to Peri's cavern for questioning,
Keene is stunned to discover that the Red Peri is a woman,
and promptly falls in love with her. It seems his affections
are not unusual, however, as all of her male followers worship her. Naturally, the female followers are more than a
little disturbed by that fact, and one woman, Elza, whose
man is enamored of Peri, agrees to help Keene and Nestor
escape.

   Meanwhile, Frank Keene learns that Peri's father, the
deceased Red Perry Maclane, was robbed by Interplanetary
of his design of a thermoid expansion chamber, a design which
made safe space travel possible. Red Perry, who by then
had a redheaded child named Peri, designed a new, faster
ship, naming it after his daughter, and became a pirate.
Now, sixteen years later, his daughter is carrying out her
father's dream--to collect enough from Interplanetary by pi-
rating to start a competitive company with the design of the
fast Red Peri ship as the product, thus putting Interplanetary
out of business.

   Frank Keene, madly in love with her, and aware that
she appears to feel something for him, too, abducts her after
the pirates repair his ship, and tries to convert her to honesty. He fails, and because she values freedom over "the
honest side" that Frank asks her to choose (which would mean
either death or imprisonment for her), Peri escapes and flees
to her own ship which is pacing his (through the vacuum of
space, by the way, with no space suit). Frank curses himself for not telling her that he couldn't let her die, that he
would have given her a new identity as his wife, and never

turned her in to the authorities.   The note Peri leaves Frank
is also filled with regret that the situation hadn't been different.
    According to Sam Moskowitz's introduction to A Mar-
tian Odyssey and Other Science Fiction Tales, this story "was
intended as the first of a series."   Weinbaum's death on December 14, 1935, prevented that series from becoming a reality.   Nonetheless, this one Red Peri story gives readers
an adventurous, courageous, determined and fiercely independent female hero who is capable of loving, but who values
freedom more.

*   WEINBAUM, STANLEY G., and RALPH MILNE FARLEY.
     "Smothered Seas," in Astounding Stories, Jan. 1936;
     in The Red Peri.   Reading, PA: Fantasy Press, 1952;
     in A Martian Odyssey and Other Science Fiction Tales.
     Westport, CT: Hyperion Press, 1974.

    Main Character: Sally Amber (also known as Princess
Stephanie Kazarovna, and the Nightshade).
    Physical Characteristics: Has "strange, dark eyes"
and "delicately penciled brows"; is nineteen years old and
"very beautiful"; is an Oriental with pale skin, and is the
daughter of Dmitri Kazarov, the Khan's Chancellor.
    Mental/Emotional Characteristics: Is a "brilliant
feminine Asiatic spy" and is considered "the greatest spy in
history"; knows "every important language"; is "at ease in
every situation and every level of society"; knows "military
science, so as to be able to identify important information";
was "taught the knowledge of human nature"; is "cold and
heartless, and immune to love"; has no feelings except "the
desire to serve Asia"; plays at being impish; says she is
wealthy and has traveled a lot; learns to love Dick Lister
which ends her usefulness as a spy.
    Story Particulars: In the year 2000, America and
Asia are at war, and Lieutenant Richard (Dick) Lister has
fallen in love with beautiful Sally Amber.   Unfortunately,
Sally is really the Asian Princess Stephanie Kazarovna, better
known as the Nightshade, a notorious spy for the Khan.   The
brilliant spy is recognized by Captain Jim Cass, who informs
Dick of her identity and leaves it to him to solve the problem.   When Dick confronts Sally with his suspicions that she
is the Nightshade, she scratches his neck, thereby drugging
him, and takes him to Asia to gain information about the
algae-clogged seas which have halted the progress of the
war.

Dick gives the Asians false information and Stephanie, torn between her love for Dick and her love for Asia, aids him in his escape, giving him an experimental boat which glides above the algae-filled waters. She gives him enough fuel to reach a neutral port, but he manages to buy fuel from a British ship stuck in the waters. Stephanie, realizing only after he'd gone that he might do such a thing, catches up with him in a helicopter and tries an unsuccessful landing in the water, nearly drowning. Dick rescues her, and ties her to prevent her from stopping him, a precaution which doesn't keep her from trying to drain the fuel tank and destroy the water purifier to slow or stop their progress towards Guam. Dick wins the struggle and takes the solution of the algae and the war to Guam where he is declared an American hero. As Khan and Captain Cass are both war casualties, no one can identify Sally as the Nightshade, which relieves Dick considerably.

Stephanie is not given an opportunity in the story to share her feelings about the defeat of her beloved country-- a defeat which is at least partly due to her failure to remain a cold, unloving spy.

ADDITIONAL READING LIST

Barnes, Arthur K(elvin). "Satellite Five," in Thrilling Wonder Stories, Oct. 1938; retitled "Jupiter," in Interplanetary Hunter. New York: Ace Books, 1972.

Gardner, Thomas S(amuel). "The Last Woman," in Wonder Stories, April 1932; in When Women Rule. Ed. Sam Moskowitz. New York: Walker, 1972.

Johnson, Owen McMahon. The Coming of the Amazons. New York: Longmans, Green, 1931.

Stone, Leslie F. (Mrs. William Silberberg). "The Conquest of Gola," in Wonder Stories, April 1931; in The Best of Science Fiction. Ed. Groff Conklin. New York: Crown, 1946 and 1963.

Stuart, Don A. (John W. Campbell, Jr.). "Cloak of Aesir," in Astounding Science Fiction, March 1939; in Cloak of Aesir. Chicago, IL: Shasta, 1952, and Westport, CT: Hyperion Press, 1976; in The Best of John W. Campbell. Ed. Lester del Rey. New York: Ballantine Books, 1976; in Isaac Asimov Presents the Great SF Stories 1 (1939).

Ed. Isaac Asimov and Martin H. Greenberg. New York: Daw Books, 1979.

_____. "Out of Night," in Astounding Stories, Oct. 1937; in Cloak of Aesir. Chicago, IL: Shasta, 1952, and Westport, CT: Hyperion Press, 1976; in The Best of John W. Campbell. Ed. Lester del Rey. New York: Ballantine Books, 1976.

Temple, William F(rederick). "The Four-Sided Triangle," in Amazing Stories, Nov. 1939; expanded to novel length as The Four-Sided Triangle. London: J. Long, 1951; story in Isaac Asimov Presents the Great SF Stories 1 (1939). Ed. Isaac Asimov and Martin H. Greenberg. New York: Daw Books, 1979.

Weinbaum, Stanley G(rauman). "The Black Flame," in Startling Stories, Jan. 1939; in The Black Flame. Reading, PA: Fantasy Press, 1948.

West, Wallace (George). "En Route to Pluto," in Astounding Stories, Aug. 1936; in The Best of Science Fiction. Ed. Groff Conklin. New York: Crown, 1946 and 1963; novelized with other material in The Bird of Time. Hicksville, NY: Gnome Press, 1959, and New York: Ace Books, 1961.

CHAPTER 3:   THE 1940s

The decade of the 1940s is generally considered the Golden Age of sf, but it certainly can't be said to be the Golden Age of Women Characters in sf. In this chapter, for example, the female main characters presented are two children, two mothers, one alien female, one woman's mind contained in a metal body, and one robot-like scientist, Dr. Susan Calvin. Asimov's Susan Calvin, in spite of her frigid demeanor, was at least a scientist--a professional in a decade when women as a whole left their war-time jobs and became occupied in the baby boom.

The two notable exceptions to this rather stereotypical group of characters are Barnes' Gerry Carlyle, the interplanetary hunter, and Moore's famous amazon, Jirel of Joiry. Both Gerry Carlyle and Jirel of Joiry made their appearances in the 1930s and, perhaps, continued their adventures under the power of previous momentum. No new women heroes appeared on the sf scene during this decade unless it could be said to be Juille in Moore's "Judgment Night." Unfortunately, Juille's pride and her preference for combat over love--both necessary traits for the warrior she is--cost her race much. This character's heroic dimensions are demonstrated to be a liability rather than a benefit to her people. The Golden Age of Women Characters in sf was yet to come.

⋆   ASIMOV, ISAAC.   "Strange Playfellow," in Super Science Stories, Sept. 1940; retitled "Robbie," in I, Robot. New York: Gnome Press, 1950; rpt. Greenwich, CT: Fawcett, 1970; titled "Strange Playfellow," in Isaac Asimov Presents The Great SF Stories 2 (1940).   Ed. Isaac Asimov and Martin H. Greenberg. New York: Daw Books, 1979.

Main Character: Gloria Weston.

Physical Characteristics: Has "chubby little" forearms; is eight years old; has "golden" curls.

Mental/Emotional Characteristics: Loves Robbie the Robot and cries when he disappears; remains certain that Robbie will return and is convinced that when her parents take her to New York City they are there to hunt for Robbie.

Main Character: Grace Weston.
Physical Characteristics: No description given.
Mental/Emotional Characteristics: Has a strong aversion to Robbie the Robot; is unscrupulous in her dealings with her husband to get what she wants; refuses to admit when she's wrong, and is not above saying an I-told-you-so when right; places her aversion above her daughter's health in importance, though she claims otherwise.

Story Particulars: In 1982, Gloria has Robbie, a Robot, as a playmate. In spite of the fact that Robbie has never been anything but gentle with Gloria and that he cost George Weston "half a year's income," Grace Weston develops an aversion to the robot and demands that her husband get rid of him. Mr. Weston, who likes the robot and doesn't want to hurt Gloria, resists Mrs. Weston's demands; however, because "his wife made full use of every art and wile which a clumsier and more scrupulous sex has learned from time immemorial to fear," and perhaps because he is still "so unutterably foolish as to love her," he finally gives in and has the robot removed from the house while he takes Gloria to the "visivox" (movies?).

When they return, a collie is waiting at home to take Robbie's place, but Gloria is unmoved and rejects the dog. She wants her friend Robbie. Mrs. Weston insists to her husband that Gloria will recover, but as time passes, it becomes obvious she is wrong. Gloria's "attitude of passive unhappiness" gradually exhausts Mrs. Weston's resolve, but she refuses to change her mind because of "the impossibility of admitting defeat to her husband."

Mr. Weston, "the lesser half," finally agrees to a trip to New York City to cheer Gloria up, which the little girl is convinced is actually a trip to search for Robbie. As the month vacation passes, Gloria still keeps her vigil for Robbie, never doubting that they will find him. Mr. Weston, realizing Gloria is not going to give up, secretly arranges a tour for the family of the robot factory where Robbie now works. Gloria, seeing Robbie, rushes to him in her joy, ignoring an oncoming tractor. Robbie saves Gloria's life, once and for all convincing Mrs. Weston that

Robbie's place is with Gloria, but not without her realizing
that the reunion had been "engineered" by her husband.

Mrs. Weston's initial aversion to the robot is quite
unlike Dr. Susan Calvin's response to robots in the robot
series by Asimov (1940s and 1950s); however, both women
are alike in their coldness and lack of likability as people.
Gloria, certain at all times that Robbie is her friend, has
no such aversion to Robbie, and is a loving, playful child.

★   ASIMOV, ISAAC.   "Liar!" in Astounding Stories, May
        1941; rpt. I, Robot.   New York: Gnome Press, 1950;
        rpt. Greenwich, CT: Fawcett, 1970

    Main Character: Dr. Susan Calvin.
    Physical Characteristics: Has "cold gray eyes"; is
38 years old; was born in 1982; has "thin pale lips"; suddenly
starts wearing lipstick, rouge, powder, and eye shadow in the
story when she thinks someone is in love with her.
    Mental/Emotional Characteristics: Is a robopsycholo-
gist; is bitter; says of herself that she is "a shriveled sixty
[years old] as far as my emotional outlook on life is concerned"; is emotionally hard, with a mind "full of pain and
frustration and hate"; is "a frosty girl, plain and colorless,
who protected herself against a world she disliked by a mask-
like expression and a hypertrophy of intellect." (This last
comment from the narrator of I, Robot.)
    Story Particulars: Asimov's Dr. Susan Calvin stories
span two decades.   This early Calvin story is unusual in that
she is in love, vulnerable, and displays some small bit of
emotion.   (In the many later stories about Dr. Susan Calvin,
she is never as vulnerable as in this story, but is more contained and robot-like.   In fact, the book that holds this story
is totally devoted to the life of Susan Calvin, and is named,
appropriately, I, Robot.)
    The vulnerability Dr. Calvin feels because of her emo-
tions is expanded by a mind-reading robot named Herbie.   Unfortunately, what no one realizes is that Herbie is lying to
everyone because he doesn't wish to hurt anyone's feelings.
After all, the First Law of Robotics strictly forbids a robot
to injure a human being, and telling Susan that the man and
co-worker she loves at U.S. Robot & Mechanical Men, Inc.,
Milton Ashe, is not in love with her would certainly hurt her.
The story's resolution is a bitter one for Susan.
    An interesting note about Asimov's presentation of Dr.
Calvin is that he rarely, in the rest of the stories about her,
allows her full human status.   She is always cold and premed-

itated in her actions and devotes her life to robots. This
brief story of her in love, wearing ineptly applied make-up
and acting "girlish," is a rare glimpse of the human being
behind the cold exterior. As Asimov wrote in "Liar!":
"Some of the woman peered through the layer of doctorhood."

★   BARNES, ARTHUR K.   "Siren Satellite," in Thrilling
        Wonder Stories, Winter 1946; retitled "Neptune," in
        Interplanetary Hunter.   Hicksville, NY: Gnome Press,
        1956; rpt. New York: Ace Books, 1972.

        Main Character: Gerry Carlyle, nicknamed Catch-'em-
alive Carlyle.
        Physical Characteristics: Has long "copper-blonde"
curls; is an "important public" figure as "queen of the space-
rovers"; is engaged to Tommy Strike; is an interplanetary
hunter of animals.
        Mental/Emotional Characteristics: Sometimes thinks
"too highly" of herself according to Tommy Strike; expresses
"hardy defiance" and remains "unshaken" in the face of im-
possibly poor odds for survival; can swing a punch when pro-
voked; is intelligent and comes up with ideas no one else
thinks of in times of adversity; is "well grounded" in math;
"characteristically" drives a hard bargain; sometimes swears
"a ladylike oath."
        Story Particulars: This story, the last in the Gerry
Carlyle series, finds Gerry and her fiancé, Tommy Strike,
traveling to Triton, a satellite of Neptune, on a mission of
mercy which they are blackmailed into performing.   Their
passenger and blackmailer, Lawrence Dacres, reports that
his brother and his crew are stranded on Triton with its
gravity of two and a half times that of Earth.   On the trip,
a portion of the crew becomes violently ill due to food poi-
soning, and Gerry is forced to replace that portion of her
crew with Martian engineers.   Little does she suspect that
Dacres and this new crew have planned from the start to take
her ship from her and leave her to die on Triton.
        Mixed in with this planted crew is Kid McCray, a
Martian middleweight boxing champion, who stumbled on board
while still in a drunken condition after a victory party.   Unfortunately for him, no one believes he is a famous boxer,
and he is put to work as part of the crew, performing the
most menial tasks.   A day away from Triton, Dacres takes
over the ship, angering Gerry so tremendously that she punches
him in the nose, bringing tears to his eyes.   As Dacres starts
towards Gerry, undoubtedly with the intention of treating her

in kind, McCray demonstrates to Gerry a better boxing technique on Dacres, an act which decides for him which side he
will be on.

In spite of the fact that Gerry, Tommy, and her part
of the crew are to be stranded on Triton without gravity suits,
which would kill them in short order, Gerry remains calm,
memorizing the faces of the mutinous crew for later reference,
and has a brilliant mathematical insight about the rapidly spin-
ning Triton which saves their lives. Though Gerry passes
out from the heavy gravity as they descend in the "life boat,"
Tommy manages to stay conscious, and following Gerry's instructions, lands on the satellite's equator. Everyone is
amazed that the gravity there, due to the body's rapid spin,
is almost Earth normal. Triton, it is discovered, has breath-
able air, except for a little chlorine which their suits filter
out, and the group discovers shaggy Shaggies which seem to
live to attack whatever is in their paths. It is a Shaggie which
figures prominently in their defeat of Dacres and his crew
when they return to plant evidence that Gerry's party died
accidentally.

At one point in the story, when it appears they will
die, Tommy inwardly regrets not insisting that Gerry marry
him and settle in "some peaceful suburban estate"; he blames
"the excitement in their blood" for the delay in his plans for
her. Gerry's internal thoughts are not mentioned in the story;
however, she is allowed to curse a "ladylike oath," whatever
that might be. Comparing the Mental/Emotional Characteristics listed in this story with those in "Hothouse Planet"
(© 1937; see the 1930s chapter) makes an interesting study
in the changing attitudes toward women. Actually, Gerry's
characteristics are not necessarily different, but Tommy's
perception of her is.

*   BRACKETT, LEIGH.   "The Halfling," in Astonishing
        Stories, Feb. 1943; in Isaac Asimov Presents the
        Great SF Stories 5 (1943).   Ed. Isaac Asimov and
        Martin H. Greenberg.   New York: Daw Books, 1981.

        Main Character: Laura Darrow.
        Physical Characteristics: Has a voice that is "sweet,
silky, guaranteed to make you forget your own name" and she
"matched her voice"; "stood about five-three on her bronze
heels, and her eyes were ... purple"; has "a funny little
button of a nose and a pink mouth" and "even white teeth";
has "gold-brown hair" and white skin; as a Cat-woman of
Callisto, has claws on her feet and hands and a tail; has been

physically altered to resemble humans, including contacts
for her eyes, the shaving of her cross-shaped mane of fur,
a wig, and the filing of her teeth from points to flat.

Mental/Emotional Characteristics: Is a highly talented
dancer; is a killer of renegades for her race, the Cat-men
from Callisto, and has killed seven so far; is very intelligent,
determined, and dedicated.

Story Particulars: John (Jade) Damien Green, owner
of the Interplanetary Carnival, "The Wonders of the Seven
Worlds Alive Before Your Eyes," tells in first-person narrative of his experience with Laura Darrow, a dancer unlike
any he's ever seen, with a mystery about her that turns out
to be quite deadly. Laura comes to the carnival while it is
in California to try out for a spot as the carnival's dancer.
She claims to be the daughter of an employee of the diplomatic corps, born in space between Earth and Mars. Now,
she tells him, her birth records are lost and she is unable
to get back to Venus where her money is unless she goes
with the carnival. Jade, who already has a dancer, is instantly taken with her appearance and manner of handling
herself and gives her an audition. Laura turns out to be the
best dancer Jade has ever seen, and he hires her in spite
of his doubts about her story.

Sindi, formerly the star dancer for the carnival, is
even more skeptical than Jade and discovers claw marks on
the stage where Laura danced. Before she can reach Jade
with the information, she is brutally murdered, supposedly
by the Cat-man from Callisto, the carnival's "prize per-
former." The Cat-man, named Laska, is high on coffee
which works on Cat-men as hashish does on humans. Jade
explains to Laura that it is a crime on Callisto for a Cat-
man to associate with humans, so if he is ever deported, he
will be killed by his own people.

As the days pass, Jade falls in love with Laura and
hopes that perhaps she will stay with the carnival even after
they arrive on Venus; however, his hopes are shattered when
"the punk" who was hired just after Laura was put on the
payroll is found murdered almost exactly as Sindi had been.
The blame is about to be placed on the Martian sand-cat that
has blood on its paws when Jade notices that the punk's eyes
are purple, not brown as before. Jade, heavy of heart, calls
Laura to the stage to confront her with the truth--that she is
a Cat-woman from Callisto in human disguise, sent to kill
Laska. The punk, actually an Immigration authority, had
discovered one pair of Laura's purple contact lenses as evidence and was wearing them on his getaway when Laura murdered him. She admits that she has already killed seven

renegades and that she was sent by her tribe to avenge Laska's
honor, to make certain he died for selling her race to humans for money. She tells Jade she loves him and runs out
of the tent.

After loosing all the carnival animals to kill the human carnival crowd and to cover her escape, Laura makes
a run for it, and Jade, wondering why he "had ever been
born," shoots her in the back. Laura, though a dead alien
hero at the story's conclusion, lived and died an honorable
member of her species, a dedicated spy and renegade killer.
Her love for Jade, which prevented her from killing him when
the opportunity presented itself, was her downfall, and the reward she expected and received for her love was death.

★ MERRIL, JUDITH.   "That Only a Mother," in Astounding
     Science-Fiction, June 1948; in Science Fiction of the
     40s.   Ed. Frederik Pohl, Martin Harry Greenberg,
     and Joseph Olander. New York: Avon Books, 1978.

     Main Character: Margaret ("Maggie") Marvell.
     Physical Characteristics: At the story's beginning, she
is pregnant and has an "increasingly clumsy bulkiness"; no
other description is given.
     Mental/Emotional Characteristics: Thinks she is prob-
ably the "unstable type" and manages to hide from herself for
nine months the fact that her newborn is limbless, a mutation
due to radiation exposure.
     Story Particulars: In 1953 in New York City, Mar-
garet and Hank are expecting a child--and both have been exposed to radiation. The war still rages on, and the use of
atomic bombs continues, causing "disproportionately" large
numbers of mutant babies to be born. Margaret reassures
herself that her baby will be normal and continues to work
at a computer job until her doctor hospitalizes her late in
her pregnancy when she has a dizzy spell at work.
     Hank, a Technical Lieutenant in the war, is gone when
the baby is born and is unable to see the baby until she is
nine months old. By then, baby Henrietta can talk in sen-
sible, understandable sentences, a fact which Margaret ignores
as being abnormal, choosing instead to call the baby "Precocious." When Hank returns on a week's leave after an ab-
sence of eighteen months, he is delighted that Henrietta can
talk, and then horrified that the child has no limbs, a fact,
he realizes, of which Margaret is unaware.
     There is some mention in the story of the number of
infanticides committed by fathers who are not prosecuted for

the crime, and at the story's end, Hank's "fingers tightened
on his child. " It is not clear whether or not Hank intends to
kill the child. Also not explained is why Margaret (and quite
possibly other mothers of mutants) remains unaware of the
limbless condition of her child in spite of conversations with
the medical staff in the hospital in which they certainly must
have discussed the infant's mutation with her. Margaret has
nine months of bathing the child in which to notice the lack
of limbs. Implied by the title is the idea that only a mother
would ignore such an obvious deformity. (See the story "When
the Bough Breaks" by Lewis Padgett, © 1944, in this chapter
for another plot dealing with an infant mutant resulting from
radiation exposure.)

★ MOORE, C(ATHERINE) L(UCILLE).   "Judgment Night, "
      in Astounding Science Fiction, Aug. 1943; in Judgment
      Night.   New York: Gnome Press, 1952; rpt. New
      York: Dell, Inc. , 1979.

      Main Character: Juille.
      Physical Characteristics: Has "a sexless face, arro-
gant and intolerant, " long "dark-gold hair, " "long, fine limbs, "
and violet eyes; wears military dress, and is trained in war-
fare; has "a face with the strength and delicacy of something
finely made of steel"; is princess of Ericon; jingles her spurs
when tension rises and when she walks.
      Mental/Emotional Characteristics: Has "the terrible
pride of a human who has tasted the attributes of divinity";
feels a "tolerant contempt" of women "who still clung to the
old standards"; embraces the amazon cult; feels it is weakness not to adhere to her principles at all costs; is uncom-
promising.
      Story Particulars: Juille, the proud princess of Eri-
con, has been trained by Helia, the amazon, in military war-
fare.   She wholeheartedly embraces the amazon cult and admires and respects Helia, herself an ex-warrior, for adhering to her principles above all else.   Juille considers mercy
for others to be foolish and calls her father, the emperor, a
fool for being merciful.   But Juille has a problem: she, as
a military amazon and leader, hard and cold, adhering to
principles, is unsure of herself as a woman.   She goes to
the resort planet Cyrille incognito and attracts Egide, an attractive blue-eyed man "with yellow curls and a short blond
beard. " Egide, a leader of the H'vani, an enemy of Ericon,
plans to kill Juille, but the resort planet weaves its web of
romance too well.   He instead falls in love with her and

shows what Juille would call weakness by not adhering to his principles and killing her.

When she returns to Ericon, who should appear as the H'vani leader of the peace talks but Egide. She becomes murderous, totally destroying the peace talks her father wants so badly, and resulting in her own capture. Helia, as it turns out, was Andarean, a conquered race, and now is ready to assist the H'vani in their efforts to overthrow the Emperor.

Juille gains reluctant admiration for Egide and is even a little in awe of him. She wants to deny it, but he excites her. When Egide goes to the Ancients for advice, Juille follows. They both receive advice and both feel certain that their race will win, but Juille, if she ever had a chance to save her race, loses it in a struggle with Egide. Instead of love, she could offer only combat. She saw Egide as weak because he could love. The adventures and battle that follow provide both Egide and Juille with the opportunity to "set into motion the juggernaut that would destroy all...." It is only at the end of the work, when it is too late for her to stop the destruction, that Juille learns to value Egide.

Also figuring prominently in the story are the llar, treated as pets but actually intelligent and wise, with "the grave animal dignity and the look of completely spurious benignity and wisdom that distinguishes all llar." To quote the story, "This race alone, of all thinking species, finds deity in itself, in the warm closed circle of its own unity." It is the llar, the Ancients decide, that offer the most promise as a species, and the llar, in their wisdom, don't trust the Ancients. The llar in their peace, oneness with self, and wisdom are an excellent contrast to the warring human species as portrayed in this work. And Juille is the epitome of the worst the race has to offer until after it's too late to save her race. This story is particularly interesting in light of the period in which it was published--during World War II.

*   MOORE, C(ATHERINE) L(UCILLE). "No Woman Born," in Astounding Science-Fiction, Dec. 1944; in The Best of C. L. Moore. Ed. Lester del Rey. New York: Taplinger, Inc., 1976; in Isaac Asimov Presents the Great SF Stories 6 (1944). Ed. Isaac Asimov and Martin H. Greenberg. New York: Daw Books, 1981.

Main Character: Deirdre.
Physical Characteristics: Before the theatre fire, she was the most beautiful woman in the world, a graceful dancer/ singer with a "soft and husky voice with the little burr in it

that had fascinated the audiences of the whole world"; after
the fire, with only her brain saved and encased in a metal
frame, she is "tall, golden," and her voice is "perfect"; has
"only a smooth, delicately modeled ovoid for her head" and
an aquamarine "crescent-shaped mask across the frontal area
where her eyes would have been if she had needed eyes"; has
arms of "pale shining gold, tapered smoothly, without model-
ing, and flexible their whole length in diminishing metal brace-
lets fitting one inside the other clear down to the slim, round
wrists," and has "more than human suppleness"; moves as
she did when she had a human body of flesh except that she
moves now "with a litheness that was not quite human"; her
brain will wear out just like it would have in a flesh body,
so she's not immortal; the maker of her metal body says
now she "hasn't any sex" and has only two of her five senses.

Mental/Emotional Characteristics: Has "strength and
courage beyond common," a stamina that is "unquenchable;"
and "serenity"; has a strong ego and is "regally confident";
is "free-willed and independent"; has "compelling charm"
which she retains and uses in her metal body; is afraid to
"draw so far away from the human race," and is lonely because she is one of a kind, a Phoenix.

Story Particulars: A year has passed since the beautiful, talented dancer/singer Deirdre was burned irreparably
in a theatre fire. Her brain saved and encased in a metal
humanoid body designed and made by "artists, sculptors, de-
signers, scientists, and the genius of Maltzer," who orches-
trated the process, Deirdre is ready to see John ("Johnnie")
Harris, her agent, and once more dance and sing for the
world. Johnnie is shocked by how much the golden metal
body and featureless metal ovoid head express her personality, until he realizes it is her motion and her voice which
make Deirdre appear to be who she was--a beautiful, graceful, fluid dancer. She is self-assured and confident that she
is ready to perform for the world on television, a surprise
performance guaranteed to shake the world. She tells Johnnie
that she doesn't want anyone's pity and plans to dance with
more versatility than the human body can manage.

Maltzer is ready for a nervous breakdown because he
fears he has done her a disservice in saving her brain just
so she could perform and receive public scorn, ridicule and
laughter. He took on the project to give hope to mutilated
people and tells Johnnie that with three of her five senses
gone she is withdrawing from humanity. Her performance is
a stunning success, and the audience, recognizing her laughter at the end, gives her a welcome that shakes the camera
with its intensity. After the show, Maltzer tells her the

crowd was pleased at the historic nature of the performance,
not at the performance itself, and insists that she retire now
before she finds out how cruel her audiences can be.

Deirdre, even after her success, goes to the country
for a week to consider the things Johnnie and Maltzer have
told her of herself. When she returns, she announces to
them that she will continue to perform, triggering an attempted suicide in Maltzer who feels he will be to blame
when she emotionally falls apart. Deirdre saves him with
faster-than-vision speed and assures both of them that she
is not the fragile being they think her to be. Physically,
she is able to tear down buildings with her metal body. Emotionally, she is unhappy and lonely and realizes that she is
drawing further and further away from humanity; however,
she insists that she is not fragile and will not lose touch
with humanity unless she wills it.

It is clear at the story's conclusion that both Johnnie
and Maltzer believe she will soon be little other than a beautiful machine. As Maltzer insists that Deirdre is now sex-
less, there was some question about including a synopsis on
this story; however, Deirdre never lost the essence of her
personality (at least not in the time frame of the story) and
for that reason "No Woman Born" has been included here.

★ PADGETT, LEWIS (Henry Kuttner and C. L. Moore).
    "When the Bough Breaks, " in Astounding Science-
    Fiction, Nov. 1944; in Isaac Asimov Presents the
    Great SF Stories 6 (1944). Ed. Isaac Asimov and
    Martin H. Greenberg. New York: Daw Books, 1981.

Main Character: Myra Calderon.
Physical Characteristics: Has red hair; is "rather
fragile, " with "a tilted nose and sardonic red-brown eyes";
ceases to wear make-up when her infant Alexander tells her
the smell makes him ill.
Mental/Emotional Characteristics: Worries a great
deal about her baby, the Superchild; has an amazing tolerance
for abuse from her infant.
Story Particulars: By about the year 1950, Myra and
her husband, Joe Calderon, both have worked with "radio-
activity and certain short-wave radiations. " This results in
the mutation of their infant, Alexander, although they are unaware of it at first. They have just moved into an apartment
--one which allows children--when four "tiny men" with "immense" craniums arrive, purportedly to "develop" Alexander,
who they claim is a "super child, " an "X Free type. " Myra

does not react kindly to the invasion of these four men who
claim to be Alexander's "descendants." To their statement
that Alexander is the first "homo superior," she responds,
"Homo nuts.... Alexander is a perfectly normal baby."
Myra instructs her husband to get rid of the little
men, adding, "I feel like a Thurber woman." The little men,
however, are not going to go, and after they freeze the Calderons in a sitting position on the couch, they settle in to
teach little Alexander. They stay two hours, then leave.
The following day, Myra and Joe take Alexander to a movie,
but Alexander simply disappears from his mother's arms.
They rush home to find the four men there once more. The
Calderons learn from the men that Alexander will be left with
them to benefit from "home and parental influence" and are
told that their parental tolerance is the factor which makes
Alexander's growth into adulthood possible. Alexander will
appear to be an eight-year-old at age twenty, and will have
slower mental and emotional maturity as well. Myra tells
Joe after the men leave that day that she feels as if she's
given birth "to a moose."
The little men return each day to give two hours of
instruction to Alexander. After a week, Alexander is able
to hold conversations, and not long after that, Alexander becomes quite "dictatorial," ordering his parents around. He
refuses to let Myra wear make-up or to allow Joe to read
the newspaper. After a month of training, Alexander has
managed to learn everything his parents know, and has learned
to teleport his mother to the store to get him candy, much
against her wishes. Alexander protects himself from spank-
ings by giving his parents electrical shocks when they touch
him.
Myra has started drinking alcohol, and stays "stewed
in the kitchen" as Joe calls it, but the final, decisive step
the little men take is to make it possible for Alexander to
have no need for sleep. Myra and Joe, frazzled and strained
to the limit even before this new development, will now be
unable to sleep either. Myra suggests to Joe in a 3:30 a.m.
conversation with him while Alexander plays in the living
room, that perhaps they are not the first parents to have a
"super-baby," and tells him that there is a breaking point in
the tolerance of parents. When Alexander starts handling a
very dangerous toy the little men have left, neither parent
can face the inevitable electrical shock they will receive if
they try to stop him. Myra rationalizes that noninterference
is best and that "a burnt child dreads the fire"; however,
Alexander doesn't survive to develop a dread. (See the story
"That Only a Mother," © 1948, in this chapter under Judith

Merril, for another plot dealing with an infant mutant resulting from radiation exposure.)

★   SCHMITZ, JAMES H.   "The Witches of Karres," in
     Astounding Science-Fiction, Dec. 1949; in The Sci-
     ence Fiction Hall of Fame, Volume IIB.   Ed. Ben
     Bova.   New York: Doubleday, 1973; rpt. New York:
     Avon Books, 1974; novelized as The Witches of Kar-
     res.   Philadelphia: Chilton, 1966; rpt. New York:
     Ace Books, 1968 and 1981.   (Novel length version
     used here.)

     Secondary Character: Goth (called Dani in mid-book
to protect her identity).
     Physical Characteristics: Is "small and lean and bone-
lessly supple"; is 9 or 10 years old; has "brown hair cut
short a few inches below her ears, and brown eyes with long,
black lashes"; has a short nose and a pointed chin ("like a
weasel").
     Mental/Emotional Characteristics: Is a witch; teleports
things, and is frequently a thief; is "a very direct sort of
small person"; wants to marry the captain when she reaches
marriageable age; uses the Sheewash Drive as proficiently
as an adult; is able to bend light and color to give a false
illusion; can change sound waves and create scents; is also
capable of being invisible ("no-shape, no-sound, no-scent").

     Secondary Character: Maleen.
     Physical Characteristics: Is about 14 years old, small-
ish, "fair-haired," and pretty; has blue eyes.
     Mental/Emotional Characteristics: Is a witch; "pre-
motes" (has premonitions) and creates mass hysteria; is "a
good all-around junior witch."

     Secondary Character: the Leewit.
     Physical Characteristics: Is a "doll-sized edition of
Maleen"; has cold, gray eyes; is about 5 or 6 years old; has
long blond hair.
     Mental/Emotional Characteristics: Is a witch; "whistles
and busts things"; is a klatha (cosmic energy) linguist who
can take a few words of a language, encompass it, and soon
be speaking it; is capable of delivering a "knock-out punch."

     Story Particulars: Captain Pausert, a young space-
traveling commercial traveler from Nikkeldepain who consistently has difficulty making smooth take-offs, saves three

young witches from slavery on Porlumma. The young witch
sisters, Maleen, the Leewit, and Goth, want to go to their
home planet, Karres, and the captain agrees to take them
there.   On the trip, he discovers that Goth has stolen jewels
to pay him for his trouble and expenses and that the law is
closing in on him.   The three witches use the Sheewash Drive
to transport the entire ship to another location in space, thus
saving him from arrest.   (Sheewash Drive is actually a use
of klatha, or cosmic energy, by witches who are teleporting
specialists.)

Once on Karres, the captain is rewarded with furs,
perfume, and other items as thanks, and he finds that he
likes the planet a great deal.   When he reluctantly leaves
Karres and returns to Nikkeldepain he discovers his betrothed,
Illyla, has married another and the authorities on Nikkeldepain
are going to lock him up until he discloses the secret of the
Sheewash Drive.   Goth, who has stowed away, uses the Sheewash Drive once more to save him, and tells him she wants
to marry him when she reaches a marriageable age.

Most of the remaining book consists of the adventures
of Captain Pausert and Goth.   During these adventures, the
captain finds out that he is distantly related to the witches of
Karres and discovers that he is also a witch.   In the process
of dealing with a vatch ("a personification of klatha, or a
klatha entity"), avoiding Worm Weather (a yellow cloud bringing death, controlled by the robot-brain of Moander, and attracted to witches), dodging the law, and coping with spies
on board ship who want to steal the Sheewash Drive, a bond
of trust and affection grows between the captain and Goth.

Schmitz treats the captain with respect, but with a
slice of humor, and presents Goth as a young, intelligent,
action-oriented witch who not only knows her own mind, but
knows how to get what she wants.   (In novelized form, this
work was nominated for a Hugo Award in 1967.)

ADDITIONAL READING LIST

Arthur, Robert.   "Evolution's End, " in Thrilling Wonder
   Stories, April 1941; in Isaac Asimov Presents the Great
   SF Stories 3 (1941).   Ed. Isaac Asimov and Martin H.
   Greenberg.   New York: Daw Books, 1980.

Barnes, Arthur K(elvin).   "Trouble on Titan, " in Thrilling
   Wonder Stories, Feb. 1941; retitled "Saturn, " in Interplanetary Hunter.   New York: Ace Books, 1972.   (See Barnes
   synopses in Chapters 2 and 3.)

_____, and Henry Kuttner. "The Seven Sleepers," in
Thrilling Wonder Stories, May 1940; retitled "Almussen's
Comet," in Interplanetary Hunter. New York: Ace Books,
1972.

Blish, James, and Damon Knight. "Tiger Ride," in Astounding Science-Fiction, Oct. 1948; in Science Fiction of the
Forties. Ed. Frederik Pohl, Martin Harry Greenberg,
and Joseph Olander. New York: Avon Books, 1978.

Bond, Nelson S(lade). "Magic City," in Astounding Science-
Fiction, Feb. 1941; in Science Fiction of the Forties. Ed.
Frederik Pohl, Martin Harry Greenberg, and Joseph Olander. New York: Avon Books, 1978. (See Bond synopsis
in Chapter 2.)

Fearn, John Russell. The Amazon series. (See Appendix
C.)

Heinlein, Robert A(nson). "It's Great to Be Back!" in Sat-
urday Evening Post, July 1947; in The Past Through To-
morrow. New York: Putnam's, 1967, and New York:
Berkley, 1975; in Science Fiction of the Forties. Ed.
Frederik Pohl, Martin Harry Greenberg, and Joseph
Olander. New York: Avon Books, 1978.

Rocklynne, Ross (Ross L. Rocklin). "Quietus," in Astounding Science-Fiction, Sept. 1940; in Adventures in Time
and Space. Ed. Raymond J. Healy and J. Francis Mc-
Comas. New York: Random House, 1946 (retitled Famous Science Fiction Stories in 1957, Modern Library);
in Isaac Asimov Presents the Great SF Stories 2 (1940).
Ed. Isaac Asimov and Martin H. Greenberg. New York:
Daw Books, 1979.

Sturgeon, Theodore (Edward Hamilton Waldo). "Maturity,"
in Analog, Feb. 1947; in The Worlds of Theodore Sturgeon.
New York: Ace Books, 1972 and 1977.

van Vogt, A(lfred) E(lton). "The Search," in Astounding
Science-Fiction, Jan. 1943; in The Best of Science Fiction. Ed. Groff Conklin. New York: Crown, 1946 and
1963; in a fix-up of stories, Quest for the Future. New
York; Ace Books, 1970, and London: Sidgwick & Jackson,
1972.

CHAPTER 4: THE 1950s

The decade of the 1950s is called the Age of Acceptance by Lester del Rey (The World of Science Fiction: 1926-1976, New York: Garland, 1980), signifying that sf was, at long last, becoming respectable. Apparently this also signified the beginning of the age of acceptance for both women characters and women writers in sf as well. (Women writers who had their first sf stories published in this decade include Rosel George Brown, Carol Emshwiller, Phyllis Gottlieb, Zenna Henderson, Anne McCaffrey, and Joanna Russ.)

This new acceptance is reflected by the changes in the characters from the 1940s. The synopses in this chapter, for example, hold five women characters who are doctors, one who is a wartime "Entertainer," two who are telepathic, two who are teachers, and even one who is a grandmother! The careers, though still limited for women characters, were beginning to broaden. Women characters were beginning to be seen not only more frequently, but also more often as main characters with pivotal positions--positions of power in stories. In addition, the age range began to broaden. In the 1950s more older women were beginning to appear in sf --the grandmother in Clingerman's "Minister Without Portfolio," for example--and one very assertive teenager--Jean Parlier in Vance's Monsters in Orbit. The acceptance of the woman character in sf had truly begun.

* BRADLEY, MARION ZIMMER. "The Wind People," in
    If, Feb. 1959; in Women of Wonder. Ed. Pamela
    Sargent. New York: Vintage Books, 1975.

    Main Character: Dr. Helen Murray.
    Physical Characteristics: Is the Starholm's doctor;
"young" and "lovely."

Mental/Emotional Characteristics: Is strong-willed;
has affairs that are "companionable, comfortable, but never
passionate," although she is "a woman capable of passion, of
great depths of devotion"; as a scientist, she denies the reality of what she has experienced because the experience
seems more like a fantasy or a dream; fears she is going
insane after years of isolation.

Story Particulars: A ship's doctor on a long layover
on "a soft, windy, whispering world," Dr. Helen Murray finds
herself pregnant. When the child arrives, Captain Merrihew
is most angry at her for her "criminal carelessness" in having the baby and reminds her that the child will die when the
ship goes into "overdrive." However, Helen refuses to have
the baby put to sleep and is determined to stay on this world
with him, although it will mean total isolation from adults for
her. The Captain finally agrees to leave her there, against
his better judgment, and Helen begins her lonely life with
Robin, her child.

On occasion, she recalls the night when Robin was
conceived, when she had sex with Colin Reynolds, a technician
on the Starholm. Then she remembers walking through the
moonlight and lying on the bank of the river, where a strange
man came to her whom she could hardly see, a man who
seemed more "living to her" than any other man she'd ever
known, though by daylight the experience seemed like a fantasy, a dream. Helen tries to deny the existence of this
second man, calling him a "hallucination," although she is
never fully certain that he wasn't real. She raises Robin on
food she gathers from the planet, bearing the loneliness fairly
well.

When Robin is fourteen years old, Helen studies his
"pearly pale" skin and wonders at his lack of similarity to
either Colin or herself. She tries to convince a skeptical
Robin that the "other people" on this world are all in his
mind because he has had no one to play with as a child; but
she never quite convinces even herself of that. The possibility that there are others on this world never ceases to
haunt and nag at Helen.

When Robin is sixteen, he sees a woman in the forest
and tells Helen of her, insisting he can see and hear the
wind people. She rebukes his argument, saying that he saw
a woman and she saw a man. "Do I have to explain more to
you?" Robin, agonized and emotionally distraught, grabs
Helen and holds her close. Helen, "her blood icing over,"
realizes that they are only a step away from incest and runs
sobbing into the forest.

When more calm, she considers that Robin, after her

death, will be all alone on this planet, and ponders the idea
of breaking her "instinctual and impregnable" taboo to give
Robin companionship.   At that moment, however, she finds
herself at the exact spot on the river bank where, sixteen
years before, she met the strange man.   Now she sees him
once more, his eyes holding "infinite sadness and compassion," and also sees his companions.   With her defenses
down, she admits the existence of the wind people and knows
that Robin's father is one of them, and that Robin has been
able to see and hear them all along.   When the man takes
two steps towards her, and she sees how much he looks like
Robin, she thinks she is "going mad."
     The story's tragic conclusion leaves Robin free to join
the wind people.   It is Helen's scientific mind which makes
it next to impossible for her to admit the existence of something she can't see or hear.

* BRUNNER, JOHN.   Echo in the Skull, in Science Fantasy
     Magazine, Aug. 1959; in double with Rocket to Limbo.
     New York: Ace Books, 1959; rev. and exp. as Give
     Warning to the World.   New York: Daw Books, 1974.

     Main Character: Sally Ercott.
     Physical Characteristics: Has "shoulder-length blonde
hair," blue eyes, and a "wide mouth"; has a lovely body and
is a "beautiful girl"; has a "husky, pleasant voice" and an
"educated accent"; is 25 years old.
     Mental/Emotional Characteristics: Has attacks of
"tolling" in her head, "like a bass-voiced scream issuing
hollow and monstrous out of an infinitely deep well"; is the
"calm type" who bottles her troubles up until they burst her
"wide open"; remembers her past lives which now endanger
her present life.
     Story Particulars: Sally Ercott, broke, destitute, de-
pressed, without a past, and certain she is going insane,
lives in London in a boarding house run by Bella and Arthur
Rowall.   She is haunted by strange memories of past lives,
quite alien from her Earth life, though she is unable to remember her past in this life.   Prior to the memories, she
has attacks in which a "tolling" in her head becomes unbear-
able.   In the midst of one such memory attack, after a night
of drink-induced sleep, Sally falls into the street, right in
the path of an oncoming car.   The car, an old MG, stops
before it strikes her, and Sally is helped to her feet by Nick
Jenkins, the attractive driver.   He sees her in dirty clothes,
her hair uncombed, and realizing that her educated voice

doesn't match her circumstances, he decides to help her.
Sally, feeling that she has dropped as low as she can go,
agrees to let him help her, and tells him her story, as
well as her amnesia will allow.   Fortunately for her, Nick
believes her incredible tale.   He gets her new clothes and
calls a doctor in to examine her.

Meanwhile, the Rowalls are plotting to get Sally back
to the boarding house to implant an alien parasitic Yem on
her back.   The Yem are parasites gradually invading all of
the habitable worlds in the universe.   They reproduce either
by spreading from the parent or by spores.   The boarding
house in which Sally lives is housing in its basement the only
Yem parent yet on Earth.   Sally, with at least two past lives
behind her in which she encountered the Yem, is somehow
drawn to the boarding house because she instinctively knows
she must stop it from spreading on Earth; yet her memory
of those past lives is hazy until Nick asks her to draw pictures of a couple of her memories.   At that point her purpose in moving into the boarding house becomes clear to her.
Without the help and encouragement of Nick, Sally would probably have merely gone insane without being able to save the
Earth from the Yem.   With Nick's faith in her, his help and
rescue, Sally proves to be the key to protecting Earth against
the parasitic invaders.

*   CLINGERMAN, MILDRED.   "Minister Without Portfolio,"
     in The Magazine of Fantasy and Science Fiction, Feb.
     1952; in The Eureka Years.   Ed. Annette Peltz Mc-
     Comas.   New York: Bantam Books, 1982.

     Main Character: Ida Chriswell.
     Physical Characteristics: Is "quite colour-blind"; is
60 years old and has a "wrinkled face."
     Mental/Emotional Characteristics: Feels "useless"
in her life of "enforced idleness" since her husband's death;
is afraid of cows and "only a little less afraid of her daughter-
in-law, Clara"; is "weak in geography."
     Story Particulars: Since her husband's death, Ida
Chriswell has been living with her son and daughter-in-law,
Clara, in what she considers "enforced idleness."   Clara insists that Ida take up bird watching in spite of the fact that
she is color-blind and, as such, unable to enjoy the beautiful
colors of the birds.   It is on one such bird-watching trip in
the country, while chasing the "ridiculous" straw "cartwheel
hat" Clara insists she wear, that Ida stumbles upon several
young men in uniforms beside "a low, silvery aircraft of

some unusual design." Ida assumes they are with the Air
Force and are connected with the war.

The boy nearest her points to her hat which is being
passed from man to man and laughed at. He then offers her
a hat like his which he places on her head. The young man
who gave her the hat tells her that she is very much like his
"Mother's Mother" and that her handkerchief reminds him of
his home in the Harmony Hills. As Ida is "lamentably weak
in geography," and has no idea where the Harmony Hills are,
she asks him to tell her about his hills. Instead, they show
her their hills by placing a "gossamer material" over her
head and making it possible for her to see colors "she had
never seen, never guessed." They then ask her questions
and request the doily she has crocheted as she talked. The
boy who gave her the hat like his asks that she exchange
photographs with him. She gives him the snapshots of her
grandchildren and he gives her pictures of his little sisters.
The parting is tearful for Ida because of their honorary treatment of her.

When she arrives home, she finds the house in turmoil, all of the radios in the house "blaring." She finds her
two grandchildren fighting and, seeing a useful purpose she
can serve, breaks up the fight and tells the girls of her adventures. At the story's end, she shows the girls the snapshots the boy had given her. They are revolted and tell her
the children in the pictures have green skin. Ida lectures
the children about not judging people by their skin color,
then wonders "where on earth" there were people with green
skin. Part of the newspaper headlines that day were "Unknown woman saves world, say men from space. One sane
human found on earth." It seems the visitors from space
like her answers.

This story is beautifully written and treats Ida with
both love and humor.

★   CLINGERMAN, MILDRED.   "The Day of the Green Velvet
     Cloak," in The Magazine of Fantasy and Science Fic-
     tion. July 1958; in A Cupful of Space.   New York:
     Ballantine Books, 1961.

     Main Character: Mavis O'Hanlon.
     Physical Characteristics: No description given.
     Mental/Emotional Characteristics: Is "timid" and un-
able to assertively say no; has been engaged to Hubert for
six years, and is unable to tell him "what a big mistake he
was"; is happy being "her old chicken-hearted, unfibered self";

does not have "courage"; collects "Victorian travel journals"
written by women between the years 1850 and 1900; is considered by Titus Graham to be "so free, so untrammeled and
brave" and to have "courage"; is honest.

Story Particulars: "Timid" and "chicken-hearted" Mavis O'Hanlon purchases a beautiful green velvet cloak only a
week before she is to be married to Hubert Lotzenhiser, the
owner of a loan company. Her six-year engagement drawing
to a close, Mavis knows she is making a mistake in marrying Hubert, just as she's made a mistake in buying the cloak.
To reward herself for the wrangles with her conscience on
both mistakes, she stops on the way home at the Book Nook,
a second-hand bookstore, to search for a new book to add to
her collection of Victorian travel journals written by women
between the years of 1850 and 1900. There she finds a journal that fits that description written by a woman named Sara,
and she goes to the counter to pay the new proprietor.

Instead of taking her money, the proprietor begins to
read the book, claiming to be a time traveler and to know
Sara. In fact, he says he is one of the people of whom she
wrote. Realizing the man is not going to give up the book
until he's read it, she pulls up a chair and waits. When he
reaches for his cigar case and can't find it, Mavis offers him
a cigarette, taking one out for herself as well. He considers
her most brave to smoke and tells her so. Pleased at his
opinion, but not given to being dishonest, Mavis tells him that
"Millions of women smoke" and once more asks for the book.
He insists once again that he is from the past and introduces
himself as Titus Graham, who should be in the year 1877 in
Heidelberg. It seems that while reading a book of short stories about the future, he suddenly found himself transported
through time and now hopes by reading Sara's journal to return to his time. Mavis, realizing that he is cold and hun-
gry, draws out the beautiful green velvet cloak, covering him
with it, and prepares to leave to get him some food. He
stops her at the door with a marriage proposal, which makes
Mavis' heart pound with pleasure at the thought of being in a
time when she would better fit in. She knows, however, that
she must heal herself of her timidness in the time in which
she was born, and refuses.

When Mavis returns, Titus is gone and only the book
remains. She takes the book with her and reads more of it,
learning that Titus returned to his time, was found by his
friends, and held Mavis in very high esteem, which Sara
finds "most provoking." Reading his account of her gives
her the courage to ask Hubert to come over so she can cancel
the engagement, but before he has time to get there, the

doorbell rings.   There before her is the great grandson of
Titus, Titus Graham the Fourth, on an errand for his now-
deceased great grandfather.   He has returned the green velvet
cloak for his great grandfather and shows promise of filling
the vacancy left by Hubert.
    Clingerman has a talent for writing with humor and
love about women, and this story is no exception.

* DE CAMP, L. SPRAGUE. Rogue Queen. New York:
    Doubleday, 1951; rpt. New York: New American Li-
    brary, 1972.

Main Character: Iroedh
Physical Characteristics: Has red skin, four digits
on hands and feet, "slit pupils," small ears, hair in "a
single strip running from the scalp down the back," and
blue teeth; is without developed breasts until she starts eating
meat, then her breasts develop and her bone structure spreads
in her pelvic region.
    Mental/Emotional Characteristics: Can fight and kill
without compunction; cares for Antis enough to risk her own
life in his daring rescue; is not jealous of Antis' sexual duties to the queen until she starts eating meat and then develops "a possessive, sentimental, and exclusive tenderness
towards him"; is fiercely independent before eating meat and
discovers she doesn't mind being bossed as much afterwards;
is called by an adamant worker a "woolly-minded antiquarian"
because she reads history; is also called intelligent.
    Story Particulars: On an alien planet, earth people
land and start a chain of events which leads to the upheaval
of the entire social/sexual structure of that planet's people.
The inhabitants have a social structure similar to that of the
earth bee; there are queens (one per community), drones
(male fertilizers of the queen), and workers (neuter females).
    Iroedh, a worker, begins the novel not entirely satis-
fied that her drone friend, Antis, has reached the age when
he must be killed.   However, the arrival of the earth people
takes her away from her concern about him.   In the time she
spends with the earth people, she learns about love and is
baffled and mystified by it.   When she sees that the earth
people have a flying machine (a helicopter) she plans a way
to rescue Antis and blackmails Winston Bloch, an earth man,
into assisting her.   Events that follow force Iroedh to eat
meat, which is supposed to kill her, but instead turns her
into a "functional female" much to Antis' distraction.   Love
(and Iroedh's body) blossoms in the wilds for Iroedh and Antis,
with Bloch and his wife Barbe Dulac as spectators.

The final event, which molds Iroedh into the Rogue
Queen the Oracle of Ledhwid wrote of, is contact with the
Oracle itself.   (It is an alien who is both male and female.)
The Oracle tells Iroedh that she has no choice but to unite
the planet by playing the conqueror, something that Iroedh
has no desire to be.   But circumstances being what they were,
she has no choice, and the planet's inhabitants begin to re-
vert, as Antis puts it, to "the happy customs of the Golden
Age."   The Oracle, before his death, tells Iroedh that religion must also be revived for this system to work.   Iroedh
and Antis, at the book's conclusion, are to go with the earth
people as intermediaries for them on the other continents of
the planet.

An amusing development in the book in the relationship
between Iroedh and Antis is that after the previously dominant
Iroedh develops breasts, Antis becomes, or attempts to become, the dominant one.   Iroedh, puzzled by this, discusses
the change with Barbe, who is not at all surprised by the situation.   It seems that after Iroedh becomes a "functional female," Antis listens to her suggestions, "grunts and says he'll
think about it," and then tells her the next day what a wonderful idea he's just had, repeating what she suggested the
day before.   However, at the book's end, when a decision
has to be made immediately and Antis tells her he'll think
it over, Iroedh takes a stand and says "Not this time" and
makes the decision herself.

With its earth people who are full of flowery romance,
its natives who have a rigid social structure for sexual activity, and its Oracle from the planet Thoth, who is both
male and female, this book is rich in its variety of sexual
roles and options.

*   HENDERSON, ZENNA.   "Pottage," in The Magazine of
        Fantasy and Science Fiction, Sept. 1955; in the noveli-
        zation of collected "People" stories, Pilgrimage.   New
        York: Doubleday, 1961; rpt. New York: Avon Books,
        1982.   (The second collection of "People" stories is
        The People: No Different Flesh.   New York: Double-
        day, 1967; rpt. New York: Avon Books, 1982.)

Main Character: Melodye Amerson.
Physical Characteristics: No physical description given.
Mental/Emotional Characteristics: At the story's beginning, she is "fed up to the teeth" with teaching in a large
school, and regrets the loss of her belief that "anything seemed
possible"; as a dedicated teacher, enjoys "the familiar Sep-

tember thrill of new beginnings"; feels as though she's behind
bars.

Story Particulars: A story based on aliens living on
Earth is not an unusual approach in sf, but Henderson's sensitive treatment of the subject is.   This is one of the early
stories she wrote about "the People," humanoid aliens who
crashed on Earth long ago and who have since scattered.   The
pockets of other Groups don't know that there are still others,
but some individuals are aware of the fact and seek out telepathic contact with the lost ones each evening.   Melodye met
Karen, one of the People, while in college.   Karen told Melodye about the People, somehow knowing she could be trusted,
and Melodye never forgot.

When this story begins, Melodye, a teacher ready for
a dramatic change in her life, chooses to accept a one-room
teaching position in Bendo, even after she is warned the residents are like "Ghost people" and Bendo a very unhappy community.   What Melodye never expects, in her entire life, is
to discover a pocket of Karen's People, but in Bendo, that's
exactly what she finds.   The youngsters she teaches there
are the third generation of People and are enough removed
from the horrors of their initial treatment on Earth to be
rebellious about hiding their talents.   They are, nonetheless,
obedient to their very strict parents and shuffle along to keep
from "lifting" off the ground.

Realizing how very unhappy the children are because
they are holding back their talents, Melodye begins gradually
allowing them to write down and draw their individual racial
memories of the Home and to lift objects and themselves with
their telepathic powers.   Unfortunately, the parents discover
her schoolhouse activities and come, en masse, to stop her,
interrupting Abie, one of the students, as he swings through
the schoolroom in an imaginary swing.   Abie, startled and
disappointed by their presence there, falls and receives a
concussion which will be fatal without proper attention.   Although Bendo is isolated, a doctor is staying at a nearby ranch
and one of the boys who can lift goes to get him.   The doctor, young Dr. Curtis, arrives and announces that Abie needs
specialists--specialists that are not available this far in the
country.   Melodye tells the People of Karen and the other
Group and words their telepathic call for them.   Karen and
three other People arrive, help Dr. Curtis with the operation
--after which he emotionally falls apart and is comforted by
Melodye--and Abie is saved.

The story's beautiful conclusion is only a beginning for
Melodye and Dr. Curtis with the People.   Melodye is single-
mindedly devoted to the well-being of her students and is a

remarkably dedicated teacher. (Many of Henderson's short story characters are teachers as devoted as Melodye is, and well worth reading about.) This particular story, with only slight modifications, was made into a television movie called The People in 1972, starring Kim Darby as Melodye and William Shatner as Dr. Curtis.

* LEIBER, FRITZ. The Big Time, in Galaxy Science Fiction, March 1958; in double with The Mind Spider. New York: Ace Books, 1961; printed as The Big Time. Boston: Gregg Press, 1976.

Main Character: Greta Forzane (frequently called "Greta girl").

Physical Characteristics: Is 29 years old; was "born in Chicago to Scandinavian parents" and was Resurrected an "action-packed ten minutes" before her natural death; is sterile and "no longer in bondage to the moon" as are all the women in the Place until the door to the Change World is shut; is a "Doubleganger" ("can operate both in the cosmos and outside of it").

Mental/Emotional Characteristics: Calls herself a "party girl"; has "a rough-and-ready charm of my own"; comforts and has sex with Soldiers of the Change War; is called an "Entertainer"; is "a nurse and a psychologist and an actress and a mother and a practical ethnologist ... and a reliable friend"; feels that women always pick her for an audience; says she has her "silly side"; is bright and sensitive to the feelings of others and nuances in conversation; has been "Resurrected" from "Man" to "Demon" ("the fourth order of evolution, possibility-binders").

Story Particulars: It is the last half of the twentieth century, in "real" time, when this "outside space and time" novel happens, at a location just called the Place. The Place, a Recuperation Station, is described in the first person words of Greta Fozane as being "midway in size and atmosphere between a large nightclub where the Entertainers sleep in and a small Zeppelin hangar decorated for a party." Greta is an Entertainer (a glorified prostitute and nursemaid) in the Place for Soldiers of the Change War, a war in which the two sides, named the Spiders and the Snakes, battle to change history to suit themselves. The recruits are either humans like Greta or Extraterrestrials (ETs) who are snatched from their lives often mere moments from the time of their natural deaths. The story is about Greta and others who are both Doublegangers (those who "can operate both in the cosmos

and outside of it") and Demons (those who "act reasonably
alive" while being Doublegangers).

Three Soldiers arrive at the Place to be entertained
by Greta, Sid, Doc, Beauregard, Maud and Lili, who are
from "quite an assortment of times and places." Their arrival sparks turmoil, but not nearly as much as when Kaby-
sia (Kaby) Labrys and Greta's "Lunan boy friend" Ilhilihis
(Illy) arrive. (Illy, it seems, looks like a "tall cross between a spider monkey and a persian cat.") Kaby brings an
atom bomb to the Place, which shocks the group only slightly
less than suddenly finding the Maintainer (which keeps a Door
in and out of the Place available) is now gone. It would
seem the group is locked in the Place for eternity. If not
for Greta's insight into the disappearance of the Maintainer,
the group might well have either stayed there indefinitely without a Door or been blown up by the atom bomb.

Greta, in spite of her heroic insight, remains an un-
sung hero, suspected of taking the very thing she has recovered. There is one character, Erich, who is convinced of
his power over women and states that women are only "Something to mess around with" in his "spare time." Greta has
no illusions about him or herself, for that is precisely what
she is there to do--to provide entertainment. Kaby, an "iron
babe" as Greta calls her, is an Amazon-type Soldier who
Greta thinks can "stand anything." A poet and a starry-eyed
poet-lover also grace the Place and complicate life there in-
credibly.

The characters in this book, including Greta, are
unique and are portrayed with irony rather than through rose-
colored glasses. (This novel was the winner of the 1958
Hugo for best novel.)

* McCAFFREY, ANNE. "Lady in the Tower," in The Maga-
    zine of Fantasy and Science Fiction, April 1959; in Get
    Off the Unicorn. New York: Ballantine Books, 1977.

Main Character: The Rowan, or Rowan.
Physical Characteristics: Is 23 years old, white haired,
and "frail."
Mental/Emotional Characteristics: Is the youngest and
the best of the five highly talented "T-1's" or "Primes" in
the service of the Federal Telepathers and Teleporters, Inc.;
is usually stormy and "peevish" in mood, but has a "miracu-
lous smile" that has a "hint of suppressed passion"; in spite
of her abundant self-confidence, is capable of being "discon-
certed"; experiences "bitter, screaming loneliness" during her

hours off duty; cannot leave her world due to the space-fear
that all Primes have; acts "with propriety face to face" in
spite of her "temperament."

Story Particulars: Rowan, the youngest Prime in the
service of the Federal Telepathers and Teleporters, Inc., is
lonely in her job, isolated as she is on a moon and unable
to travel elsewhere after work. She was trained by Siglen
of Altair and told by her that she, as a T-1, was unable to
travel in space. Physically frail, white-haired Rowan subdues
her passions and stoically accepts that handicap until, at age
twenty-three, she hears a previously unknown Prime struggling
to protect his planet from an attack force of invading "ET's"
(Extraterrestrials) who are bombarding the planet with viruses
to kill off the population.

Rowan, calling the man Deneb because that is his
planet's name, is at first shocked by his existence, then
"peevish," and finally happy. She thrusts his medicine halfway to his planet, and he takes it from there. When he contacts her again, it is after working hours and he is getting
desperate for help. He asks for two "germdogs" for help
with the viruses and for three patrol squadrons. Rowan,
wanting to help in spite of the fact that her station is currently behind Jupiter from him, agrees to go out in her shell
and throw the germdogs towards him, an act which is rewarded by a "passionate and tender kiss" blown to her across
"eighteen light-years of space." Rowan goes to her quarters
in the station and fights off her loneliness until she remembers the kiss, then falls into a restful sleep. Deneb wakes
her in the middle of her sleep for more help. The invaders
have now begun to bombard the planet with missiles and he
is the only one there capable of thrusting them away. He
wants her to come there and help him, but he knows she can't
because she is unable to tolerate space-travel. Rowan pleads
for help for Deneb from another Prime, Reidinger, who
roughly refuses her in the hope that she will be the Prime
who overcomes her space-fear.

ET missiles then begin to arrive at Rowan's station,
and quick action must be taken. She notifies all the Primes
that they will be merging with her to rid the station of the
missiles and offers to "handle the ego-merge" with Deneb to
help him ward off his attackers once and for all. The Primes,
merged and focused through Rowan, impress upon the invaders
the immensity of their powers and warn them not to return,
successfully driving off the ET's.

After all the Primes have withdrawn, Deneb catches
Rowan's mind and asks her to come live with him. Rowan,
though passionately wanting just that, refuses and retreats

back into her body, withdrawing from mental contact for two
days.   When she emerges she is distant, tragic, and subdued,
depressing the crew who work with her.   Reidinger, who tells
Deneb that Rowan needs him, furnishes her with a joyous first
meeting with Deneb, whose name is really Jeff Raven.   Jeff
came to Rowan, thus proving to her that a Prime can travel
in space.   He explains to her that Siglen of Altair, who
trained all the Primes but him, has an inner-ear imbalance
which made free-fall traumatic for her and she instilled this
fear into all of her students.   It is decided that Rowan can
live with Jeff--and commute to work.   At the story's end,
the reader knows that Rowan has found an outlet for her passions and a cure for her loneliness.

*   MacLEAN, KATHERINE.   "And Be Merry," in Astounding
       Science-Fiction, Feb. 1950; retitled "The Pyramid in
       the Desert," in The Diploids.   New York: Avon Books,
       1962; rpt. Boston: Gregg Press, 1981.

       Main Character: Dr. Helen Berent.
       Physical Characteristics: Is thirty-eight years old at
the story's beginning, but rejuvenates herself to appear eighteen years old; has a surprised expression on her new face
and is pale; has a "warm voice"; is an expert endocrinologist
and the wife of an archeologist.
       Mental/Emotional Characteristics: Experiments on
herself and has the desire to be "one of the best cockeyed
endocrinologists practicing"; feels she can "strike a blow for
evolution at last"; is, according to her husband, "just too
rational. "
       Story Particulars: Dr. Helen Berent, an expert endo-
crinologist, decides to spend the summer alone, experiment-
ing on herself while Alec, her archeologist husband, traipses
all over the wilds in search of finds.   Knowing Alec will for-
bid her experimentation on herself, she feigns a broken foot
and stays home to use herself as a human guinea pig "to investigate the condition of old age. "
       The bulk of the story is in the form of letters and tapes
being read and heard by her husband after his return.   She
begins by making herself a home in her laboratory and re-
duces her calcium intake below the necessary level before
she begins to use her treatments on herself.   Her once-
broken arm, which healed with a bump on it, heals this time
with no bump, rejuvenated as if new.   Next she goes to work
on the replacement of "soft tissues" and, quite by accident,
makes herself appear not the thirty-eight year old she is, but

eighteen years old. She realizes that her new face looks surprised from all angles and that her new, much younger appearance will cause her husband as well as herself tremendous problems. She asks her husband on tape, "... what if one of our friends happens to see me on the street looking like an eighteen year old? What am I supposed to say?" She adds, "... we will have to change our names and move to California." She considers giving him treatments too and is concerned that people will think he is "a cradle snatcher."

In spite of Helen's reservations and concerns, she is pleased to be able to "strike a blow for evolution at last." Immortality seems to be within reach for her. There is only one further tape beyond this point. On it, Helen expresses her concern about her sudden interest in "violence and slaughter." Realizing that Helen has probably had a nervous breakdown under the "fear" and "terror" that sprang from her sudden immortality, Alec searches for and finds Helen in a mental hospital. Finding her just coming out from under some drugs, Alec is forced to knock out the doctor so he can tell his "too rational" wife that she is dying of cancer. This revelation sets Helen's scientific mind to work, giving her the final insight she's needed--she has not discovered immortality after all. Because all cells mutate, she tells Alec, not yet fully realizing he is there, the longer the life, the larger the chance for someone to die of "something." Then she really sees Alec and both welcome the other "back."

Helen's eighteen-year-old appearance remains the same and the reader is left to ponder what she and Alec can or will do about her sudden youthful appearance. Helen is determined and devoted as a scientist and is as thoroughly dedicated a professional as her husband. She is capable of completely losing herself in her work and follows a "straight and narrow track of formulas" in her scientific reports. One of her dreams, when she thinks immortality is in her grasp, is that both she and her husband can study the other's field of expertise, thus fully "covering the field of human behavior" between them, and "talk the same language."

★   MacLEAN, KATHERINE. "Contagion," in Galaxy Science
        Fiction, Oct. 1950; in Women of Wonder. Ed. Pamela
        Sargent. New York: Vintage Books, 1975.

     Main Character: June Walton.
     Physical Characteristics: Is "tall and tanned"; has
"a few freckles," "wavy red hair," "dark blue eyes," and
"a good figure."

Mental/Emotional Characteristics: Is a doctor; is married to Dr. Max Stark; is analytical and a good thinker; has a high degree of self-control and logic.

Story Particulars: After traveling 36 light years from Earth, June Walton and a group of close to 100 earth people are testing the planet Minos for possible human habitation capability when a tall, rugged, red-haired man appears out of the forest bearing greetings, in English, from the "mayor." It seems that a small group of earth people have already been on Minos for three generations. The greeter, Patrick Mead, is surprised to see the diversity of appearances among the new arrivals, a fact which doesn't disturb the newcomers until much later. Pat is invited back to their ship, carefully cleaned and rid of all his germs, and allowed to meet all the people on board.

As the hours wear on and the husbands on board grow increasingly jealous of all the attention Pat is getting, it becomes obvious to June that the disease Pat had mentioned, called melting sickness by residents of Minos, has been caught by the men on board. From then on, it's a fight against time, and June and her doctor husband, Max, work together to try and find the key to the illness. It behaves like a fast-acting leukemia, so the men are hurried into the "womblike life tanks." It is June who has the insight that Pat Mead's cells are attacking the cells of every man on board and that all they need is a "week's cure," during which they will all come to look exactly like Pat.

At the week's end, with June guarding and locking the door to the tank room all week so as not to panic the women on board with the truth, the men emerge, all looking exactly like Pat Mead, though with the same individual internal memories, capabilities, reactions, and physical gestures that they always had. And who should appear at the airlock at that moment but a "handsome, leggy, red-headed girl who could have been his [Pat's] sister," Patricia Mead. Sheila, who considers herself the most beautiful woman on board, panics, and all but six of the women share Sheila's desire to remain the same. However, logic wins out. First, the men who have changed cannot survive on ship's food due to a molecular change. Second, the women can either leave the planet, and their men, or face the change the men have made. June and Max make logical arguments to the women, pointing out that there is "only one solution" and that is the one that's made.

Vanity and the human reaction to losing one's unique outward appearance are the emphasis in this interesting story.

* MERRIL, JUDITH. "Daughters of Earth," in The Petrified

Planet. Ed. Fletcher Pratt. New York: Twayne,
1952; in Daughters of Earth. New York: Doubleday,
1968; in The Best of Judith Merril. New York: Warner Books, 1976.

Main Character: Emma (Em) Malook Tarbell.
Physical Characteristics: Is tall and slim; is a doctor, a medic "specially trained for the job of defrosting"
space travelers; becomes an "unofficial specialist in obstetrics."
Mental/Emotional Characteristics: Is "too direct, too
determined, too intellectual, too strong" to marry, but meets
a man who has the "audacity" to marry her; finds "pleasure
past and lost ... excruciating to remember"; is hate-stricken
rather than grief-stricken at her husband's death and throws
herself into her work; enjoys working alone; learns how to
have men friends "without intensity"; enjoys men who have
"enthusiasm, the ability to participate completely" as she
does; is "rebelliously 'idealistic'" and must explore a new
world; has as her passion a desire to establish communication with the intelligent silicone life forms on Uller, and because of that is "in disrepute"; is thought by her mother to
have "'coldblooded' and 'unnatural' experimental attitudes."
Story Particulars: This story, though an epistle about
six generations of mothers and daughters, focuses on the
fourth generation, Emma Malook Tarbell, the so-called writer
of the letters. Em is writing the letters for her granddaugh-
ter Carla as a history of her heritage for her to take with
her into space. The very act of writing the letters as a way
of continuing family heritage might seem more traditionally
typical of the man of the family; however, it is the women
in this family who are the adventurers and explorers and who
pass that birthright down to their daughters.
The desire to explore space for these Earth descendants seems to affect only every other generation. Martha,
who lived on Earth and visited the moon only once, had no
desire to explore space, but her daughter Joan refused to
follow the "normal course of events" and to go to "work as
a biophysicist until she found a husband." It seems that the
"prospect appalled her." Joan instead studied for nineteen
months under an accelerated program during which time she
met and married Alex, who was also in the program, and
left to settle on Pluto. Joan's daughter Ariadne, whose father died when she was ten, grew up and married on Pluto,
there having the baby Emma. Emma, who grows up to be
a doctor, inherits Joan's "personal effects" and a "box of
papers and letter-tapes" which contains the first heritage papers to be written.

Emma Malook, like her grandmother Joan, "rebelliously 'idealistic'" and having explorer's blood, seems to be "doomed to single bliss" because she is "too direct, too determined, too intellectual, too strong"; however, she meets Ken Tarbell, a man who has the "audacity" to marry her. Together they go with the first explorers to settle a world out of our solar system, Uller, a planet "twenty-one light years from home." There, after a brief idyllic period, Em, pregnant with Leah (Lee), loses Ken to an attacking intelligent native life form. Her grief takes the form of overpowering anger and hard work. Eventually she learns to love men without them being "the beloved," which frees her from her fear of overwhelming emotional hurt again and cures her loneliness.

Leah is born on Uller and soon learns that her mother is "somehow in disrepute" because of her belief that they should try to communicate with the intelligent life form rather than exterminate them. She, Jose Cabrini, and sixty-five other dissenters form Josetown, separate from Firstown, and are given ten years to establish communication with the Ullerns. During that time, as always, Em throws herself joyously into her work, knowing "the kind of total purpose in living" that Martha, Ariadne, and Leah would never experience. Leah grows up trying to hate Em for the loss of her playmates and her isolation in Josetown. She can never understand "how her mother could be so stupid as to try to attract a man by being bright."

Carla, Leah's daughter and the alternate generation with explorer's blood, decides to leave Uller for Nifleheim on the first joint venture with the native Ullerns in a ship built for time travel. Em gives her the "film" on which she has recorded her heritage, and realizes only after the ship leaves that it is "imperfect," lacking some of Leah's history. In the story, the standard question and reply of mother (planet-lover) and daughter (explorer) as the ship stands ready to leave is always "aren't you afraid?" and "I'm terrified!" (or "petrified," or "scared stiff"). In spite of the fear, the explorer blood always wins. The story is well written and offers believable characters and a beautiful heritage for Earth's daughters.

* MERRIL, JUDITH. "Stormy Weather," in Startling Stories, Summer 1954; in The Best of Judith Merril. New York: Warner Books, 1976.

Main Character: Catherine (Cathy) Andauer.
Physical Characteristics: Is 25 years old; is one of

the "expert psichosomanticists" of the "Traffic Control Service."

Mental/Emotional Characteristics: Is competent and
enjoys her work; did well in her "psi-training"; has fallen in
love which is dangerous for a psichosomanticist; curses when
sufficiently angered.

Story Particulars: The chances are indeed slender for
a trained psichosomanticist to find a man "worth having" who
can psi, but Cathy was able to find Mike. Now, stuck in
space on a thirty-day shift in a one-woman ball of a spacecraft, her oxygen need higher than the algae on board can
keep up with, Cathy bounces between boredom with her surroundings, anger at Mike for not communicating, and fear
for his safety. She has been unable to mentally reach him
since she woke from a dream screaming on this shift. Fear
and boredom bring on memories of words from blues tunes,
and Cathy is thoroughly irritated, depressed, and worried.
Her duties--to monitor "chunks of rock" and blow up any that
will intersect space traffic--are vital to the Traffic Control
Agency in the Space Service, but they are usually not very
time consuming, leaving her lots of spare time, in this case,
to worry. The salary and retirement pay for this job are
good and the experience sets a woman for life, because "there
were always jobs waiting for the glamorous heroes and heroines
of the Space Service," and psichosomanticists like her were
offered "the best jobs of all."

On this thirty-day shift, Cathy performs her duties
rather mechanically, preoccupied with why Mike has cut their
mental contact. She decides against the ideas that he has
been doped, or is drunk, or that he is dead, and wonders if
pride has forced him to cut contact. "A man can afford to
be proud," she thinks, and adds that a woman couldn't afford
to be proud. "A Servicegirl couldn't take chances," and does
"better in psi-training than men." She wants to contact Mike
but making contact would cost her enough oxygen for two
meals. Even smoking two cigarettes would cost her enough
oxygen for one meal.

Cathy finally decides to concentrate on now and talks
herself to sleep--just in time for the chrono speaker to wake
her with its alarming "Alert for action" call which gives
Cathy something useful to do. A "parti-cloud" has drifted
into the solar system and it is in her sector and therefore
her job to bomb it before it crosses "the busiest space-lanes
in the System." Thoughts of Mike are pushed to the background as she calculates the path the bomb must follow. After the calculations, time weighs heavy on her hands, and
she indulges herself once more by calling Mike again, still

receiving no response. The call makes her late sending the
bomb, but all is not lost. Cathy manages to destroy the
"parti-cloud" of gravel with no difficulty. Her eventual reunion with Mike is a joyful one, thoroughly dissipating Cathy's
blues.

★ MERRIL, JUDITH. Shadow on the Hearth. Garden City,
     NY: Doubleday, 1950; rpt. London: Compact Books,
     1966.

     Main Character: Gladys Mitchell.
     Physical Characteristics: Is 37 years old; has "long
lines of haggard middle age"; applies "powder and lipstick";
is still very physically attracted to her husband. (Absent
are references to build, weight, height, eye or hair color.)
     Mental/Emotional Characteristics: Is set in an estab-
lished routine and unyielding/inflexible to new and strange
situations; has a poor memory; is fearful; is dependent on
her husband, Jon, for direction and security; protects her
daughters with motherly love.

     Secondary and Minor Characters: 1) Barbara--Is 15
years old; is Gladys' daughter; is flexible in crisis; has a
good memory; handles her own fears well; is just discovering
her attraction to men; wants to take on responsibilities; calls
her mother "mother" to show how mature she is. 2) Veda--
Is Gladys' main/housekeeper; is self-sufficient; knows her
own mind and expresses it freely; is independent and loaded
with common sense. 3) Edith--Is one of Gladys' neighbors;
is alcoholic, frivolous, prone to hysteria in emergency (sur-
prisingly, a foil to Gladys), dependent, and self-righteous.

     Story Particulars: Gladys Mitchell, a suburban home-
maker/mother, begins her day as usual--except for the maid
calling in sick and the strange sound and bright flash which
she became aware of while she was doing the laundry in the
basement. It isn't until afternoon when her daughters Barbara
and Ginny, aged 15 and 5 respectively, return home from
school, that Gladys discovers that atomic bombs have been
dropped on Washington and New York City. This book takes
place almost exclusively within this suburban home, the news
available only from radio and from men dressed in frightening impenetrable suits. Veda arrives at the house in the
hands of several men in these suits. And the next door
neighbor, Edith, appears, drunk and certain she's dying from
radiation sickness. Gladys's husband, Jon, was in New York

City when the bomb was dropped there, and by some miracle
manages to survive and find his way home at the end of the
book.
     The "action" of this book is primarily internal: how
does a homemaker/mother with no interests in life but the
care of her family react when she is suddenly placed in
charge alone, with no partner to protect her from harsh realities, to make decisions for her? With no resources but
her own inner strengths, which until now have never been
called into use, Gladys manages to survive the ordeal and
finds the strength to care for her injured husband as well.
     This book takes a stereotypically dependent, middle-
class wife/mother, puts her in an extreme crisis situation,
and allows a stronger person to emerge. In 1954, this novel
was made into a television play called "Atomic Attack" and
starred Walter Matthau, Phyllis Thaxter, and Robert Keith.
("Atomic Attack" was the last play aired on the short-lived
Motorola Television Hour.)

 ★   RUSSELL, ERIC FRANK. "Fast Falls the Eventide," in
          Astounding Science-Fiction, May 1952; in The Best
          of Eric Frank Russell. New York: Ballantine Books,
          1978.

     Main Character: Melisande.
     Physical Characteristics: Has "pale, long-fingered"
hands; can live "at a pinch" without oxygen; is seven hundred
years old and has "just finished her final examinations and
gained the status of an adult"; goes to Zelam to be a teacher.
     Mental/Emotional Characteristics: Is "superb in the
liquid" forms of communication; chooses a world to go to
through logic rather than through fear of loneliness; is diplomatic and determined.
     Story Particulars: In a far-future Earth time, when
the human species evolves to the point of living thousands of
years and the sun is nearing its death, Melisande graduates
from school at seven hundred years old and must make a
choice about which planet and what intelligent species to teach.
For many years Terrans had been sending their young as
teachers to the far reaches of the universe in an effort to
ensure the survival of the human species. Now Earth has
only one million people left on it and even those are gradually being sent out as teachers.
     Melisande, because of her excellent store of "general
knowledge" and her "superb" grasp of "liquid languages," has
a total of eleven worlds from which to choose. She decides

to move to Zelam, the only one that has, to that point, no
Terrans on it. Though her tutor tells her that they would
prefer the first Terran on Zelam be "masculine," Melisande
is firm and determined, asking "Why?" The tutor's answer
is "There is no reason at all except that we would prefer it."
Melisande cuts to the heart of the illogical response, telling
him that it would be "quite unworthy of us to insist upon
something without any reason." Nonetheless, her tutor prefers to see that no other recent graduates have chosen Zelam
before admitting defeat and permitting her to go there.

During her trip to Zelam, Melisande puts her time to
good use, and learns the language of the Zelamites. The
nocturnal inhabitants of Zelam, resembling "erect alligators"
in appearance, welcome Melisande to her new home and show
her the college in which she will teach. The chief cultural
supervisor on Zelam, Nathame, tells her that Terrans are
"supremely clever" in spreading themselves "over a hundred
million worlds," an act which has made the species "invin-
cible." He tells her that Terrans have been able to accomplish that goal by becoming teachers on less advanced worlds,
and thus providing those worlds with "self-esteem." By not
increasing their numbers on their host worlds, he continues,
they have eliminated in the inhabitants the fear of being over-
run with Terrans. He gives her as her teaching goal the
task of teaching the Zelamites how to survive as the Terrans
have, and Melisande sets to work.

The emphasis of this story seems to be on the evolved
nature of the human species at some future time, a positive
statement that Terrans will survive wars and go on to greater,
more peaceful pursuits. Melisande is representative of our
evolved species in that future time.

*   VANCE, JACK (John Holbrook Vance). Monsters in Orbit,
    in Thrilling Wonder Stories, Feb. 1952 and Aug. 1952
    (as the stories "Abercrombie Station" and "Cholwell's
    Chickens," respectively); in double with The World Be-
    tween and Other Stories. New York: Ace Books, 1965.

    Main Character: Jean Parlier.
    Physical Characteristics: Is a "pretty girl" with "sharp
white teeth," "ivory" skin, and black hair and eyes; is thin
and flat-chested compared to residents of Abercrombie; carries herself with "swash-buckling fervor"; has a "wide and
flexible" mouth; is 17 years old.
    Mental/Emotional Characteristics: Is intelligent and a
quick thinker; is fully in charge of herself; sees herself as

sophisticated and flexible; has killed people when necessary;
claims she has no morals; is aware of her attractiveness and
uses it with men; has "unnerving charm" and is "wary and
wild"; is "characterized by a precocious feral quality, a reck-
lessness that made ordinary women seem pastel and insipid";
has "élan"; considers men "silly jackasses"; secretly longs
to know her parents.

    Story Particulars: Jean Parlier, a 17-year-old who
is sophisticated and wise beyond her years, answers an ad
for a job which offers to pay her a million dollars. She can
earn this money, it seems, by marrying wealthy Earl Abercrombie, a mentally twisted heir who keeps monsters sus-
pended in deep freeze in a room on his orbiting space-
community station. Jean turns one million dollars into two
(and doesn't even have to marry Earl!) by informing his older
brother Lionel that their eldest brother Hugo is in one of
Earl's freezer cases. Jean turns her money over to Attorney
Richard Mycroft for investing and lives off the income from
the investments; however, money doesn't buy her all she wants
as she has thought it would.

    One thing Jean desperately wants is to know her par-
ents, although she was deserted by them as an infant. Jean
decides to seek out her history on the planet Codiron. (Until age 10, she was raised by a gambler named Joe Parlier,
who was "lascivious, wild and dangerous." Jean killed him
when she was ten and stowed away on a space ship. When
she was discovered, she was put in a "Waif's Home" on Bella's
Pride, from which she ran away just before the superintend-
ent was found dead. Five additional years are left unac-
counted for.)

    Jean, in seeking out her parents' whereabouts, dis-
covers seven more young women identical in appearance to
herself and being held captive. All are the result of the
multiple division of the initial fertilized egg by the resident
physician at the Codiron Women's Home, Cholwell, who got
the cells as a result of a liaison between the director of the
Home and a young social worker. Jean rescues the seven
women from his clutches and returns to Earth with them,
there discovering that kind Mr. Mycroft and his secretary
Ruth are the parents of all eight. Jean is rough, worldly-
wise, intelligent, independent and no one's fool.

* WYLIE, PHILIP. The Disappearance. New York: Rine-
     hart, 1951; rpt. New York: Warner Books, 1978.

     Main Character: Paula Gaunt.

Physical Characteristics: Was born with "copper pink" (red) hair (which, at the book's beginning, she pridefully dyes, a fact she hides from her husband); is 46 years old and graceful and supple. After the men disappear, she has gray hair, "smooth skin," "bright eyes," and a "vigorous body."

Mental/Emotional Characteristics: Has an aptitude for languages which she studied in college about which her husband was "pleased and proud, but perhaps slightly patronizing"; is "a woman of warmth, of engagingly varied moods, and of many capacities"; is "perceptive and sympathetic" and "good-tempered"; has "good nerves," a good mind, and "common sense"; learns of herself that she has a desire to lead, to run things, much as a man would have before the disappearance.

Secondary Character: Edwinna
Physical Characteristics: Is the daughter of Paula and Bill; has blond hair, dark eyes, and winged eyebrows; is 26 years old; has been divorced twice; has a young daughter; is tall; After the disappearance, her eyes develop a "hunter's squint." She had "an Indian's skin color; her once sleek hair was cropped short ... bleached ashen by the sun."

Mental/Emotional Characteristics: Is highly educated, has "energy, youth and intelligence," but is irresponsible, "stony, emotionless and often cruel," hard, selfish, and pleasure-seeking, contemptuous of "everything and everybody." When the men disappear, she first panics and wants to kill herself (probably because men have been supporting her all her life), and then takes control of herself. She becomes a provider for others, insightful and caring.

Story Particulars: On February 14, all the men disappear from the world of women and all the women disappear from the world of men. The book is fairly evenly divided between the stories of both, as seen through the eyes of Dr. Bill Gaunt and Paula Gaunt, husband and wife. Paula, a 46-year-old homemaker, whose main concern seems to have been maintaining the exact tint of red hair she'd had when Bill Gaunt married her, is suddenly thrust into a position of command, primarily because she is one of the few women who stays calm about the shocking event. She organizes Miami into committees to handle almost everything and is asked to act as translator when a ship full of Russian women come to New York with the threat of submission or war. Edwinna, Paula's daughter who acts at first like the 26-year-old spoiled brat she's been, gradually matures, and finally she takes on the responsibility of hunting game for the others.

Disaster follows disaster in the novel, beating down
the spirits of the women and the men alike.   The book is an
excellent study of human nature: man's lust for power and
control, and woman's struggle for self-sufficiency and equality.   The women discover they know how to run very little
in the world of machinery (except vacuum cleaners, can open-
ers, and automobiles) and struggle valiantly to continue against
impossible odds.   The men, after a brief atomic war, allow
their homes to decay into chaos and eventually break into
physical violence, looting and killing each other.   The women
come to blame the men for their separation, and Paula, who
always thought herself happy, or at least content as a homemaker, is surprised to find herself in agreement; if all men
weren't as astute, at least Bill Gaunt realizes (and as a phi-
losopher, expounds on) that he and all mankind had refused
humanity to the women, "So they ceased to exist."
At the end of four years (to the day), both sexes are
returned to the exact spot where they disappeared and cele-
brations abound the world over.   Various reasons are considered for the disappearance, but the most substantial given
was that people--men and women--had become, by their adop-
tion of unnatural social, sexual, and political roles, schizo-
phrenic.   The cure, of course, was to allow each person,
regardless of sex, full expression, full humanity, and to love
the individual as is without forcing the person into a role.
Also briefly touched on was the idiocy of "-isms"--material-
ism, communism, Americanism, etc.--and the destruction
such segregation brings with it.
This fascinating sf novel is must reading.   Displaying
a maturity beyond the social, sexual, and political philosophy
of its time, it cuts to the heart of the problems between
women and men, and, in this writer's opinion, surpasses in
depth the clarity of vision, almost all (if not all) of the writing on the subject before or since.   Paula Gaunt is truly a
heroic, and a very real human, character.

*   WYNDHAM, JOHN (John Wyndham Parkes Lucas Beynon
     Harris).   "Consider Her Ways," in Sometime, Never.
     London: Eyre & Spottiswoode, 1956; rpt. New York:
     Ballantine Books, 1956; in Neutron Stars.   Ed. Greg-
     ory Fitz Gerald.   Greenwich, CT: Fawcett Books,
     1977.

     Main Character: Called Mother Orchis, but really
originally Jane Summers, and now Jane Waterleigh.
     Physical Characteristics: At the story's beginning,

she has an arm like "a plump, white bolster with a ridiculous
little hand attached at the end"; her body is a "monstrous
form that billowed," "an elephantine female form, looking
the more huge for its pink swathings"; "the hands, though
soft and dimpled and looking utterly out of proportion, were
not uncomely"; is pretty, about 21 years old; "Her curling fair
hair was touched with auburn lights, and cut in a kind of bob";
her complexion "was pink and cream, her mouth was gentle,
and red without any artifice"; "has blue-green eyes beneath lightly
arched brows." Later in the story, she returns to her own
body which has an oval face with a "faintly sun-tanned" complexion, with a small, neat mouth; "chestnut hair that curled
naturally," "brown eyes rather wide apart"; her body was
"slender, long-legged, with small, firm breasts."

Mental/Emotional Characteristics: Throughout the
story, Jane tries to be objective as is normal for her profession as a Bachelor of Medicine; she observes the strange
events, tries to analyze and file them away for future reference; she finds herself capable of killing to save the male population and is called a "thought-child" of her time.

Story Particulars: Slender, attractive Jane Waterleigh
suddenly finds herself in a monstrous, unmanageable body
and called by the name of Mother Orchis. She is taken to
her "home," where five other "Mothers" are puzzled by her
wanting to read and write, and by her talk of "men." At
first, Jane is certain it is all a hallucination, but as time
passes, she realizes it is only too real. She painfully gains
the memory of her own time, recalling her "recently" deceased husband, her profession as a Bachelor of Medicine,
and the drug chuinjuatin, which is responsible for her visit
to the future. The drug for which she agreed to play human
guinea pig had sent her into an earth future without men.

Jane is horrified at this world and irate about her fat
body and her status as a Mother, one of the world's reproductive organisms and nothing more. When she continues to
insist that everything and everyone there is a hallucination,
they finally take her to see the historian in the area, Laura.
There Jane learns of a future world which stuns her. The
men died in Jane's time of a mutated virus developed by a
Dr. Perrigan. Now, in this future world, the women have
learned to create other female babies and have a social structure similar to that of ants. Laura considers the women of
Jane's time to be slaves, owned and ruled by their husbands.
In spite of all of Jane's refutations and explanations, Laura
is not to be swayed in her viewpoint. After all, Laura reasons, Jane cannot possibly be objective about her own time.
Jane begs for a shot of chuinjuatin, in the hope that it will

return her to her own time--which it does. She then tries
to change the present to prevent the future without men. The
ironic twist at the story's close gives the reader pause for
thought. Jane's careful documentation of her experiences reflects the habits of her profession as a Bachelor of Medicine.

ADDITIONAL READING LIST

Anderson, Poul. Virgin Planet, in Venture, Jan. 1957; ex-
    panded under same title, New York: Thomas Bouregy,
    1959; New York: Warner Paperback Library, 1970 and
    1973.

Brackett, Leigh. "The Woman from Altair," in Startling
    Stories, July 1951; in The Best of Leigh Brackett. Ed.
    Edmond Hamilton. New York: Ballantine Books, 1977.
    (Not the viewpoint character but a main character none-
    theless.)

Bradbury, Ray (Douglas). "The Veldt," in Saturday Evening
    Post, Sept. 1950; in Past, Present, & Future Perfect.
    Ed. Jack C. Wolf, and Gregory Fitz Gerald. Greenwich,
    CT: Fawcett, 1973; in Tomorrow, & Tomorrow, & Tomor-
    row. Ed. Bonnie L. Heintz, Frank Herbert, and Donald
    A. Joos. New York: Holt, Rinehart & Winston, 1974.

Brunner, John (Kilian Houston). "The Wanton of Argus," in
    Two Complete Science Fiction Adventure Books, Summer
    1953; retitled The Space-Time Juggler, in an Ace Double
    with The Astronauts Must Not Land. New York: Ace
    Books, 1963; under title "The Wanton of Argus," in Inter-
    stellar Empire. New York: Daw Books, 1976 and 1978.

deFord, Miriam Allen. "Throwback," in Startling Stories,
    Dec. 1952; in Future Tense. Ed. Kendall Foster Crossen.
    New York: Greenberg, 1952; in Xenogenesis. New York:
    Ballantine Books, 1969.

del Rey, Lester (Ramon Felipe Alvarez-del Rey). "Wind
    Between the Worlds," in Galaxy Science Fiction, March
    1951; in The Early Del Rey, Vol. 2. Garden City, NY:
    Doubleday, 1975, and New York: Ballantine Books, 1976.
    (Not the viewpoint character but a main character nonethe-
    less.)

Dick, Philip K(endred). "Human Is," in Startling Stories,

Winter 1955; in The Book of Philip K. Dick.   New York:
Daw Books, 1973; in The Best of Philip K. Dick.   Ed.
John Brunner.   New York: Ballantine Books, 1977.

Fearn, John Russell.   The Golden Amazon series.   See in
Appendix C: Amazon Women.

Heinlein, Robert A(nson).   The Puppet Masters.   New York:
Doubleday, 1951; rpt.   Boston: Gregg Press, 1979.

_____.   The Rolling Stones.   New York: Scribner's, 1952.

Henderson, Zenna.   "And a Little Child," in The Magazine
of Fantasy and Science Fiction, Oct. 1959; in The Anything
Box.   New York: Doubleday, 1965, and New York: Avon
Books, 1969.

_____.   "The Anything Box," in The Magazine of Fantasy
and Science Fiction, Oct. 1956; in The Anything Box.   New
York: Doubleday, 1965, and New York: Avon Books, 1969.

_____.   "Ararat," in The Magazine of Fantasy and Science
Fiction, Oct. 1952; in Pilgrimage.   New York: Doubleday,
1961, and New York: Avon Books, 1963.

_____.   "Captivity," in The Magazine of Fantasy and Sci-
ence Fiction, June 1958; in Pilgrimage.   New York:
Doubleday, 1961, and New York: Avon Books, 1963.

_____.   "Loo Ree," in The Magazine of Fantasy and Sci-
ence Fiction, Feb. 1953; in Holding Wonder.   New York:
Doubleday, 1971, and New York: Avon Books, 1972.

_____.   "Wilderness," in The Magazine of Fantasy and
Science Fiction, Jan. 1957; in Pilgrimage.   New York:
Doubleday, 1961, and New York: Avon Books, 1963.

Holly, J. Hunter (Joan Carol Holly).   Encounter.   New York:
Thomas Bouregy, 1959.

Knight, Damon.   "Dio," in Infinity, Sept. 1957; in The Arbor
House Treasury of Great Science Fiction Short Novels.
New York: Arbor House, 1980.

_____.   "Not with a Bang," serialized in The Magazine
of Fantasy and Science Fiction, Winter and Spring 1950;
in The Eureka Years.   Ed. Annette Peltz McComas.   New
York: Bantam Books, 1982.

_____. "Stranger Station," in The Magazine of Fantasy
and Science Fiction, Dec. 1956; in The Year's Greatest
Science-Fiction and Fantasy, Second Annual Volume. Ed.
Judith Merril. New York: Dell, 1957; in Modern Science
Fiction. Ed. Norman Spinrad. Garden City, NY: Anchor
Press/Doubleday, 1974, and Boston: Gregg Press, Inc.,
1976.

Leiber, Fritz (Reuter). "Little Old Miss Macbeth," in The
Magazine of Fantasy and Science Fiction, Dec. 1958; in
The Best of Fritz Leiber. New York: Ballantine Books,
1974 and 1979.

Merril, Judith. "Dead Center," in The Magazine of Fantasy
and Science Fiction, Nov. 1954; in The Best of Judith Merril. New York: Warner Books, 1976.

_____. "Homecalling," in Science Fiction Stories, Nov.
1956; in Daughters of Earth. Garden City, NY: Doubleday, 1968, and New York: Dell, 1970.

Merwin, (W.) Sam(uel), Jr. The House of Many Worlds.
Garden City, NY: Doubleday, 1951.

Miller, Walter M(ichael), Jr. "Command Performance," in
Galaxy Science Fiction, Nov. 1952; retitled "Anybody Else
Like Me," in The Best of Walter M. Miller, Jr. New York
York: Pocket Books, 1980.

_____. "I, Dreamer," in Amazing Stories, June./July
1953; in The Best of Walter M. Miller, Jr. New York:
Pocket Books, 1980. (Not the viewpoint character but a
main character nonetheless.)

_____. "The Triflin' Man," in Fantastic Universe, Jan.
1955; retitled "You Triflin' Skunk," in The Best of Walter
M. Miller, Jr. New York: Pocket Books, 1980.

_____. "Vengeance for Nikolai," in Venture Science Fic-
tion, March 1957; in The Best of Walter M. Miller, Jr.
New York: Pocket Books, 1980.

Neville, Kris (Ottman). "Bettyann," in New Tales of Space
and Time. Ed. Raymond Healy. New York: Holt, 1951;
novelized as Bettyann. New York: Tower, 1970; story
version in Science Fiction of the Fifties. Ed. Martin
Harry Greenberg and Joseph Olander. New York: Avon
Books, 1979.

Nourse, Alan E(dward). "The Canvas Bag," in The Magazine
of Fantasy and Science Fiction, April 1955; in The Counterfeit Man and Others. New York: David McKay, 1963;
rpt. The Counterfeit Man and Other Science Fiction Stories. New York: Scholastic Book Services, 1975.

Pohl, Frederik. "The Midas Plague," in Galaxy Magazine,
April 1954; in The Best of Frederik Pohl. New York:
Ballantine Books, 1975, and New York: Taplinger, 1977.

_____. "The Snowmen," in Galaxy Magazine, Dec. 1959;
in The Best of Frederik Pohl. New York: Ballantine
Books, 1975, and New York: Taplinger, 1977.

St. Clair, Margaret. "Brightness Falls from the Air," in
The Magazine of Fantasy and Science Fiction, April 1951;
in Special Wonder: The Anthony Boucher Memorial An-
thology of Fantasy & Science Fiction. Ed. J. Francis
McComas. New York: Random House, 1970; in Special
Wonder, Vol. 2. Ed. J. Francis McComas. New York:
Beagle Books, 1971.

_____(under Idris Seabright). "The Wines of Earth," in
The Magazine of Fantasy and Science Fiction, Sept. 1957;
in The Best from Fantasy and Science Fiction, Seventh
Series. Ed. Anthony Boucher. New York: Doubleday,
1956; in Change the Sky and Other Stories. New York:
Ace Books, 1974.

Schmitz, James H(enry). "The Second Night of Summer,"
in Galaxy Science Fiction, Dec. 1950; in Agent of Vega.
Hicksville, NY: Gnome Press, 1960; rpt. New York:
Pocket Books, 1962, and New York: Grosset & Dunlap,
1972.

_____. "Space Fear," in Astounding Science-Fiction,
March 1951; retitled "The Illusionists," in Agent of Vega.
Hicksville, NY: Gnome Press, 1960; rpt. New York:
Pocket Books, 1962, and New York: Grosset & Dunlap,
1972.

_____. "The Truth About Cushgar," in Astounding Science-
Fiction, Nov. 1950; in Agent of Vega. Hicksville, NY:
Gnome Press, 1960; rpt. New York: Pocket Books, 1962,
and New York: Grosset & Dunlap, 1972.

Smith, Edward E(lmer). The Galaxy Primes, serialized in

Amazing Stories, March 1959; in novel form, New York: Ace Books, 1965 and 1976.

Smith, Evelyn E. "The Last of the Spode," in The Magazine of Fantasy and Science Fiction, June 1953; in The Eureka Years. Ed. Annette Peltz McComas. New York: Bantam Books, 1982.

Sturgeon, Theodore (Edward Hamilton Waldo). "The Other Man," in Galaxy Science Fiction, Sept. 1956; in The Worlds of Theodore Sturgeon. New York: Ace Books, 1972 and 1977.

_____. "Saucer of Loneliness," in Galaxy Science Fiction, Feb. 1953; in Science Fiction of the Fifties. Ed. Martin Harry Greenberg and Joseph Olander. New York: Avon Books, 1979.

Wyndham, John (John Wyndham Parkes Lucas Beynon Harris). "Heaven Scent," in Tales of Gooseflesh and Laughter. New York: Ballantine Books, 1956.

_____. "Perforce to Dream," in Beyond Fantasy Fiction, Jan. 1954; in Jizzle. London: D. Dobson, 1954; in Beyond the Barriers of Space and Time. Ed. Judith Merril. New York: Random House, 1954.

_____. "Wild Flower," in Fantastic Universe, Nov. 1955; in Tales of Gooseflesh and Laughter. New York: Ballantine Books, 1956.

CHAPTER 5: THE 1960s

A period called the Age of Rebellion by Lester del Rey (The World of Science Fiction: 1926-1976, New York: Garland, 1980), the 1960s saw the advent of the "New Wave" writers in sf. Listing, among others, John Brunner, Samuel Delany, Michael Moorcock, and Joanna Russ as New Wave writers, Neil Barron in Anatomy of Wonder says, "They explored with often painfully ruthless objectivity topics once taboo in most SF, such as sex, radical politics, and religion. Simultaneously, they attacked SF's sacred cows: the conquest of space, human progress through technology, the success of the male-dominated capitalistic state." With the New Wave writers also came a new wave of speculation about women (rather than men) in positions of power and control. Increasingly, women began to read sf. Isaac Asimov writes in "The Feminization of Sci-Fi" (Vogue, October 1982) that television's Star Trek, first aired in 1965, was directly responsible for popularizing sf with women. "The result is that from 1965 on, we have seen the gradual feminization of the audience for printed science fiction. The readers of the science-fiction magazines and novels are women to an extent of 25 percent at the very least. I suspect that the percentage is now nearer the 40 percent mark." One of the "enormous changes" Asimov sees as a result of this change in reading audience is that "to satisfy reader demand, the stories have to contain women as people" (Asimov's emphasis).

Whether it was the New Wave writers, Star Trek, a change in composition of the sf magazine audience, or some other equally plausible reason, sf changed during this time period. Researchers generally agree that the 1960s saw a marked increase in the number of sf works with women, not as secondary characters, appendages to the hero (to paraphrase Sam Lundwall in Science Fiction: What It's All About, New York: Ace Books, 1971), but as main characters in their

own right.   This resulted in fewer two-dimensional and a
greater number of three-dimensional women characters.   The
female hero was born.

With the inclusion of the female hero also came a new
openness about sexuality.   Suddenly there were both male and
female heterosexual, homosexual, or bisexual main characters.   Sf became a genre suitable for the exploration of sexuality, sensuality, and androgyny.   (Ursula K. Le Guin's
award-winning novel The Left Hand of Darkness, published
in 1969, seemed to epitomize the acceptability of the exploration of alternatives to a set gender and to a set of characteristics to match.)

Men were finally portrayed not only as strong but as
capable of fear, weakness, and insecurity.   Women were allowed not only to be emotional, but to be strong and flexible,
to know their own minds, to control their own destinies.
Both women and men were finally being portrayed as whole
human beings.

*   ANDERSON, POUL.   "Kyrie," in The Farthest Reaches.
        New York: Trident, 1968; in The Best of Poul Ander-
        son.   New York: Pocket Books, 1976; rpt. New York:
        Pocket Books, 1979.

        Main Character: Eloise Waggoner.
        Physical Characteristics: Is "scrawny, big-booted, big-
    nosed," and has "pop eyes and stringy dust-colored hair";
    was a librarian who had "a wild talent" (telepathy) and is
    now special communications technician on board the Raven;
    has a harsh voice; is "barely out of her teens"; seems ugly
    to the captain.
        Mental/Emotional Characteristics: Is a telepath and
    communicates with and loves a "living vortex," an Aurigean;
    to the Aurigean, she is "the coolness of water, the patience
    of earth"; is a Christian; is "gauche and inhibited."
        Story Particulars: Eloise Waggoner, a telepathic hu-
    man who is ugly by human standards, loves and is loved by
    Lucifer, an Aurigean which is a "living vortex ... a fireball
    twenty meters across, shimmering white, red, gold, royal
    blue, flames dancing like Medusa locks, cometary tail burn-
    ing for a hundred meters behind, a shiningness, a glory, a
    piece of hell."   Eloise, as special communications technician
    on the Raven, communicates to Lucifer for the ship and
    spends hours playing him music.   The mutual love is romantic
    in nature, Lucifer calling her "moonlight on an ocean."

Eloise, who thinks she will soon be returning to the "four walls of an apartment above a banging city street," never to communicate with Lucifer again, struggles to prevent feeling sorry for herself. Lucifer explains to her that if she wishes it, he will be with her always because, he says, there is no distance limit in telepathic communication. Eloise is overjoyed at the news.

When the ship makes the "jump" of twenty-five light-years, they come relatively near to a supernova, emerging into "a lethal radiation zone." The radiation doesn't affect Lucifer, but the humans scramble to get their screen generator started to protect themselves and send Lucifer out to look at a dangerous "radiation source on an intercept orbit" with the ship. He finds the "million-kilometer ball of ionized gas" the captain sends him to look over and spends exhausting hours wrestling it out of their path. He succeeds, but is "merged" with the gas cloud and tumbling towards the supernova. He assures Eloise that he can spiral out and return to her; but the supernova is unlike anything in his experience and he fails, falling to his death. Eloise knows from the captain that Lucifer is dead, but to her, he is alive, his thoughts continuing to come to her due to the "time dilation" caused by the supernova. Eloise will telepathically receive his thoughts as he falls to his death for "an infinite number of years."

In retrospect, it is apparent that the nun at the story's beginning who is always "praying for her own dead" is Eloise. She turns out to be emotionally stronger than the captain anticipated, dealing with the experience of lifelong death of a loved one by devoting herself to the care of "the sick, the needy, the crippled, the insane," rather than having a breakdown herself.

* BOYD, JOHN (Boyd Bradfield Upchurch). The Pollinators of Eden. New York: Weybright and Talley, 1969; rpt. New York: Penguin Books, 1978.

Main Character: Dr. Freda Janet Caron.
Physical Characteristics: Is "Caucasian, aged 24," and is descended on her mother's side from a Mexican prostitute; is a cystologist; is a "blond and ovately willowy" administrative director in the Bureau of Exotic Plants; is large breasted and a virgin.
Mental/Emotional Characteristics: At the beginning of the book, she is coldly in control of her emotions, has a revulsion to human contact which subsides after four drinks,

and "a strong libido," which is under strict control; she feels
she is "condemned forever to psychic virginity," a "potent
combination of beauty and brains," but "frigid." After contact with the plants of Flora, she discovers she is really hu-
manistic ("antiorganization; proindividual, anticivilization;
pronature, nonaltruistic; hedonistic") and sensuous.

Story Particulars: In the earth year 2237, Dr. Freda
Caron, Administrative Director of the Cystological Section of
the Bureau of Exotic Plants in the Department of Agriculture,
expects her fiancé, Paul Theaston, to be aboard the ship returning from the newly discovered planet Flora, the Planet
of the Flowers. However, although he isn't aboard, he has
sent Hal Polino, an assistant, with two tulips from Flora
named after her, a letter with seeds in it, and a verbal message to be delivered in private. Freda disapproves of even
being seen with Hal as it is against strict bureau policy regarding underlings. But Hal is discreet and takes her to a
quiet eating place where no one from the bureau will see
them. What he tells her over dinner convinces her that her
stable, "empirical scientist" is approaching insanity on Flora.
Yet Paul has chosen to stay for an extension period to conduct more research on the manner in which the orchids on
the planet pollinate. Freda sets to work to discover how the
tulips pollinate, thinking that will be a help, and Hal is assigned to her, against her wishes, to assist in the hand pol-
lination of the tulips.

Meanwhile, the Navy is trying to block any human
habitation of Flora, and Freda is chosen to be among a few
who go to Washington to try to turn the tide for an earth
colony there. Unfortunately, unbeknownst to Freda, she has
also been chosen by her boss as a sacrifice pawn to take the
blame if they fail. On the trip, frigid Freda is seduced after
four drinks by Dr. Hans Clayborg, "a dynamic little man
with a brain so charged with wit and ideas that his hair stuck
out at right angles from the static electricity his brain gen-
erated." She spends the rest of her time in Washington re-
searching frigidity in women and concludes that it's hopeless
for her. Naturally, Freda is blamed when the Senate Committee announces that Flora is closed as an earth colony, but
is still open for scientific exploration, and she returns to her
research with Hal.

It is at this point that the flowers, who, as thinking
beings, consider Freda their mother, begin to awaken Freda's
sensuality, and she, still the scientist, is aware of the change,
and charts the crests of this phenomenon. Her attraction to
Hal is almost at its peak when he is killed by the tulips for
directing painful sound waves in their direction. Freda re-

alizes she must move fast and tries to have the tulips plowed
under (which results in the death of the tractor driver) and
then sprayed by a plane (resulting in the death of the pilot).
She finally manages to get a remote-controlled bulldozer and
has them buried. She also finds a way to blackmail her boss
into letting her go to Flora and arrives overjoyed to see Paul.
His long hug and her lack of revulsion convinces her that her
aversion to being touched is now gone, and he admits he's
been afraid to hug her because her "veneer" might crack and
cut him. Thus frigid Freda takes that final step that trans-
forms her into the "Earth Mother" by allowing both male and
female orchids to make love to her, making her a pollinator.
The orchids give her her very first orgasm.

　　　　The remainder of the book consists of her capture by
the Navy, placement in an earth-based mental hospital, and
the conversion of all people she comes in contact with to "humanism." What is odd is that her previous cold, insightful,
analytic mind is trained lovingly on the understanding of the
human minds and emotions of the doctors trying to cure her.
The result is that she cures each one who comes in contact
with her, and part of that cure is usually sex. She is pro-
claimed "Earth Mother" by her last doctor when she gives
birth to a bouncing baby seed pod. The reader may get the
feeling that Freda has planted a few seeds of her own by con-
verting her doctors to "humanism." Freda is preoccupied
for a large portion of the book with sex and the cure for her
frigidity.

*　　BROWN, ROSEL GEORGE. Sibyl Sue Blue. New York:
　　　　Doubleday, 1966; retitled Galactic Sibyl Sue Blue. New
　　　　York: Berkley Medallion Books, 1968.

　　　　Main Character: Sibyl Sue Blue.
　　　　Physical Characteristics: Has bright green eyes; has
"little bitty," tiny wrinkles around eyes and mouth and natural
black-and-gray striped hair which is naturally curly; is nearly
40 years old and smokes cigars; has a good figure; is a great
fighter even with someone twice her size; has rouged knees;
is the mother of a 16-year-old daughter named Missy (who is
a beautiful, long brunette); uses perfume; uses many disguises.
　　　　Mental/Emotional Characteristics: Is committed to
her work as a sergeant in the police force; is intelligent; is
a good detective and is "clever and dependable"; hasn't allowed
herself to be tied down during the last ten years since the expedition of her husband, Kenneth, was lost; still loves and
misses Kenneth; knows "the depths of death, desire and fear";

sometimes dislikes herself for what her job does to other
people's lives; loves freely and is very sexually attracted
to strong, intelligent, animal-type men; is quite able to fall
in and out of love and does; is occasionally afraid, admits
it, and overcomes it.

Story Particulars: Murders of young teen females are
occurring, strange murders in which the victims die because
they lack a liver. Sibyl, as a sergeant in the police force,
suspects that Centaurians and Stuart Grant, a young million-
aire, are somehow connected with these benzale (a drug that
is smoked) murders. After fending off several attacks from
Centaurians, Sibyl tries one of these cigarettes, too, and
barely escapes the experience with her life. During her experience she receives a message from her supposedly-dead
husband, who never returned from Radix, the same planet
that the benzale drug comes from! Because of this, she decides she must go there, seeks out Stuart Grant who is going,
convinces him to let her go, then falls madly and irrationally
in love with him. During the trip, Sibyl recovers from this
infatuation, becoming rational about him once more, and
spends the remainder of the book trying to unravel the mys-
teries of the murders, of the life form on Radix, and of her
missing husband. Sibyl has no inhibitions about sex with human males or Centaurian males, but states that she will
never marry again. She briefly tells her daughter the "secret of life" before her space trip with Stuart: "The Secret
of life is for you to enjoy being you. If you can do that,
everything else happens by itself."

There is another book about this hard-kicking/hitting,
cigar-smoking female hero called The Waters of Centaurus
(Doubleday, 1970).

*   BRUNNER, JOHN. A Planet of Your Own, in double with
    The Beasts of Kohl. New York: Ace Books, 1966;
    edited version "The Long Way to Earth," in If, March
    1966.

Main Character: Kynance Foy.
Physical Characteristics: Is "five and a half feet tall"
and "exotically gorgeous, having inherited dark eyes and sin-
uous grace from a Dutch ancestor who had fallen from grace
in Java in the company of a temple dancer"; has "hair of a
curious iron-gray shade ... against which her tanned skin
burned like new copper"; is 25 years old.

Mental/Emotional Characteristics: Majored in "qua-
space physics" and minored in "interstellar commerce," but
also is "well grounded in the unfeminine combination of business

law and practical engineering"; had great confidence that either
her education or her looks would win her employment in space
and is scared when she realizes that neither helped; is intelligent and enjoys knowing more than the men who expect her
to know little; is called "an extraordinary person" by Horst.

    Story Particulars: Kynance Foy--attractive, intelli-
gent, and well-educated--decides to seek her fortune in space
and is determined to return to Earth sporting one of the ex-
orbitantly expensive Zygra pelts. What she doesn't expect is
that there is no demand in space for her skills in "qua-space
physics," "interstellar commerce," and "business law and
practical engineering." At the end of her rope financially
and at the end of her journey when she reaches Nefertiti,
Kynance jumps at the chance to work for Zygra Company and
is shocked to learn that she has been accepted as the next
supervisor of the harvesting machines on Zygra, the planet
on which the Zygra pelts, really moss-like parasites, grow.
Certain that there are snags in the job, but assured by Zygra
Company employee Shuster that there are none, Kynance settles in her new job on Zygra where she is to be the sole in-
habitant for her one year stay.

    Her legal training has made Kynance wary and she
has already begun to alter the equipment to protect herself
from violating her contract when she is shocked to see four
naked men on a makeshift raft making their way towards the
main station. As even waving to other people would be considered a breach of contract, Kynance reenters the station
without acknowledging their existence and rapidly disconnects
the autochef, the domestic services, and the medicare unit
from the main computer so that she can have access to them
when the men arrive. All the men, as it turns out, are
former supervisors just like Kynance, and all were tricked
into violating their contracts in some minor way and were
turned out into the swamp to live or die as they might. Kynance, using her abundant legal knowledge, finds a way to
force Zygra Company to relinquish its control of the planet
to her and the four men, and when the ship returns for pelt
harvest, she declares the planet legally the property of the
five inhabitants, and expels Shuster from their planet.

    One of the four men, Horst Lampeter, is fascinated
by Kynance, telling her she's "an extraordinary person."
He also thinks to himself, when he first sees her, that she
is "still a girl" in spite of her twenty-five years. At the
successful conclusion of their confrontation with Shuster,
Horst tells Kynance, "You seem like a machine, a computer
full of miracles," and seems pleased that it appears she will
now "stop behaving like a machine and start acting like a
woman."

In spite of Horst's viewpoint and comments and Kynance's inane statement about her dynamic insight and handling of the problem ("Well, I've hated it. And thank you for
reminding me before it was too late and I got into the habit
for life!"), the overall impression that Kynance makes is that
she is an intelligent, compassionate, adventure-seeking person with more than her share of ingenuity, enterprise, and
initiative.

* COOPER, EDMUND. The Last Continent. New York:
    Dell, 1969; rpt. London: Hodder & Stoughton, 1970.

   Main Character: Dr. Mirlena Stroza (shared with
Kymri op Kymriso).
   Physical Characteristics: Has "black skin" and "black
hair" and is "large-breasted"; is said to have "erotic splen-
dor" and to have a high capacity for alcohol; is a psychologist
from Mars; is "strangely beautiful" and has "thick lips,"
"broad nostrils" and "prominent cheekbones"; has "short,
stiff" hair that "curled magically like black moss over her
head" which has turned white at the story's end.
   Mental/Emotional Characteristics: Is an "interplanetary explorer" and a "woman of considerable intellectual power,"
but is afraid of the stars and of unfamiliar wild animals; is
"a very complicated woman"; is amused by her reactions at
times; is capable of learning to speak a language quickly; according to Kord Vengel, she is a "woman who presumed to
be more than a woman but lacked the necessary force and
ruthlessness to compete in a world of men"; initially is
afraid to expose her body to a white man; has an "immense
curiosity" and a hunger for "knowledge."
   Story Particulars: In a future Earth time, black humans war against white humans for "the freedom of space,"
a war which results in the destruction of the moon and near-
destruction to Earth. The black people who went into space
survived to take over Mars, leaving the rest of the Earth for
dead. There were a few survivors on Earth, however, in
the International Antarctic Research Station. The station was
built to be self-supporting for a team of scientists, including
hydroponic gardens.
   This small group of Earth people, initially mostly
white and finally all white, survive for 2000 years until the
black Martians return to Earth to search for minerals. In
this Martian exploration party is ship psychologist Dr. Mirlena Stroza, who is fortunate enough to be the first Martian
to set foot on Earth and who is stunned by the sight of a white

human who tries to kill her on sight. Her quick reflexes
prevent her death, and she and the landing party take the
"white savage" to their orbiting spacecraft where Mirlena
learns his language, which is similar to early Martian language, and discovers that he is "mature, intelligent, and re-
sourceful." Mirlena thinks these people should be studied
and states her case to the ship's captain, who allows four
people (including Mirlena) to form a survey party to study
the "level of development" of the white people. They allow
the white man, Kymri op Kymriso, to lead them to his city,
the only city left, called Noi Lantis. On the trip, made on
foot through the jungle from the spot where they first found
Kymri, a sexual relationship begins between Mirlena and Kymri, which is initially cause for shame to them both.

The arrival of the black Martians in Noi Lantis creates conflict among its white citizens. They consider killing
the blacks to warn off any who might follow, but the city's
leader, Kymri's father, Urlanrey, wisely takes no hostile
action. The Martian party has one hostile, prejudiced member, Kord Vengel, who insists on sneaking off into the forbidden Abode of the Dead, which in actuality is the entrance
to the International Antarctic Research Station. There he is
crushed by the fall of a robot he shoots. Kymri and Mirlena
search for him there and are followed by Urlanrey, who must
punish Mirlena for entering the forbidden area.

Meanwhile, back on Mars, President Timon Harland
kills Kastril, the leader of the group who still hates whites,
the Vaneys, because of the secret police state under which
Kastril kept Mars. This change in politics along with the
death of Vengel makes possible the positive interaction between blacks and whites, making the story's conclusion a happy
one.

Mirlena is a prime force in the story. It is due to
her leadership and understanding that Urlanrey comes to accept the black people as friends. When the "sloop," capable
of picking up the survey party, crashes, thus stranding the
remaining three on Earth, Mirlena initiates an exchange of
information and they teach the white people about "atomic
theory," radio-telescopes, and "electrics." Mirlena, as a
psychologist, gives lectures and demonstrations and has a
clinic. (Mirlena mentions at one point the woman "American
Negro psychiatrist called Sigma Freud," whose works are the
basis for the society in which the whites live.) Mirlena marries Kymri and, at the story's conclusion, is pregnant with
"the first child of two worlds."

* DeFORD, MIRIAM ALLEN. "The Crib Circuit," in The Magazine of Fantasy and Science Fiction, Nov. 1969; in Elsewhere, Elsewhen, Elsehow. New York: Walker, 1971.

Main Character: Alexandra Burton.
Physical Characteristics: Is about 26 years old; was a "skilled computer operator" and programmer in the twentieth century, and also claims to have been "an undercover agent" for extraterrestrials.
Mental/Emotional Characteristics: Claims to have had "strong Psi powers" in the twentieth century, which were probably destroyed by her freezing and storage in "cryolosis"; is intelligent and well educated for her time; is shrewd in her efforts to save her own life; is emotionally strong in the face of her own death.
Story Particulars: Alexandra Burton, with inoperable throat cancer in the twentieth century, had spent her last penny on being frozen and for the maintenance costs of cryolosis. When she awakens, it is the year A.D. 2498, and she is in a place where everyone goes nude and speaks "Mercan." She is relieved to find out her throat cancer is cured and struggles to understand the words of the doctor and nurse. They send for a "twenny centry [sic] specialist" from the IBIS ("International Bureau Investigate Speech"). The expert is about her own subjective age of 26 and calls himself Dr. Loren Watts. He speaks twentieth-century English quite well, if somewhat stiffly.
It is from Loren that Alexandra has her first indication that she has not been revived and cured to begin a normal life once more. When she is taken before the CRIB (Cryolosis Revival Investigation Board) she learns that she will be terminated after she has been examined by all the interested subsidiaries of CRIB. They have, it seems, what they call "op pop" or "optimum population" and Alexandra just doesn't fit into their plans. She is understandably shocked, and one CRIB member objects to so cruelly telling the revived people of their fate. Nonetheless, the law is the law and Alexandra lies awake that night, searching her mind desperately for a plan. Escape is unrealistic because she can't speak the language and has no way to support herself. Suicide is out because she is looking for a way to live, not a way to die. Getting Dr. Watts to fall in love with her isn't possible because his interest in her is strictly professional. Finally a plan occurs to her, a plan she decides to implement as soon as the HIP (Historical Investigation Project), the next CRIB subsidiary, takes her for investigation.

When Alexandra meets Dr. Ann Mayhew of the HIP,
Alexandra launches her plan and tells her that she was not
only a computer programmer, but an undercover agent for
extraterrestrials as well, recruited because of her high Psi
powers. She tells Dr. Mayhew that she's been sent into the
future to warn her species that they will be destroyed if they
don't mend their ways. The extraterrestrials didn't stay the
first time, Alexandra tells her, because it was already too
late to reeducate them to prevent the "catastrophe" that occurred after the twentieth century, a catastrophe which took
humans a century from which to recover. So instead, the
extraterrestrials sent her into the future with a message.
Alexandra adds the final touch to her story: her memory of
their message in her mind will be blocked until she is accepted as "a full citizen" in that society. Naturally, Dr.
Mayhew doesn't believe her, another CRIB meeting is called,
and in spite of the fact that she holds to her story, no one
else believes her either. In one month, she knows she will
face death. The odd twist at the story's end makes Alexandra realize she is anything but a liar.

* DELANY, SAMUEL R(AY). Babel-17. New York: Ace
    Books, 1966; rpt. Boston: Gregg Press, 1976; rpt.
    New York: Bantam Books, 1982.

Main Character: Rydra Wong.
Physical Characteristics: Has copper eyes that "slant
like astounded wings," and an Oriental face; is 26 years old;
has "hair like fast water at night"; has perfect pitch.
Mental/Emotional Characteristics: Is a poet with total
verbal recall; is a cryptographer/linguist; calls herself "neu-
rotic as hell"; is called "this age's voice"; takes command
unobtrusively; writes poetry by reading minds, and is disturbed that her ideas are not her own; is uninhibited; is sensitive to others due to psychic ability; reads body and muscle
language; is unafraid of love and affection; experiences psychic
communication transcending language barriers.
Story Particulars: Rydra is called in by the military
to decipher an Invasion-related language named Babel-17.
After partially deciphering the language, she gathers a crew
and flies to the place she has learned will be the site of the
next attack. Rydra, her ship sabotaged to take off without a
pilot, is saved from annihilation by an enormous ship called
Jebel Tarik ("Tarik's Mountain"). While on board, she and
her crew are plunged deep into the fighting. There she meets
Butcher, who appears to be a branded convict from the penal

caves of Titin, and delves even more deeply into the mystery
of Babel-17 as she gets to know him. Together, Rydra and
Butcher discover the truth behind Babel-17--that "it 'pro-
grams' a self-contained schizoid personality into the mind of
whoever learns it, reinforced by self-hypnosis." Her solution
to the language and invasion concludes the story. (This novel
was nominated for a Hugo Award in 1967 and tied for a first-
place slot for a 1967 Nebula Award.)

★ GOTLIEB, PHYLLIS. Sunburst, in Amazing Stories,
       March-May 1964; exp. version, New York: Berkley,
       1964; rpt. New York: Berkley, 1978; rpt. Boston:
       Gregg Press, 1978. (Expanded version used here.)

     Main Character: Shandy (Sandra) Ruth Johnson.
     Physical Characteristics: Is "a very tall cranelike
girl, rather sallow, with narrow torso"; has "a high forehead
and pointed chin" which "gave her face the look of a brown
egg poised on the small end, and her long crinkly black hair
was tied in a ponytail with a shoelace"; is thirteen years old
(born June 3, 2011) and 5'7" tall; runs like an ostrich in a
loping trot.
     Mental/Emotional Characteristics: Is bright and an
Impervious (no one can read her mind); is "solitary, incon-
spicuous," and unemotional (always got all of her emotions
from books) until she goes to the Dump (the place where all
the psi children are kept under control); is capable of taking
care of herself; was orphaned at an early age; wants "ultimate discovery," and "permanence"; longs for security; wants
to be useful; is always observing and gaining insight; is a
voracious reader (she admires Margaret Mead) and steals
books from the library in order not to be on any official record anywhere.
     Story Particulars: An explosion of a reactor at a nu-
clear power plant in a small mid-western town is, in itself,
a serious matter, but the resulting birth of a number of children with psi ability is, if possible, even more serious. It
seems that most of the psi children are psychopathic and are
kept behind a wave-scrambling device called the Marczinek
Field at a place called the "Dump" just outside of town. Although Shandy has always felt herself to be special in some
indefinable way, she is glad she isn't a psi. She contentedly
lives with Ma Slippec, a bootlegger, and makes deliveries
for her.
     One day Shandy is chased and caught by Jason Hem-
mer, the 18-year-old "Dumper's peeper" (the psi who locates

other psi children for placement in the Dump).   He, much
to his surprise, cannot read her mind, which means she is
an Impervious, or someone whom no one can read.   She is
taken to the Dump, talked to, tested, and kept for possible
future usefulness in dealing with the psi children.   Being the
bright, inquisitive individual she is, Shandy asks for and is
given the files on all the children kept at the Dump.   After
she reads the files, a pattern gradually begins to form in her
mind, and a theory emerges--almost all of the psi children
are of a delinquent nature, so the mutation caused by the
radiation is not a good one for humanity.   She thinks a more
gradual evolution into the psi realm would be healthier for
the human race.

Shandy and Jason develop a special rapport, possibly
because he can't read her mind, and she is always a little
of a mystery to him.   Shandy grows very comfortable and
secure at the Dump, and her opportunity to be useful occurs
much sooner than anyone expected.   The Dumplings (psi children) escape and are on a destructive rampage.   Only Jason
and Shandy, with the help of a deformed Dump child called
Doydoy, are in a position to save the world from their destruction.   In this novel, Shandy matures, develops her first
emotions, learns what it's like not to be lonely, and projects
a future for herself which is still totally uncertain--uncertain
because it is she who carries the mutant psi gene which can
safely be passed on.

*   HEINLEIN, ROBERT A.   Podkayne of Mars, in If, in
       three issues beginning in Nov. 1962; New York: Put-
       nam's, 1963; rpt. New York: Berkley Medallion Books,
       1975.

Main Character: Podkayne (Poddy) Fries.
Physical Characteristics: Is 157 centimeters tall and
has blue eyes ("Five feet two and eyes of blue," as her father says); weighs 49 kilograms; is 8 in Mars years (15 in
earth years); has long legs, a 48-centimeter waist, and a
90-centimeter chest; has enough Swedish ancestry to have
pale wavy blond hair; is pretty.
Mental/Emotional Characteristics: Has an IQ of 145;
has ambitions to be a pilot and a commander; exaggerates to
such a degree that humor is the result; possesses aplomb
(according to a suitor); has no patience and is predictable
(according to her brother); is lovingly called a "savage" by
her uncle; cracks under the threat of being caged with a Ve-
nerian native.

Story Particulars: Podkayne (named after a Martian
saint), at 15 earth years of age, is a Marsman who wants
to see Venus and Earth.   (Martians are native to Mars; Mars-
men are transplanted earth people.)   Unfortunately, due to an
accident in the "deep-freeze" holding Poddy's infant sisters
and brother, Mrs. Fries, a Master Engineer skilled in "karate and kill-quick" who travels quite a bit in the performance of her job, finds herself the instant mother of the three
babies she was planning to save until later in her life to
raise.   Mrs. Fries' "primitive instincts" take over and her
behavior with the infants is compared to that of a mother cat
that feels uneasy whenever a human touches her kittens.   Nat-
urally the trip to|Earth is out of the question.

Uncle Tom (who is black), however, saves the day.
Wielding his influence as a Senator, he gets Poddy and 11-
earth-year-old Clark passage on the trip.   Clark, as it turns
out, is smarter than Poddy and lies to her.   He also gambles
and ends up killing.   He, all in all, is a horrible younger
brother for a young woman with ambition.   Poddy's greatest
passion in life is to grow up and be first a pilot and then "a
commander of deep-space exploration parties"; unfortunately,
in Heinlein's future world, women are still as excluded from
so-called male professions as they were in 1963 when this
book was written.   So Poddy's chances of success are rather
slender at best.   But she's had a lot of math and gets herself admitted to the control room of the spaceship, using her
"puzzled kitten" expression, as she calls it, on the captain.
However, in the book, she discovers Dexter, a man she likes,
and asks herself "Is anyone going to let Poddy captain one of
those multimegabuck ships?"   She decides that changing a
ship's nursery full of wet babies is "lots more fun than dif-
ferential equations."   Anyway, she reasons, "a woman who
... undertakes to beat men at their own game might have ...
a fairly limited social life, wouldn't you think?"   So Poddy's
ambitions fall by the wayside.

Uncle Tom, who is deeply involved in a political intrigue, has used the kids as a cover on the trip, and Clark
and Poddy are captured and are to be put to death.   This is
when Clark displays behavior somewhat pathological in nature,
and a partially successful escape is the result.   He also ex-
pends a lot of energy insulting Poddy with comments like
"... don't try to use your head, it leaks," and "... let that
cut in your face heal; you're making a draft."   Clark also
smacks her "behind" as they separate on the escape.

Between Uncle Tom calling Poddy a "savage" and
Clark's verbal bombs aimed at her intelligence, it is surprising Poddy ever had ambitions at all.   Uncle Tom's lecture

about Poddy's mother caps Heinlein's didactic verbiage in this
novel. He instructs Poddy's father to tell his wife that she
had no business raising a family and "gallivanting off God
knows where.... You should tell your wife, sir, that building bridges and space stations and such gadgets is all very
well ... but that a woman has more important work to do."
The overwhelming emphasis in this novel seems to be that
women should be mothers, and that mothers should not also
have careers. It appears at the book's end that Poddy will
succumb to that pressure.

*   HENDERSON, ZENNA. "J-Line to Nowhere," in The
        Magazine of Fantasy and Science Fiction, Sept. 1969;
        in Holding Wonder. New York: Doubleday, 1971; rpt.
        New York: Avon Books, 1972; in The Venus Factor.
        Ed. Vic Ghidalia and Roger Elwood. New York: Mac-
        fadden-Bartell, 1977.

        Main Character: Twixt Garath.
        Physical Characteristics: No physical description given
except that she is approximately sixteen years old.
        Mental/Emotional Characteristics: Feels that she will
"die" if she doesn't get to "touch the soil" soon; has "un-
truthed by silence" in the past, but now decides not to anymore; feels twisted and "funny" until she touches soil, then
feels enthusiastic and as though she's "split a hard, crippling
casing clear up my back"; gets angry at her situation and
argues "in wordless savage gusts with no one."
        Story Particulars: Twixt Garath lives with her par-
ents and her younger brother Chis in an enclosed city, never
seeing the sun, trees, or ocean and not allowed to "touch the
greeneries" inside the city because they are "the breath of
the complex." In her mid-teens, she feels cramped and
twisted and, like her parents and Chis, longs for life on the
outside. Unlike her parents, Twixt has not yet given up the
hope of seeing the outer world.
        In the enclosed city, no one looks at anyone else in
public and permission must be granted to touch another.
Twixt remarks at how unusual it is for her mother to touch
her. When Twixt embarrasses herself horribly by causing
Engle Faucing, a potential suitor, to fall down on the dance
floor with another partner, she is humiliated as only a teen
can be. Terribly upset, she pours a beverage into her teaching computer and leaves school to take a series of glides and
finally blindly "hammered the controls" of a "jerkie" which
delivers her to open spaces where no one else is in sight, a
situation which is highly unusual.

She is enchanted with ants, trees, and wind, runs bare-
foot on the grass, and wades in the water of the ocean.   She
has found the dream of her entire family in this spot, but
suddenly feels fear and panic because there are no people,
or "humming of wheels."   In the distance she sees "a huddle
of small buildings" which have "sky showing between them,"
and is terrified that she is "the only person in the world."
Clutching her skirts, she runs back to the J-line.   There,
before the jerkie comes, she picks a white flower, and then
is stunned when a man arrives in a jerkie and offers it to
her.   She obligingly gets in and the door shuts before the
man can tell her where she is.   She thinks he mouthed "Nowhere," but is not sure.

Twixt returns home overjoyed, free of what feels like
"a hard, crippling casing" on her back.   Unfortunately, her
parents don't believe her experience was real, and she must
go to a counselor the next day to help her "conform."   Twixt
confronts her parents with the fact that the whole family is
"non-conform" and her father agrees, but tells her that at
least they label their fantasies as "fantasies" instead of claiming they are true.   Twixt knows differently.   Chis privately
corners Twixt and tells her that he'll find the spot again for
her, which Twixt seems to be willing to allow though he is
younger than she is.   She goes to bed, dreaming of him finding the spot, of her father putting in "for locale amends"
which will allow them to go there, and of being able to say
"foof to you, Engle Faucing!"

Except for her one act of truancy and her new feeling
of freedom to grow, Twixt seems content to let her world
decide things for her.   She lets her brother take over the
job of finding the outdoor spot she accidentally stumbled upon,
and she seems content to let the boys choose her if she is
the one they want, thus removing all responsibility of freedom of choice from her.   If Chis never finds Nowhere,
Twixt's thoughts of saying "foof" to Engle Faucing may be
only a memory.

★ LE GUIN, URSULA K.   Planet of Exile, in double with
      Mankind Under the Leash.   New York: Ace Books,
      1966; printed alone New York: Garland, 1975; rpt.
      New York: Ace Books, 1977.

Main Character: Rolery of Wold's Kin (shared with
Jakob Agat).
      Physical Characteristics: Is slight in build and the
daughter of Shakatany; is twenty "moonphases" old; has yellow
("amber") eyes and a "light, sweet voice"; is of a humanoid
species on an alien world.

Mental/Emotional Characteristics: Was raised not to look another in the eye; is "indolent, impudent, sweet-natured, solitary"; refuses to be intimidated; is "stubborn, willful, and very proud"; can send and receive "mindspeech."

Story Particulars: Six hundred years before the story begins, space travelers from Earth were deserted on an alien world when their ship was needed in the war which broke out at that time. As time passed, the stranded Earth people realized that, like it or not, they had been abandoned and were essentially colonists on this world. Naturally inhabiting the planet was a humanoid species with whom the Earth people were originally physiologically incapable of interbreeding. This biological fact kept the two basically human species not only from interbreeding, but from a successful blending of cultures; however, at the time the story begins, both the fortress-building humans on this alien world and the colonists from Earth are considering joining forces to fend off the attacking Gaals.

Since winters there last 5000 days, the migrating Gaals usually travel southward in small bands; but this winter they are attacking as a united group. The leader of the colonists, Jakob Agat Alterra, contacts Wold, the leader of the native people and father of Rolery, in order to encourage them to join forces against their common enemy. Rolery and Agat are able, they learn, to mindspeak to one another and come to love each other in spite of their alien backgrounds. The war with the Gaals is fought and won, but losses are great.

Rolery's quiet supportiveness and her love for Agat help him survive the ordeal. The reader learns near the book's end that the colonists have not only adapted enough to be susceptible to local viruses, but that now the two human species can interbreed. Rolery's part in the drama of the beginning of the blending of the two species is important. It is her quietly powerful presence in the colonists' camp which turns the tide of thinking towards a united world; in addition, her eventual acceptance by the colonists changes Wold's attitude towards the colonists. Rolery doesn't revolutionize the world, but quietly changes it with her love for Agat.

* McCAFFREY, ANNE. "The Ship Who Sang," in The Magazine of Fantasy and Science Fiction, April 1961; in Women of Wonder. Ed. Pamela Sargent. New York: Vintage Books, 1975; in Looking Ahead: The Vision of Science Fiction. Ed. Dick and Lori Allen. New York: Harcourt Brace Jovanovich, 1975.

Main Character: Helva.
Physical Characteristics: Was "born a thing" with
twisted limbs, and is destined to be "a guiding mechanism"
for a spaceship; is a Shell-person, her mind put in a metal
shell, "an encapsulated 'brain'"; she's kept physically small
by "pituitary manipulation" to prevent the transfer into a
larger shell; resembled a mature dwarf in size; is known for
her lovely voice because she hums and sings when she works,
but does not breathe as "oxygen and other gases were ... sus-
tained artificially by solution in their shells"; is age 16 when
she is given her ship.
Mental/Emotional Characteristics: Has a "receptive
and alert" mind; is "destined to be the 'brain' half of a scout
ship, " to be partnered with a mobile person (called a "brawn");
has an "above normal" IQ and a high "adaptation index"; is
capable of love, though she never feels love until partnered.
Story Particulars: Helva is born deformed, but as
she has a good mind, she is allowed to live to become the
"brain" part of a brain and brawn partnership on a spaceship.
Her training and conditioning is extensive and takes many
years. Along the way, she develops the hobby of "singing"
while she works. (Actually she doesn't sing because she
doesn't breathe, but she has learned to "manipulate her dia-
phragmic unit to sustain tone," and to manipulate her throat
muscles so as to enable her to produce sounds that others
interpret as singing.)
When she is 16 years old, she is given her ship and
chooses one of the nine brawns (mobile partners) available
at that time. She chooses Jennan, the only brawn who actually looks at her or where her physical presence is hidden
within the central control pillar. They begin their missions
together and Helva falls in love with this warm, thoughtful
brawn. But life does not remain idyllic for the two. A difficult rescue of a religious group on a planet which is rapidly
overheating due to its sun becoming unstable results in the
death of Helva's brawn. Helva is contacted by another shell
person who also has her own ship, and who suggests that,
considering Helva's current emotional crisis, she might want
to turn rogue rather than to accept a new brawn. Helva's
decision not only concludes this story, but also sets the stage
for a series of stories about her in The Ship Who Sang. (An
additional story about this character is "Honeymoon" in Get
Off the Unicorn, © 1977, Ballantine Books, New York, NY.)

★ MITCHISON, NAOMI. Memoirs of a Spacewoman. Lon-
        don: V. Gollancz, 1962; rpt. New York: Berkley
        Medallion Books, 1973.

Main Character: Mary.
Physical Characteristics: No physical description is
given as the book is in memoir form.
Mental/Emotional Characteristics: Is confident, knowl-
edgeable, and self-possessed; is attracted to a variety of
types of men and has children by several of them; is a communications expert, meaning she establishes empathy and communication with alien life forms easily; is a vegetarian.
Story Particulars: Remarkable Mary, communications
expert for Terra with alien life forms on numerous galactic
voyages, offers in first-person narrative the story of her
early years of exploration. The expeditions, taking many
Terra years to complete, require a period of "blackout" for
the team while in transit. The obvious result is that infant
children left behind are nearly grown when the parents return
to Terra, which originally created a set of moral problems
until a "few major scandals" helped to clear up the moral
ground rules.

Mary's exploration of various planets and their intelligent (and not so intelligent) life forms is the skeletal work
for this novel, with personal relationships, experiments, and
childbearing providing the meat of the story. Mary has several lovers--Vly (the bisexual Martian who communicates
nonverbally by touch and who triggers Mary's pregnancy of
a haploid child), T'o M'Kasi (the black Terran who fathers
a pale brown baby girl for Mary), and Peder Pedersen (the
Terran leader of her first expedition, the father of her blond-
haired son Jon, and a very close friend). During her pregnancies and the first year of the children's lives, Mary stays
on Terra to get the children "stabilised" and "integrated."
She writes that she felt just like a twentieth-century mother.
"It must have been just like that in the old days, being a
Mum. Only I could get away, that was the difference. How
marvellous it was, in spite of tiny prickles of regret, to be
back in a ship among my instruments and tables, thinking
intently and uninterruptedly."

Mary's life is her expeditions, her studies, research,
and communication with alien life forms. It is therefore not
surprising that she would twice volunteer for the grafting of
an alien life form onto her body for the purpose of experimentation. One expedition, to a planet on which the party
studies and communicates with caterpillars and butterflies,
results in one of the party being left for life on Terra, the
penalty for interfering with the development of an alien life
form. The party, all women, felt badly for the punished
member and visit with her on their return from other expeditions. Mary's other friendships are exclusively with col-

leagues who would age like her, through the centuries rather
than during one solid, unbroken time period.

She is somewhat surprised at the mutual affection which
develops between herself and Peder after the disaster of her
second alien graft. But this affection will not tie either of
them to the planet for long, or keep them from their work,
for she writes at the book's beginning that she is preparing
for a return expedition to the butterfly planet. Soon Mary
will once more be off on an expedition, pursuing her life's
work, meeting and loving men, and returning at expedition's
end to see her rapidly maturing offspring, perhaps to have
another child, and to catch up on news with her colleagues
and friends. Mary's memoirs are a joy to read.

*   NORTON, ANDRE (originally Alice Mary Norton, now
     Andre Alice Norton). Ordeal in Otherwhere. Cleve-
     land, OH: World Publishing Co., 1964; rpt. New
     York: Ace Books, 1965 and 1982.

     Main Character: Charis Nordholm.
     Physical Characteristics: Has shoulder-length, light
brown hair, tanned skin, a wide mouth, clearly defined cheekbones, and pale gray eyes; is of Terran stock; was born on
the planet Minos; is of medium height.
     Mental/Emotional Characteristics: Thinks things out,
and assembles her information before she acts; is innately
curious; has a thirst for knowledge; always has to know "why";
has a previously undeveloped telepathic ability and compassion and empathy.
     Story Particulars: As the daughter of a government
Education Officer, Charis had lived on a variety of planets--
seven in all. But her father's last appointment on Demeter
had been fatal to him; he was taken by the "white death" as
were many of the native male population. Unfortunately, the
natives blame the government party for the deaths and trade
her to a Free Trader for more men. Charis is taken to the
planet Warlock where she is under contract to establish trade
with the sea-dwelling female rulers of the planet. What she
isn't told is that the Wyvern witches "dream" themselves
where they want to be and, in fact, their whole political and
social structure is based on their ability to "dream to a purpose."
     Charis, deposited in cell-like quarters by the Free
Traders once on Warlock, is surprised the first time she
dreams she is elsewhere. The dream is so real that she
is certain it could not be just a dream. She is transported,

as if in a dream, to a spot near the sea, from which she
starts on a journey on foot. While walking, she rescues
and adopts a curl-cat calling herself Tsstu with whom Charis
has telepathic communication. It is after her telepathic contact with Tsstu that Charis is drawn back to the sea, where
she meets with the female Wyverns and is given a disk which
allows her to transport herself to anyplace she can clearly
envision.

　　　Charis and Tsstu teleport back to the Free Traders'
camp which has been destroyed, and there meet Shann Lantee,
a ranger from the Survey party whom she had tried to signal
to rescue her from the Free Traders. He, too, can "dream,"
as the Wyverns have learned, although none of their males
are capable of it. It turns out to be a fateful meeting because it takes their joint efforts to begin to heal the schism
that exists between the male and female Wyverns. And it
will take the combined efforts and cooperation of the Wyvern
males and females to protect their planet from a "Company
grab," the illegal control of a planet by a large company.

　　　Charis rescues Chann twice using her telepathic powers
(with the help of Tsstu and Taggi, Shann's wolverine). After
her rescues of Shann, she at first resists further mind links
with him, but gradually comes to accept his occasional, unspoken order to "Link!" The resulting intimacy and oneness
of mind changes their lives and offers the Wyverns an example of male and female telepathically in contact and not at
war. Charis decides Warlock is the place she wants to live
because she feels so at home there, and becomes the diplomatic liaison who is to "conduct a treaty with the witches."
It would seem that both Shann and Charis have found a place
for themselves on Warlock.

*   PANSKIN, ALEXEI.   Rite of Passage.   New York: Ace
　　　Books, 1968; rpt. Boston: Gregg Press, 1976; rpt.
　　　New York: Pocket Books, 1982.

　　　Main Character: Mia Havero.
　　　Physical Characteristics: Is age 12 at the start of the
book, and small for her age; has close-cut black hair; is
"black-eyed," dark skinned, occasionally mistaken for a boy,
and age 19 when she writes the book.
　　　Mental/Emotional Characteristics: Is studying to be
an ordinologist (one who orders and catalogs information,
similar to a librarian); is "smarter than most people"; is
clumsy until after her survival class; considers herself "hell
on wheels."

Story Particulars: Young Mia Havero lives with her
father on board a six-level, hollowed-out astroid ship which
is "roughly thirty miles by twenty by ten." (Seven such ships
were completed and out colonizing space when Earth was destroyed in war on March 9, 2041, due to overpopulation.)
All children on the ship, at age 14, are put out on a planet
to survive Trial for a month. Basic supplies and a horse
are given to each 14-year-old, and those who survive the
month are picked up by a scout ship. Though somewhat bar-
baric, the process does cull out the less intelligent children
and is an effective means of population control. It also signifies the transition into adulthood, a "rite of passage" as it
were, and those who survive are considered adults and have full
voting privileges.

When Mia is 12, her father, who is in a powerful position on the ship, has them moved to a different level where
she meets Jimmy Dentremont, whom she gradually grows to
know, respect, and love. As time passes and her Trial date
approaches, Mia has an adventure with Jimmy (they don space
suits and go to the outside of the ship while it is traveling
faster than the speed of light), decides to become an ordinologist, develops strong feelings for Jimmy, and grows quite
confident about her ability to survive Trial on a planet of
Mudeaters (any people who are colonists and live on a planet).
After all, she has become quite competent in all areas covered in her Survival Class.

But Mia has some surprises in store. She learns
that Mudeaters call ship dwellers by the name of Grabbies
because they hoard all technology and science, offering portions of information only in trade for the raw materials the
colonists have to offer. When Mia is dropped on planet for
Trial, she considers herself "hell on wheels," but quickly
realizes she's not as capable as she thought. She is beaten
by a man and nursed back to health by another. It is from
the latter, an old man who takes her in despite her status
as a Grabbie, that Mia learns to consider Mudeaters people.
When she learns that Jimmy has been captured and is in jail,
she cleverly finds a way to rescue him.

Their adventures on the planet include exploring one
another sexually because Mia thinks that waiting to have sex
until adulthood seems ridiculous when they might not even
survive Trial. Mia's rite of passage into adulthood is exciting and memorable for her, and she vows that as her generation gains power on board ship that changes will be made in
the policies toward the colonists. (This novel won the 1969
Nebula Award for best novel, and came in second place for
the 1969 Hugo Award for best novel.)

★ SCHMITZ, JAMES H. A Tale of Two Clocks. New
     York: Torquil Book, 1962; retitled Legacy. New
     York: Ace Books, 1979.

Main Character: Trigger (Miss Farn) Argee (a.k.a.
Comteen Lod and Birna Drellgannoth).
    Physical Characteristics: Is 24 years old, is "slim
and trim"; has "shoulder-length, modishly white-silver hair,"
but usually has red hair; has "gray eyes"; is the winner of
"small-arms" medals and carries a "Denton"; is "fairly pro-
ficient at the practice of unarmed mayhem"; walks "attrac-
tively" with what her friends call "the Argee Lilt"; has "warm
mahogany brown" hair in mid-book.
    Mental/Emotional Characteristics: Is the "secretary
and assistant of the famous Precolonial Commissioner Holati
Tate"; has a "temper" and is "obstinate"; has an extremely
high IQ; is an individualist, "ready to fight for her own rights
and anyone else's"; has been "taught to improvise."
    Story Particulars: A long-lived, slow-moving, plastic-
based life form, the Old Galactic plasmoids, has been discovered in the universe. The problem is that no one can
communicate well enough with them to learn their science
secrets, but plenty of people are trying, among them the official Federation Plasmoid Project. Trigger Argee, the competent, intelligent assistant to the famous Precolonial Commissioner Holati Tate, has drawn the guard duty command
on Maccadon for a portion of the project. Yet Trigger feels
compelled to return to the Manon system to guard the affections of Brule Inger from a woman there--a jealous reaction
Trigger has never displayed before now. Nonetheless, when
she prepares to transfer to another job and finds her transfer blocked, she plots an escape which is thwarted by Federation employee Major Heslet Quillan.
    It is only after Trigger attempts the escape that the
Federation begins to inform her of the full situation. It
seems a plasmoid unit--a paired 112-113 unit--is the key unit
in the running of the entire Old Galactic Station, a station
which has continued to run for 30,000 years. When the 112
and the 113 are paired, the unit is self-regulating. Unfortunately, the 112 unit needing regulating is not paired with
a 113 unit because it was stolen; however, for some unknown
reason, Trigger has won the affections of the 113-A unit, a
duplicate 113 unit probably capable of regulating the 112.
Trigger unwillingly adopts the 113-A, a "dark green" creature "marbled with pink streakings" and "rather like a plump
leech a foot and a half long," and names it Repulsive. With
the help of Quillan, with whom she develops a relationship,

Trigger begins a difficult but successful attempt to take the
113-A unit to the 112 unit, struggling almost constantly with
people who are trying to take the 113-A unit and are tamper-
ing with her memory and her inclinations; Trigger is a strong
character, an individualist who isn't afraid of a fight.

★   SMITH, CORDWAINER (Paul Myron Anthony Linebarger),
      and GENEVIEVE LINEBARGER.   "The Lady Who
      Sailed the Soul," in Galaxy Magazine, April 1960; in
      Galaxy: Thirty Years of Innovative Science Fiction.
      Ed. Frederik Pohl, Martin H. Greenberg, and Joseph
      D. Olander.   New York: Wideview Books, 1981.

      Main Character: Helen America.
      Physical Characteristics: Is a "little brunette" with
"brown eyes, and very pronounced eyebrows" who is "a wonderful sailor"; is the daughter of Mona Muggeridge, "a feminist beyond all limits," who campaigned for "the lost cause
of complete identity of the two genders"; is a "compact little
person" and "black-haired, dark-eyed, broad-bodied but thin";
is "pale" and "short."
      Mental/Emotional Characteristics: Is "grim, solemn,
sad" and "deadly serious"; she is "challenged by lessons,
haunted by publicity" and is "careful and reserved about friendships" therefore "desperately lonely"; is "competitive only on
a coldly professional basis"; is a "quiet girl" who "always
knew her subject" in school; has "a lively, rich personality";
is "a leader" and has good "nerves"; is "brave" and "obstinate" and has "determination."
      Story Particulars: Every age has its romantic couple,
the pair who overcome tremendous adversity and impossible
odds to be together.   This story of Helen America and Mr.
Grey-no-more, future sailors between the stars, is one such
story.   Helen America was born to the "celebrated she-man"
feminist Mona Muggeridge, who refused to identify the father
of her child and raised her among constant publicity and under tremendous pressure to excel in her studies.   In spite
of Helen's desire to be her mother's "embodied antithesis,"
she does manage to succeed in her studies.
      After Mona elopes with her "perfect husband," who
was a "skilled machine polisher" and still married, and they
are killed in an accident, Helen attends college, listing as
her last choice the profession of sailor.   Sailors, in spite
of the human life expectancy of 160 years by this time, spent
forty of their physical years on one flight during a subjective
time frame that is merely a month.   Because she is the first

woman to apply to be a sailor who is young enough and has
"also passed the scientific requirements," Helen becomes
the intended victim of the press once more as they try to
play matchmaker by giving Helen and the sailor Mr. Grey-
no-more a "holiday in New Madrid." Both of them refuse
the offer, and then Helen agrees to go if she will not be
forced to meet Mr. Grey-no-more and if no press is per-
mitted. Mr. Grey-no-more, an "odd, intense old man whose
hair was black," also changes his mind and goes on holiday,
and is introduced to Helen quite casually by "a master of the
dances."

After a brief period of getting to know one another,
they have an intense "bittersweet love affair." Helen asks
him to marry her, but he refuses, seeing their age difference of nearly fifty years as too much of a barrier. He
came to Earth from New Earth for the adventure of seeing
the planet, and as a sailor because he couldn't afford to be
sent in a pod. Now he plans to return to New Earth in a
pod and wants them to have their "separate lifetimes to remember" their affair. Helen lets him go and has the child
she's carrying aborted, never telling him she had been pregnant. She is given the Soul, a ship full of "religious fanat-
ics," and leaves for New Earth, knowing she will be sixty
years old when she arrives, a loss of forty years of her life.

During the voyage, one of the sails needs repairs and
Mr. Grey-no-more appears as a hallucination to help her.
His advice works and she arrives on New Earth at sixty years
of age, now the same age as Mr. Grey-no-more. Their love
story survives to be acted for audiences for "centuries to
come," though none of the actresses ever portrayed her as
"a grim, solemn, sad, little brunette who had been born amid
the laughter of humanity." The story is faced with the dialogue
of a mother and child discussing the romance. The mother,
the "sentimental" one of the pair, loves the story of Helen
America and Mr. Grey-no-more just as she loves the aging
"spieltier" (an animal so versatile in its appearance that it
is kept as a children's toy) her daughter has discarded and
thinks should be destroyed.

In this well-written story, a feminist is portrayed in
an absurd extreme, and a romantic, equally extreme, sacrifices forty years of her life to be with her lover. Further,
romanticism is equated with the love of a pitiable, "worn-
out" spieltier, clinching reader sympathy for the aging Helen.
This story gives the reader ample material for critical anal-
ysis regarding its antithetical presentation of feminism and
romanticism.

⋆   TIPTREE, JAMES, JR. (Alice B. Sheldon).   "The Snows
        Are Melted, the Snows Are Gone," in Venture Science
        Fiction, Nov. 1969; in Ten Thousand Light Years
        From Home.   New York: Ace Books, 1973 and 1978;
        rpt. Boston: Gregg Press, 1976.

        Main Character: No name given.
        Physical Characteristics: Has a "flood" of blonde
hair, blue eyes, and no arms (a "phocomorph"); is "young"
and "too thin"; has "slim prehensile toes" which she uses
like fingers; gets to her feet like "a human spring"; has an
intelligent wolf as a partner with her on "Patrol"; has "small
breasts"; is as "agile as a hare" and has endurance.
        Mental/Emotional Characteristics: Is devoted to find-
ing a physically whole man to bring to her deformed group;
has an easy laugh; has curiosity and compassion and is fearless.
        Story Particulars: On Earth, in what is probably a
post-atomic-holocaust time, a nameless hero (simply called
"she" here for the sake of simplicity) has the task of searching for, isolating, luring out, and capturing a physically normal man in what had once been Ethiopia. She comes from
an area where the survivors are apparently born either without arms or without legs. In her case, the deformity is no
arms, but she has tremendous endurance as a runner and
can manipulate things with her "prehensile toes." Her partner in this venture is an intelligent protective, "bulge-headed"
wolf which helps her dress and undress and carries a pack
filled with food for them both. Together she and the wolf
find a village and study the inhabitants from a hiding place,
looking for a strong, large man.
        When they are ready, the wolf uncovers her breasts
and pulls down her pants so she can expose herself to a man,
thus inspiring him to chase her. The plan works and she
begins a long run, lasting for two full days with him at her
heels with only periodic rest stops for them both. The wolf
is solicitous, guarding her and forcing her to rest when she
has reached her limit, but otherwise staying out of sight,
keeping the man under surveillance.
        She and the wolf have a rather symbiotic relationship.
He helps her on and off with her clothes. She unhitches the
pack from his back with her toes. He pushes her in the direction he wants her to go. She holds his mouth open with
her knees when he has a spasm which resembles an epileptic
attack. The partnership is a good one, but on this venture,
she begins to limp short of their goal and must spray a gas
in the man's face to drug him, using a "syringe fastened
between teeth and cheek."

She and the wolf have managed to get far enough towards their goal that Bonz, her human male partner on this patrol, can reach them on a tractor. Bonz, who has no legs, drives the tractor, but cannot leave his seat to help her tie or load the captured man. Bonz's attitude towards the man is hateful and resentful. "There's your damned Y-chromosome," he tells her.

She is a strong character, her lack of arms never making her feel sorry for herself. Her adjustment to her handicap is remarkable, even considering the help she receives from the wolf. She takes on the most strenuous of tasks, having been "trained hard" for it, and has no fear of the physically-able man following her.

* WYNDHAM, JOHN (John Wyndham Parkes Lucas Beynon Harris). <u>Trouble with Lichen</u>. London: M. Joseph, 1960; rpt. New York: Ballantine Books, 1960 and 1982.

<u>Main Character</u>: Diana Pricilla Brackley.
<u>Physical Characteristics</u>: At first, she is 18 years old and 5'10" tall; she is "slender and straight," with "dark chestnut" hair "with a glint of russet lights," and has a face with a "classic quality," and grey eyes; is considered "decorative." As time passes, only her age changes, because after about age 25, she doesn't age.
<u>Mental/Emotional Characteristics</u>: Feels that "being just a woman and nothing else" is "one of the deadend jobs"; is extremely independent, restless, and highly intelligent, even "brilliant"; keeps questioning things "that don't <u>need</u> questioning"; is a biochemist; is "personable," determined, and farsighted; becomes wealthy from an inheritance at age 25.
<u>Story Particulars</u>: Diana Brackley, a brilliant biochemist hired by the elite Darr House Development, discovers that a particular lichen retards the aging process. She is fairly certain that this discovery has also been made by Francis Saxover, owner and director of Darr, whom she is in love with. Unfortunately, Francis is twice her age and Diana is certain he doesn't share her feelings. During a conversation with Francis' daughter Zephanie on the subject of women, it becomes obvious to Diana just what her career should be--to extend the lives of people to give them a reason and time to "put the world to rights."

Diana sets about her task by leaving Darr, traveling around the world to locate all the sources of this particular lichen that she can, and opening an exclusive and expensive

"beauty place" in London.   There is, as it turns out, a severely small supply of the lichen, and she realizes that eventually a synthetic supply will have to be formulated, but that
is not her first and primary goal.   In the 14 years that follow, Diana treats only the wives and relatives of the most
powerful and influential men in England.   The result is a
group of a thousand women who, when the news breaks about
the age-retarding treatments, refuse to give up the benefits.
Diana has her army which forms itself under the name of the
League for the New Life.   But prior to the news leak, Diana
contacts Francis to inform him of her covert use of the lichen.   Though he doesn't approve of Diana's decision to reveal the truth about the lichen, he does tell his children,
Zephanie and Paul, who have also been receiving covert treatments of the lichen.   It would seem that everyone would be
overjoyed by the prospect of a longer life, but many have
their own reasons for not wanting people to live longer.
Diana, realizing this, lets herself be "killed" in a staged
assassination, and disappears to a farm "abroad."

The League continues its work, the world accepts long
life as an attractive possibility, and scientists set to work to
create a synthetic antigerone ("against age").   Francis tracks
her down, certain that the murder was a fake, and at the
book's conclusion, they finally begin to work together.   Diana
is a world-shaker, and achieves her own ends in a back-door
approach, requiring much singleness of purpose, planning, and
insight.

ADDITIONAL READING LIST

Aldiss, Brian W(ilson).   "The Night That All Time Broke
    Out," in Dangerous Visions.   Ed. Harlan Ellison.   Garden
    City, NY: Doubleday, 1967, and New York: The New
    American Library, 1975; in Earth Is the Strangest Planet.
    Ed. Robert Silverberg.   Nashville: Thomas Nelson, 1977.

Bester, Alfred.   "They Don't Make Life Like They Used To,"
    in The Magazine of Fantasy and Science Fiction, Oct.
    1963; in The Dark Side of Earth.   New York: Signet
    Books, 1964; in Star Light, Star Bright, The Great Short
    Fiction of Alfred Bester, Volume II.   New York: Berkley,
    1976.

Bloch, Robert.   "A Toy for Juliette," in Dangerous Visions.
    Ed. Harlan Ellison.   Garden City, NY: Doubleday, Inc.,
    1967, and New York: The New American Library, 1975;

in Partners in Wonder. Ed. Harlan Ellison. New York:
Walker, 1971.

Brunner, John (Kilian Houston). "The Totally Rich," in
Worlds of Tomorrow, June 1963; in Out of My Mind. New
York: Ballantine Books, 1967; in The Late Great Future.
Ed. Gregory Fitz Gerald and John Dillon. New York:
Fawcett Books, 1976.

Carter, Angela. Heroes & Villains. London: William Heinemann, 1969, and New York: Pocket Books, 1979.

Chandler, A(rthur) Bertram. Empress of Outer Space. New
York: Ace Books, 1965. (In a double with The Alternate
Martians.)

Cooper, Hughes. Sexmax. New York: Paperback Library,
1969. (Several of the main characters are women.)

deFord, Miriam Allen. "Against Authority," in The Magazine
of Fantasy and Science Fiction, Feb. 1966; in The Venus
Factor. Ed. Vic Ghidalia and Roger Elwood. New York:
MacFadden-Bartell, 1972, and New York: Woodhill Press,
1977.

Delany, Samuel R(ay). "Corona," in The Magazine of Fantasy
and Science Fiction, Oct. 1967; in Driftglass. New York:
The New American Library, 1971, and Boston: Gregg
Press, Inc., 1977; in Looking Ahead: The Vision of Science
Fiction. Ed. Dick and Lori Allen. New York: Harcourt
Brace Jovanovich, 1975.

_____. "Driftglass," in If, June 1967; in Driftglass.
New York: The New American Library, 1971, and Boston:
Gregg Press, 1977. (Secondary character. This story
was nominated for a 1968 Nebula Award for best short
story.)

_____. "We, in Some Strange Power's Employ, Move on
a Rigorous Line," in The Magazine of Fantasy and Science
Fiction, May 1968; in Driftglass. New York: The New
American Library, 1971, and Boston: Gregg Press, 1977;
in Those Who Can. Ed. Robert Scott Wilson. New American Library, 1973. (Not the viewpoint character, but a
main character nonetheless.)

Dorman, Sonya. "Go, Go, Go, Said the Bird," in Dangerous

Visions. Ed. Harlan Ellison. Garden City, NY: Doubleday, 1967, and New York: The New American Library, 1975.

Elgin, Suzette Haden (Patricia A. Suzette Elgin). "For the
Sake of Grace," in The Magazine of Fantasy and Science
Fiction, May 1969; in World's Best Science Fiction: 1970.
Ed. Donald A. Wollheim and Terry Carr. New York:
Ace, 1970; incorporated into At the Seventh Level.
New York: Daw Books, 1972; in Communipath Worlds.
New York: Pocket Books, 1980.

Emshwiller, Carol. "Animal," in Orbit 4. Ed. Damon
Knight. New York: Putnam's, 1968; in Joy in Our Cause.
New York: Harper & Row, 1974.

_____. "Lib," in Triquarterly, March 1968; in The Best
SF Stories from New Worlds 6. Ed. Michael Moorcock.
New York: Berkley, 1970; in Joy in Our Cause. New
York: Harper & Row, 1974.

_____. "Sex and/or Mr. Morrison," in Dangerous Vi-
sions. Ed. Harlan Ellison. Garden City, NY: Doubleday, 1967, and New York: The New American Library,
1975; in Women of Wonder. Ed. Pamela Sargent. New
York: Vintage Books, 1975.

Frayn, Michael. A Very Private Life. New York: The
Viking Press, 1969; rpt. New York: Dell, 1969.

Henderson, Zenna. "Angels Unawares," in The Magazine of
Fantasy and Science Fiction, March 1966; in The People:
No Different Flesh. Garden City, NY: Doubleday, 1967,
and New York: Avon Books, 1968.

_____. "Deluge," in The Magazine of Fantasy and Science
Fiction, Oct. 1963; in The People: No Different Flesh.
Garden City, NY: Doubleday, 1967, and New York: Avon
Books, 1968.

_____. "The Indelible Kind," in The Magazine of Fantasy
and Science Fiction, Dec. 1968; in Holding Wonder. Garden City, NY: Doubleday, 1971, and New York: Avon
Books, 1972.

_____. "No Different Flesh," in The Magazine of Fantasy
and Science Fiction, May 1965; in The People: No Different Flesh. Garden City, NY: Doubleday, 1967, and
New York: Avon Books, 1968.

_____. "Return," in The Magazine of Fantasy and Science Fiction, March 1961; in The People: No Different Flesh. Garden City, NY: Doubleday, 1967, and New York: Avon Books, 1968.

_____. "Shadow on the Moon," in The Magazine of Fantasy and Science Fiction, March 1962; in The People: No Different Flesh. Garden City, NY: Doubleday, 1967, and New York: Avon Books, 1968.

_____. "Something Bright," in Galaxy Magazine, Feb. 1960; in Galaxy: Thirty Years of Innovative Science Fiction. Ed. Frederik Pohl, Martin H. Greenberg, and Joseph D. Olander. New York: Wideview Books, 1981.

_____. "Subcommittee," in The Magazine of Fantasy and Science Fiction, July 1962; in The Anything Box. Garden City, NY: Doubleday, 1965, and New York: Avon Books, 1969.

_____. "Troubling of the Water," in The Magazine of Fantasy and Science Fiction, Sept. 1966; in The People: No Different Flesh. Garden City, NY: Doubleday, Inc., 1967, and New York: Avon Books, 1968.

Henneberg, Nathalie-Charles (Nathalie and Charles Henneberg zu Irmelshausen Wasungen). "Ysolde," in International Science Fiction, June 1968; in The Best From the Rest of the World: European Science Fiction. Ed. Donald A. Wollheim. New York: Daw Books, 1976.

Herbert, Frank. Dune. Philadelphia: Chilton, 1965; rpt. New York: Ace Books, 1967; rpt. New York: Berkley, 1975 and 1982. (Woman character is a strong secondary character. This book was first published in two series in Astounding Science-Fiction under the names of "Dune World" and "The Prophet of Dune," starting in Dec. 1963 and Jan. 1965 respectively. Dune won the 1966 Nebula Award for best novel, and tied for the first place 1966 Hugo Award for best novel.)

Leiber, Fritz (Reuter). "Mariana," in Fantastic Science Fiction Stories, Feb. 1960; in The Best of Fritz Leiber. New York: Ballantine Books, 1974 and 1979.

_____. "No Great Magic," in Galaxy Magazine, Dec. 1963; in Changewar. New York: Ace Books, 1983.

L'Engle, Madeleine. A Wrinkle in Time. New York: Far-
rar, Straus and Giroux, 1962; rpt. New York: Dell, 1976.
(Juvenile novel which was the winner of the 1963 Newbery
Award.)

Lightner, A(lice) M(artha). The Day of the Drones. New
York: W. W. Norton, 1969; rpt. New York: Bantam
Books, 1970.

McAllister, Bruce. "Prime-Time Teaser," in The Magazine
of Fantasy and Science Fiction, Dec. 1968; in Twenty
Years of Fantasy and Science Fiction. Ed. Edward L.
Ferman and Robert P. Mills. New York: Putnam's,
1970.

McCaffrey, Anne (Inez). "A Meeting of Minds," in The Magazine of Fantasy and Science Fiction, Jan. 1969; in The
Liberated Future: Voyages into Tomorrow. Ed. Robert
Hoskins. New York: Fawcett Books, 1974; in Get Off
the Unicorn. New York: Ballantine Books, 1977.

_____. Restoree. New York: Ballantine Books, 1967
and 1977.

_____. "Weather on Welladay," in Galaxy Magazine,
March 1969; in Get Off the Unicorn. New York: Ballantine Books, 1977. (Woman is one of the main characters.)

_____. "Weyr Search," in Analog Science Fiction/Science
Fact, Oct. 1967; incorporated into Dragonflight. New
York: Ballantine Books, 1968. ("Weyr Search" tied for
first place for a 1968 Hugo Award for best novella and
was nominated for a 1968 Nebula Award for best novella.)

_____. "A Womanly Talent," in Analog Science Fiction/
Science Fact, Feb. 1969; in To Ride Pegasus. New York:
Ballantine Books, 1973. (To be reprinted.)

MacLean, Katherine (Anne). "Interbalance," in The Magazine
of Fantasy and Science Fiction, Oct. 1960; in The Best
from Fantasy and Science Fiction, 10th series. Ed. Robert P. Mills. New York: Doubleday, 1961, and New
York: Ace Books, 1961.

Merril, Judith. "The Deep Down Dragon," in Galaxy Magazine, Aug. 1961; in Galaxy: Thirty Years of Innovative
Science Fiction. Ed. Frederik Pohl, Martin H. Greenberg,

and Joseph D. Olander. New York: Wideview Books, 1981.

Moore, Ward. "The Fellow Who Married the Maxill Girl," in The Magazine of Fantasy and Science Fiction, Feb. 1960; in The Best from Fantasy and Science Fiction, 10th series. Ed. Robert P. Mills. New York: Doubleday, 1961, and New York: Ace Books, 1961.

Norton, Andre (Alice). "Toys of Tamisen," in If, April and May 1969; included in novel Perilous Dreams. New York: Daw Books, 1976.

Reed, Kit (Lillian Craig Reed). "Cynosure," in The Magazine of Fantasy and Science Fiction, June 1964; in Other Stories and The Attack of the Giant Baby. New York: Berkley Books, 1981.

_____. "Winston," in Orbit 5. Ed. Damon Knight. New York: Putnam's, 1969; in Other Stories and The Attack of the Giant Baby. New York: Berkley Books, 1981.

Russ, Joanna. "The Adventuress," in Orbit 2. Ed. Damon Knight. New York: Putnam's, 1967; retitled "Bluestocking," in Alyx. Boston: Gregg Press, 1976; in The Adventures of Alyx. New York: Pocket Books, 1983.

_____. "The Barbarian," in Orbit 3. Ed. Damon Knight. New York: Putnam's, 1968; in Alyx. Boston: Gregg Press, 1976; in The Adventures of Alyx. New York: Pocket Books, 1983.

_____. "I Gave Her Sack and Sherry," in Orbit 2. Ed. Damon Knight. New York: Putnam's, 1967; in The Best from Orbit 1-10. Ed. Damon Knight. New York: Berkley Books, 1975; retitled "I Thought She Was Afeard Till She Stroked My Beard," in Alyx. Boston: Gregg Press, 1976; in The Adventures of Alyx. New York: Pocket Books, 1983.

_____. "My Dear Emily," in The Magazine of Fantasy and Science Fiction, July 1962; in The Best from Fantasy and Science Fiction, Twelfth Series. Ed. Avram Davidson. New York: Ace Books, 1963.

_____. Picnic on Paradise. New York: Ace Books, 1968; rpt. New York: Berkley, 1979; included in Alyx. Boston: Gregg Press, 1976; in The Adventures of Alyx. New York: Pocket Books, 1983.

St. Clair, Margaret. The Games of Neith. New York:
    Ace Books, 1960. (In double with The Earth Gods Are
    Coming.)

Saxton, Josephine. The Hieros Gamos of Sam and An Smith.
    Garden City, NY: Doubleday, 1969; rpt. Philadelphia, PA:
    Curtis Books, 1972.

Schmitz, James H(enry). "Lion Loose," in Analog Science
    Fiction/Science Fact, Oct. 1961; in A Pride of Monsters.
    New York: Macmillan, 1970. (Secondary character. "Lion
    Loose" was nominated for a Hugo Award in 1962.)

_____. "The Pork Chop Tree," in Analog Science Fiction/
    Science Fact, Feb. 1965; in A Pride of Monsters. New
    York: Macmillan, 1970.

_____. "The Searcher," in Analog Science Fiction/Science
    Fact, Feb. 1966; in A Pride of Monsters. New York:
    Macmillan, 1970.

_____. "The Star Hyacinths," in Amazing Stories, Dec.
    1961; retitled "The Tangled Web," in A Nice Day for
    Screaming and Other Tales of the Hub. Philadelphia:
    Chilton Books, 1965.

_____. The Tuvela, serialized in Analog Science Fiction/
    Science Fact, starting Sept. 1968; retitled The Demon
    Breed. New York: Ace Books, 1968 and 1981.

_____. The Universe Against Her. New York: Ace
    Books, 1964 and 1982; rpt. Boston: Gregg Press, 1981.

_____. "The Winds of Time," in Analog Science Fiction/
    Science Fact, Sept. 1962; in A Nice Day for Screaming and
    Other Tales of the Hub. Philadelphia: Chilton Books,
    1965; in A Pride of Monsters. New York: Macmillan,
    1970.

Sheckley, Robert. "Can You Feel Anything When I Do This?"
    in Playboy Magazine, Aug. 1969; in The Fiend. Chicago,
    IL: Playboy Press, 1971; in Science Fiction Argosy. Ed.
    Damon Knight, New York: Simon & Schuster, 1972.

Smith, Cordwainer (Paul Myron Anthony Linebarger). "The
    Ballad of Lost C'Mell," in Galaxy Magazine, Oct. 1962;
    in The Science Fiction Hall of Fame, Volume IIA. Ed.

Ben Bova. New York: Doubleday, 1973, and New York:
Avon Books, 1974; in The Best of Cordwainer Smith. Ed.
J. J. Pierce. New York: Ballantine Books, 1975. (Sec-
ondary character.)

_____. "The Dead Lady of Clown Town," in Galaxy Maga-
zine, Aug. 1964; in The Best of Cordwainer Smith. Ed.
J. J. Pierce. New York: Ballantine Books, 1975; in
Galactic Dreamers: Science Fiction. Ed. Robert Silverberg. New York: Random House, 1977.

_____. "Mother Hitton's Littul Kittons," in Galaxy Maga-
zine, June 1961; in The Best of Cordwainer Smith. Ed.
J. J. Pierce. New York: Ballantine Books, 1975.

Smith, Evelyn E. The Perfect Planet. New York: Thomas
Bouregy, 1962; (Woman is one of two main characters.)

Sturgeon, Theodore (Edward Hamilton Waldo). "When You
Care, When You Love," in The Magazine of Fantasy and
Science Fiction, Sept. 1962; in The Best from Fantasy and
Science Fiction: A Special 25th Anniversary Anthology.
Ed. Edward Ferman. Garden City, NY: Doubleday, 1974;
in Case and the Dreamer. New York: The New American
Library, 1974. (This story was nominated for a 1963 Hugo
Award for short fiction.)

Vinge, Vernor (Steffen). Grimm's World. New York: Berkley Books, 1969.

Vonnegut, Kurt, Jr. "Harrison Bergeron," in The Magazine
of Fantasy and Science Fiction, Oct. 1961; in Welcome to
the Monkey House. New York: Delacorte Press, 1968,
and New York: Dell, 1970.

_____. "Welcome to the Monkey House," in Playboy Maga-
zine, Jan. 1968; in Welcome to the Monkey House. New
York: Delacorte Press, 1968, and New York: Dell, 1970;
in Past, Present, & Future Perfect. Ed. Jack C. Wolf
and Gregory Fitz Gerald. Greenwich, CT: Fawcett, 1973.

Wilhelm, Kate. "Stranger in the House," in The Magazine
of Fantasy and Science Fiction, Feb. 1967; in Abyss.
New York: Doubleday, 1971, and New York: Bantam
Books, 1973 and 1978.

Wilson, Richard. "Mother to the World," in Orbit 3. Ed.

Damon Knight.   New York: Berkley Books, 1968; in The
Science Fiction Hall of Fame, Volume III.   Ed. Arthur C.
Clarke and George W. Proctor.   New York: Avon Books,
1982.   (This story won the 1969 Nebula Award for best
novelette and was in fourth place for a 1969 Hugo Award
for best novelette.)

CHAPTER 6: THE 1970s

The 1970s saw rapid growth in the number of women characters in sf. Not only were many more women characters included in sf, but they were usually more than the ornamenta-
tion they had been in the past. The female characters of this
decade were frequently leaders--world-changers. It was common for a woman character in the 1970s to hold the fate of
her world in her hands; she left her mark on her world. She
was, like the male characters in sf in the past, larger than
life, admirable, even heroic. She was often called upon to
lead the fight against domination of normals (in the case of
the proposed destruction of mutants), robots, corporations,
religious groups, aliens, and, yes, males.

Predictably, the exceptional or unique person who had
always been present in fiction with male main characters became the norm in works with female main characters. But
this didn't occur without an occasional twist of plot; some of
these female characters were alienated from the human species because they were aliens, mutants, or elderly in a world
of only young people. The theme of woman as alienated person was explored. James Tiptree, Jr., who turned out to be
Alice B. Sheldon, broke ground on the alienated woman theme.
Her so-called masculine writing style made her popular with
both women and men, a fact which resulted in widespread exposure to the theme of the alienated woman.

Certainly, many women characters in sf were still
secondary to the plot and were weak, dependent, afraid, and,
stereotypically speaking, "normal" for women. Edmund
Cooper's Gender Genocide (1972, with British title of Who
Needs Men?) is one example of a work which has a radical
anti-male woman main character, who eventually agrees with
the man she's been sent out to kill--that biology is destiny
for women. However, for the most part, as the breakthroughs

of the 1960s continued, an increasing number of women characters were created in molds other than the stereotypical
molds of the past. As Peter Nicholls wrote under "Women"
in The Science Fiction Encyclopedia, "At least it can be said
that in the sf of the 1970s we are seeing fewer heroines like
Podkayne of Mars ... and more who are real people." The
characters created in stereotypical molds were gradually giving way to more real, more human, and even more heroic
characters.

This breaking of molds was also seen in the works of
writers who did not typically write about one strong, central
female character, but preferred male main characters or a
variety of characters. For example, Marion Zimmer Bradley's Darkover series, though initially introduced in the 1960s,
became increasingly popular as more Darkover books were
published in the 1970s. Although she has few sf works with
women as viewpoint or main characters, all of the works
contain women characters who are strong and interesting as
secondary characters. Ursula K. Le Guin and Marta Randall
are two additional writers whose works are filled with strong
and interesting, though not always viewpoint or main women
characters. Among the works of Ursula Le Guin which should
not be missed, not only because of their quality but because
of their speculation on androgyny and sex roles, are The Dispossessed (1974) and The Left Hand of Darkness (1969), both
Hugo and Nebula award winners. Marta Randall's book Journey (1978) and its sequel, Dangerous Games (1980), are epic
in proportion and are filled with strong, interesting women
(and men) characters. Women characters in sf were, at long
last, beginning to appear in greater proportion as real people
with goals, dedication, and a willingness to work hard.

During the 1970s, a flood of sf works by and about
women began to pour into the market. Not only were there
more women writers producing fiction with women main characters, but men also began to write more frequently about female heroes who were brave, intelligent, strong (physically
and emotionally), talented, adventure-seeking, and, if not
without fear, at least capable of dealing with it.

*   BRADLEY, MARION ZIMMER.   The Shattered Chain: A
    Darkover Novel.   New York: Daw Books, 1976; Bos-
    ton: Gregg Press, 1979.

    Main Character: Jaelle n'ha Melora.

Physical Characteristics: Is twelve years old at the beginning of the book, maturing to age 24 by the end of the novel. At age 12, she was "tall for her age, lightly built, with delicate bones, her hair flowing red, hanging halfway down her back." At age 24, she is beautiful, has large eyes framed in thick dark lashes, a slender, feminine body and hair "the exact color of new-minted copper bars."

Mental/Emotional Characteristics: At age twelve, she was set in the restrictive ways of Dry Towners and was hesitant to wear even breeches and boots. At age 24, she is a Free Amazon, leader of the band of Amazons she is with, and fiercely outspoken and open. At age twelve, she was deeply upset at her mother's death, and emotionally made the decision to go with the Free Amazons so as never to "be in subjection to any man." At age 24, she has some laren (psychic ability) and a fiery temper.

Secondary Female Characters: 1) Lady Rohanna is an aristocrat with short flame-red hair at the beginning and long heavy auburn hair with grey twelve years later. She is a tower-trained telepath of the Comyn (ruling caste on Darkover) and fosters Jaelle's infant brother. She realizes, after her trip with the Free Amazons to rescue Jaelle's mother from a Dry Towner, that she has chosen her life with her mate in spite of being given to him by her parents. 2) Kindra is a tall, slender, swift-moving woman, with gray eyes, sunburned calloused hands, and graying, close-cropped hair. She has a gaunt and pleasant face, is middle-aged, and a mercenary soldier and leader of the Free Amazons. She is a kind and steady person with some telepathic ability. 3) Magda Lorne is a Terran agent (an alien anthropologist and translator in Empire Intelligence work) who was briefly married to Peter, another agent. She has high psi potential, has long dark hair worn coiled low on her neck and fastened with a butterfly-shaped clasp at her introduction, and cuts her hair short to travel incognito as a Free Amazon. Although born to Terran parents, she was brought up as a Darkovan and has to deal with some confusion within herself about how she should behave, especially as a Free Amazon.

Story Particulars: In a book as rich as this one is in strong, interesting female characters, it seems a shame to concentrate on only one; however, only one truly fits the definition of a main character as set down in the beginning of this book, and that is Jaelle. (All of Marion Zimmer Bradley's books have strong, interesting women characters, but, as most are told from a man's point of view, few have been

included in this volume. All of her books are recommended,
however, for their usually inoffensive treatment of female
characters.) Jaelle is only twelve years old at the start of
the book when she and her pregnant mother are rescued from
a life of imprisonment in a Dry Town (desert town) by Lady
Rohanna and Kindra, leading a small band of Free Amazons
on the planet Darkover. (The word "amazon" as used in this
book does not fit the dictionary definitions. The women of
the Free Amazons are neither masculine women nor necessarily warriors, although all do learn to defend themselves.
Some are fighters but most follow other trades.) Lady Rohanna was a close friend to Jaelle's mother and it is she
who learns of her whereabouts and arranges a rescue. When
Jaelle's mother dies in childbirth, Jaelle states her intention
to be a Free Amazon so as never to "be in subjection to any
man" as her mother was, and goes with Kindra and the Amazons who rescued her.

The second third of the book takes place twelve years
later when Jaelle is 24. Magda Lorne, an alien anthropologist with Empire Intelligence, grows concerned when her
former husband and childhood friend Peter, also in Empire
Intelligence on Darkover, does not return from his mission.
Lady Rohanna, a telepath of the Comyn (ruling caste of Darkover) once more plays an important role in the book by providing Magda with the location of Peter and with a means of
safely reaching him: Lady Rohanna instructs Magda to dress
as a Free Amazon. It is on Magda's trip through the mountains in winter, on her way to rescue Peter, that she runs
into Jaelle in a traveler's shelter, and, after unsuccessfully
trying to convince her she is an Amazon, Magda tells Jaelle
her true mission. Jaelle, impressed by the safe passage
papers Magda carries from Lady Rohanna, spares her life
and forces Magda to take the oath of the Free Amazons. The
two of them go to rescue Peter and he and Jaelle fall in love.

In the last third of the book, in spite of the barriers
Jaelle's oath as a Free Amazon places in her path, Jaelle
finds a way for Peter and herself to make a life together on
Darkover. Magda takes her own oath as a Free Amazon seriously and discovers that she has laran, or psychic abilities.
Jaelle tells Peter at one point in the story, "... you must
sometimes let me be a woman and not always reasonable ..."
as though she thinks women have a monopoly on being occasionally unreasonable--an out-of-character statement for the
fiery, proud Jaelle.

Magda seems more independent at the end of the book
than any of the other women, for Kindra is dead, Lady Rohanna is still in her marriage, and Jaelle has chosen to live

as Peter's freemate and seems to want an even closer commitment to him than being a Free Amazon allows. Nonetheless, it is a very readable book containing in it four very
interesting and diverse female characters. (The story of
Magda and Jaelle continues in Thendara House, published in
1983 by Daw.)

* BUSBY, F. M. Rissa Kerguelen. New York: Berkley,
  1976. (Originally published as two novels: Rissa Kerguelen and The Long View, both by Berkley in 1976.)

Main Character: Rissa Kerguelen (a.k.a. Antonia Du-
val, Lysse Harnain, Tari Obrigo, and Cele Metrokin).
Physical Characteristics: Seldom climaxes in sex until her marriage to Bran Tregure, and then has quite normal
sexual desires; has dark hair, cropped close to her skull
when Welfared, grown "sitting-length" by the book's end; begins the book as a young child and is in her late twenties,
bio-time, at the book's end; learns to fight and kill with only
her body as a weapon; is a fifth generation Hulzein.
Mental/Emotional Characteristics: Is highly intelligent, independent, strong-willed and practical, and never
makes "the same mistake twice"; is one of the "adrenaline
freaks" for whom time slows down in case of "life or death";
is, at first, considered "not a very feminine woman" by Tregare (leader of the armed Escaped ship); has "guts and honesty" and always holds something of herself back to protect
herself from others; must grieve when she kills someone.
Story Particulars: Snatched away from her uncle as
a child in the twenty-first century after the deaths of her
parents and placed in a welfare institution run by the notorious UET (United Energy Transport), Rissa Kerguelen struggles to survive the indignities of having her head shaved
nearly bald; of having no rights, possessions, or identity as
a person; and finally of being used sexually against her will
by her boss in Welfare. When, against impossible odds,
Rissa wins the lottery and can buy her way out of Welfare,
she is contacted by an old friend of the family who arranges
to have her trained by the Hulzein Establishment in Argen-
tina, one of the few places on Earth UET doesn't control.
Rissa learns there, among other things, to kill with her body,
to take on a variety of identities and to survive as one who
has Escaped UET--always ready to protect herself.
Rissa manages to ruin the life of the man who had her
parents killed, and to escape Earth, her wealth from the lottery intact. Afterwards she reaches Number One, a planet

full of Escaped people, and immediately insults Provost Sta-
gon dal Nardo, who forces her to fight him to his death.
While still in the fight arena, she marries the pilot of the
ship which brought her there, Bran Tregare, who happens to
be the son of Liesel Hulzein, the head of the Hulzein Establishment on that planet.   Though she, at that time, doesn't
know whether she can love him, Bran's position as a Hulzein
protects her from further challenges.   She learns that Bran's
dream, as an Escaped pilot from the UET academy, is to destroy UET, to return control of Earth to the people there,
and to rectify the Welfare situation.   Rissa insists that he
let her take an active part in his plans and becomes as respected by Bran's followers as he is.

        This saga of Rissa tells of a woman who takes care
of herself first, but who learns of love, who knows how to
and doesn't hesitate to kill people, but who grieves for them
afterwards, who enjoys being a mother but who never lets
motherhood keep her from changing the course of the world.
She is a hero who, after fighting her way up from the bottom,
and becoming the Chairman of the Board of Trustees of Earth,
learns she is a fifth generation Huzlein and has inherited a
position of power.   Rissa's story is a long one and one well
worth reading.   Her life is full and action-packed by her own
choice.   She is a strong, dynamic character who is both
compassionate and deadly.   An interesting facet of this work
is that women who are bruised, scarred, or mutilated in the
course of their fighting are not perceived as less attractive
or appealing by their lovers, but instead are loved for the
inner qualities which make them who they are.   (Zelde M'tana,
of the book by that name, appears in this work intermittently.
A synopsis of that work is in the 1980s chapter.)

*   BUTLER, OCTAVIA E.   Survivor.   New York: Doubleday,
      1978; rpt. New York: New American Library, 1979.

      Main Character: Alanna Verrick (or Lanna).
      Physical Characteristics: Is nearly two meters tall
and slender; has long black hair; had a daughter who was
killed; is Afro-Asian; is in her early twenties; is large boned.
      Mental/Emotional Characteristics: Struggles and ad-
justs to survive regardless of odds against her or cost to
her; is of strong mental fiber and has a strong self-concept;
is stubborn; is noble and loving (risks the hatred of her people in trying to save them); is a solitary person; is a "wild"
human on Earth between the ages of 8 and 15 (when her parents were killed and until she was captured by the Mission-

aries), and is still basically a "wild" person who demands
her freedom and knows how to survive; is a fighter; doesn't
believe the Missionary teaching about a God or a soul and
is disgusted by the double standard for women and men.

Story Particulars: The main character of this sf book,
as the title suggests, is a survivor. She is a child called
"wild" on Earth because at age eight she is orphaned and is
forced to fend for herself for seven years. Alanna learned
in those years how to lie, steal, appear to conform, forage
for food, toughen physically--to survive. The impact of that
time on her life and personality is permanent. The Missionaries who find her try to change her ways, to get her to accept their beliefs. To survive, Alanna pretends conversion
and conforms to their customs. She becomes with them what
she later calls a mental chameleon without losing herself.

When the Missionaries take a space ship from Earth
to another earth-like planet, they take Alanna with them. The
intelligent, fur-covered beings ("animals" the Missionaries
call them) who inhabit the planet are, in shape and size,
much like humans, and call themselves the Tehkohn and the
Garkohn. Their remarkable fur changes color to reflect their
emotions as they talk, and to camouflage them in the hunt.
When at rest, or at ease, the beings have a natural color
which tells their job or status.

The Garkohn, warring against the Tehkohn and wanting the Missionaries as slaves, addict the Missionaries to
the meklah tree (fruit and leaves) and force submission by
threatening withdrawal. When Alanna is captured by the
Tehkohn, she is taken off meklah because they abhor the ad-
diction. She is then asked to mate with their leader, the
blue-furred Tehkohn Hao called Diut. She agrees to the liaison when she is told she will be free among the Tehkohn after her training in their skills and customs. Her subsequent
affection for Diut and her pregnancy by him almost totally
convert her to the Tehkohn way of life. She becomes a
fighter, a hunter, and a respected member of the Tehkohn
group.

When Alanna and a number of Tehkohn are captured
by the Garkohn, Alanna's child is killed in the process. Diut,
who was also captured, tells Alanna's foster father, who is
the leader of the Missionaries, that they must suffer withdrawal from the meklah (death is one possible result) to free
themselves from the Garkohn, because the meklah tree doesn't
grow where they will be going to escape. Alanna's survival
philosophy aids her in her triple-deception role and she becomes the key person in the conflict between the three groups.
Her decision about which group she will stay with at the book's
end reflects where her real loyalties lie.

The book is written not in chronological order, but in a mixture of times (not really flashbacks), and partly in first person by Alanna and by Diut, and partly in third person. In spite of--or perhaps because of--the blend of speakers and times, the book makes interesting reading. Alanna's survival ability makes her truly heroic.

* CARR, JAYGE. Leviathan's Deep. Garden City, NY: Doubleday, 1979; rpt. New York: Playboy Paperbacks, 1980.

Main Character: The Kimassu Lady, called Val by Neill (after a Valkyrie, a "sword-maiden").
Physical Characteristics: Is a little taller than a tall Terren (sic) male; is bald; doesn't have the orange pigmentation in her skin as do the rest of her race, but is "pallid, bleached-pale" and considers herself "loathsome"; is not allowed to reproduce because of her skin color; has tawny-colored eyes; laughs by hissing; is amphibious; is strong; has six fingers on each hand and webbed toes; has a smile-like expression which is, in reality, threatening.
Mental/Emotional Characteristics: Is a Lady of the House of Morningstar; is an expert at "opening minds" of people who are unwilling to disclose information; is contemptuous of cowardly, begging behavior; has a collection of "boys" who work for her and sleep with her on command; is a specialist in Terrene torture; rose to her position by "diligence and wit and force of personality"; is intelligent; had been self-conscious of her color in the past but came to deal with it; is determined to help her people survive, even if it means disobeying the orders of the Goddess; sets a high standard of honor for herself; is full of purpose; has strength of mind; hates Terrens; has courage; calls herself a "cloud-walker, earth-shaker, sea-drainer, temple-destroyer."
Story Particulars: In a future time, there is a world called Delyafam by its intelligent, orange-skinned, bald, amphibious inhabitants. On this planet, controlled and run by the female population, the Kimassu Lady is a specialist in Terren (sic) interrogation and torture. She, like other powerful females on her planet, has her household, her "boys," as they are called. But unlike others on the planet, Kimassu has no orange pigmentation in her skin and her pale complexion made her feel like an alien among her own people as she grew up. She learned to accept her difference and to succeed in spite of it, a quality which quite possibly is the reason she becomes the key person in the survival of her race and her planet.

Kimassu hates the Terrens who visit her planet, but her hatred is tempered when she gets to know Neill, who fondly calls her Val (after a Valkyrie, who, she is told, was a sword-maiden who "chose the bravest of the brave" after they fell in battle to fight at the "Battle at the end of Time"). From Neill she learns the concept of war and discovers that the Terrens want to take over her planet. She also learns that in Neill's world, it is the females who are submissive and controlled by the males. Her total disbelief that this could even be possible is most convincing in this first person narrative, and her internal debate and reasoning continue as an important thread throughout the book.

When Kimassu takes Neill to a deserted island to protect him from the death her people have planned for him (he commits a sacrilege by touching those Bound to the Goddess), he tries to rape her and is shocked to learn that she cannot be raped. It is that factor in her species which has placed the females in control of the males. She is likewise shocked to learn that Terrene females can be raped and begins to understand why things developed differently on the Terren planet. Neill, however, introduces a new concept to her--partnership. She learns to think of him as a friend, "a mind delectable to explore, a dear, loving comrade," and she finds that she will never again be content with boys "who could never grow into men."

In the book, she is taken captive by the Terren Admiral Alexei Gorky who desires her as his mate--with the emphasis on the possessive "his." Although this appalls her, it also gives her insight into the effect the social structure of her own people has on the male population. Her escape from him costs her a hand and part of her arm, but it sets her free to begin to make the changes necessary to save her race. She learns from her experiences how to go about making her planet uninteresting to Terrens by making it unprofitable. The final pages of the book deliver an ending (or a beginning) that is powerful and perhaps unexpected. The Kimissu Lady, although alien to human culture, is a dynamic and fascinating individual.

★ CHARNAS, SUZY McKEE. Walk to the End of the World.
New York: Ballantine Books, 1974; rpt. New York:
Berkley, 1978 and 1979.

Main Character: Alldera (doesn't appear until a third into the book, but is the main character of this book and of Motherlines, New York: Berkley, 1978).

Physical Characteristics: Has wide jaw and cheekbones, "wide-set eyes of an unremarkable pale hazel color,
a nose that had been broken and healed flat-bridged, and a
heavy-lipped mouth with a sullen turn to the corners"; has
skin of a "dirty coppery cast"; is unusual for a "fem" in that
she could speak and "her legs and buttocks were strongly developed" (an illegal, speed-trained runner); is not beautiful;
has small breasts; has had two "kit-cubs" (female infants)
but didn't stay in the milkery long because she had so little
milk.

Mental/Emotional Characteristics: Hates men and is
disgusted by their touch; hides her intelligence behind a mask
of dull stupidity; loves to run; is tired of "this process of
figuring out the subtlest, safest course to take" with men;
has a trained memory so she can do her work as a messenger; remembers every song she's ever heard; would like to
run away to the "heart of the Wild" if she believed that free
fems actually existed; is not allowed to use "I" in speaking
with men; considers men who want to sexually please women
to be perverted.

Story Particulars: In this book, when the "predicted
cataclysm" comes, only those officials with access to shelters
survived.   All were white and most were male.   The few
women who survived were blamed for the disaster and told
to keep to themselves and be quiet.   The women agree to do
as the men say for the time being (after all, the men were
sick with guilt and grief, they reasoned), but that time lengthened and to men, women became the "unmen," the "enemies
of men."   Women, considered by men to have no souls,
eventually became cattle used for physical labor, bearing
stock for future generations, and some few for pets for
wealthy men.   Male children are separated from women at
an early age and raised by men in Boyhouses so to remove
the harmful female influence from male children.

Into this world is born Alldera, a fem who is a speed-
trained runner and messenger.   She learns to hide her intelligence from men, a trick which has saved her from beatings
and sexual encounters many times.   She is chosen by Servan
d Layo to travel with him and his male lover, Eykar Bek,
to find Bek's father.   For a man to try and identify and locate his father is strictly taboo, so it is a dangerous under-
taking.   On the trip, the group learns that riots have started
due to the food shortage that year, and that 'Troi, their destination, is likely to be attacked because they are reported
to have stockpiled food.

Bek, injured and carried in a camper on the shoulders
of six fems, insists on hearing Alldera's life history, which

she carefully edits. Alldera hides the fact that she has a mission--something unheard of for fems. Her mission on this journey is to prevent the slaughter of the fems who call themselves The Pledged. They are a group dedicated to fighting men to the death if more fems are culled (killed) because they are not docile. Alldera, though in sympathy with them and faintly hopeful that they will succeed, is realistic enough to realize that they, too, would be killed. In order to prevent that, a scheme is devised to send the runner Alldera to pretend to ask help of the free fems, who she doesn't believe exist. It is hoped that this anticipation of outside assistance will prevent The Pledged from making any aggressive moves.

Unfortunately, a crisis situation develops, The Pledged, Alldera must assume, are probably killed, and Alldera learns she has no place to call home. Her conversations with Bek figure prominently in the story, as he turns out to be a reluctant sympathizer to the fem plight. Both Alldera and Bek learn to say no to the system as it exists.

Though Alldera is not introduced until a third into the novel, her position and actions are at the crux of the work. The sequel, Motherlines, chronicles her new life, alien to her past, but promising a future filled with hope. Together, these books, written by a feminist, paint a future world in which the men are homosexual and become insulted if they are called "fem-lovers," and the women lead either brutally harsh lives without dignity, or rebellious lives with danger or death as the probable reward. The fems Alldera finds in Motherlines are colorful, tough, pragmatic, proud warriors who ride horseback--the antithesis of the fems she left behind.

★ CLAYTON, JO. Diadem from the Stars. New York: Daw Books, 1977.

Main Character: Aleytys (nicknamed Leyta), which means "wanderer" in her mother's tongue.

Physical Characteristics: Has "fine red hair" that is really red-gold in color, and "blue-green" eyes; will live a particularly long life because of her Vryhh bloodline; strong "beyond the ordinary"; has a "brown-amber face."

Mental/Emotional Characteristics: Is a "Xenopath" and is "gifted" in "esper" skills; is an "empath," can "mind touch" animals, can see through their eyes, and can heal them with her mind; can burn with her touch; is "claustrophobic" and wants no "ties" like marriage; has an exceptional "memory, faster than ordinary reflexes"; has "an instinct

for ... machines" and learns "languages in minutes rather
than weeks"; has "endurance" and "cunning"; is a "survivor
type"; can heal herself and others with her powers; has
"courage, generosity, even a little wisdom" at her young age;
with the help of the diadem, she can cast time-spells to slow
time; wants to fix it so she doesn't "have to depend on anyone else again for anything."

Story Particulars: This book is the first in a series
about young Aleytys, the red-haired esper who is half Vryhh.
In this book, Aleytys, who still lives in her father's household on the planet Jaydugar, is disturbed by the two facts
that she is the only one in the valley with red hair and that
she is treated cruelly by most of the people in the household.

As the story unfolds, sentiment against her skyrockets
when a spaceship crashes on the planet. Her lover, Vajd,
tells her about her mother, the red-haired Vryhh named Shareem, who crashed on Jaydugar many years before and was
bought by Azdar while ill and unable to defy her captor.
Azdar took her to bed many times until Shareem was well
and, by then, she was pregnant with Aleytys. After Aleytys'
birth, Shareem escaped, leaving the young Vajd with a letter
and a book for Aleytys when she is ready for them. When
Aleytys learns that she is to be burned as a demon, she
makes her escape, following her mother's instructions to
find an operable space beacon.

During her journey, while pregnant with the child she
and Vajd created, she learns of more of her esper skills,
finding that she can control animals, heal wounds, burn with
her hands if angry, and speak an alien tongue within moments
of hearing it. When she catches a cold, she is carried off
by Tarnsian, a cruel caravan leader whom she'd helped in
the past, and is raped repeatedly by him. She finally escapes
from his camp but is tailed by him. It isn't until she is
found by a group of witches and is given the diadem, a con-
struct of "fine golden wires, spun into a half dozen exquisite
flowers around jeweled hearts" set with "singing stones,"
that Aleytys is finally able to defeat Tarnsian. The fact that
the diadem is stuck on her head, a permanent fixture, horrifies Aleytys, but she calms herself and asks the witches to
take her to the location where the ship beacon should be according to her mother. Along the way, she meets Stavver,
the thief who stole the diadem from the RMoahl, intelligent
spider-like creatures, and they join forces to get off world.
Their narrow escape from Jaydugar and the RMoahl at the
book's end is the beginning of Aleytys' adventures as a wanderer in space, which is appropriate as her name means
"wanderer" in her mother's tongue.

In the books that follow, she loses and relocates her
son Sharl, continues to discover her powers, learns that the
diadem (and now her head) contains three imprisoned souls,
and becomes a Hunter for the Company. These books shouldn't
be overlooked by readers searching for a character who is a
strong, space-wandering individualist with esper powers. (The
series so far includes the following: Lamarchos, 1978; Irsud,
1978; Maeve, 1979; Star Hunters, 1980; The Nowhere Hunt,
1981; and Ghosthunt, 1983, all published by Daw Books. Another in the series is already being written.)

★ EISENSTEIN, PHYLLIS. Shadow of Earth. New York:
    Dell, 1979.

Main Character: Celia Ward.
Physical Characteristics: Is twenty years old; has
"long blond hair," pale skin, blue eyes, and is slender.
Mental/Emotional Characteristics: Has a flair for
languages and speaks French, Italian, Portuguese, and Spanish (with "a distinct Argentine accent"); tutors people in language to help pay her way through college; is curious, inquisitive, and intelligent; has a nervous breakdown while in the
"parallel world"; learns to be devious, to plan in advance;
learns to make her own decisions.
Story Particulars: In Chicago in the not-too-distant
future, Celia Ward, who lives with her parents, is preparing
to enter her senior year of study at Northwestern University
after spending her summer tutoring Larry Meyers in Spanish
and having sex with him on their breaks. Her discovery of
guns carefully hidden under his closet floor plunges Celia into
a world of danger in a "parallel world" in which the Spanish
settled on the continent instead of the British. Rather like
a mad scientist, Larry, who is in his sixth year of graduate
study, has built a piece of equipment that propels people and
matter into a "parallel world"--one of the "alternate prob-
abilities" which might have occurred "if" any of thousands
of factors had been different.
Larry takes Celia into the world of Spanish rule in
North America with the assistance of his activator/belt and
pays to have her killed to protect the secret of his invention.
He, in his greed, is taking advantage of the fact that there
are only limited weapons in that "parallel world" and is sup-
plying the people with guns and ammunition so they can start
wars. Thanks to the greed of the hired killers, Celia is not
murdered, but sold as a slave and then auctioned off to Rio,
a lute-playing trovador who takes her to a wealthy Marques.

His Grace, the Marques, has been hunting for a blond beauty
like Celia to have blond sons by, and takes Celia, an unwilling, unhappy victim, to his bed repeatedly until he is certain
she is pregnant. Celia is disappointed that Rio turned her
over to the Marques, but continues to see him and finds she
cares deeply for him. It is Rio who tells her that Larry had
not been killed by their attackers, but had hired them to kill
her.

In spite of the relatively good treatment Celia receives
as the Marques' betrothed and later as the Marquesa, Celia
hates her life there, filled with embroidering, knitting, and
confessions to the padre. As a prisoner who is not allowed
to leave the Palace, Celia doubts that she can ever return to
her own world until the arrival of Larry as a prisoner, still
with his activator-belt, renews her hopes. After Larry's
death from pneumonia and Celia's recovery from a nervous
breakdown (caused by Larry's death and by Rio disbelieving
her story about the "parallel world"), Celia decides she must
escape. She plots her escape weeks in advance, carefully re-
questing odd foods at all hours which must be purchased from
vendors in town so that guards would be unsuspecting when
she, dressed as a maid, leaves one evening, supposedly to
get the Marquesa some special delicacy.

Her struggle to survive her year in the parallel world
and to return to her own world, although successful, changes
Celia's life, and probably the lives of everyone in the "parallel world" as well. Celia, initially a dependent woman
who has never been forced to take on very much responsibility, matures in her year of slavery and pregnancy into a
woman who will never again allow someone to make her decisions for her. She tells Rio that she wants to manage her
own life, to pursue her own future, and to live "without fear
of the fever" which she had because of her pregnancy. Celia
is also glad to return to her Morning-After Pills so that she
will once again have sexual freedom without pregnancy, a
control over her own body which she sorely missed in the
"parallel world."

*   HOLLAND, CECELIA. Floating Worlds. New York:
      Alfred A. Knopf, 1976 (©1975); rpt. New York: Pocket
      Books, 1977 and 1979.

      Main Character: Paula Mendoza.
      Physical Characteristics: Is short and 29 years old;
grew up in Havana; has "kinky red-gold hair," a pointed chin,
and "eyes tipped up at the outer corners"; is called "cat-faced"
by a lover; has "mouse-brown" colored skin.

Mental/Emotional Characteristics: Plays the flute; is
the daughter of the late Akim Morgan (well-known behaviorist)
and of an architect; speaks Styth (the language of the mutants
of Uranus and Saturn); is philosophically an anarchist, but
wants peace at all costs also; is capable of the secrecy and
subversion necessary to make a good spy; is intelligent, brave,
and highly controlled; is seemingly very cool emotionally, but
is sexually active with both Styth and human males.

Story Particulars: This novel is an epic, both in its
length (it is easily long enough for two or three novels of
average length) and in its heroic characterization of Paula
Mendoza. Born in a future earth world where Manhattan is
a museum half a mile below the ocean's surface and the cities are enclosed in domes because the outside air is polluted,
Paula becomes dissatisfied with her life: her job on the Committee for the Revolution (which is called simply the Committee), her lover, Tony, and the prospects of having his child
and spending the next 20 years in the same rut she's in now.
Her work for the Committee, translating Styth (the only other
language still spoken in the solar system), opens for her an
opportunity for change; Paula becomes the pregnant mistress
of a Styth Akellar.

The Styth, mutants, and considered "genetic pollution"
by some, plan to become the rulers of all the solar system
and consider themselves, because of their normal height of
seven feet and their strength, to be the "natural masters" of
the earth people. Saba, Paula's Styth lover, who already has
several wives (and whom Paula refuses to marry), agrees to
a truce with the Committee on the condition that he take Paula
back to Uranus with him as a lover for a period of ten years,
which was Paula's idea to begin with. (The reader is never
openly informed of Paula's motives in this plan, and the Committee is also doubtful of her loyalty, but her strong, peace-
loving anarchist views should be a big clue. As one Styth
says of her, "Part of her is everybody's enemy.") The truce
is agreed upon, Paula lives on Uranus, loosely maintaining
her status as a Committee informant and negotiator and watching her son mature in the harsh Styth society. When the
Styth, through their own leadership upheavals, decide to become aggressive once more, it is Paula who becomes the
key figure in a peace movement on earth.

The pivotal part Paula plays in Styth and earth politics
and agreements, the gradual changes in her relationship with
Saba, and other Styth and earth people, and the unexpected
end of this book make Paula a highly intricate and fascinating
woman, who, throughout the book, affects everyone touching
her life. She is truly a character of epic proportions.

* KILLOUGH, LEE. The Doppelganger Gambit. New York:
Ballantine Books, 1979.

Main Character: Janna Brill.
Physical Characteristics: Is "bony thin" and "one
hundred eighty-three centimeters of whipcord sinew"; has
pale skin and "smoky-blond" hair which is described as a
"lion's mane" in "thick curls"; can't tolerate alcohol.
Mental/Emotional Characteristics: Is strong-willed
and mentally tough; frequently swears "a string of profanities"
when angered; distrusts "intuition on principle, as emotional
and therefore unreliable"; intentionally chooses a hard life
rather than one of ease; is against relationships which require
"sacramental marriage"; loves her work as a police officer.
Story Particulars; In this police-investigated murder
mystery set in a future Earth time, Janna Brill, a tough law
enforcement officer (leo) with a grade of Investigator, nearly
loses Wim, her partner of five years, in their attempt to
capture some robbers. As it turns out, Wim, who is leaving
in a few weeks on a ship with his wife to colonize a planet,
is blind for life and Janna is assigned a new partner, Mahlon
Maxwell, better known as Mama, who makes it a point to
follow his intuition and ignore department regulations. Janna,
as senior officer, struggles to control the towering bald black
man in their investigation of the death of Andy Kellener, a
philanthropist executive involved in the arrangement of galactic colonization voyages. Kellener's partner, Jorge Hazlett,
is motivated by greed when he arranges for the installation
of less expensive equipment for a number of colony ships--
equipment which, at least in the case of the ship called the
Invictus, is inadequate for the job and fails, costing innumerable lives. Jorge is a bright, if dangerous man, and
kills Andy when he refuses to falsify the computer records
of the transactions. In order to provide himself with an
ironclad alibi, Jorge hires someone to find him a double who
purchases a number of items on his credit, using a plastic
fingerprint, while Jorge is killing Andy.
When Mama and Janna go out on the case, Mama in-
tuitively knows Jorge is the murderer and Janna, in spite of
her objections, gradually decides that he is right. Janna's
tough and thorough police work gives them almost all the leads
they need to prove Jorge's guilt, and their unorthodox tailing
and confrontation of Jorge make the difference and nearly cost
Mama his life. In spite of the insistence of Wim and his
wife, Veda, that Janna join them in their trip to colonize
another planet, and Janna's near-loss of Mama, Janna realizes
that police work is what she's best suited for. "I'm a leo,
Wim, blood and bone."

Interesting touches in the book are legalized drugs,
the references to heterosexual and homosexual people as "het"
and "ho," and floatcars that inspire the squad commander's
use of "sail" instead of "roll" when sending the "lions and
she-lions" out on duty. Rape is no longer a criminal charge
but is prosecuted as a battery. In addition, Janna has a
"cohab" by the name of Sid and an old lover by the name of
Paul, with whom she refused to have "a sacramental marriage."
Janna Brill is a tough "leo" of the future who loves her work.

★ LEE, TANITH. Drinking Sapphire Wine. New York:
      Daw Books, 1977.

Main Character: Unnamed in this first-person "auto-
biography," so will be called "she/he" as mentioned in the
transcriber's note in the front of the book.
Physical Characteristics: She/he is "predominantly
female," however is living in a society where suicide results
only in a body change. She/he begins the book in a male
body like those of "consumptive" poets with "masses of loosely
curling dark hair, slight and graceful builds, aquilinity of fea-
ture, and large shadow-smudged blue opals for eyes...."
She/he spends the majority of the book as a female with a
beauty which "draws its charm from a measure of imbalance."
She/he has "a slim, agile body, ... excellent muscle tone,
long legs, long fingers, breasts not too large.... Good bone
structure in a face light and versatile...." Her/his skin is
"tawny-tan," her/his hair straight and "one shade fairer"
than her/his skin, and she/he kept the eyes of the poet,
"large blue opals."
Mental/Emotional Characteristics: She/he is "inclined
to violence, chivalry, and general moodiness" as a male or
a female. As a female her/his maternal urge returns occasionally. She/he is vain; as described by a lover, "There
is something about your unique brand of boorish, arrogant
stupidity that ties me up in a bow. So adventurous, so cyn-
ical, such a funny combination of valor and cowardice, idiocy
and intelligence." While still in the city, she/he haunts the
History Museum, delving into old records; she/he is a misfit
in the Jang (teen) circles, a loner, and therefore bossy.
("Loners need to be bossy. They quickly learn it's the only
method they have of shoving people off their backs," says an
android of her.) She/he describes her/himself as "emotional
and impulsive."
Story Particulars: She/he lives in a society where
robots (also Q-Rs, short for Quasi-robots, or androids) are

caretakers of the human race.   Suicide to a human meant
only that a Limbo robot would gather together the pieces and
place the life spark in another body, memory still intact.   In
this world, there are children, Jang (adolescents), and Older
People.   The period of Jang, which is what she/he is in,
lasts up to half a century, and is a time when adolescents
explore ecstasy (a drug-induced euphoria) and marriage.
Marriage is required before sex and can be set at a time
period lasting from an afternoon to a vrek (400 days).   Jang
have their own slang, used to such a degree that it is almost
a language in and of itself.

        She/he, a misfit in this suicidal, drug-taking, slang-
using group, haunts the History Museum (quite alone, as no
one else is interested in history), digging up antiquated words
and codes of honor.   She/he, unfortunately, discovers the
word "duel" and is challenged to one over Danor (a woman
friend she/he is a lover to while in her/his male body).   It
is the result of this duel--to the death--that gets her/him
exiled from the city by the Q-Rs (Quasi-robots).   When she/
he leaves her/his body-changing, lover-friend Jangs, she/he
has a great deal of fear to overcome.   Humans at this time,
pampered and protected (and hated) by robots, have no exposure to life outside the city, for the most part, a desert
wasteland, and are generally fearful of open spaces, loneliness, and other life on the planet.   However, in her/his new
female body, her/his maternal instinct reasserts itself, and
her/his attempt to adopt a small desert pet she/he calls
Gray-Eyes results in the explosion of her/his "provision-
dispenser" which showers the surrounding desert with "combined semi-synthesized food and ready-mixed water."   When
the desert suddenly bursts into blossom with the moisture of
the unexpected shower, she/he sets to work to make that
growth a lasting garden paradise.

        A flash (news bulletin) on her/his garden spot, meant
by the robots to discourage other people from also leaving
the city, has the effect of bringing a trickle of Jang and
Older People out from the city to live in or near her/his
garden.   In spite of this, she/he is still lonely.   A final
revealing betrayal of the robots and the resolution of her/his
loneliness climax this book.

        Glossaries of Jang Slang, General Terms and Conven-
tions, Institutions, and Devices open and close the book.
This novel is not only enjoyable reading, but funny, too.
(This is actually the second book about this character.   The
first, Don't Bite the Sun, also published by Daw Books, precedes the action of this book and was printed in 1976.   It
covers her first trip to the desert, her first pet, and the
beginnings of her discontent with Jang life.)

* McCAFFREY, ANNE. Dinosaur Planet. New York:
Ballantine Books, 1978.

Main Character: Varian (shared with Kai, male main
character).
Physical Characteristics: Is tall (1.75 meters); has
a slender but muscularly fit body and a trim waist; is a vegetarian (as all "civilized" people are at the time of this book);
has gray eyes and springy dark curly hair; is a young woman.
Mental/Emotional Characteristics: Is interested in
everything; is a xenob vet and avidly curious about alien life-
forms ("Making friends with alien creatures is my business.");
is a Disciple of Discipline (personal defense training in which
the mind controls the body's reactions and strengths--training
which is required by the Exploration and Evaluation Corps of
the Federated Sentient Planets for leadership); is gaily happy,
bubbling with humor; can argue "pleasantly and effectively
without losing her temper or wit"; has a ready laugh; is repulsed by killing and blood-lust; is capable of rage at people
attacking intelligent life forms.
Story Particulars: Explorers and evaluators, Varian
and her co-leader Kai, both Disciples of Discipline and lightweights, lead both lightweights and heavy-worlders in their
work on the planet Ireta. In the midst of the identification of
flora and fauna and the search for new energy sources, the
lightweights begin to suspect that the heavy-worlders are re-
verting to their hunting/killing/meat-eating ways. As evidence
grows to support this theory, Varian and Kai grow increasingly uneasy. Rumors flow that they have been "planted" or
left stranded to survive and reproduce on this alien planet as
communication has been cut off.
Two interesting things about this novel are the Theks
and the expletive language. The Theks are "a silicate life
form, much like a rock and extremely durable, and though
not immortal, certainly the closest a species had evolved toward that goal." Unfortunately for the reader, there are no
Theks on the planet Ireta, and communication with them is cut
off early in the book due to some sort of storm. The expletive language in this book is unique. A few curse words or
expletives are "raking ramjets," "scorch it," "fardles," and
"muhlah," with variations such as "too scorching old," "scorch
the raker," and "what in the name of raking."
Sexual advances for the lightweights, at least between
Kai and Varian, are initiated by the male with the silent ac-
quiescence of the female. However, the two do lead as equals
with a ready exchange of information and ideas. The lightweights, at least, fully recognize their joint leadership and

respect it.   Among the lightweights, respect was high for
Varian's capabilities as both a xenob-vet and a leader.   Varian performs her duties with enthusiasm and usually has a
light-hearted attitude.   It is this contrast between the positive,
light-hearted Varian, and the destructive, negative attitudes
of the heavy-worlders which makes the actions of the heavy-
worlders seem so wantonly destructive and cruel at the book's
end.

* McINTYRE, VONDA N.   Dreamsnake.   New York: Hough-
     ton Mifflin, 1978; rpt. New York: Dell, 1979.   (The
     first chapter of this novel, "Of Mist, and Grass, and
     Sand" was first published in Analog, Oct. 1973; rpt. in
     Women of Wonder, ed. Pamela Sargent, in 1974 by Vintage
     Books, in The Best of Analog, ed. Ben Bova, in 1978 by
     Baronet, and in The Road to Science Fiction #4, editor
     James Gunn, in 1982 by The New American Library.)

     Main Character: Snake.
     Physical Characteristics: Has short black curls; has
arthritis as do all healers.
     Mental/Emotional Characteristics: Is a healer using
snakes to help her heal people; willing to drive herself physically if saving a life is involved; is "proud and self-reliant";
is courageous, passionate and compassionate; feels tears are
a good release of emotion for both women and men; enjoys
casual sexual encounters, but prefers a partner she can
"share with" rather than one who is "grateful to her"; has a
strong sense of responsibility and is committed to her life
as a healer; has self-respect; loves her snakes and hates to
see the wasting of any life form.
     Story Particulars: In a future earth world, when the
effects of a nuclear war have nearly dissipated, Snake is a
healer who uses serpents to aid her in her work.   Although
healers are mountain people, Snake chooses to go to the desert for a portion of her proving year, and there, while healing a young boy with a tumor, suffers the loss of her dreamsnake Grass, a rare off-world snake which eases the pain of
one dying.   The healers have been unable to get the dreamsnakes to reproduce on earth and the healers have been able
to successfully clone only a few, one of which was Grass,
cloned by Snake.   Arevin, one of the desert nomads and probably the future leader of his people, is attracted to Snake,
and she to him, but Snake, now crippled as a healer without
Grass, must return to her teachers to tell them of her loss.
     On her trip, she meets several people who affect her
life deeply, one of whom is Melissa, a fire-scarred twelve-

year-old child whom Snake adopts to protect her from further
sexual abuses and beatings from her guardian. The beautiful
mountain people with whom Melissa lives are uncomfortable
looking at her disfigured face, in spite of her skill as a horse
trainer. Snake, knowing she must try to find a way to replace
the dead dreamsnake before returning to her teachers, risks
her life as well as Melissa's in her effort to do so. She is
followed and attacked several times by a "crazy" who, it
turns out, is after the dreamsnake she no longer has. The
crazy, once captured, is helpful in leading Snake and Melissa
to a place where many dreamsnakes live.

Arevin, who feels compelled to help Snake, goes to her
teachers in the mountains and tells them that his people were
to blame for the death of Grass. He finds that they are not
unforgiving, but merely unable to replace the dreamsnake to
make Snake's ability to heal whole once more. He sets out
once more in search of Snake and fortuitously is at the right
place at the time when Snake and Melissa need him the most.
Snake's success at finding dreamsnakes and her realization
that as off-world creatures, their mating differs from that of
earth serpents, ensures growth in the ranks of the much-
needed healers and wins her a freshly-hatched dreamsnake.

A number of interesting future-world concepts are expressed in the book, among them bio-control by both women
and men to prevent unwanted pregnancies, and the difference
in customs between desert and mountain people. Desert people give their names only to friends, and mountain people are
sexually very free with one another. For example, Arevin
is shocked by the openness he meets in the mountains, where
sexual companionship is offered by saying, "Is there anything
I can do for you?" The images struck in this book remain
remarkably clear long after a first reading, and Snake is a
hero, worth her weight in healing snakes, who is not soon
forgotten. ("Of Mist, and Grass, and Sand" won the 1974
Nebula Award for best novelette and took second place in the
1974 Hugo Awards in the same category. The novel won both
the Hugo and Nebula awards for best novel in 1979.)

* McINTYRE, VONDA N. "Screwtop," in The Crystal Ship.
    Ed. Roger Silverberg. Nashville: Thomas Nelson,
    1976; in The New Women of Wonder. Ed. Pamela
    Sargent. New York: Vintage Books, 1978; in Fire-
    flood and Other Stories. Boston: Houghton Mifflin,
    1979; rpt. New York: Pocket Books, 1981.

    Main Character: Kylis.

Physical Characteristics: Is about 20 years old; has short black hair and auburn-colored skin; has a "silver tattoo on the point of her left shoulder" which signifies acceptance by spaceport rats ("people who sneak on board starships and live in them and in spaceports"); has scars on her back from being whipped in prison.

Mental/Emotional Characteristics: Is independent and self-sufficient in the past, but now cares for two men, and sometimes feels "exposed and vulnerable"; can be stubborn; is too experienced to be an optimist; was driven away from home by fighting, hitting parents and became a spaceport rat at age ten; still hallucinates occasionally due to the sensory deprivation she was tortured with in prison.

Story Particulars: For ten years, Kylis has led a life of freeloading as a spaceport rat. Then she goes to a planet where she is caught, put in the prison Screwtop, and made to work in a drilling pit on the hot, wet equator of the planet Redsun. There she gradually changes her independent, self-sufficient ways and allows herself to care for Gryf and Jason, two men who are also prisoners. Jason is a famous author who has been imprisoned under another name, and Gryf, a product of genetic experimentation and a native of Redsun, is being pressured to hold a particular job for the government which he refuses to do. They can't be said to be a happy threesome because they are in prison, but they do manage to make life a little more bearable for one another.

Kylis is surprised by her concern and need for these two men and is uneasy with her vulnerability because of them. At the novella's beginning, Jason has just gotten off his shift, prepared for his one day off from labor every forty days, and he and Kylis comfort one another. Kylis is still recovering from her punishing stay in the sensory deprivation box, which resulted in hallucinations, and Jason, who is not physically built for the demanding labor required of him, is exhausted. Kylis, who got off from an earlier shift and took her rest then, leaves him to sleep and shifts her concern to Gryf, who is always taking on other workers' loads.

As the day progresses, Kylis finds herself adding a third person to her concerns in spite of her past history of not caring for anyone but herself. She becomes sympathetic towards Miria, another prisoner, and after seeing her secretly crying, impulsively asks her to join their group, and to eventually escape with them. Miria refuses the offer, and later Kylis sees her go inside the office of the prison warden, Lizard, unhampered by the guards, and naturally suspects her of being one of the camp's many spies. Kylis fears she has exposed Jason and Gryf to punishment by telling Miria that they, too, plan to escape.

Later in the day, Kylis is approached by Lizard about her becoming his sex partner and the mother of a child for him. She flatly refuses and remains steadfast in spite of her subsequent imprisonment in a cell. Oddly enough, it is Miria, supposedly a spy, who makes the difference for the threesome and offers Kylis the first real hope that she has had in a long while.

This story presents the reader with a fascinating, believable view of hard labor in a prison camp on an alien planet, full of sweat, torture, hard work, too little food, parasites and jungle dangers. Kylis is a character with a strong will to live, who, nonetheless, almost gives up hope.

* MAXWELL, ANN. Change. New York: Popular Library, 1975.

Main Character: Selena Christian or Selena of the Spirit (called Golden Eyes by Mark).

Physical Characteristics: Has "golden eyes, " and long "lustrous dark hair"; has a body with "finely turned curves"; is a "Branlow mutant" with "paranormal powers" (a "paran"); is 26 years old and slow to mature physically.

Mental/Emotional Characteristics: Is a "paran" (slang for paranormal) which means her "response to every type of stimulus is exaggerated" (pleasure and pain thresholds, sexuality, hunger/thirst etc.); has very "superior intelligence"; has precise empathy with animals; has dreams of "a strange desolate planet" inhabited by "cat-like" beings that have telepathy or empathy; has a "flawless" memory; has "acute invasion phobia" which means she refuses "to give up any control" of her actions "to another person"; can't be hypnotized because she distrusts people so much; is called "damned stubborn"; is willful which gives her "the strength" to push herself "to the limit" of her "potential"; discovers she is a "natural healer"; is mature enough to admit when she's wrong.

Story Particulars: In the twenty-first century, an epidemic of mutations started and continued on into the century of this book. One mutation, called the Branlow mutation, caused yellow eyes and paranormal powers, called "paran" for short. The "normals" feared and hated the Branlow mutants, and tried to kill them all. As a result, a planet, appropriately named Paran, was secretly populated by parans and normals "to develop any and all paranormal abilities" and was headed by an exceptional paran, Mark Curien.

Scheduled to die by order of an Earth court, and supposedly tricked by Mark into confessing she is a paran, Selena

Christian is snatched from the jaws of death and taken to
Paran.   There she is given extensive tests to determine the
extent of her paran ability and is assigned wild Arabian horses
and wolves to work with since she has an exceptional empathy
with them.   Her progress with the animals is rapid partly
because of her mixed feelings about Mark who is still on
Earth as a spy.
      Her initial fumbling attempt to mind-speak with Mark
from Paran results in his incorrect assumption that she is
a spy trying to identify him as a spy to an Ear (paran re-
ceiver) on Earth.   Shortly after, Mark and three other parans
are captured, two of whom are killed slowly.   Mark, however,
and another paran escape and return to Paran, and Selena
avoids his presence by taking some of her animals into the
mountains.   She is recalled when one of the cat-like creatures she has dreamed of is brought to Paran by Rhanett,
one of the alien Rynlon pilots who has been helping transport
the Earth-bound parans to Paran.   On her way to the creature,
Selena passes Mark who appears to be very friendly with another woman and is hurt by what she sees.   Emotionally in
pain, Selena encounters the cat-like creature who wraps her
tail around Selena and telepathically comforts her.   Mark
realizes how he's hurt Selena and wants to be physically and
telepathically close to her, but Selena fears his contact and
insists that she return with the cat-like creature she's named
Shimm to her own planet to further develop her paran powers.
      Selena discovers on Shimm's planet, named Change,
that she is a natural and quite powerful healer.   She is told
that Change is gradually killing all of the Changlings due to
the planet's sharp axial tilts and food shortages.   Selena is
recalled to Paran when Tien, the leader of the anti-paran
movement on Earth, plans to attack Paran.   All of the parans
but Mark are to be removed to Rynlonne for safekeeping.
When Selena arrives on Paran, she finds Mark dying, and
joins with the four Changlings who returned with her to heal
him.   That is the turning point in their relationship, and the
beginning of a joint struggle to save Paran from Tien and to
find a planet for the Changlings.
      Called Golden Eyes by Mark, Selena, though alien to
the "normal" human because of her abilities, is a thoroughly
likeable and admirable character, one who tries valiantly to
overcome her one major flaw: her fear, not of love, but of
losing love as she had lost her parents' love by their death.

*   PAUL, BARBARA.   Bibblings.   New York: The New
      American Library, 1979.

Main Character: Valerie (Val) Chester.

Physical Characteristics: No physical description given as this was a first-person narrative.

Mental/Emotional Characteristics: Has a sense of humor about her work and the aliens she meets; is the leader in meeting and greeting the aliens; is a contributor of ideas and options; occasionally gets in a mood about the fact that she feels they have no right to interfere in alien lives but gets over that mood quickly; is a "blunt talker" rather than a diplomat; is an admitted manipulator of aliens in her efforts to help them; is full of ironic quips and piercing insight, and recognizes and pokes fun at human self-righteousness and other shortcomings; is resilient.

Story Particulars: In a future time, Valerie Chester is the group leader of what has been ironically nicknamed the Anglo-Saxon Invaders, a team of Earth descendants more officially called the Chester Commission of the Diplomatic Corps of the Federation of United Worlds. She, her pilot husband (Adam), and four other team members are given assignments on troubled planets. Their job is to solve whatever problem the planet has. On this assignment, they are sent to Lodon-Kamaria where the greedy Federation Council says there are rich deposits of the mineral alphidium, which is an interstellar ship fuel. There is also a war between the Lodonites and Kamarians which is taking place in the mountains where the deposits are buried, thus making mining of the mineral impossible. The team is stunned on their arrival on the planet because the Lodonite half of the planet's population is insane--burning buildings, raping, dancing mechanically (as though they had eaten ergot-infested rye and were taking an LSD trip). The only portion of the population immune to the insanity is the neuter gender who feed the effected group and provide them with sleep-producing liquor.

A quick trip across the mountains assures the team that the Kamarians are quite sane--and covered with very friendly birds they call bibblings. It isn't until the bibblings leave the area that the Kamarian also become insane, and the team finds that it is not invulnerable to the disease. It is only the sterile team member, Justin, who is unaffected, and who saves their lives by taking them across the mountain once more to follow the migration of the bibblings. The war, it seems, is caused by the people trying to follow the migration of the birds against the will of whichever people happen to have them at the time. Substance X, carried by the bibblings, reacts with hormones to cause the madness, and anti-X, also carried by the bibblings, cures it.

The solution is fairly simple, and the team doctors

set to work on a vaccine with which they promise to inoculate everyone--as soon as peace is declared. The peace talks between the two warring commanders, though not smooth, are eventually successful, though sabotage and war (under the guise of commercial competition) remain with them. Says Valerie of them "They'd traded one kind of sickness for another."

Valerie, throughout the book, thinks and speaks with heavy irony, tempered by realistic tolerance of the inevitable and unchangeable. She has rare "who-the-hell-do-we-think-we-are moods" which she recovers from quickly. As leader of the team and the one known for her "blunt" talking, Valerie wisely maintains a sense of humor throughout her experiences. In fact, the first person narrative can hardly be read without an occasional smile or laugh. Valerie is a well-adjusted, realistic team leader who views strange or difficult situations with her own unique brand of ironic humor which she shares with the reader.

* PISERCHIA, DORIS. Star Rider. New York: Bantam Books, 1974.

Main Character: Lone (her mount's name for her) or Jade (Valdar's name for her).

Physical Characteristics: Is a jak (an offshoot of the human race called Jakalowars--"he who races with the stars"); is a Ridge Runner (a jak from the Ridge Cluster, a place where infant jaks and mounts were abandoned); is about 14 years old, "big, muscular, yellow-haired, black-eyed."

Mental/Emotional Characteristics: Is able to jink (get the aura of a thing close up and swarm all over it with her mind); is a hedonist; is intelligent enough to solve riddles that no one else has solved; curses freely at her mount and others; feels she is too tough to cry; makes room in her head for anyone who loves her.

Story Particulars: Lone and her mount/partner Hinx are like other jaks and their mounts: able to jink (get the aura of a thing close up and swarm all over it with their minds) and skip (go into another dimension and "skip" to somewhere else). They are hunting for the legendary planet Doubleluck, supposedly a rich planet, with streets lined with gold and lakes of perfume. When they stumble across Big Jak and he tells them he knows where Doubleluck is and wants them as partners, Lone foolishly believes him and narrowly escapes entrapment on Bounding Winter, a planet where homeless adolescent jaks are dumped when they get in the way.

In spite of her narrow escape, Lone is far from
through with Big Jak. From him, she receives the new name
of Jade, gains an awakened sexuality, and hears several stories.
One of these stories is about people living on an island in
despair because they couldn't get to other islands. So someone came up with the idea to hide a jewel to provide the people with something to search for nearby. This, they think,
will remove the longing for the other islands--as long as no
one discovers the jewel is no jewel. Jade is not dumb, but
the reader doesn't know she understands this allegory until
late in the novel when she searches for and finds the planet
of the varks (flying creatures able to skip with no mount).
Once there, she talks to the varks about "going to glory"--
skipping out of the galaxy or, in other words, getting off the
"island." And she realizes she is the key to enabling the
jaks to leave the galaxy. Why else would everyone be trying
to kill or imprison her?
     In her next confrontation with Big Jak (whose real
name is Valdar), he calls her a "do-gooder" for wanting to
find other jaks to skip the galaxy. But Jade continues her
plan to organize willing jaks, mounts, and varks for a grand
skip. Valdar admits to being under the employ of the varks
as a watcher and later, in the midst of their skip across
space to another galaxy, admits he loves her. The varks,
by the way, have hope that the human race is growing up
and make the skip with them. Jade matures from a willful,
cursing adolescent to a jak holding much promise.

*   RANDALL, MARTA. Islands. New York: Pyramid
    Books, 1976; rpt. New York: Pocket Books, 1980.

     Main Character: Tia Hamley.
     Physical Characteristics: Has "drug-resisting" body
which refuses to accept the "Immortality Treatments" and is,
therefore, old in a time when no one else ages; has a "flat
stomach crossed again and again by lines, breasts hanging
low but never large enough to make much difference"; has a
"wrinkled" rump, "sinewy and shrunken" thighs and "skinny,
skinny arms ending in big, square, capable hands"; has a
face which is "weathered around brown eyes, skin dried and
lined as driftwood, hair streaked with grey and dry from constant exposure to the sun"; is sixty-seven years old at the
book's beginning but flashes back to as early as age 14; is
1.6 meters tall.
     Mental/Emotional Characteristics: At age 14, she ex-
periences "a transcendental merging of individual and absolute

truth" and discovers that she is elated and joyful in her existence, that she is "sufficient" in and of herself; is angry
and bitter that her body would not accept Immortality Treatments; as a mortal among Immortals, feels isolated like a
freak and deals with the awkward brushes with Immortals by
being sarcastic and distant.

Story Particulars: Young Tia Hamley, who is all too
mortal, lives in an era when seemingly everyone else has
been successfully made Immortal. Unfortunately, her treatments failed to work. Angry and bitter, she runs away from
her love, Paul Ambuhl, and spends the next fifty years trying
to survive the reality of her mortality with new experiences,
new encounters, forever aware that the Immortals were both
repulsed and fascinated by her.

At the book's beginning when Paul reappears in her
life with his lover, Jenny Crane, Tia (now a wrinkled sixty-
seven-year-old) has flashbacks about her life. She recalls
the moment she became aware of herself as a unique individual, sufficient in and of herself. She also recalls a lover
with whom she experimented with a drug which first opened
the doors of her ability to monitor her own body, an ability
which fascinates her doctors. Now, at sixty-seven years old,
she spends her time diving for relics on a sunken island in
the Pacific Ocean near her home, a relic in itself with its
fixed walls, solid furniture, sculptures, old paintings, hand-
woven rugs, and woodburning fireplace.

Tia also feels like a relic as the sole and rather popular patient of an entire branch of medicine--geriatrics--and
is understandably surprised when Paul, an Immortal who will
forever be youthful in appearance, wants to have sex with
her. What she doesn't realize, however, is that Paul is attracted to her because of her link with mortality. In reaction
to his fear that Tia has died during a dive, he talks her
through a sexual encounter which borders on necrophilia,
horrifying Tia. Though she has had sexual encounters with
women before, Tia is not physically attracted to Jenny, but
does find herself liking her, a fact which surprises Tia.
But what fascinates and compels Tia the most is finding her
own key to immortality. When she stumbles upon an airtight
chamber in an underwater city, she discovers the final key
she needs to make a transition into a new level of awareness.

In spite of Tia's anger and bitterness, and no small
dose of distrust of the motivations of others, she is an intelligent, strong, dynamic character with mystical inclinations
and a passion for discovering an immortality of her very own.
(This novel was nominated for a 1977 Nebula Award for best
novel.)

* RUSS, JOANNA. <u>The Female Man</u>. New York: Bantam
  Books, 1975; rpt. Boston: Gregg Press, 1975.

<u>Main Character</u>: Janet Evason.
<u>Physical Characteristics</u>: Is a "Safety Officer" (S &
P or Safety and Peace); is about 40 years old; has "fought
four duels" and "killed four times"; has "fair" hair which is
"streaked"; is from Whileaway, which is one possible form
of "the Earth ten centuries from now" where there have been
no men for nine centuries because of the plague; has a "big
ass" and "callouses on the feet"; is "white-skinned" and tall;
is hardy with "sun-bleached hair" and "muscles"; has none
of the ailments that Jeannie and Joanna are prone to have.
<u>Mental/Emotional Characteristics</u>: Handles her af-
fairs with "hard-headed innocence"; loves and works with the
"same exalted, feverish attention fixed on everything"; weeps
"those strange, shameless, easy, Whileawayan tears. "

<u>Main Character</u>: Jeannine Nancy Dadier.
<u>Physical Characteristics</u>: Is a librarian, 29 years old,
and has sex with Cal even when she doesn't want to; is "a
long-limbed, coltish girl in clothes a little too small for her";
is "white-skinned" and "tall. "
<u>Mental/Emotional Characteristics</u>: Enjoys hiking and
"being a girl"; can be talked into buying what she doesn't
want; is comfortable fading into woodwork and walls, and
would be happy to be "relieved of personality at last and forever"; thinks she ought to get married and sometimes believes
in astrology, palmistry, and occult signs; sees herself as
lonely and is a "coward. "

<u>Main Character</u>: Joanna.
<u>Physical Characteristics</u>: Had a poor appetite until
Janet appeared; is "white-skinned" and "tall. "
<u>Mental/Emotional Characteristics</u>: Before Janet's ar-
rival, her life revolved around "The Man" and all she did
was done in an effort to impress or interest him; thinks she
made Janet up; has good senses of "female irony" and "female teeth. "

<u>Secondary Character</u> (secondary only in that she enters
the story late in the book): Alice-Jael Reasoner (also initially
called "The Woman Who Has No Brand Name" and has the
code name of "Sweet Alice").
<u>Physical Characteristics</u>: Has "silver hair" and eye-
brows, "silver" eyes, a "lined face, " a "rather macabre
grin, " a "crooked, charming smile, " steel teeth with fake

"real teeth" for show, and "almost crippled hands" with "folds
of loose, dead skin" over a set of surgically-implanted
"Claws"; is "an employee of the Bureau of Comparative
Ethnology, and a specialist in disguises"; is "white-skinned"
and "tall"; is capable of "voluntary hysterical strength" in
which adrenaline is intentionally pumped into the body to attain a killing strength; is "an assassin" who never gives
"warning."

Mental/Emotional Characteristics: Is "truly violent,"
and has "independence of mind"; as an assassin, she "must
decline all challenges" because her job is not to show off
her killing ability; resists "curiosity, pride, and the tempta-
tion to defy limits"; hates men; takes the "easiest way out
whenever possible"; defines her "art" as "slow, steady, responsible work."

Story Particulars: It is difficult to call any one of
the four women characters of this novel the main character
(all are called "Everywoman"); however, most of the first
person narrative is from Joanna's (Russ's?) point of view.
The story is about four women who are "less alike than identical twins ... but much more alike than strangers have any
right to be." They are their "other selves out there in the
great, gray might-have-been." Janet is from the "far future," Jeannine and Joanna are from "almost the same moment of time," and Jael is from a near future time, though
none of them are in the same world.

Janet, "an official ambassador" from idyllic Whileaway (which has no men) and secretly their "savior from utter despair," is happy "living as she does in a blessedness
none of us will ever know," though she frequently gets emotionally depressed also.

Jeannine, still living in a prolonged economic depression, is compelled at age 29 by everyone she knows to marry
anyone she can find, and almost succumbs to the pressure
until Jael appears in her life.

Joanna, who lives in a world much like our own, attends cocktail parties, has a "pink book" of "WHAT TO DO
IN EVERY SITUATION" (to match the blue book carried by
men), but on occasion expresses with "divine relief" her "female irony" and uses her "female teeth." (In fact, the whole
novel is an expression of that poignant irony and those honed-
on-hard-truth teeth.)

Jael, assassin and man-hater, coordinates the "J" con-
vention to "do business." She wants to enlist their help in
the war in her world, the war between "the Haves and the
Have-nots," "Us and Them"--between the men and the women.

She needs to find places for the women of her world "to re-
cuperate and places to hide an army," places to store their
machines, places to get raw materials, and, most important,
"places to move from--bases that the other side doesn't know
about. "
    This feminist novel is written from varying points of
view, each character expressing her own feelings and thoughts
about the life she lives, and the men (or lack of men) with
whom she must contend. This novel, in this author's opinion,
will be hard to beat for character studies of women in a variety of societies and for a fearless feminist statement in the
genre of sf. (This novel was nominated for a 1976 Nebula
Award for best novel.)

★ RUSS, JOANNA. We Who Are About To.... New York:
    Dell, 1975; Boston: Gregg Press, 1978.

    Main Character: unnamed (first person, "recorded
on a pocket vocoder").
    Physical Characteristics: Wears body-suits and san-
dals; looks like "little, dark, Sephardic Jews"; is 42 years
old and 1. 50 meters tall.
    Mental/Emotional Characteristics: Is a musicologist
and travels a lot in the course of her lectures; is a "scrounge";
hides "pharmacopoeia" in her neckband and belt; is a filcher,
a "Trembler" (a religion or attitude which has as its principal subjects "work and mortality"; they call themselves "No-
bodies"); is a vegetarian; is arrogant and pro Death in an
uncivilized world.
    Story Particulars: The basic story line--space travel-
ers marooned on an unknown, but inhabitable world with no
chance of rescue--has been approached by authors in many
ways, but not one, in this author's opinion, has been as
unique as this one. The unnamed hero, who will be called
"she" here, prefers death to trying, against all odds, to survive on an alien world. She provides the four other women
and three men with a multitude of reasons why survival on
the alien planet is impossible. The usual plan to propagate
the species (impractical for so small a gene pool) rears its
ugly head, and she, deciding she can't stand becoming a
"walking womb," leaves before she is forced into sex and
child bearing. She records, "You must understand that the
patriarchy is coming back, has returned (in fact) in two days.
By no design. You must understand that I have no music,
no books, no friends, no love. No civilization without indus-
trialization. I'm very much afraid of death. But I must.
I must. I must. "

She isolates herself from the rest in a cave, 240 ki-
lometers from the camp, but part of them come after her,
call her mad, and promise to take her back to camp and imprison her.   She, in her desperation, kills all of them but
one, Cassie.   (And Cassie requests one of her drugs for instant death and leaves to kill herself.)   She returns to camp
alone and kills the remainder of the group, and once more
isolates herself in the cave, waiting for death.   There, visited by all of the marooned group and an old love via hallucinations, she begins to see all those she has killed as helpless sparrows and suffers tremendous guilt and self-hate for
her actions.

The end of the book, though definitive, gives the reader
room for a variety of reactions.   Russ has provided, in this
book, rich fodder for self-discovery and debate on the subject
of death.

★   RUSS, JOANNA.   "When It Changed, " in <u>Again Dangerous</u>
    <u>Visions</u>.   Ed. Harlan Ellison.   Garden City, NY:
    Doubleday, 1972; in <u>The New Women of Wonder</u>.   Ed.
    Pamela Sargent.   New York: Vintage Books, 1977; in
    <u>The Zanzibar Cat</u>.   Sauk City, WI: Arkham House, 1983.

Main Character: Janet.
Physical Characteristics: Is 34 years old, 1 meter
80 centimeters tall in her "bare feet, " and scarred from
fighting three duels ("a fine line that runs from temple to chin").
Mental/Emotional Characteristics: Is rational and
perceptive, "with the self-confidence of someone who has
always had money and strength to spare"; is unaware of what
it feels like to be "second-class or provincial"; has "popular
influence" as she is chief of police; is strong and not given
to emotional outbursts; is homosexual with no one playing "the
role of the man"; is worried about men coming to Whileaway.
Story Particulars: Human life on Whileaway was cut
in half 30 generations ago by a plague, which took with it all
males of the population.   Perhaps at first necessary as an
"economic arrangement, " as the Earth man from space tells
them, the women have since adjusted and learned that marriage, commitment, and child rearing among themselves (accomplished by a merging of ova) is a very happy arrangement.   They run their government, are professionals, radio
operators, machinists, farmers, etc., and have industry.
They number 30 million people.   They feel they need no men.
Enter four men who think they do.

The main character has difficulty even bringing herself

to shake hands with the "apes with human faces." The men talk to them about men coming to Whileaway and the advantages it will mean in "trade, exchange of ideas, education." They also tell the Whileaway citizens that "sexual equality has been reestablished on Earth," a statement Janet sorely doubts. Katy, Janet's wife (a mechanic), tries to kill one of the men with a gun, and Janet stops her. However, Janet agrees with Katy's intentions. Even Janet's "tactful child," Yuki, "whooped derisively" at the thought of falling in love with "a ten-foot toad."

Janet worries that she will be mocked, that Katy will be considered weak, that Yuki will be made to feel unimportant or silly. She realizes that once men arrive, her achievements will be considered "not-very-interesting curiosa ... things to laugh at sometimes because they are so exotic, quaint but not impressive, charming but not useful." Janet, more a hero than any man she's met, says in this story, "Take my life but don't take away the meaning of my life." (This story was the winner of the 1973 Nebula Award for best short story and took fifth place for a Hugo Award the same year.)

* SARGENT, PAMELA. "IMT," in Two Views of Wonder.
     Ed. Thomas N. Scortia and Chelsea Quinn Yarbro.
     New York: Ballantine Books, 1973; in Starshadows.
     New York: Ace Books, 1977.

Main Character: Lisa Fernandez.
Physical Characteristics: As a teenager, she had an "acne-scarred face," an "oversized nose," and teeth that never saw a dentist. Now she's in a loveless marriage, is in her late thirties, is of Spanish descent, had one child who was killed at age 12 in a collapsing subway tunnel, and is city manager of New York City. She is called "a gutter rat" to her face by an enemy.
Mental/Emotional Characteristics: Has imagination and foresight; can "make decisions and get things done"; learns things quickly; understands the problems of the city from firsthand experience; scratches her fingernails on her desk when tension gets too intense; is able to control her emotions even when pressured by the press; sometimes doubts her own ability to handle a situation, but always rises to the occasion when the time comes.
Story Particulars: The cities, now prisons and traps, are dying. People can't get to work on time for poor transportation and overcrowding, but even those who leave are

forced to return for employment. As city manager of New
York, Lisa, born and raised in the slums of that city, asked
a committee for help. What she was given was a plan for
an instantaneous matter transmitter (IMT), and she decides
to sit on it. She knows its release would mean a continua-
tion of the cities. Dan, her former lover, and assistant to
the mayor, fights for the release of the plans, not trusting
her judgment on the matter. When he finally does understand,
he decides to help her, but his initial distrust would be a
barrier for a while.

      Lisa has a vision of how the world could be and con-
tacts Russia and Japan to make them partners in the IMT.
But she realizes what others don't--that before its use, the
cities must die. And she realizes she is the one who is at
the right place at the right time to do the coordinating of the
entire operation. Lisa's husband, Ramon, is a dreamer and
won't work to put foundations under those dreams. Their love
is gone, and his leaving isn't even an event causing emotion
in Lisa. She even stifles a yawn when he tells her goodbye.

      There is one other female character, minor, but im-
portant in pointing to Lisa's compassion for people. She is
Linda Marat, Lisa's mentally retarded receptionist. She is
beautiful and dumb and is the perfect receptionist--she doesn't
listen to excuses or explanations because she couldn't understand them. Lisa admits that some men think she's the perfect woman: "She's beautiful and doesn't say much." Linda
is an excellent contrast to Lisa. Lisa is an insightful, strong
character who doesn't mind using "bastard" or "hell" at
times. She sometimes doubts her own abilities but always
comes through in the end. Lisa is a visionary individual
and is in a position to do something about her visions. She
also has the courage to do it.

★ SHELDON, RACCOONA (Alice B. Sheldon). "Your Faces,
     O My Sisters! Your Faces Filled of Light!" in
     Aurora: Beyond Equality. Ed. Vonda McIntyre and
     Susan Anderson. Greenwich, CT: Fawcett, 1976;
     James Tiptree, Jr., in Out of the Everywhere. New
     York: Ballantine Books, 1981.

     Main Character: no name given.
     Physical Characteristics: Thinks she is "a walking
sister," a courier for the sisters in the midwestern United
States; has "slim strong legs," a "tough enduring wiry body,"
and short brown hair; is "medium-height" and young.
     Mental/Emotional Characteristics: Wants to act re-

sponsibly as a courier; is happy with her life, sees good in people, and feels free; is "proud of the vitality in her"; has headaches and "bad hallucinations" but insists to herself she is "well"; thinks men are "sick" and "so different from the good natural way"; is "completely trusting" and believes "everybody is her friend."

Story Particulars: This story is sf only in the mind of the unnamed woman main character (who will be called "she" here). She is a married mother of one child, an "affluent young suburban matron" who completely loses touch with the realities in her life and is committed to, then escapes from, a mental hospital. In her mind, she lives in a world containing no men and is a courier for the sisters, a messenger who is free and happy in her travels on foot. She believes the world is now safe, a "beautiful peaceful free world," because men no longer exist in it. "They were sick, poor things," she thinks.

In her travels, she meets a variety of "sisters" (as there are no men in her world, she sees all people as sisters) with whom she chats openly. The people she meets talk about her after she's gone on her way, thinking she is either crazy or on drugs. A woman police officer says of her "A spoiled brat if you ask me, all those women's lib freaks." Oblivious to people's opinions of her, the story's hero is happy and free, and according to one woman she meets in her travels, "fun." That woman's husband responds, "That's the sick part, honey."

Our hero is horrified when she remembers the history of women, a history in which women were treated like a "caged-up animal." She thinks of what it must have been like. "Don't go outside, don't do this, don't do that, don't open the door, don't breathe. Danger everywhere." When she thinks about this kind of past for women, she gets severe headaches, but most of the time she walks happily along, a "courier going west" to Des Moines from Chicago, openly greeting sisters she meets along the way. Fortunately, the story's very real, very brutal conclusion does not force her back to the cruel reality she has managed to escape.

* TIPTREE, JAMES, JR. (Alice B. Sheldon). "The Women Men Don't See," in The Magazine of Fantasy and Science Fiction, Dec. 1973; in Warm Worlds and Otherwise. New York: Ballantine Books, 1975; in The New Women of Wonder. Ed. Pamela Sargent. New York: Vintage Books, 1977.

Main Character: Ruth Parsons.
Physical Characteristics: Was a "librarian" with
"GSA records" in "Foreign Procurement Archives"; has a
"tiny voice" and is "neat but definitely not sexy"; has had
some "first-aid training"; is about forty years old, "trim"
and "mousy"; is the daughter of a woman who never married
and has a daughter of her own under the same circumstances.
Mental/Emotional Characteristics: Remains "sane as
soap" in a crisis situation; is "stoic and helpful" and doesn't
complain in adverse situations; is "uninterested in together-
ness" with a man, and doesn't consider herself "very memorable"; maintains superb control over her anger; feels that
men are alien to her, and dreams of "going away."
Story Particulars: Ruth Parson, government librarian
and mother to Althea, wants to leave the world of men, a
world which is alien to her. She is seen through the eyes
of Don Fenton on an aborted plane trip to Chetumal. Captain
Estéban, Don Fenton, Ruth Parsons, and Althea Parsons
crash into mangroves at the end of a sandbar on the Carib-
bean. Stranded with no radio communication, there they
wait for rescue. Captain Estéban has been wounded and Ruth
uses the "little first-aid training" she's had on him. As
time passes, Don becomes increasingly aware of the fact that
the women don't complain, are "stoic and helpful" but definitely not "sexy." The women even insist upon sleeping out-
doors in the hammock rather than in the plane.
Don sees Mrs. Parsons (as he calls her) as a "Mother
Hen" about her daughter and is therefore surprised when she
wants to come with him into the thick growth to find fresh
water inland, leaving Althea alone with Estéban. Nonetheless, Don agrees and they find a fresh water stream near
"an alligator nursery." As it is by then almost dark, they
stay the night on the ground, next to each other, during which
time Don gets "aggressive notions" about Ruth on which he
doesn't act. He realizes her lack of fear of him had sound
basis. "If I were twenty years younger. If I wasn't so
bushed.... Mrs. Ruth Parsons has judged these things to a
nicety."
During the night, they awake to a harsh light held by
unidentified visitors, and their attempt to communicate is unsuccessful. The visitors leave them there alone once more,
but not before Don steps into a hole and injures his knee so
badly that they are forced to stay there another day and night.
During the next day, Ruth becomes increasingly agitated and
tense. As she fishes for them and brings Don water, she
distractedly answers Don's questions about herself and Althea,
telling him that she grew up "happily" without a father just

as Althea has, and that "women's lib" ("the lib") is "doomed."
She tells him, "Women have no rights, Don, except what men
allow us," and that with the "next real crisis," their "so-
called rights will vanish," Women's freedom "will be blamed."
for "whatever has gone wrong." She adds that she dreams
of "going away," then terminates the conversation.

Don is highly suspicious of her nervousness and her
willingness to stay there an extra night, thinking that perhaps
she is expecting someone to meet her there. He sees her as
alienated, therefore vulnerable to "some joker who's promising to change the whole world." Don confronts her with "Expecting company?" which visibly shakes her, and leaves Don
ready to make a run for it--away from "Mrs." Parsons and
her friends. At sunset, the visitors from the night before
arrive and Don realizes that they are "Extraterrestrials,"
in fact "Peace-loving cultural-exchange students--on the interstellar level." Ruth clutches to herself something they need
or want and asks their help. Don accidentally shoots her in
his efforts to protect her. Ruth tells him to stop and convinces the aliens to take them to the crashed plane. There
she picks up Althea and leaves, destination unknown, with the
aliens, leaving the confused Don with the memory of portions
of their last words. "For Christ's sake, Ruth, they're aliens!" he tells her. 'I'm used to it," she says absently.
(This story was nominated for a 1975 Nebula Award for best
novelette.)

* VAN SCYOC, SYDNEY J(OYCE). Saltflower. New York:
    Avon Books, 1971.

Main Character: Hadley Greer.
Physical Characteristics: Has a slim body, silver hair
that "hung across her shoulder like a silken animal" and that
"stirred sometimes of its own will," and silver eyes ("the
color of mercury"); has headaches that start in her head and
seem to send out rootlets until she recognizes them as barriers to finding out why she feels like an alien; is 17 years
old; in alien passion, her lips engorge with blood and her
hand throbs; has eyesight that is extendable which she calls
"reaching vision."
Mental/Emotional Characteristics: Has her doctorate;
has visions or flashes of another world; has two personalities:
one of the earth world she was born on and one that comes
at night when her silver hair comes alive and she feels called
to run on the salt flats; is determined to find out the reason
for the desert seeding and alien deaths; is passionate.

Story Particulars: In the year 2024, 17-year-old,
silver-haired, silver-eyed Hadley Greer steps out of her
everyday earth routine of dating Richard Brecker and working on her research project to find out why she feels like an
alien.   She has had innumerable flashes of another world, a
white one, and has headaches with these visions.   And she
knows that her hair (which moves of its own accord as if
having a life of its own) and her silver eyes have no match
on this planet--unless that match is Jacob Pastern, assistant
in the New Purification Colony in the Great Salt Lake Desert
in Utah, whose picture she has seen in the newssheets.   She
feels compelled to seek him out there.

On her trip she researches that desert and learns that in
1979, three space ships reportedly "seeded" the desert but
all that could be found by scientists was salt.   And she knows
that her mother, Marley Greer, was on that desert in 2006,
just before she became pregnant with Hadley.   Arriving at
the Colony, Hadley finds not only Jacob, but five children
like herself in appearance; they have knowledge of the white
world, too.

Dr. Braith, the mad leader and founder of the New
Purification Colony, creates a bizarre atmosphere for the
primarily elderly congregation of Sheep, leading the group
in prayers for the return of the three ships that seeded the
desert.   Richard, Hadley discovers, is not merely an ardent
suitor, but a Special Investigations Branch agent (SIBling) assigned to watch her because she is a transracial--the product
of both earth humans and alien beings.   An additional twist
is that 26 people have disappeared from the Colony and are
suspected by the SIBlings of being murder victims.   Richard,
ever the SIBling, has several suspects in mind.

The salt-crusted desert, stimulating "some near-
dormant area of her brain," awakens alien racial memories
in Hadley, sending her running to exhaustion across the salt
flats until she reaches the "place of visions," a portal to
what becomes known as Earth Two a world in which the
children can safely grow and multiply.

The fate of the alien beings, the reason for the desert
seeding, and the identity of the murderer all become clear in
the novel.   And Hadley discovers which of the two worlds,
the two races, and the two men is correct for her.

★   VAN SCYOC, SYDNEY J(OYCE).   "When Petals Fall,"
       in Two Views of Wonder.   Ed. Thomas N. Scortia
       and Chelsea Quinn Yarbro.   New York: Ballantine
       Books, 1973; in Best SF: 1974.   Ed. Harry Harrison

and Brian W. Aldiss. Indianapolis, IN: Bobbs-
Merrill, 1975.

Main Character: Kelta West.
Physical Characteristics: Is "tall, lean"; has "straight
brows," long, dark hair, and long thighs.
Mental/Emotional Characteristics: Is Federal Inspector for old age facilities, and quite probably a coordinator
for the Messengers of Mercy (those who infiltrate old age
homes and unplug the entire ward they are covering, thus
in effect, killing most of the people on that ward); is tough-
minded, precise, to the point, and decisive.
Story Particulars: Kelta West, in her capacity of a
Federal Inspector of old age homes, presents herself at Taylor-
Welsh nursing home at 2 a.m. to make a surprise inspection
of the ward most recently hit by the Messenger of Mercy.
This most recent action by the Messenger resulted only in a
60 percent loss of old people as opposed to the usual 95 percent loss, and Inspector West has come to investigate. What
she finds is a surprise: someone has been using the old people in this home for an experiment in a serum for immortality.
     Kelta meets with the facility director the next morning
and takes the client files, under protest from the director,
to a hotel where she is certain an investment company will
contact her to try and interest her in stock in nursing homes.
She is not disappointed, but the meeting has a bonus: the
developer of the serum also attends the meeting. Between
them, while Kelta secretly records the conversation, they
try to convince her that the old age homes and the serum
(which prolongs the body functions but not the brain functions)
are in the best interest of society. Her very convincing
"personal" response is that there isn't enough water for everyone now, and that there's too much poor air and radiation.
She wears a radiation badge and intimates that due to a radiation accident fifteen years before, she is devoting her life
to a career or a social cause because she can't have normal
children. She tells the men that the homes were started
"because their clients were human beings," but that now the
homes are full of "objects" instead. She adds that it's time
for the older generation to move over and give "a clear field
for the next generation to deal with these problems."
     After the meeting, Napp, the man who is recording
this conversation by remote control, confronts Kelta with his
suspicions that she is the coordinator of the Messengers.
Kelta doesn't deny or admit her involvement, but the reader
is convinced of her dedication to what she believes in. And

Napp, in spite of his confrontation, is very much on her side. This very well-written story offers much food for thought on the subject of death.

★ VARLEY, JOHN. Titan. New York: Berkley, 1979.

Main Character: Captain Cirocco ("Rocky") Jones.
Physical Characteristics: Is taller than most men and has a "hatchet" nose; is 34 years old and is "not black, but not white either."
Mental/Emotional Characteristics: Has few friends, but is "fiercely loyal" to those she has; doesn't "cry easily, nor often"; likes "space, reading, and sex, not necessarily in that order"; knows how to use hand guns and karate and can sing and dance; is bisexual "with a strong preference for the male sex"; is "highly intelligent," "individualistic" and "independent"; prefers an abortion to having a child at this time and situation in life; has always desired adventure and wanted "to do something outrageous and heroic"; wants love only if it leaves her freedom to act; enjoys cocaine when given the opportunity; would have been best suited as "an adventurer, a soldier of fortune" rather than a ship captain.
Story Particulars: Cirocco ("Rocky") Jones is a woman filled with a passion for adventure; however, the only adventure open to her in this future Earth time is leading the crew of the DSV (Deep Space Vessel) Ringmaster on the first exploratory mission made by Earth in eleven years. It is during the mission that Rocky and her crew stumble upon a previously undiscovered moon of Saturn which they soon realize is a hollow, wheel-shaped object 1300 meters in diameter with enough spin to create one-fourth gravity on the interior surface.

In spite of their preparation for unknown dangers, they are still unprepared when the moon sends out tentacles, snatches them from their approach, and destroys their ship. After they have spent a year in comatose states, the crew emerges from the ground of this world at various locations on the interior, in various degrees of alteration. With the abundantly loving assistance of female crew member Gaby, who is now in love with Rocky, Captain Cirocco Jones begins a lengthy pilgrimage to the hub of this world. Along the way, she meets a variety of life forms including a blimp-like creature which furnishes air transportation in its stomach; innocently friendly, singing centaur-like creatures called Titanides who have loud, carousel-horse color combinations of hair and skin; and human-appearing "angels" who swoop down on their large wings to kill the friendly Titanides.

When she discovers that one of her crew is prepared to supply the secret of gunpowder to the Titanides, Rocky decides to seek out the supposedly all-powerful, god-like Gaea in the hub of this world to ask for peace for the warring angels and Titanides and for an explanation of the treatment which had been received by the Ringmaster's crew; however, she must leave her injured lover Bill in order to accomplish this. In making her decision to leave, Rocky learns that though she needs and wants his love, she finds it more important to have the freedom to act, to have her need for adventure filled.

Gaby accompanies Rocky on the journey to the hub, a journey which takes them nearly a year. Gaea, they discover when they reach the hub, is a 3,001,266-year-old intelligent life form who is the creator of all the life forms in this world and who is gradually, due to advanced age, losing control over her various lands. Rocky not only finds Gaea at her journey's end, but is recognized by Gaea as heroic, "an adventurer," and is offered the position of "Wizard" by her. Rocky, realizing that she isn't cut out for a desk job back on Earth, accepts the position as Gaea's representative on the rim, and begins her job by averting the bombing of that world by a rescue ship from Earth. Gaby stays on Gaea with Rocky and is made "Minister of Tourism and Conservation" by her.

Though not the main character, Rocky does have a major role in Wizard (New York: Berkley, 1980). This novel came in third place for a 1980 Nebula Award and was nominated for a Hugo Award.

*   VINGE, JOAN. "Eyes of Amber," in Analog Science
    Fiction/Science Fact, June 1977; in Eyes of Amber.
    New York: The New American Library, 1979.

Main Character: Lady T'uupieh; also called T'uupieh the Assassin, and Demon's Consort. (Main character status is shared with Shannon Wyler.)

Physical Characteristics: Is nobility on Titan, orbiting Saturn, though dispossessed of her lands at the story's start, and the leader of a band of outlaws; speaks in what is recognized as "music" on Earth, in "chords"; has an "almost flat profile," a "moon-white face," a "fragile mouth," "long, sharp teeth," "red pupilless" eyes, "crescent" nose-slits, and "wing membranes"; is a life form which is "nitrogen-and ammonia-based."

Mental/Emotional Characteristics: Has "nerve, and

cunning, and an utter lack of compunction"; is "carved from
ice" and is a "competent" killer and "a realist"; believes
that "Love is a toy" which she has put behind her.

    <u>Story Particulars:</u> Somewhere around the year A. D.
2000, an Earth probe is sent to Titan, which orbits Saturn,
and intelligent life is discovered there. The probe's " 'eyes'
or subsidiary units" fail to release properly on the probe's
descent, destroying the possibility of relaying varied information about the entire body. But the probe is not a total loss
because Lady T'uupieh, nobility dispossessed of her lands and
now leader of a band of outlaws, and a hired assassin, adopts
the probe as her own "demon" and carries an "eye" with her
everywhere. She waits patiently during the hour between
transmissions from the demon. Communicating through the
probe is Earth musician Shannon Wyler, who operates the
"IBM synthesizer" thus speaking to T'uupieh in the chords
of music that compose her language.

    The story opens on Lady T'uupieh's visit with the very
one who stole her lands, Lord Chwiul, in his townhouse.
Ironically, he hires her to kill his brother Klovhiri and his
brother's wife, Ahtseet, who happens to be T'uupieh's sister.
As T'uupieh hates Klovhiri, who helped Chwiul take her lands,
and feels contempt for her sister for marrying Klovhiri just
to keep the "family lands," she is more than willing to take
the job of killing them. Chwiul explains his plan to her of
leading them into an ambush where he can watch the assassination. Her reward will be Chwiul's townhouse, in other
words, part of her own property back.

    Shannon, on the Earth side of this latest news from
T'uupieh, is disheartened because she's already killed eleven
of her species in the past year. He decides to try and stop
her from killing this time and discusses morality and love
with her, much to T'uupieh's disgust. She counters his arguments with "How can one droplet change the tide of the sea?
It's impossible! ... There is no 'good,' no 'evil'--no line
between them. Only acceptance." T'uupieh closes the lengthy
conversation with the demon with a challenge. "I cannot change
tomorrow. Only you can do that. Only you." Shannon, exhausted from the long period without rest or sleep, is ready
to give up, but is encouraged by his mother, who is also "a
skilled engineer," and offers him a method to get around the
"time-lag problem" inherent in his communication with
T'uupieh.

    The next morning, when T'uupieh awakens, she grows
angry with the demon for not talking to her and strikes it,
only to receive an electrical shock as retaliation. The demon
then tells her his name, Shang'ang, which does not harm her

in any way, proving to her that she is truly "chosen" as the "Demon's Consort." Later, at the ambush, the demon warns the party to be ambushed that they are approaching a trap, angering Chwiul into a murderous rage. The demon strikes Chwiul dead as he attacks T'uupieh, saving her life, and returning her lands to her. (This story won the 1978 Hugo award for best novelette.)

★ WILHELM, KATE. Juniper Time. New York: Harper
   & Row, 1979; rpt. New York: Pocket Books, 1980.

Main Character: Jean Brighton (shared with Arthur Cluny, the male main character).
Physical Characteristics: Is 5'2" tall; weighs 100 pounds; has dark blue eyes and hair bleached almost white by the sun; has a body deceptively delicate looking; has "the scattering of freckles across her nose" and "the boyish way of moving with strides longer than women usually took"; becomes one with the desert and moves like a dancer.
Mental/Emotional Characteristics: Worked as a doctoral candidate on a computer terminal in a linguistics lab; was the "key" to the development of a method of translating a language with no Rosetta stone; says of herself that she is competent but not brilliant; others say she is brilliant on the computer; is honest; loves and is able to cry with her own hurt, and with compassion for others; after her brutal rape by three men, she becomes apprehensive when she hears someone approach; afraid of men most of her life until she comes to grip with her fears, becoming self-contained and assured.
Story Particulars: Jean's father was an astronaut who was killed in a space accident while she was still young. He tells her she has a gift or magic with words. When she matures, she attends college to get a doctorate in linguistics and finds she has a special talent with language computers.
   A worldwide drought drives people out of the areas hit the worst into newly populated places called Newtowns, towns filled with poverty, crime, despair, and no privacy. When Jean proves to be the "key" to her professor's research into translating language with no Rosetta stone, and when the government steps in because of the importance of the discovery, Jean leaves her job. After this her male roommate (with whom she is in love) leaves her, and Jean decides to go to a Newtown. There she is raped and beaten by three men. When she is physically recovered, she decides to go to her grandfather's old house in Bend, Oregon which he has

deeded to her. It all seems very familiar and comfortable
to her there, although most of the people have left and all
the trees but the junipers and sagebrush have died because
of the drought. She walks out into the desert to kill herself
and is saved, or rather stopped, by Robert Wind-in-the-Tall-
Trees. She lives with the Indians and learns oneness with
the desert. She gradually comes to grips with her fears of
her past and of men, and achieves self-containment and as-
surance.

Arthur Cluny, Jean's childhood playmate, meets the
changed Jean and is baffled by her. He finds he cannot manipulate her to translate the message the government has found
in space, but she decides to do it for her own reasons. Her
discovery of the meaning of the message, and her father's
connection to it, may be just what the world needs to decide
to join in a unified effort to solve the drought problem. At
the very least, it will buy the world time.

*   YARBRO, CHELSEA QUINN. "False Dawn," in Strange
     Bedfellows. Ed. Thomas N. Scortia. New York:
     Random House, 1973; in Women of Wonder. Ed.
     Pamela Sargent. New York: Vintage Books, 1975;
     story became first chapter of False Dawn. Garden
     City, NY: Doubleday, 1978.

     Main Character: Thea.
     Physical Characteristics: Is 27 years old; has "dark,
hard skin" which was "burned red-brown"; has "nictitating
membranes" that slide over her eyes, making her a Mutant
in a post-disaster Earth time; uses a crossbow for protection.
     Mental/Emotional Characteristics: Has always had to
fight for survival; fears rape and mutilation; is a self-contained,
solitary person.
     Story Particulars: Thea, a Mutant in a post-disaster
Earth time, travels cautiously through California, seeing
along the way not only human illness, vicious dog packs, and
killer water spiders, but also terrible rapes and mutilations
performed by the Pirates, packs of men who stole from the
people who were left and who hated Mutants like herself. She
overhears some Pirates talking about the death of Evan Montague, the former leader of the Pirates who had kept them
in tow and protected the Mutants to a degree. With the word
that Montague is dead and that a brutal man by the name of
Cox has taken over, Thea is certain that she will be raped
and killed if she doesn't leave the area and begins her journey
to safety.

Along the way, she finds a man in his forties in a silo, his right arm cut off with a chain saw by the Pirates the week before. Thea compassionately takes a chance and gives the man (who claims to be either Seth Pearson or David Rossi) penicillin from her pack. They decide to travel together but are accosted by Lastly, one of Cox's deserters who wants to travel with them. Lastly frequently threatens to rape Thea and makes it clear that he hates Mutants. Fortunately, Thea's only obvious mutation is the second set of eyelids she has, a mutation which isn't normally visible to others.

Distant dog packs eventually drive them into a summer cabin and Rossi is sent out to hunt for firewood. While he is gone, Lastly ties Thea to a bed and cuts her nipple, creating such pain in Thea that her nictitating membranes cover her eyes. Lastly, triumphant that he has a Mutant to brutalize, cuts off her nipple completely and proceeds to beat and rape her. Rossi returns and angrily slams Lastly's head against the wall, mortally wounding him. Thea, emotionally battered and vulnerable, tells Rossi she wanted him, and Rossi quietly admits that his name is Montague. They hear the approach of the vehicles of Cox and his men, and quickly flee together into the forest.

The novel continues with the trials, tribulations, and travels of these two characters as they search for a quiet place to settle together, for trust in each other, and for survival in an ecologically hostile environment.

ADDITIONAL READING LIST

Anderson, Poul. "The Bitter Bread," in Analog Science Fiction/Science Fact, Dec. 1975; in Best Science Fiction Stories of the Year, Fifth Annual Collection. Ed. Lester del Rey. New York: E.P. Dutton, 1976, and New York: Ace Books, 1977. (Not the viewpoint character but a main character nonetheless.)

_____. The Byworlder, serialized in Fantastic Science Fiction & Fantasy Stories, June and Aug. 1971; as a novel, New York: The New American Library, 1973; rpt. Boston: Gregg Press, 1978.

_____. A Stone in Heaven. New York: Ace Books, 1979.

_____. "The Ways of Love," in Destinies (Vol. 1, No. 2), Jan./Feb. 1979; in The Best of Destinies. Ed. James Baen. New York: Ace Books, 1980. (Not the viewpoint character but a main character nonetheless.)

Anthony, Piers (Piers Anthony Dillingham Jacob). Chaining the Lady. New York: Avon Books, 1978.

Arnason, Eleanor. "The Warlord of Saturn's Moons," in New Worlds Quarterly, June 1974; in The New Women of Wonder. Ed. Pamela Sargent. New York: Vintage Books, 1978.

Bear, Greg. "Scattershot," in Universe 8. Garden City, NY: Doubleday, 1978; in The 1979 Annual World's Best SF. Ed. Donald A. Wollheim. New York: Daw Books, 1979.

Benford, Gregory. "Old Woman by the Road," in Destinies, Nov./Dec. 1978; in The Best of Destinies. Ed. James Baen. New York: Ace Books, 1980.

Bradley, Marion Zimmer. The Ruins of Isis. Norfolk, VA: The Donning Company, 1978; rpt. New York: Pocket Books, 1979.

Brown, Rosel George. The Waters of Centaurus. Garden City, NY: Doubleday, 1970; rpt. New York: Lancer Books, 1971.

Cherryh, C. J. (Carolyn Janice Cherry). "Cassandra," in The Magazine of Fantasy and Science Fiction, Oct. 1978; in The 1979 Annual World's Best SF. Ed. Donald A. Wollheim. New York: Daw Books, 1979; in Nebula Winners 14. Ed. Frederik Pohl. New York: Harper & Row, Inc., 1980. (This story won the 1979 Hugo Award for best short story and took second place in the 1979 Nebula Awards in the same category.)

Clayton, Jo. Irsud. New York: Daw Books, 1978 and 1981. (A novel of the Diadem.)

_____. Lamarchos. New York: Daw Books, 1978. (A novel of the Diadem.)

_____. Maeve. New York: Daw Books, 1979. (A novel of the Diadem.)

Coney, Michael G. The Hero of Downaways. New York: Daw Books, 1973.

Cooper, Edmund. Prisoner of Fire. London: Hodder and Stoughton, 1974; rpt. New York: Walker, 1976.

_____. Who Needs Men? London: Hodder & Stoughton, 1972; retitled Gender Genocide. New York: Ace Books, 1972.

deFord, Miriam Allen. "Lone Warrior," in Two Views of Wonder. Ed. Chelsea Quinn Yarbro and Thomas N. Scortia. New York: Ballantine Books, 1973.

_____, and Juanita Coulson. "Uraguyen and I," in Cassandra Rising. Ed. Alice Laurance. Garden City, NY: Doubleday, 1978.

Dickson, Gordon R(upert). The Spirit of Dorsai. New York: Ace Books, 1979. (Both the story teller and one of the main characters are women.)

Dorman, Sonya. "Building Block," in Analog Science Fiction/ Science Fact, March 1975; in The New Women of Wonder. Ed. Pamela Sargent. New York: Vintage Books, 1978.

Effinger, George Alec. "How It Felt," in Universe 5. Ed. Terry Carr. New York: Random House, 1974, and New York: Popular Library, 1976; in Irrational Numbers. Garden City, NY: Doubleday, 1976.

Eklund, Gordon. "Stalking the Sun," in Universe 2. Ed. Terry Carr. New York: Ace Books, 1972.

Elgin, Suzette Haden (Patricia A. Suzette Elgin). The Communipaths. New York: Ace Books, 1970; in the collection Communipath Worlds. New York: Pocket Books, 1980.

_____. Furthest. New York: Ace Books, 1971; in the collection Communipath Worlds. New York: Pocket Books, 1980. (Woman is important secondary character.)

Ellison, Harlan. "Dr. D'arqueAngel," in Viva, Jan. 1977; titled "The Diagnosis of Dr. D'arqueAngel," in Strange Wine. New York: Harper & Row, 1978, and New York: Warner Books, 1979.

_____. "Killing Bernstein," in Mystery Monthly, June 1976; in Strange Wine. New York: Harper & Row, 1978, and New York: Warner Books, 1979. (Not the viewpoint character but the subject of the story.)

_____. "Sleeping Dogs," in Analog Science Fiction/Science Fact, Oct. 1974; in Best Science Fiction Stories of the Year, Fourth Annual Collection. Ed. Lester del Rey. New York: Ace Books, 1975; in Paingod and Other Delusions. Moonachie, NJ: Pyramid, 1975.

Emshwiller, Carol. "Debut," in Orbit 6. Ed. Damon Knight. New York: Putnam's, 1970, and New York: Berkley, 1970; in The New Women of Wonder. Ed. Pamela Sargent. New York: Vintage Books, 1978.

_____. "Maybe Another Long March Across China 80,000 Strong," in Joy in Our Cause. New York: Harper & Row, 1974.

Felice, Cynthia. Godsfire. New York: Pocket Books, 1978 and 1982.

_____. "No One Said Forever," in Millennial Women. Ed. Virginia Kidd. New York: Delacorte Press, 1978, and Dell, 1979.

Foster, Alan Dean. "Dream Done Green," in Fellowship of the Stars. Ed. Terry Carr. New York: Simon & Schuster, 1974; in Best Science Fiction Stories of the Year, Fourth Annual Collection. Ed. Lester del Rey. New York: E.P. Dutton, 1975, and New York: Ace Books, 1977.

Gaskell, Jane (Jane Gaskell Lynch). A Sweet Sweet Summer. New York: St. Martin's Press, 1972.

Girard, Dian. "No Home-Like Place," in The Endless Frontier (I). Ed. Jerry Pournelle. New York: Ace Books, 1979 and 1982.

Gloeckner, Carolyn. "Earth Mother," in Long Night of Waiting by Andre Norton and Other Stories. Ed. Roger Elwood. Nashville: Aurora, 1974; in Best Science Fiction Stories of the Year, Fourth Annual Collection. Ed. Lester del Rey. New York: E.P. Dutton, 1975, and New York: Ace Books, 1977.

Goldberg, Beverly. "Selena," in Cassandra Rising. Ed. Alice Laurance. Garden City, NY: Doubleday, 1978.

Goldin, Stephen. Assault on the Gods. New York: Doubleday, 1977; rpt. New York: Fawcett Crest Books, 1981.

Haldeman, Joe (William). "The Pilot," in Destinies (Vol. 1, No. 3), April/June 1979; in The Best of Destinies. Ed. James Baen. New York: Ace Books, 1980.

Henderson, Zenna. "The Believing Child," in The Magazine of Fantasy and Science Fiction, June 1970; in Holding Wonder. Garden City, NY: Doubleday, 1971, and New York: Avon Books, 1972.

_____. "Crowning Glory," in Holding Wonder. Garden City, NY: Doubleday, 1971, and New York: Avon Books, 1972.

_____. "Incident After," in Holding Wonder. Garden City, NY: Doubleday, 1971, and New York: Avon Books, 1972.

_____. "Love Every Third Stir," in Holding Wonder. Garden City, NY: Doubleday, 1971, and New York: Avon Books, 1972.

_____. "Sharing Time," in Holding Wonder. Garden City, NY: Doubleday, 1971, and New York: Avon Books, 1972.

_____. "The Taste of Aunt Sophronia," in Holding Wonder. Garden City, NY: Doubleday, 1971, and New York: Avon Books, 1972.

_____. "The Walls," in Holding Wonder. Garden City, NY: Doubleday, 1971, and New York: Avon Books, 1972.

Hoover, H. M. The Delikon. New York: The Viking Press, 1977; rpt. New York: Avon Books, 1978.

_____. The Lost Star. New York: The Viking Press, 1979; rpt. New York: Avon Books, 1980.

_____. The Rains of Eridan. New York: The Viking Press, 1977; rpt. New York: Avon Books, 1979.

Hughes, Zach (Hugh Zachary). The Legend of Miaree. New York: Ballantine Books, 1974.

Karl, Jean. "Accord," in The Turning Place. New York: E. P. Dutton, 1976; rpt. New York: Dell, 1978.

_____. "Catabilid Conquest," in The Turning Place. New York: E. P. Dutton, 1976; rpt. New York: Dell, 1978.

_____. "Enough," in The Turning Place.   New York:
E. P. Dutton, 1976; rpt. New York: Dell, 1978.

_____. "Over the Hill," in The Turning Place.   New York:
E. P. Dutton, 1976; rpt. New York: Dell, 1978.

_____. "Quiet and a White Bush," in The Turning Place.
New York: E. P. Dutton, 1976; rpt. New York: Dell,
1978.

_____. "The Turning Place," in The Turning Place.   New
York: E. P. Dutton, 1976; rpt. New York: Dell, 1978.

Kingsbury, Donald.   "The Moon Goddess and the Son," in
Analog Science Fiction/Science Fact, Dec. 1979; in The
Endless Frontier, Vol. II.   Ed. Jerry Pournelle and John
F. Carr.   New York: Ace Books, 1982.

Lee, Tanith.   The Birthgrave.   New York: Daw Books,
1975.   (This novel was nominated for a 1976 Nebula Award
for best novel.)

_____. Don't Bite the Sun.   New York: Daw Books, 1976.

_____. Electric Forest.   New York: Daw Books, 1979.

Le Guin, Ursula K(roeber).   "The Day Before the Revolution,"
in Galaxy, Aug. 1974; in More Women of Wonder.   Ed.
Pamela Sargent.   New York: Vintage Books, 1976; in
Galaxy: Thirty Years of Innovative Science Fiction.   Ed.
Frederik Pohl, Martin H. Greenberg, and Joseph D. Olander.   New York: Wideview Books, 1981.   (This story
was winner of both the Jupiter and Nebula Awards for
best short story of 1975.   It was also nominated for a
Hugo Award in the same category in the same year.)

_____. "The Eye of the Heron," in Millennial Women.
Ed. Virginia Kidd.   New York: Delacorte Press, 1978,
and Dell, 1979; published in hardback form under The Eye
of the Heron.   New York: Harper & Row, 1982.

_____. "The New Atlantis," in The New Atlantis and
Other Novellas of Science Fiction.   Ed. Robert Silverberg.
New York: Hawthorn Books, 1975; rpt. New York: War-
ner Books, 1976.

_____. "SQ," in Cassandra Rising.   Ed. Alice Laurance.

Garden City, NY: Doubleday, 1978; in The 1979 Annual
World's Best SF.   Ed. Donald A. Wollheim.   New York:
Daw Books, 1979; in The Compass Rose.   New York: Har-
per & Row, 1982, and New York: Bantam Books, 1983.

Leiber, Fritz (Reuter).   "Do You Know Dave Wenzel?" in
Fellowship of the Stars.   Ed. Terry Carr.   New York:
Simon & Schuster, 1974.

Lundwall, Sam J(errie).   "Nobody Here But Us Shadows," in
Galaxy, Aug. 1975; in The Best from the Rest of the
World: European Science Fiction.   Ed. Donald A. Wollheim.   New York: Daw Books, 1976.   (Not the viewpoint
character but a main character nonetheless.)

_____.   2018 A. D., or The King Kong Blues.   New York:
Daw Books, 1975.   (The woman character is one of several main characters.   The book was originally published
in Sweden in 1974 under the title King Kong Blues.)

Lynn, Elizabeth.   "Jubilee's Story," in Millennial Women.
Ed. Virginia Kidd.   New York: Delacorte Press, 1978,
and Dell, 1979.

McCaffrey, Anne (Inez).   "Daughter," in The Many Worlds of
Science Fiction.   Ed. Ben Bova.   New York: E.P. Dutton,
1971; in Get Off the Unicorn.   New York: Ballantine
Books, 1977.

_____.   Dragonsinger.   New York: Atheneum, 1977; rpt.
New York: Bantam Books, 1978.   (Part of the Harper
Hall trilogy.   The third in the series, Dragondrums, fo-
cuses on a male character.)

_____.   Dragonsong.   New York: Atheneum, 1976; rpt.
New York: Bantam Books, 1977.   (Part of the Harper
Hall trilogy.   The third in the series, Dragondrums, fo-
cuses on a male character.)

_____.   "Dull Drums," in Future Quest.   Ed. Roger El-
wood.   New York: Avon Books, 1973; in Get Off the Unicorn.   New York: Ballantine Books, 1977.

_____.   "The Greatest Love," in Futurelove: A Science
Fiction Triad.   Ed. Roger Elwood.   Indianapolis, IN:
Bobbs-Merrill, 1977.

_____. "The Thorns of Barevi," in The Disappearing Future. London: Panther, 1970; in Get Off the Unicorn. New York: Ballantine Books, 1977.

McIntyre, Vonda N. "Aztecs," in 2076: The American Tricentennial. Ed. Edward Bryant. New York: Harcourt Brace Jovanovich, 1977; in Fireflood and Other Stories. Boston: Houghton Mifflin, 1979, and New York: Pocket Books, 1981.

_____. The Exile Waiting. Greenwich, CT: Fawcett, 1977. (This novel was nominated for a 1976 Nebula Award for best novel.)

_____. "Fireflood," in The Magazine of Fantasy and Science Fiction, Nov. 1979; in Fireflood and Other Stories. Boston: Houghton Mifflin, 1979, and New York: Pocket Books, 1981. (This novelette was nominated for a 1980 Hugo Award for best novelette.)

_____. "The Genius Freaks," in Orbit 12. Ed. Damon Knight. New York: Putnam's, 1973; in Fireflood and Other Stories. Boston: Houghton Mifflin, 1979, and New York: Pocket Books, 1981.

_____. "The Mountains of Sunset, the Mountains of Dawn," in The Magazine of Fantasy and Science Fiction, Feb. 1974; in Fireflood and Other Stories. Boston: Houghton Mifflin, 1979, and New York: Pocket Books, 1981.

Malzberg, Barry N. "A Galaxy Called Rome," in The Magazine of Fantasy and Science Fiction, July 1975; novelized as Galaxies. New York: Pyramid, 1975, and Boston: Gregg Press, 1980.

Martin, George R. R. "A Song for Lya," in Analog Science Fiction/Science Fact, June 1974; in A Song for Lya & Other Stories. New York: Avon Books, 1976; in The Best of Analog. New York: Baronet, 1978, and New York: Ace Books, 1979. ("A Song for Lya" was the winner of the 1975 Hugo Award for best novella and took second place for the 1975 Nebula Award in the same category. Not viewpoint character, but a woman main character nonetheless.)

Maxwell, Ann. A Dead God Dancing. New York: Avon Books, 1979.

_____. The Singer Enigma. New York: Popular Library, 1976.

Monteleone, Thomas F. "Breath's a Ware That Will Not Keep," in Dystopian Visions. Ed. Roger Elwood. Englewood Cliffs, NJ: Prentice-Hall, 1975; in Nebula Winners Twelve. Ed. Gordon Dickson. New York: Harper & Row, 1978, and New York: Bantam Books, 1979. (This story was nominated for a Nebula Award in 1977 for best short story.)

Moorcock, Michael. The Adventures of Una Persson and Catherine Cornelius in the Twentieth Century, A Romance. London: Quartet Books, 1976; bound with Black Corridor. New York: Dial Press, 1980. (See Hilary Bailey's story on Una Persson in the 1980s reading list.)

_____. "Ancient Shadows," in New Worlds Nine. Ed. Hilary Bailey. London: Corgi Books, 1975; in Legends from the End of Time. New York: Harper & Row, 1975, and New York: Daw Books, 1977.

Moore, Raylyn. What Happened to Emily Goode After the Great Exhibition. Norfolk, VA: The Donning Company, 1978.

Morgan, Dan, and John Kippax (John Charles Hynam). A Thunder of Stars. New York: Ballantine Books, 1970.

Morris, Janet E. The Carnelian Throne. New York: Bantam Books, 1979 and 1981. (Book four in the Silistra Series.)

_____. The Golden Sword. New York: Bantam Books, 1977 and 1981. (Book two of the Silistra Series.)

_____. High Couch of Silistra. New York: Bantam Books, 1977. (Book one of the Silistra Series.)

_____. Wind from the Abyss. New York: Bantam Books, 1978 and 1981.

Norton, Andre (Alice). Dread Companion. New York: Harcourt Brace Jovanovich, 1970; rpt. New York: Ace Books, 1972 and 1977.

_____. Forerunner Foray. New York: The Viking Press, 1973; rpt. New York: Ace Books, 1975 and 1982.

_____. Outside. New York: Walker, 1975; New York: Avon Books, 1975.

_____. Wraiths of Time. New York: Atheneum, 1976; rpt. New York: Fawcett Crest Books, 1978.

_____. Yurth Burden. New York: Daw Books, 1978.

_____, and Dorothy Madlee. Star Ka'at. New York: Walker, 1976; rpt. New York: Pocket Books, 1977. (Juvenile.)

_____, and _____. Star Ka'at World. New York: Walker, 1978; rpt. New York: Pocket Books, 1979. (Juvenile.)

_____, and _____. Star Ka'ats and the Plant People. New York: Walker, 1979; rpt. New York: Pocket Books, 1980.   (Juvenile.)

O'Brien, Robert C(arroll). Z for Zachariah. New York: Atheneum, 1974; rpt. New York: Dell, 1977.

Panskin, Alexei, and Cory Panskin. "Lady Sunshine and the Magoon of Beatus," in Epoch. Ed. Roger Elwood and Robert Silverberg. New York: Berkley, 1975; in Farewell to Yesterday's Tomorrow. New York: Berkley, 1975.

Paul, Barbara. An Exercise for Madmen. New York: Berkley, 1978.

_____. "The Slow and Gentle Progress of Trainee Bell-Ringers," in Cassandra Rising. Ed. Alice Laurance. Garden City, NY: Doubleday, 1978; novelized as Pillars of Salt. New York: The New American Library, 1979.

Paxson, Diana L. "The Song of N'Sardi-el," in Millennial Women. Ed. Virginia Kidd. New York: Delacorte Press, 1978, and Dell, 1979.

Piercy, Marge. Woman on the Edge of Time. New York: Alfred A. Knopf, 1976; rpt. New York: Fawcett Crest Books, 1976. (An excerpt from this novel, "Woman on the Edge of Time," was printed in Aurora: Beyond Equality, editors Vonda N. McIntyre and Susan Janice Anderson, Fawcett Publications, prior to its publication in novel length.)

Piserchia, Doris. Earthchild. New York: Daw Books,
1977.

_____. Spaceling. New York: Daw Books, 1978.

Plauger, P. J. "Child of All Ages," in Analog Science
Fiction/Science Fact, March 1975; in Best Science Fiction
Stories of the Year. Ed. Lester del Rey. New York:
Ace Books, 1977; in Nebula Award Stories Eleven. Ed.
Ursula K. Le Guin. New York: Harper & Row, 1977,
and New York: Bantam Books, 1978; in Best of Analog.
Ed. Ben Bova. New York: Baronet, 1978. (This short
story came in second place for a 1976 Nebula Award and
came in third place for a 1976 Hugo Award.)

Rackham, John. The Anything Tree. New York: Ace, 1970.
(In Ace double with The Winds of Darkover, by Marion
Zimmer Bradley.)

_____. Flower of Doradil. New York: Ace, 1970. (In
Ace double with A Promising Planet, by Jeremy Strike.)

Reamy, Tom. "San Diego Lightfoot Sue," in The Magazine
of Fantasy and Science Fiction, Aug. 1975; in Nebula Award
Stories Eleven. Ed. Ursula K. Le Guin. New York: Harper & Row, 1977, and New York: Bantam Books, 1978; in
San Diego Lightfoot Sue and Other Stories. Kansas City, MO:
Earthlight, 1979 and New York: Ace, 1983. (This story won
the 1975 Nebula Award for best novelette and came in fourth
place for a 1975 Hugo in the same category.)

Reaves, J. Michael. "Passion Play," in Universe 5. Ed.
Terry Carr. New York: Random House, 1974; rpt. New
York: Popular Library, 1976.

Reed, Kit (Lillian Craig Reed). "Across the Bar," in Orbit
9. Ed. Damon Knight. New York: Putnam's, 1971, and
New York: Berkley Books, 1972; in Other Stories and The
Attack of the Giant Baby. New York: Berkley Books,
1981.

_____. "In Behalf of the Product," in Bad Moon Rising.
Ed. Thomas M. Disch. New York: Harper & Row, 1973;
in Other Stories and The Attack of the Giant Baby. New
York: Berkley Books, 1981.

_____. "The Food Farm," in Orbit 2. Ed. Damon Knight.

New York: Berkley, 1967; in Women of Wonder. Ed.
Pamela Sargent. New York: Vintage Books, 1974; in
Other Stories and The Attack of the Giant Baby. New
York: Berkley Books, 1981.

_____. "Songs of War," in Nova 4. Ed. Harry Harrison.
New York: Walker, 1974; in The New Women of Wonder.
Ed. Pamela Sargent. New York: Vintage Books, 1978;
in Other Stories and The Attack of the Giant Baby. New
York: Berkley Books, 1981.

Robinson, Spider. "Antinomy," in Destinies, Nov./Dec. 1978;
in The Best of Destinies. Ed. James Baen. New York:
Ace Books, 1980.

Russ, J. J. "M Is for the Many," in Universe 5. Ed.
Terry Carr. New York: Random House, 1974, and New
York: Popular Library, 1976.

Russ, Joanna. Alyx. Boston: Gregg Press, 1976; retitled
The Adventures of Alyx. New York: Pocket Books, 1983.
(These books contain four Alyx stories and Picnic on Para-
dise, 1968.)

_____. And Chaos Died. New York: Ace, 1970; rpt.
Boston: Gregg Press, 1978; rpt. New York: Berkley,
1979. (One of the main characters is a woman. This
novel tied for second place in 1971 for the Nebula Award
for best novel.)

_____. "Gleepsite," in Orbit 9. Ed. Damon Knight.
New York: Putnam's, 1971; in The Best from Orbit.
Ed. Damon Knight. New York: Berkley Books, 1975.

_____. "Nobody's Home," in New Dimensions Two.
Garden City, NY: Doubleday, 1972; in Women of Wonder.
Ed. Pamela Sargent. New York: Vintage Books, 1975; in
The Best of New Dimensions. Ed. Robert Silverberg.
New York: Pocket Books, 1979.

_____. "The Second Inquisition," in Orbit 6. Ed. Damon
Knight. New York: Putnam's, 1970, and New York:
Berkley Books, 1970; in More Women of Wonder. Ed.
Pamela Sargent. New York: Vintage Books, 1976; in
Alyx. Boston: Gregg Press, 1976; in The Adventures
of Alyx. New York: Pocket Books, 1983. (This story
came in fifth place for a 1971 Nebula Award for best nov-
elette.)

_____. The Two of Them. New York: Berkley, 1978.

Ruuth, Marianne. Outbreak. New York: Manor Books, 1977.

Sargent, Pamela. "Bond and Free," in The Magazine of Fantasy and Science Fiction, June 1974; in Starshadows. New York: Ace Books, 1977.

_____. "If Ever I Should Leave You," in If, Feb. 1974; altered version in Starshadows. New York: Ace Books, 1977.

_____. "Shadows," in Fellowship of the Stars. Ed. Terry Carr. New York: Simon & Schuster, 1974; in Starshadows. New York: Ace Books, 1977.

Saxton, Josephine. "Alien Sensation," in Cassandra Rising. Ed. Alice Laurance. Garden City, NY: Doubleday, 1978.

_____. Group Feast. New York: Doubleday, 1971.

_____. "Heads Africa Tails America," in Orbit 9. Ed. Damon Knight. New York: Putnam's, 1971, and New York: Berkley Books, 1972.

Schmitz, James H(enry). "Company Planet," in Analog Science Fiction/Science Fact, May 1971; in The Telzey Toy and Other Stories. New York: Daw Books, 1973, and New York: Ace Books, 1982. (A Telzey story.)

_____. "Compulsion," in Analog Science Fiction/Science Fact, June 1970; in The Telzey Toy and Other Stories. New York: Daw Books, 1973, and New York: Ace Books, 1982. (A Telzey story.)

_____. The Lion Game, serialized in Analog Science Fiction/Science Fact, Aug. and Sept. 1971; as a novel, New York: Daw Books, 1973, and New York: Ace Books, 1982. (A Telzey novel.)

_____. "Resident Witch," in Analog Science Fiction/Science Fact, Jan. 1971; in The Telzey Toy and Other Stories. New York: Daw Books, 1973, and New York: Ace Books, 1982. (A Telzey story.)

_____. "The Telzey Toy," in Analog Science Fiction/

Science Fact, Jan. 1971; in The Telzey Toy and Other Stories. New York: Daw Books, 1973, and New York: Ace Books, 1982. (A Telzey story.)

Scott, Robin. "Maybe Jean-Baptiste Pierre Antoine de Monet, Chevalier de Lamarck, Was a Little Bit Right," in Orbit 6. Ed. Damon Knight. New York: Putnam's, 1970, and New York: Berkley, 1970.

Sheffield, Charles. "Transition Team," in Destinies, Nov./ Dec. 1978; in The Endless Frontier (I). Ed. Jerry Pournelle. New York: Ace Books, 1979.

Skal, Dave. "The Mothers, the Mothers, How Eerily It Sounds," in Aurora: Beyond Equality. Ed. Vonda N. McIntyre and Susan Janice Anderson. Greenwich, CT: Fawcett, 1976.

Sky, Kathleen. "Motherbeast," in Cassandra Rising. Ed. Alice Laurance. Garden City, NY: Doubleday, 1978.

Spinrad, Norman (Richard). A World Between. New York: Pocket Books, 1979.

Sturgeon, Theodore (Edward Hamilton Waldo). "The Girl Who Knew What They Meant," in Sturgeon Is Alive and Well. New York: Berkley Books, 1971, and New York: Berkley/Jove, 1978. (Secondary character.)

_____. "Slow Sculpture," in Galaxy, Feb. 1970; in The Hugo Winners, Vol. 3. Ed. Isaac Asimov. Garden City, NY: Doubleday, 1977; in Galaxy: Thirty Years of Innovative Science Fiction. Ed. Frederik Pohl, Martin H. Greenberg, and Joseph D. Olander. New York: Wideview Books, 1981. (This story was the winner of both the 1971 Hugo Award for best short story and the 1971 Nebula Award for best novelette.)

Sullivan, Sheila. The Calling of Bara. New York: Elsevier-Dutton, 1975; rpt. New York: Avon Books, 1981.

Thompson, Joyce. The Blue Chair. New York: Avon Books, 1977.

Thorp, Roderick. "Sunburst," in Orbit 6. Ed. Damon Knight. New York: Putnam's, 1970, and New York: Berkley Books, 1970.

Tiptree, James, Jr. (Alice B. Sheldon). "Forever to a Hudson Bay Blanket," in Fantastic, Aug. 1972; in Ten Thousand Light Years from Home. New York: Ace Books, and Boston: Gregg Press, 1976; in Interfaces. Ed. Ursula K. Le Guin and Virginia Kidd. New York: Ace Books, 1980.

_____. "Houston, Houston, Do You Read?" in Aurora: Beyond Equality. Ed. Vonda N. McIntyre and Susan Janice Anderson. Greenwich, CT: Fawcett, 1976; in Star Songs of an Old Primate. New York: Ballantine Books, 1978. (This story was the winner of the 1977 Jupiter and Nebula Awards for best novella and tied for first place for the 1977 Hugo Award in the same category.)

_____ [under Raccoona Sheldon]. "The Screwfly Solution," in Analog Science Fiction/Science Fact, June 1977; (under James Tiptree, Jr.) in Out of the Everywhere, and Other Extraordinary Visions. New York: Ballantine Books, 1981. (This story was the winner of the 1978 Nebula Award for best novelette and took third place for a 1978 Hugo Award in the same category.)

_____. "She Waits for All Men Born," in Future Power. Ed. Jack Dann and Gardner R. Dozois. New York: Random House, 1976; in Star Songs of an Old Primate. New York: Ballantine Books, 1978.

_____. "Time-Sharing Angel," in The Magazine of Fantasy and Science Fiction, Oct. 1977; in Out of the Everywhere, and Other Extraordinary Visions. New York: Ballantine Books, 1981. (This story was nominated for a 1978 Hugo Award for best short story.)

_____. Up the Walls of the World. New York: Berkley, 1978. (Several secondary characters are female.)

Trimble, Louis (Preston). The Bodelan Way. New York: Daw Books, 1974. (Two of the major characters are women, although the main character isn't.)

_____. The Wandering Variables. New York: Daw Books, 1972. (Woman character shares main character position with a man.)

Van Scyoc, Sydney J(oyce). "Nightfire," in Cassandra Rising. Ed. Alice Laurance. Garden City, NY: Doubleday, 1978.

_____. Starmother. New York: Putnam's, 1975.

_____. "Sweet Sister, Green Brother," in Galaxy, Dec. 1973; in Best from Galaxy III. Ed. James Baen. Hauppauge, NY: Award Books, 1975.

Varley, John (Herbert). "Air Raid," in Isaac Asimov's Science Fiction Magazine, Spring 1977; in Best Science Fiction Stories of the Year, Sixth Annual Collection. Ed. Gardner Dozois. New York: Dutton, 1977; in The Persistence of Vision. New York: Dial Press, 1978, and New York: Dell, novelization Millennium. New York: Berkley, 1983. (This story came in second place for both the 1978 Nebula Award and the 1978 Hugo Award for best short story.)

_____. "Bagatelle," in Galaxy, Aug. 1974; in The Barbie Murders. New York: Berkley, 1980.

_____. "The Barbie Murders," in Isaac Asimov's Science Fiction Magazine, Feb. 1978; in The Best Science Fiction of the Year No. 8. Ed. Terry Carr. New York: Ballantine Books, 1979; in The Barbie Murders. New York: Berkley, 1980. (This story was nominated for a 1979 Hugo Award for best novelette.)

_____. "The Black Hole Passes," in The Magazine of Fantasy and Science Fiction, June 1975; in The Persistence of Vision. New York: Dial Press, 1978, and New York: Dell, 1979.

_____. "Equinoctial," in Ascents of Wonder. Ed. David Gerrold. New York: Popular Library, 1977; in The Arbor House Treasury of Great Science Fiction Short Novels. New York: Arbor House, 1980; in The Barbie Murders. New York: Berkley, 1980.

_____. "In the Bowl," in The Magazine of Fantasy and Science Fiction, Dec. 1975; in Nebula Winners Twelve. Ed. Gordon Dickson. New York: Harper & Row, 1978, and New York: Bantam Books, 1979. (Not the viewpoint character but a main character nonetheless.)

_____. "Lollipop and the Tar Baby," in Orbit 19. Ed. Damon Knight. New York: Harper & Row, 1977; in The Barbie Murders. New York: Berkley, 1980.

_____. "Manikins," in Amazing Science Fiction Story Magazine, Jan. 1976; in The Barbie Murders. New York: Berkley, 1980.

_____. The Ophiuchi Hotline. New York: The Dial Press, 1977; rpt. New York: Dell, 1978.

_____. "The Phantom of Kansas," in Galaxy, Feb. 1976; in The Persistence of Vision. New York: Dial Press, 1978, and New York: Dell, 1979.

Vinge, Joan D. "The Crystal Ship," in The Crystal Ship. Ed. Robert Silverberg. Nashville: Thomas Nelson, 1976; in Eyes of Amber and Other Stories. New York: The New American Library, 1979.

_____. "Mother and Child," in Orbit 16. Ed. Damon Knight. New York: Harper & Row, 1975; in Fireship. New York: Dell, 1978. (Not viewpoint character but a main character nonetheless.)

_____. The Outcasts of Heaven Belt, serialized in Analog, Feb.-April 1978; in novel form, New York: The New American Library, 1978 and 1982. (The woman character is one of the main characters.)

_____. "Phoenix in the Ashes," in Millennial Women. Ed. Virginia Kidd. New York: Delacorte Press, 1978, and Dell, 1979.

_____. "Tin Soldier," in Orbit 14. Ed. Damon Knight. New York: Harper & Row, 1974; in More Women of Wonder. Ed. Pamela Sargent. New York: Vintage Books, 1976; in Eyes of Amber and Other Stories. New York: The New American Library, 1978 and 1982. (Not the viewpoint character but a main character nonetheless. This story came in third place for a 1975 Jupiter Award for best novelette.)

_____. "View from a Height," in Analog Science Fiction/ Science Fact, June 1978; in Eyes of Amber and Other Stories. New York: The New American Library, 1978 and 1982. (This short story came in third place for a 1979 Hugo Award.)

Wells, (Frank Charles) Robert. The Spacejacks. New York: Berkley, 1975.

White, Jane. Comet. New York: Harper & Row, 1975.

Wilder, Cherry. "Mab Gallen Recalled," in Millennial Women.
    Ed. Virginia Kidd. New York: Delacorte Press, 1978,
    and Dell, 1979.

Wilhelm, Kate. The Clewiston Test. New York: Farrar,
    Straus & Giroux, 1976; rpt. New York: Pocket Books,
    1977 and 1982. (Woman is one of several main characters.)

_____. "A Cold Dark Night with Snow," in Orbit 6.   Ed.
    Damon Knight. New York: Putnam's, 1970, and New
    York: Berkley, 1970.

_____. Fault Lines. New York: Harper & Row, Inc.,
    1977; rpt. New York: Pocket Books, 1978 and 1981.

_____. "The Funeral," in Again Dangerous Visions. Ed.
    Harlan Ellison. Garden City, NY: Doubleday, Inc., 1972,
    and New York: The New American Library, 1972; in The
    Infinity Box. New York: Harper & Row, 1975, and New
    York: Pocket Books, 1977; in More Women of Wonder.
    Ed. Pamela Sargent. New York: Vintage Books, 1976;
    in Alpha 9. Ed. Robert Silverberg. New York: Berkley,
    1978. (This story came in fourth place for a 1973 Nebula
    Award for best novelette.)

_____. Margaret and I. Boston: Little, Brown, 1971;
    rpt. New York: Pocket Books, 1978 and 1980. (This
    novel was nominated for a 1972 Nebula Award for best
    novel.)

_____. "The Plastic Abyss," in Abyss. New York:
    Doubleday, 1971, and New York: Bantam Books, 1973
    and 1978. (This story was nominated for a 1972 Nebula
    Award for best novella.)

_____. "State of Grace," in Orbit 19. Ed. Damon Knight.
    New York: Harper & Row, 1977; in Somerset Dreams &
    Other Fictions. New York: Harper & Row, 1978 and 1979.

Wolfe, Gene. "How the Whip Came Back," in Orbit 6. New
    York: Putnam's, 1970, and New York: Berkley, 1970.

Yarbro, Chelsea Quinn. "Allies," in Chrysalis 1. Ed. Roy
    Torgeson. New York: Zebra Books, 1977; in Cautionary
    Tales. Garden City, NY: Doubleday, 1978, and New York:

Warner Books, 1980. (This work has been included because of Yarbro's intentional omission of all male or female pronouns throughout the story. Are the characters
male or female? Yarbro keeps her own counsel on that.)

_____. "Dead in Irons," in Faster than Light. Ed. Jack
Dann and George Aebrowski. New York: Harper & Row,
1976, and New York: Ace Books, 1982; in Cautionary
Tales. Garden City, NY: Doubleday, 1978, and New
York: Warner Books, 1980; in The New Women of Wonder.
Ed. Pamela Sargent. New York: Vintage Books, 1978.

_____. "Frog Pond," in Galaxy, March 1971; in Cautionary
Tales. Garden City, NY: Doubleday, 1978, and New York:
Warner Books, 1980.

_____. "Time of the Fourth Horseman," in Infinity 3.
Ed. Robert Hoskins. New York: Lancer Books, 1972; in
novel form New York: Ace Books, 1976 and 1981. (Woman
is one of two main characters.)

CHAPTER 7: THE 1980s

Far from being hampered by strict definitions of what it can
be, science fiction continues to grow in dimensions and seems
to have sprouted into a variety of new directions.   Isaac Asimov attributes much of the change in sf to the "feminization"
of sf.   In "The Feminization of Sci-Fi" (Vogue, October 1982)
he writes, "It is the feminization of science fiction that has
broadened and deepened the field to the point where science-
fiction novels can now appear on the bestseller lists."   This
"feminization" also includes the appearance of more women
characters for the increased number of women readers.

One example of this change can be seen in the evolution of the Star Trek novels.   The stock characters--Captain
Kirk, Dr. McCoy, and Mr. Spock--continue to be included,
of course; however, unlike the TV series, women characters
(other than Lt. Uhura) are beginning to appear as main characters.   For example, a strong, important woman character
appears in Death's Angel by Kathleen Sky (New York: Bantam
Books, 1981).   Kathleen Sky's husband, Stephen Goldin, believes the real main character of Sky's book to be Colonel
Elizabeth Schaeffer, not any of the usual Star Trek characters.
Although the character doesn't fit the definition of main character used in this reference book, I tend to agree.   Colonel
Schaeffer doesn't appear until nearly a third of the way into
the book; however, she rapidly takes over the focus of the
story and is the active character throughout the rest of the
novel.

Science fiction in the 1980s is being written for, and
is therefore appealing to, a more mature audience than ever
before.   And according to Isaac Asimov, sf is appealing to a
"steadily increasing percentage of women readers" (Vogue,
October 1982).   If this is true, sf readers can look forward
to an increasing number of stories and novels containing

women as main characters worthy of reader respect and admiration.   As Andre Norton wrote in her foreword to Cassandra Rising (ed. Alice Laurance, New York: Doubleday, 1978), "The girl with the B. E. M. [Bug-Eyed Monster] is past history.   Now let us have the girl who can take her own chances and stand shoulder to shoulder with any hero."   From all indications, the 1980s is an era in which sf readers can look forward to many more remarkable, three-dimensional women characters --heroes.   The "girl" in sf is maturing into a "woman" and none too soon.

*   BUSBY, F. M.   <u>Zelde M'tana</u>.   New York: Dell, 1980.

   <u>Main Character</u>:   Zelde M'tana.
   <u>Physical Characteristics</u>:   Is strong, black-skinned, and 15 to 16 years old at the start of the book; talks in slang ("Wasn't out to mad you up") and often begins a sentence with a verb; is trained to be a lethal fighter by the Wild Children on Earth who call themselves the Kids.
   <u>Mental/Emotional Characteristics</u>:   Is shrewd and street-wise; learned to command at an early age; thinks on her feet; is self-confident, fearless, and a born leader; is emotionally strong even at the book's beginning, but even so, manages to grow from needing someone at the beginning of the book to not needing someone ("My men--<u>I'm</u> the one as does the picking"); is bisexual.
   <u>Story Particulars</u>:   Zelde M'tana, one of the Wild Children on Earth who call themselves the Kids, is captured by UET (United Energy and Transport), the enemy.   It is determined that she is to be shipped out to a brothel on a mining planet.   When the crew mutinies in transit, she and the other women prisoners are freed to help in the fight.   The mutiny is a success, and they achieve the status of Escaped from the UET.   Zelde has four lovers in the book: Honcho, a male gang head on Earth; Tillya, an emotionally weak female prisoner on the ship; Ragir Parnell, the male captain once they attain Escaped status; and, Torra Defose, a strong female "Policebitch" turned Escaped.
   After Parnell dies Zelde takes over command of the ship and manages to bring the ship to safety in spite of the fact that the crew resents her leadership because of her youth and her lack of ship experience.   Zelde ends the book as second hat (third in command) on a different ship, the only Escaped <u>fighting</u> ship in existence.   Her new captain sees her as having a future as a leader in her own right and as a fearless fighter.

Zelde is a strong, tough leader who is able to think in action and whose story makes captivating reading. She also appears as a character in Busby's Rissa Kerguelen (June 1977, Berkley). (See the 1970s chapter for the synopsis of Rissa Kerguelen.)

* CHERRYH, C. J. (Carolyn Janice Cherry). Serpent's Reach. New York: Daw Books, 1980.

Main Character: Raen a Sul hant Meth-maren.
Physical Characteristics: Is a "long-boned" woman; is aged fifteen when the story begins and ages to nearly 100 years old at the book's end; has "aquiline features"; bears "a pattern on her right hand, chitinous and glittering, living in her flesh" which is "her identity, her pledge to the hives, such as all Kontrin bore"; is "blue-hive"; is a "skilled marksman"; is "potentially immortal" because the majat have granted it; has black hair.
Mental/Emotional Characteristics: Is "atypical," "random," "a survivor," "intelligent, and dangerous"; enjoys gambling and doesn't mind taking risks.
Story Particulars: Fifteen-year-old Raen and her family, the Kontrins, have been granted immortality by the majat (large, intelligent hive-dwelling creatures in Hydri Reach who dislike the idea of humans dying). Beta humans, though, imported in egg form, live and die at the human rate and clone the azi, the workers, who die at age forty. As the only immortal humans in that region of space, the Kontrins control alpha Hydri III; however, a power play on the part of other Houses of the Family results in the murder of all of Raen's House except herself.

Injured and certain she is dying, Raen instinctively flees to the safety of the blue hive. Flinging herself into the hive itself, Raen is fed and cared for until she heals. The majat of the blue hive assist her in her efforts to regain control of Kethiuy--an effort which fails in spite of her valiant attempt. Afterwards, she is expelled from her world and from the majat and begins wandering the universe. The "chitin-pattern" on her hand signifies that she is Kontrin, thus affording her unlimited credit.

At age 34, Raen buys the contract of an attractive azi named Jim, who is "engineered for pleasing appearance and intelligence," when he loses at a game of Sej played against her aboard ship. She is irritated by Jim's passivity and lack of initiative, but is grateful for his companionship. She buys him clothes and jewelry and offers him the use of her

unlimited credit which she long ago grew bored with. Raen
establishes herself with Jim on Istra, planning a confrontation both with the Kontrin, now headed by Moth, and with the
Outside element which plan on expanding the hive, a move
which would ultimately cause its collapse. Moth, the only
Kontrin still alive who once had only an average human's life-
expectancy, somehow senses that a majat cycle is drawing
to a close. As the Eldest, Moth leads the Families for many
years, but destroys them and herself as the cycle closes,
solving Raen's problem with possible Kontrin intervention into
her plans.

      Raen, as the only surviving Kontrin female, eventually
becomes the representative of the new cycle of majat and re-
establishes trade with humans once more. Jim is given a
lengthened life-span by the majat and remains Raen's companion, perhaps acting as a second self to her. His illegal
and unpermitted absorption of Raen's tapes containing knowledge of the Families, though necessary in the light of her
disappearance, changes Jim's "mind-set," making him very
much like Raen herself and permanently altering his own servant training. (Implied here is that the tapes which program
people--Kontrin, beta and azi alike--as to who they were and
what was expected of them made them who they were rather
than any basic genetic differences.)

      Both Moth and Raen can be seen as hive-Mothers or
Kontrin queens--Moth of the old hive cycle, Raen of the new.
Raen is a strong character who is compared to James Bond
in Mary T. Brizzi's article "C. J. Cherryh and Tomorrow's
New Sex Roles" (in The Feminine Eye, ed. Tom Staicar, New
York: Frederick Ungar, 1982). Raen is not only an expert
marksman, but, writes Brizzi, "is cosmopolitan, sophisticated,
even a bit jaded, not just a world traveler, but a planet-
hopper.... Like Bond, she is the object of many assassination attempts which she foils with humor and ease." Raen
is a survivor who gains compassion for the betas and azi; she
is the new Kontrin queen-to-be who seeks her destiny, rarely
doubting that she will succeed.

  * EISENSTEIN, PHYLLIS. In the Hands of Glory. New
      York: Pocket Books, 1981.

     Main Character: Dia Catlin.
     Physical Characteristics: Has short dark hair which
is bleached blond late in the book for the purpose of hiding
her identity; is pretty.
     Mental/Emotional Characteristics: Is a Patroller and

"a hell of a pilot"; is "bright" and "capable" and "pragmatic";
has wanted to do "combat flying" all her life and loves flying;
is proud; derives great inner satisfaction and peace in physical exercise; is very competitive and has "the call to glory"
according to her brother; is an excellent shot on the target
range and when shooting at moving targets; is a star gymnast
and has trophies to prove it; commits herself completely to
what she believes in, whether it be the Patrol or the rebel
cause; wants to base her life on honor; is cool and in control
in crisis situations; loves deeply when she gives her love.

Story Particulars: The Patrol, headed by Brigadier
General Marcus Bohannon, was the last remnant of the Federation Patrol. His memoirs contain the truth about the
Brigadier's motives in planting a base on the planet Amphora
and in putting the agrarian inhabitants to work mining and re-
fining ore for the Patrol and its ships. Now, eighty years
later, the rebels on the planet still fight the Patrol and see
the planet as theirs. Most members of the Patrol are unaware of the Memoirs and believe they are there to protect
the inhabitants, not realizing that the Patrol is the aggressor.

One Patrol member convinced of the benevolent protective nature of the Patrol is Lieutenant Dia Catlin, who is
proud to come from a family of Patrol officers. Her mother,
father, sister, and brother are all connected with the Patrol,
and Dia shows much promise in her Patrol career. She is
a superb shot, a trophy-winning gymnast, an excellent pilot,
and totally committed to her career in the Patrol. When her
lover Michael Drew and she are shot down by rebel fire, he
is killed instantly, but Dia, though critically wounded, lands
the aircraft safely. She is captured and brought back to
health by a doctor who finally lets her call him Talley and
by a furry alien creature who calls himself Strux. Though
in deep grief over the loss of Michael, Dia finds herself attracted to Talley, and the attraction appears to be mutual.

When it is apparent that the rebels may be captured
if they don't relocate, Talley leaves Dia where she will be
found and escapes. Dia is returned to the Citadel by the
attacking Patrol members, is instantly a hero, and is given
a promotion to second lieutenant by the Patrol's leader,
Brigadier Arlen Velicher. Velicher has an ulterior motive,
however, and offers to share his bed and the apartment next
door to his quarters with Dia. Dia, although still deeply
grieved over Michael's death, and thinking occasionally about
her attraction to Talley, thinks that, like other women in the
past, she stands to gain additional career promotions from
Brigadier Velicher and coolly, unemotionally, even logically
chooses to accept his offer. As she prepares to move from

the apartment she shared with Michael into the apartment
ajoining Arlen's rooms, she reflects on her decision and sees
it merely as another step in her career, "as if she had been
given an assignment by a strict instructor."

In the weeks that follow, her exposure to the little
lies of the upper echelon of the Patrol and Velicher's refusal
to let her see Brigadier Bohannon's Memoirs destroy her
idealistic vision of the Patrol's purpose. When Gordon Tal-
lentyre Magramor (Talley) is captured and tortured, she is
just as cool, unemotional, and logical as when she moved in
with Velicher. She releases Talley and takes him to rebel
headquarters. Naturally some rebels are skeptical of her
motives, seeing her as a potential spy, but Talley, their
leader, insists that she be given a chance. With Dia leading them, the rebels take over Patrol headquarters, and Dia
must face her father feeling very much like a traitor.

Dia is a capable, dedicated, hardworking, committed
hero with the ability to shake the prejudices of her upbringing
in the face of logic.

★ HALDEMAN, JOE. Worlds. New York: The Viking
   Press, 1981; rpt. New York: Pocket Books, 1982.

Main Character: Marianne O'Hara (Scanlan is her
"root name"); a.k.a. Mary Hawkings.
Physical Characteristics: Has "thick dark red hair,
eyes the color of copper, skin as pale as wax"; is sixteen
years old at the book's beginning and in her forties at the
book's end; is of small build; is "striking, magnetic, charis-
matic" but not beautiful.
Mental/Emotional Characteristics: Considers herself
"morose" but never "serious"; is "single-minded and broadly
talented"; is "agnostic" and "intelligent"; loves to play jazz
on the clarinet; spent a time in her life "going through mates
as if they were changes of underwear," and always enjoys a
variety of male companionship; is said to have "the soul of a
compassionate machine."
Story Particulars: By the latter part of the twenty-
first century, the population of the forty-one Worlds or "orbiting settlements" is nearly half a million and increasing.
New New York, the largest of the Worlds, is really a hollowed-
out asteroid sealed and then filled with "air, soil, water,
plants, lights," and is populated by a quarter of a million
people. Among the native residents of New New York is
Marianne O'Hara, a bright, "broadly talented" young woman
with political ambitions who moves to Earth to attend college.

This book, the first in a proposed trilogy by Haldeman, chronicles Marianne's adventures on Earth during the
six months prior to the world war and plague there. During
this period, she has a difficult time understanding the differences in culture and social norms between Earth and New New
York. For example, in keeping with the social norms in New
New York, Marianne enjoys open sexual relations with men
and has a difficult time understanding the mentality of "groundhogs" who find rape so very appealing. (She is attacked twice
while on Earth.)

While attending classes on Earth, she learns to care
for Benny, the poet, and like him, becomes peripherally active in an underground group which is planning a revolution.
Marianne's involvement with classmate Jeff Hawkings becomes
serious while she is on vacation with him in Europe and becomes even more intense after Benny is killed by unknown
murderers. Jeff, who is an FBI agent, marries Marianne,
and they take a brief honeymoon in New Orleans. There,
after Jeff's departure, Marianne becomes an instant celebrity
as a clarinet soloist for a jazz band, and is consequently kid-
napped by mercenaries from Nevada as the most prominent
Worlds citizen then on Earth.

Jeff rescues her and takes her to the launch facility
at Capetown, Florida to remove her from danger. It is
there they learn that bombs have been dropped on Earth and
on the Worlds, and that Jeff will not be allowed to immigrate
with Marianne to New New York. Earth has bombed all of
the Worlds and only New New York survived the bombings
well enough to sustain life; however, as overcrowding will
now be a problem on New New York, no groundhogs are being allowed to immigrate. Nonetheless, Marianne, at Jeff's
insistence, leaves Earth on the last flight out and eventually
becomes a political leader on New New York. The story is
told, for the most part, from Marianne's first person account of
that period of time; however, also included are first person ac-
counts of John (later to be one of her husbands) and Benny.

★ HEINLEIN, ROBERT A. Friday. New York: Holt, Rine-
        hart and Winston, 1982, rpt. New York: Ballantine Books,
        1983. (Took fourth place in the 1983 Hugo Awards.)

Main Character: Friday (a.k.a. Friday Jones, Mar-
jorie Baldwin, and Hannah Jensen).
Physical Characteristics: Is a "field agent," a "courier"; doesn't consider herself to have a pretty face, but others
do; has a "possum pouch, created by plastic surgery" behind

her navel, used for carrying microfilm; can kill with her
hands; has "an unusually comely body"; is not "human" but
is an "artificial person" and is fully functional as a human
woman, though having faster reflexes than is considered normal for a human and "immune to cancer and to most infec-
tions"; has the "built-in suntan" of an "Amerindian" though
she has "Finnish, Polynesian, Innuit, Danish, red Irish, Swazi,
Korean, German, Hindu," and English blood as well; becomes
the "staff intuitive analyst."

Mental/Emotional Characteristics: Is held in "high
esteem" by her "colleagues"; is married to an S-group (syn-
thetic-group) of three men and three other women when the
story begins; needs a sense of belonging she has never had
as an AP (artificial person); is of strong emotional fiber but
finds she needs people more than they need her; is more
highly intelligent than even she will admit to herself.

Story Particulars: In a future Earth time when APs
(artificial persons) are a rejected but definite portion of the
population and when the civilization on Earth is in one of its
cyclic declines, Friday, an AP who has never felt like she
really "belongs," is a highly valued courier for Dr. Hartley
"Boss" Baldwin in his establishment of couriers and assassins.
Friday can, due to her "enhanced" human powers, kill with
her hands in the process of doing her job and is admired and
respected by all of her associates. She carries the stigma,
however, of being an artificial person (essentially a test tube
baby who has been carefully genetically engineered for improve-
ments) who is thought by most uninformed and prejudiced people to be less than human, to have no soul, to have no rights
as a human. Because of her desperate need to belong, Friday marries into an S-group, a synthetic family, without telling them she is an AP. When she finally spills her secret,
seven years into the marriage, they immediately divorce her,
leaving her with an even deeper conviction that she is not
fully human.

Drowning her sorrows in the arms of a man--in this
case, the arms of two men and another woman--is just the
medicine she needs, and a chance liaison develops into a
lasting, loving family group, with several additional family
members later. However, before this happy ending occurs,
the world is given Red Thursday, a day when assassins
around the world kill major political figures to bring the globe
under their control. This begins a gradual, chaotic decline
in the civilization of the world and precedes what Friday predicts will be another Black Death epidemic. Before his death,
Boss advises Friday to leave Earth and settle elsewhere, advice which she fully intends to take, eventually, but which
circumstances force on her much earlier than she'd planned.

Friday is a shrewd, self-protecting, and tough woman,
a killer, a fighter, a genius who never fully admits her intelligence. She is an AP who admits to herself that she, too,
is human, but only after carrying an implanted fetus to full
term, an act which convinces her psychologically that she is
a fully functional woman--human.

This first person book is fast-paced and fun reading,
with interesting viewpoints and comments on politics, unisex
bathrooms, democracy, credit cards, bisexuality (Friday and
several other characters in the book are bisexual), AP and
racial prejudice, corporations/monopolies, the decline of
civilization (and the signposts which warn of it) and male
vanity. Friday's rape by a gang at the book's beginning is
not repeated; her other sexual encounters in the book, with
both sexes, are entered of her own volition. It is unfortunate, though, that it takes motherhood to make Friday feel
fully human, because in every biological sense, she is not
only fully human, but an enhanced human (in physical strength,
powers and intelligence)--one who never allows her full potential to develop, perhaps because her drive to "belong" is
always stronger than her drive for self-development.

*   LEE, TANITH. The Silver Metal Lover. New York:
    Daw Books, 1981.

Main Character: Jane (also Jain).
Physical Characteristics: At first she is 16 years
old, 5'4" tall, with "pale bronze" hair, green eyes, almost oval
face, but with a pointed chin, a "Venus Media" body type
("voluptuous" and "highly sexed"). Later in the book, she
discovers her real hair is "blond ash" or "barley blond" and
she loses 30 pounds to become slender. Some say attractive,
others say like a boy.
Mental/Emotional Characteristics: At first, she is
wealthy, falls in love easily "with characters in visuals, or
books, or with actors in drama," but not with attainable
men; is "unsubtle," "hypercondriacal" (sic), "not very good
at being alive," intelligent and bright according to her mother,
feels herself a failure as a "wit," finds being kissed by men
boring, "maladjusted." She grows into a loving, giving, self-
sufficient, confident, independent young woman, who knows
pain because she has loved and lost.
Story Particulars: A poorly adjusted, wealthy, 16-
year-old who is out of touch with the world around her, falls
irrationally and totally in love with a silver robot called, appropriately, Silver. He is a new model, a life-like robot

with musical talent, red hair, and just a shade (no pun intended) different from his prototypes. In fact, his makers
are prepared to disassemble him and try again, until Jane,
uncharacteristically, works up the courage to find a way to
purchase him. As it turns out, her friend Clovis purchases
him for her in someone else's name (she is legally too young
to own a sexually active robot), and she sells all her belong-
ings to repay him.

Jane and Silver go to live in the slums, which is all
they can afford when Jane's mother takes away her credit
card. There Jane loses her fear of herself and life under
Silver's careful nurturing. And there they play and sing for
money for rent and food. People love their music, and Jane
discovers that her mother was wrong when she told her she
couldn't sing--and that her real hair color is beautiful, not
unattractive as her mother told her. Jane becomes Jain,
and discovers the beauty of who she is and learns to love
and give, all because of Silver. And she is convinced that
Silver is much more than a robot--that he has emotions and
can love and be hurt. She is overjoyed with her life with
him. However, she, in the midst of her joy, hears that
Silver is being recalled by his manufacturer to be melted
down, and devises a plan of escape for them, which fails.
Jain feels her life is over and tries to kill herself, but is
instead assisted once more by Clovis.

The book's end provides the reader and Jain with
evidence that Silver has a soul, and gives Jain a depth and
spirit that is rare in someone her age. This book is written
in an autobiographical form. (See the 1930s chapter for a
synopsis of Lester del Rey's "Helen O'Loy," a story in which
a female android is loved by two men.)

*   MARTIN, GEORGE R. R., and LISA TUTTLE. Wind-
       haven. New York: Pocket Books, 1981. (Parts One
       and Two of this book were published in slightly differ-
       ent form as "The Storms of Windhaven," Analog, May
       1975 and as "One-Wing," Analog, Jan. and Feb. 1980,
       respectively.)

    Main Character: Maris of Lesser Amberly.
    Physical Characteristics: The story progresses from
her childhood to her death; has "short, dark hair"; has very
strong arms to enable her to use the wings to hold herself
aloft; is born the daughter of a fisher.
    Mental/Emotional Characteristics: Feels she can't be
whole without her wings; loves the flyer Dorrel and has a

number of other lovers in her life; argues persuasively and
contributes valuable ideas to the flyers; is courageous, determined, and in control of her emotions; loves flight more
than anything else including love with a man; is one of the
best flyers on Windhaven; has "good sense" and is perceptive; as a flyer, she has "precision, control, reflexes, a feel
for the wind"; becomes the cohesive force between the one-
wings and flyer born.

    Story Particulars: Give a little girl a dream, the
talent to succeed at that dream, and the courage and determination to defend it, and you have the essence of Maris of
Lesser Amberly on the planet Windhaven. Windhaven is a
planet spotted with islands rather than continents on which
an Earth ship crashed eight centuries before. The survivors,
in an effort to maintain communication with all of the people
scattered on various islands, made a number of "wings" for
people to use, perhaps much like hang gliders. Now, eight
centuries later, the tradition-bound society allows only the
first-born of flyers to learn to use the wings, and the flyers
are considered the equals of the Landsmen, the lords over
the islands, much like kings.

    Maris of Lesser Amberly has a dream of flying in
spite of the fact that she was born to a fisher. Her chance to
fly comes when her widowed mother marries a flyer Russ, and
Maris is allowed to learn to fly. Flying gives her great joy
in life, and she loves it more than anything else. When her
stepfather and mother have a son, she knows it's only a matter of time until he will take her wings from her as he is
the true first-born of a flyer, but she isn't prepared for the
overwhelming heartache she feels.

    Maris and her brother Coll, who wants to be a
singer and is afraid to fly, humiliate Russ by telling him
before a party of flyers that Maris is the flyer in spite
of tradition. Maris steals the wings and goes to her lover
Dorrel to ask him to call a council of flyers for her so they
can make a determination on the issue. In an unprecedented
decision by the Council, nineteen-year-old Maris is given her
stepfather's wings, and Maris becomes a hero to hordes of
children eager to learn to fly. In addition, an academy is
set up for teaching "Woodwings" (children born of parents
who are not flyers) how to fly. Yearly competition between
Woodwings and flyers gives the Woodwings the chance to become flyers, although they are forever derisively called one-
wings even when they win. The tension between flyer-born
and one-wings continues throughout Maris' life, until a mad
Landsman hangs a one-wing with her wings still on and Maris
finds a way to unite the flyers and one-wings against the mad-
man.

Maris' life is full of the joy of flying, good friends
and lovers, and purpose. When a flying accident permanently
grounds her, she feels dead, but thanks to the care and love
of the healer Evan, she once more finds the courage to have
purpose in life. Maris is a remarkable hero who reshapes
the world in order to fulfill her desires. ("The Storms of
Windhaven" came in second place in the category of novella
in 1976 for both Nebula and Hugo Awards.)

* MEZO, FRANCINE. The Fall of the Worlds, Unless She
    Burn, No Earthly Shore (trilogy). New York: Avon
    Books, 1980, 1981, 1981, respectively.

Main Character: Areia Darenga (a.k.a. Chaeya, or
wife, to the priest M'landan).
    Physical Characteristics: Is tall, long-legged, red-
haired, and 280+ years old.
    Mental/Emotional Characteristics: Is highly rational
and very intelligent; as a clone of the Lambda House, Areia
is suppose to have no emotions (such as love, hate, or the
ability to kill); however, during the course of the books, she
discovers that clones, too, are fully human.
    Story Particulars: Areia, captain of a space ship, is
a clone of the Lambda House, created to become a Maintainer,
or an instrument to protect human civilization from itself,
while never being a part of it herself. Members of her House
are commanders of the great ringed space ships that cruise
the galaxy and are treated at ten-year intervals for Longlife.
A clone is given an indefinite length of life, but is never allowed fully human status. Clones are merely an instrument
to protect human civilization, to keep peace for a species in-
tent upon self-destruction and conquest; they are human robots in essence. Humans (as opposed to clones) feel subservient to the clones, as in a police state, overprotected
from themselves. Both "clones" and "humans" suffer from
the arrangement, but the alternative is war. Even within
this highly structured system, Areia discovers that she and
other clones have emotions; and humans finally are able to
receive Longlife, thus reducing some of the resentment held
for the long-lived clones.
    In her painful journey of self-discovery, Areia loves
three men, learns to hate, and finds out she can kill others--
all strictly "impossible" for clones. There are elements of
psychic awareness with one lover, also a clone, and of mys-
ticism with another lover, the alien priest M'landan. In her
love for M'landan, Areia most fully discovers herself. Their

love is taboo for both of them, yet they do not deny it.   And
from his hands, she receives Longlife from a new source.

★   PAUL, BARBARA. Under the Canopy. New York: The
    New American Library, 1980.

Main Character: Margo Kemperer.
Physical Characteristics: Is middle-aged; dresses up
even in a rain forest.
Mental/Emotional Characteristics: Likes a supply of
fine wines; takes her culture with her (portable culture); enjoys routines and rituals; is polite; is trained by the Academy;
is willing to compromise if met halfway; is a stickler for
propriety; projects the "image of the cool, unflappable ad-
ministrator"; looks the other way when it accomplishes more;
has unshakable self-assurance; according to Stephanie, she is
"a hidebound, autocratic snob"; is content, controlled, and
sensitive to the unspoken in her dealings with the people of
Gaea; is unafraid (Stephanie says "too vain to be afraid") and
inflexible.

Main Character: Stephanie Leeds.
Physical Characteristics: Is 27 years old; dresses in
men's cut-off slacks, blouses tied at her midriff, and sandals;
is tall and lean; has mouse-colored hair; wears no make-up;
is dirty (according to Margo).
Mental/Emotional Characteristics: Speaks her mind
with unrestrained abandon; throws herself enthusiastically
into a job, but pushes others to keep up her pace (Margo
says she plunges in "headfirst"); wants equality between all
people; Margo says she's opinionated and disdainful, and
thinks of her "as close to being Public Enemy Number One
as anyone could be on this world"; feels and expresses contempt for traditions (Margo says "envy-ridden"); gets angry
easily; Margo says "temperamental ... ninety-nine percent
temper and one percent mental."

Story Particulars: In a future world where both women
and men participate in wars and command planets, there is
a quiet, primitive jungle planet called Gaea, where Margo
Kemperer has been appointed the Interplanetary Union director
of the planet and things are run smoothly, with culture, style,
order, and the respect of the inhabitants. Stephanie Leeds,
self-appointed crusader, is sent to be Margo's assistant, and
the well-ordered world must deal with her lack of adjustment
to the native customs.

An interesting dilemma that develops in this book is
that the reader is never certain who the hero really is.
Margo, as director of the planet, opens and ends the book.
Her thinking is followed closely in the novel, and she views
Stephanie as too immature to know what's best. She runs
the planet with a blend of aristocratic superiority (she went
to the Academy), and acceptance of provincial customs.
Margo thinks the Gaean people will let her know if they want
to work harder and bring in more money. She respects their
pace, their lack of ambition. But Stephanie, a crusader for
equality for the Gaeans and of their bettering themselves (seeing and doing things her way, in other words), is also of
major importance and she sees Margo as a hypocrite. Stephanie wants the inhabitants of the planet to develop their
world, to improve their lives. Stephanie's first-person diary
of her days lost in the jungle is also in the book.

Since the two characters stand at opposite poles, in
opinion and approach, and since almost equal objective attention is given to each, the reader must decide which one of
them is the hero, if either. The book, perhaps because of
this dilemma, is interesting reading and both female main
characters, for better or worse, are allowed to be exactly
who they are. And both the good and the bad are exposed.
Barbara Paul has given sf two memorable female characters.

* PRATCHETT, TERRY. Strata. New York: St. Martin's
    Press, 1981.

Main Character: Kin Arad.
Physical Characteristics: Is 210 years old; has an
appearance which varies from skin of "midnight-black, like
her wig" to "silver" skin with black hair "shot with neon
threads"; is a Company Sec-exec in charge of supervising
the building of new worlds with strata machines.
Mental/Emotional Characteristics: Has been married
seven times, "once even under the influence of love"; has
had "memory surgery"; doesn't hesitate to punch someone in
the face with "a scientific fistful of rings" when the occasion
arises; is "unorthodox"; wrote Continuous Creation, "the first
book published in four hundred years"; has a strong sense of
self and an equally strong sense of humor; is adaptable and
flexible without sacrificing her identity in the least; is willing
to take risks; enjoys adventure and exploring the unknown;
has "done just about everything."
Story Particulars: The undaunted hero of this book is
the only book writer to be published in 400 years, and at that,

she had to learn how paper was made and hire robots to
build a printing press! She is none other than Kin Arad,
the 210-year-old Earth-born Sec-exec of a planet-making
team. The Company for which Kin works makes planets with
strata machines, the prototype of which was left by the Great
Spindle Kings, the now-extinct planet-makers of the past.
(They ceased to reproduce when they learned that they weren't
the first planet-makers, but that "the Wheelers had beaten
them to it, half a billion years before.") In each planet the
Company builds, they carefully include fossiliferous rock and
add a geologic stratification to make the world appear quite
old and filled with a history of life.

Kin is just finishing up a planet when Jago Jalo literally pops into her office, using a light-bending machine
that makes him invisible. This strange little man intrigues
Kin with his tale that he has found a Spindle world. Because
of her innate curiosity, Kin finds herself off and jumping
Elsewhere in a ship programmed by Jago. She is accompanied
by a four-armed kung pilot called Marco Farfarer (a seven-
foot-tall male with a "red coxcomb" on top, two "saucer
eyes," and a grin that resembles "a red crescent with harp
strings of mucus"), a three-meter-tall cannibalistic female
shand nicknamed Silver ("a bear with binocular vision and a
domed skull and several walruses in its ancestry"), and an
intelligent raven that talks and that is actually a spy.

The ship takes them to a flat world which looks a lot
like Earth and which is contained inside a protective dome
with little planets circling around inside it, a structure which
students of astronomy's history will find familiar. As the
ship is not built to land and is doomed to crash, they evacu-
ate it with power suits and a dumbwaiter which can feed the
human, the kung, and the shand indefinitely. (They errone-
ously think the raven is dead, but it dons a power suit on
its own initiative, and follows them at a good spying distance.)
Their trek across this flat world, filled with fire-breathing
dragons and flying carpets, ends at the planet's hub. There
Kin, the human and therefore the "essential lunatic element,,"
learns that the entire universe is only 70,000 years old and
solves not only the problem of their return to their own respective corners of the universe, but also of the gradual dis-
integration of the machinery that keeps the flat world safe
for the life forms living on it. Kin decides to write a new,
very brief edition of her book, Continuous Creation, correct-
ing her previously faulty information, and to build a new
world for the people on the flat world, even if it takes "a
thousand years."

This humorous, tongue-in-cheek novel never REALLY

spells out for the reader whether it is set in a far past or a
far future time.   References to Rome instead of the Reme of
which Kin knows (based on the names Romulus and Remus),
to the "Christ-Creator religion" (which says that "Everyone
is evil until proved holy" and that the Earth was created in
six days), and to a second "Leiv Eiriksson" all point to the
possibility that the flat Earth, soon to be the round Earth,
was actually the origin of our own Earth.   Whatever the reader
decides, Pratchett has written a fun-filled novel with a main
character who is, nonetheless, a thinker, a doer, an adventurer, a builder, an unorthodox hero with a sense of humor.

*   SALMONSON, JESSICA AMANDA.   The Swordswoman.
    New York: Pinnacle Books, 1982.

   Main Character: Erin Wyler (a.k.a. Erin of Thar and
Merilia of the Black Mountain).
   Physical Characteristics: Has "brown eyes" and hair
that is "shoulder length and black"; is beautiful and has "an-
drogynous strength"; has "a third degree black belt in karate,
a fourth dan in kendo and iaido sword styles, with at least
a working knowledge of jujutsu."
   Mental/Emotional Characteristics: Has "a history of
emotional problems" though they are "minor problems" because she is "consistently calm" and has a "generally disconnected attitude"; feels that reality had always been "a fleeting
sensation" until she suddenly appears in Endsworld; feels
"lust" for "a battle" and is impatient until she learns patience
from Kiron; strives to learn to act from compassion rather
than in anger or indignation.
   Story Particulars: Erin Wyler, resident of San Fran-
cisco, a third degree black belt in karate and a fourth degree
dan in kendo and iaido sword styles, constantly lives with a
"generally disconnected attitude" from life and reality.   Earlier in her life, she created in her diary a world alien to
Earth, a world in which she was a sword fighter and enemy
to the cruel Shom Bru.   It isn't until she fights Jerry Mason,
who kept a diary about a very similar world and who is Shom
Bru's counterpart on Earth, that what had served as a harm-
less fantasy becomes a horrible reality--she kills her oppo-
nent in competition.
   Erin is consequently placed in a mental institution
where she is visited by Válkyová Idaska, the Czech para-
medic who rode with her to the sanatorium.   Val, as she
calls him, has been given a "rhinestone-bright trinket carved
in the shape of a sword" by a sandy-eyed man, which is to

be given to Erin. The sword both repels and fascinates her
and the "diamond" blade sends both Erin and Val to the world
of Erin's diary, Endsworld. They are separated in the transfer, and Erin finds herself lying naked on the shore of a sea.
         Suddenly, Erin finds that "reality had sharpness and
clarity." She finds a blind priest who gives her clothes and
who insists that she battle him for two swords, a battle which
Erin wins. Thus equipped, Erin finds an unhappy couple in
a fishing village and becomes a fisher's apprentice to Rud.
Rud and his wife, Orline, come to think of Erin as the daughter they never had and present her with a fisher's girdle. On
the day that all the fisher folk have been dreading, Rud tricks
Erin and ties her to a tree to keep her from interfering in
the sacrifice which is to come; however, she works her way
free and returns to the village, only to find Rud held before
the villagers by human-sized insects, who are nipping off his
arms with their large mandibles. Erin attacks the insects,
an act which brings about a total, rather than a controlled,
partial destruction of the village's people. Erin survives
only because the insects see her diamond blade which she
wears around her neck.
         The next morning, stunned and depressed, Erin is
discovered by Teebi Dan Wellsmith, a "fishmonger" who
regularly buys the villagers' fish to take to the city of Ter-
wold. Their meeting is the beginning of a relationship destined to be long, but cut short by the new, disturbing influence of Val in Endsworld. In this world, Erin learns that
the two-swords and three-swords co-operate with the insects
by organizing periodic sacrifices of the crippled, the beggers,
the old. Val organizes a group of followers who are pacifists
against the brutal sacrifices. It is Val's impact on this world
which costs Teebi his life. Erin's sword apprenticeship with
Kiron, the four-legged immortal of Endsworld, teaches her
patience and to act only from compassion, not in anger or
indignation. It is there that she sees her dead, but pre-
served double in this world, Merilia, and receives from her
additional sword-fighting skills. Erin uses these skills in
her efforts to totally destroy the insects and to maim Shom
Bru.
         The book's resolution is a disturbing one in its impli-
cations both for Earth and for Endsworld. Erin's return to
Earth is for her somewhat like going to hell; it is only when
she meets Teebi's Earth counterpart, Daniel Wells, that she
begins to hope Earth won't be so bad after all.

★ SANDERS, SCOTT. "Touch the Earth," in Edges.   Ed.

Ursula K. Le Guin and Virginia Kidd. New York:
Pocket Books, 1980.

Main Character: Marn
Physical Characteristics: No description given, except
that at the beginning, she wears a mask, gloves and a hood
like the other residents of Ohio City.

Mental/Emotional Characteristics: Is a chemist; was
raised in a closed environment called Ohio City, probably after a nuclear war or other holocaust and is fearful of the
outside world; is determined to stay outside with the other
eight in spite of her fears; realizes in the story that she
doesn't mind touching others in spite of her training to the
contrary.

Story Particulars: As the story opens, nine renegade
members of the physically self-contained system called Ohio
City are breaking out to the green world of the outside. They
are all fully clothed, gloved, and masked, as are all members of their society, and all but one have their hoods in
place, too. (The actual reason behind the hidden bodies and
faces in Ohio City is never explained and the reader is left
to speculate on the whys.) When they reach the extreme of
the pipe-tunnel, they torch through the steel pipe to their
freedom, and a young, green forest welcomes them. The
small group, awed at first, soon sets to work on setting up
the dome, and by evening, due to the hot work, they have
dared to throw back their hoods, a first step toward change.

Marn, the main character, in a moment of rest with
Hinta, another woman, admits to her that she has never
touched another human, which is common in Ohio City, but
refuses Hinta's offer to touch her hand. Marn becomes increasingly aware, as time passes, of just how difficult this
adjustment will be for all of them. Not only are they facing
a world with unknown dangers, but they are also facing the
obsolescence of their own deeply instilled thinking and habits
regarding keeping every inch of skin hidden and not touching
another. However, Marn seems to have more difficulty with
shedding the habits than the others and is scared by the "raw
flesh" she sees when one night they all remove their masks
and chant "touch the earth" with palms in the dirt. But gradually she begins to adjust to the naked faces and to others
being able to see her feelings on her face, and they work
hard to make their new home livable.

When, on a work detail, Jurgen is bitten by a snake,
Marn reacts quickly and intelligently and helps him back to
camp, touching him without thinking in the process. And
when they arrive at camp, Hinta, going through the medical

file, discovers no antivenin exists. Marn removes her
gloves, cuts the wound with a scalpel, and has the courage
to suck the wound clean of its poison. The others, watching,
are "shocked into silence," and Marn confronts them with
"What are you gawking at? You rather he die?" The process serves to bind Marn to Jurgen, creating a much-needed
bridge for her to the world of touching others, and perhaps
breaking a barrier for the others as well. Marn has shed
her fear.

★ SARGENT, PAMELA. Watchstar. New York: Pocket
    Books, 1980.

    Main Character: Daiya AnraBrun.
    Physical Characteristics: Is 14 cycles (years) old;
has a "thick, dark curly mass" of hair; has "dark skin."
    Mental/Emotional Characteristics: Can mindspeak
(communicate with her mind) and can soothe animals to sleep
before killing them for food; can place a mental barrier
around her mind; can control her "monthly bleeding" and
ovulation by mind control; can lift objects with her mind including her own body; has the power to erase her memories;
is mentally the strongest person her lover Harel knows; can
heal herself with her mind; is willful and curious; seeks
knowledge and, in doing so, loses her ability to be mentally
open with others in her village; finds she can survive without
Harel's love; questions the concepts of God and the Merged
One; differs from her peers in that she is skeptical of the
wisdom of her people's traditions; questions the "why" of
things which no one else does, and thus creates uneasiness
among her people.
    Story Particulars: A future Earth, seemingly tech-
nologically primitive, is the setting for this novel about
Daiya, a 14-year-old villager who is very different from her
peers. Born and raised in huts in their village, and always
in touch with the minds of others (the Net), she and others
of her age group are toughening their bodies and mental powers for their "ordeal," a rite which results in death for
many.
    While Daiya is training, she stumbles upon a craft
not of this world, piloted by a boy who she realizes is a
"solitary," one who cannot mindspeak, lift himself with his
mind, or heal himself with his mental powers. Daiya knows
he is not of the Earth, for no babies who are born unable to
mind-speak are allowed to live. She and Reiho haltingly establish communication after he is able to quickly learn her

language with the assistance of Homesmind, a gigantic machine mind of his world. She learns he lives on the comet she has seen recently in the night sky, and her faith in the belief system to which her village adheres is severely shaken. Her villagers, as the people in other villages on Earth, believe that only people who are able to speak to other minds are truly human. The "ordeal" must be experienced and survived before young people are allowed to form partnerships and have children. As people grow older, they become part of the Merging Ones, community leaders, and when death comes, they are taken to live with the Merged One, or God. The boy Reiho defies all of her beliefs because he is her age, very much alive, a solitary and can speak with a mind far away, although not to her. She flees from him, erases her memories of him, and faces her ordeal with her peers, including Harel, her lover. She doubts her ability to survive it because of her uncontrollable doubts and curiosity and the "dark spot" where her memories of Reiho have been erased.

During the ordeal, Reiho once more appears, making it impossible for Daiya to see the ordeal as anything but an illusion, and ruining her chance to become one with the village. Now having no home to return to, Daiya goes with him to the mountains where he uncovers the secret of her people's power--vast towers of machinery buried, hidden beneath the mountains. She communicates with the mind of the machinery and sees the history of the Earth's people, which further shakes her belief in the village people's view of truth.

Her subsequent trip with Reiho to the comet, his home, is frightening but eye-opening for Daiya. It is there, after she speaks with Homesmind, that she decides she must return to Earth and try to make her people accept her even with her new, alien knowledge. She has learned that Reiho and his people were originally from Earth, but had not contacted it for 2000 years. Meanwhile, the Earth people remaining there continued to receive their mental powers from the machines in the mountains, but had forgotten that the machines were the source of their powers, not God.

The book's conclusion is not a resolution, but the beginning of vast changes for Earth people. Daiya, brave and courageous and isolated from the village in which she was born, finds security in the Net--not in the minds of her village's people, but in the minds of machines across the universe which are seeking "consciousness in all forms." She, at age fourteen, is mentally stronger than all the minds of her village's people combined and has seen and accepted knowledge which kills many of them. Daiya, it appears, is

destined to be the pivotal point in the changes to come, the
new awareness of people on Earth. Readers who feel out of
step with those around them and feel they are at the forefront of changes to come will probably relate to Daiya in this
novel.

★ TIPTREE, JAMES, JR. (Alice B. Sheldon). "With Delicate Mad Hands," in Out of the Everywhere. New
York: Ballantine Books, 1981.

Main Character: Carol Page or CP (also called "Snotface" and "Cold Pig" by her adolescent and adult peers, respectively).
Physical Characteristics: Is "a sweetly formed,
smallish girl of the red-hair-green-eyes-and-freckles kind"
with a face spoiled in appearance by "a huge, fleshy, obscenely
pugged nose"; has skin of "dry angry workhouse red"; is an
orphan; has herself sterilized so she can go into space; as
a sexual being, is called "a human waste can"; has certi-
fication for solo flight in space.
Mental/Emotional Characteristics: Is "a hard, smart
worker--tireless, unstoppable" aiming for "Space Crew Training"; learns "fast and well"; as a "realist," learns all the
"menial" arts, takes "a minor in space medicine," and learns
about all kinds of engines; writes poetry; is not sane; desires
only "never to be pursued, touched, known of by man or humanity" and to go to the "Empire of the Pigs" where she will
be finally at home; believes she is a "ship-wrecked traveler"
or a "spy" from the Empire of the Pigs.
Story Particulars: Orphaned, red-haired, green-eyed,
and ugly because of her pig-like nose, Carol Page (CP for
short; called Snotface by her peers), grows up with an
inner "Voice" which calls to her and guides her, and an unquenchable thirst for the stars. Her hard work and lack of
peer distraction lead to her successful completion of Space
Crew Training where she learns all "menial" arts including
"space cookery," massage, "space laundry" and "the twenty-
seven basic sexual stimulations." She also learns all about
engines, takes a minor in space medicine, and gets her pilot's license.
When assignment time comes, CP is chosen for "long-
run work," not just because of her skills, but because what
they need is "a human waste can" who will not "incite competition or any hint of tension for her services." She accepts all the menial work given to her on these runs and, in
fact, is considered lucky after a while because missions she

goes on run so smoothly. She comes to be known by her cruel adult peers as Cold Pig, because she can feel no real desire for the crew who sexually use her.

On one mission, Carol is the only pilot left to fly the fifth scout ship because the fifth pilot has a broken hip. Bob Meich, captain of the Calgary, responds to Carol's request to pilot the scout by telling her, "No cunt is going to fly off my ship while I'm breathing." He proceeds to rape her and make fun of her poetry, acts which determine his future. Carol, now insane from a lifetime of emotional abuse, poisons the remaining pilot and kills Meich in such a way that he knows she is responsible for his death. She dumps their bodies into space, and heads "outward" towards the "Empire" that she has imagined to be there somewhere, the place where she has always felt she belonged--with her people, the Pig people. Her inner Voice encourages her to change her direction, which she does even though she believes the voice is just a "delusion she knew perfectly well was born of her human need for support amid ugliness, rejection, and pain." Even knowing that she has only 140 days of oxygen left does not make her unhappy, because she is, for the first time in her life, "Alone and free among her beloved stars." She spends her days studying the "starfields on all sides" and writing down "wise, witty, or beautiful" words and "the names of a few people, mainly women, she'd respected."

Then the unexpected occurs: a star-like planet, "highly radioactive" and glowing from within, appears before her. She lands on the planet and there meets the owner of her mysterious Voice, Cavaná, a creature who looks a great deal like a kangaroo with a short tail and floppy pig-like ears. She considers Cavaná male, though she is unable to tell the sex of these beings. Cavaná, as ugly to his own people as Carol was to hers, is a Star Caller, a profession considered severe because a Star Caller must give up all for their love of the stars, and of the one with whom they make "Contact." Carol is eventually driven out onto the planet by the end of the oxygen on the ship, and the planet's radiation kills her within a few days; but during those days, Cavaná and Carol share a love which, though not consummated due to vast physical differences in the species, is "intense and silent and all-consuming." He eases the pain of her death considerably and dies with her. She is happier in the last 140 days of her life than she has ever been before. Cavaná, by the way, was female.

* VINGE, JOAN D. The Snow Queen. New York: The Dial Press, 1980; rpt. New York: Dell, 1981.

Main Character: Moon Dawntreader Summer.

Physical Characteristics: Has hair "as white as cream" and eyes "the color of mist and moss agate"; has small breasts and a slender girlish body; is beautiful.

Mental/Emotional Characteristics: Has a very strong will and desires to be a sibyl, "the Sea's daughter," with the ability to go into trance and answer any question; is "Flexible and independent"; loves deeply and devotedly; wants to make a difference in the course her world takes.

Story Particulars: It is difficult, in a way, to name only one main woman character in this epic of the period of change in the cycles of winter to summer on a world where the seasons change only once every 100 years. The novel contains Arienrhod, the Snow Queen of the world, who is strong, powerful, and visionary, but ruthless; however, the story centers upon Moon Dawntreader Summer, Arienrhod's clone and potential replacement as Queen, who is not only strong, powerful, and visionary, but also compassionate and a sibyl. (Sibyls are people who are chosen ones, infected with "a man-made disease, a biochemical reaction" which enables them to communicate instantly through space, to transfer their minds into the bodies of other sibyls, and to answer any question--because a being somewhere will know the answer.) Jerusha, as head of the planet's police force, sent from off-world, is also a powerful woman character whose story is interwoven throughout the fabric of the novel. Fate Ravenglass, a blind mask-maker, though a minor or secondary woman character in the book is the sibyl who draws Moon back to her home world after she is (accidentally and illegally) snatched from it in a smuggler getaway.

In spite of this array of characters, it is Moon's story which serves as the focus of the change from the Snow Queen (Arienrhod) to the Summer Queen (Moon); in addition, it is Moon's love for her childhood playmate, Sparks Dawntreader Summer, which Fate uses to draw Moon back to her home world. Unfortunately, the Snow Queen, as Moon's identical physical twin, also loves Sparks, and when Moon suddenly disappears from the planet, Arienrhod takes Sparks as her Starbuck (lover), which eventually lessens Spark's self-respect. Moon manages to return to her world in time to win the mask of the Summer Queen made by Fate and to perform the necessary transitional sacrifice of the Snow Queen to the sea. Restoring Spark's pride in himself and altering her world's attitude towards both sibyls and technology are challenges Moon courageously takes on at the book's conclusion.

ADDITIONAL READING LIST

Ames, Mildred. Anna to the Infinite Power. New York:
Scribner's, 1981.

Bailey, Hilary. "Everything Blowing Up: An Adventure of
Una Persson, Heroine of Time and Space," in Interfaces.
Ed. Ursula K. Le Guin and Virginia Kidd. New York:
Ace Books, 1980. (See Michael Moorcock's book on Una
Persson in the 1970s chapter reading list.)

Benford, Gregory. "Cadenza," in New Dimensions 12. Ed.
Marta Randall and Robert Silverberg. New York: Pocket
Books, 1981.

Bradley, Marion Zimmer. "Blood Will Tell," in The Keeper's Price and Other Stories. Ed. Marion Zimmer Bradley. New York: Daw Books, 1980.

_____. Hawkmistress! New York: Daw Books, 1982.

_____. "The Lesson of the Inn," in Sword of Chaos. Ed.
Marion Zimmer Bradley. New York: Daw Books, 1982.

_____. "A Sword of Chaos," in Sword of Chaos. Ed.
Marion Zimmer Bradley. New York: Daw Books, 1982.

_____, and Elisabeth Waters. "The Keeper's Price,"
in The Keeper's Price and Other Stories. Ed. Marion
Zimmer Bradley. New York: Daw Books, 1980.

Carr, Jayge. "Blind Spot," in Omni, July 1981; in The 1982
Annual World's Best SF. Ed. Donald A. Wollheim. New
York: Daw Books, 1982.

_____. Navigator's Sindrome. Garden City, NY: Double-
day, 1983. (A second book with the same woman character, The Treasure in the Heart of the Maze, is to be
published in 1984.)

_____. "The Wondrous Works of His Hands," in Alien
Encounters. Ed. Jan Howard Finder. New York: Taplinger, 1982.

Carr, Terry, and Leanne Frahm. "Horn o' Plenty," in
Stellar #7, Ed. Judy-Lynn del Rey. New York: Ballantine
Books, 1981.

Carter, Paul A.   "The Mystery of the Duplicate Diamonds,"
    in Stellar # 7.   Ed. Judy-Lynn del Rey.   New York: Bal-
    lantine Books, 1981.

Castell, Daphne.   "Household Gods," in Interfaces.   Ed. Ur-
    sula K. Le Guin and Virginia Kidd.   New York: Ace
    Books, 1980.

Charnas, Suzy McKee.   "Scorched Supper on New Niger," in
    New Voices III.   Ed. George R. R. Martin.   New York:
    Berkley Books, 1980.

Cherryh, C. J. (Carolyn Janice Cherry).   Downbelow Station.
    New York: Daw Books, 1981.   (This novel won the 1982
    Hugo Award for best novel.)

_____.   The Dreamstone.   New York: Daw Books, 1983.

_____.   Forty Thousand in Gehenna.   Huntington Woods,
    MI: Phantasia Press, 1983.

_____.   Port Eternity.   New York: Daw Books, 1982.

_____.   The Pride of Chanur, in Science Fiction Digest,
    Oct.-Nov., 1981; novelization, New York: Daw Books,
    1982.   (Took second place in the 1983 Hugo Awards.)

Christensen, Kevin.   "Bellerophon," in Destinies, Spring
    1980; in The Endless Frontier, Vol. II.   Ed. Jerry Pour-
    nelle and John F. Carr.   New York: Ace Books, 1982.

Clayton, Jo.   The Ghosthunt.   New York: Daw Books, 1983.
    (A novel of the Diadem.)

_____.   The Nowhere Hunt.   New York: Daw Books,
    1981.   (A novel of the Diadem.)

_____.   Star Hunters.   New York: Daw Books, 1980.
    (A novel of the Diadem.)

Coney, Michael.   Cat Karina.   New York: Ace Books, 1982.

Coulson, Juanita (Ruth).   Outward Bound.   New York: Bal-
    lantine Books, 1982.

Duntemann, Jeff.   "Marlowe," in Alien Encounters.   Ed. Jan
    Howard Finder.   New York: Taplinger, 1982.

Elgin, Suzette Haden (Patricia A. Suzette Elgin). <u>And Then</u>
<u>There'll Be Fireworks</u>. New York: Doubleday, 1981.
(Part of the Ozark Trilogy.)

_____. <u>The Grand Jubilee</u>. New York: Doubleday, 1981.
(Part of the Ozark Trilogy.)

_____. <u>Twelve Fair Kingdoms</u>. New York: Doubleday,
1981. (Part of the Ozark Trilogy.)

Felice, Cynthia. <u>Eclipses</u>. New York: Pocket Books, 1983.

_____. "A Good Place to Be," in <u>Chrysalis 9</u>. Ed. Roy
Torgeson. Garden City, NY: Doubleday, 1981, and New
York: Zebra Books, 1981.

_____. <u>The Sunbound</u>. New York: Dell, 1981.

_____, and Connie Willis. <u>Water Witch</u>. New York: Ace
Books, 1982.

Florance-Guthridge, George. "The Quiet," in <u>The Endless</u>
<u>Frontier, Vol. II</u>. Ed. Jerry Pournelle and John F. Carr.
New York: Ace Books, 1982.

Frankel, Linda. "Ambassador to Corresanti," in <u>The Keep-</u>
<u>er's Price and Other Stories</u>. Ed. Marion Zimmer Brad-
ley. New York: Daw Books, 1980.

Girard, Dian. "Invisible Encounter," in <u>The Endless Fron-</u>
<u>tier, Vol. II</u>. Ed. Jerry Pournelle and John F. Carr.
New York: Ace Books, 1982.

Hansen, Karl. "Sergeant Pepper," in <u>The Berkley Showcase,</u>
<u>Vol. 1, New Writings in Science Fiction and Fantasy</u>. Ed.
Victoria Schochet and John Silbersack. New York: Berkley Books, 1980.

Hewitt, Margaret C. "A Gift of Space," in <u>Stellar #6</u>. Ed.
Judy-Lynn del Rey. New York: Ballantine Books, 1980.

Holdom, Lynne. "The Way of a Wolf," in <u>Sword of Chaos</u>.
Ed. Marion Zimmer Bradley. New York: Daw Books,
1982.

Hoover, H. M. <u>The Bell Tree</u>. New York: Viking Press,
1982.

Hughes, Zach (Hugh Zachary). Thunderworld. New York:
   The New American Library, 1981.

Johnson, Annabel, and Edgar Johnson. An Alien Music.
   New York: Four Winds Press, 1982.

Kellogg, Bradley M. A Rumor of Angels. New York: The
   New American Library, 1983.

Kenin, Millea. "Where the Heart Is," in Sword of Chaos.
   Ed. Marion Zimmer Bradley. New York: Daw Books,
   1982.

Killough, Lee. "Bête et Noir," in Universe 10. Ed. Terry
   Carr. Garden City, NY: Doubleday, 1980; in Aventine.
   New York: Random House, 1981, and New York: Ballan-
   tine Books, 1982.

_____. "Corpus Crytic," in Stellar #5. Ed. Judy-Lynn
del Rey. New York: Ballantine Books, 1980.

_____. "The Lying Ear," in Alien Encounters. Ed. Jan
Howard Finder. New York: Taplinger, 1982.

_____. The Monitor, The Miners and The Shree. New
York: Ballantine Books, 1980.

Lafferty, R(aphael) A(loysius). Aurelia. Norfolk, VA: The
   Donning Company, 1982.

Lee, Tanith. "Gemini," in Chrysalis 9. Ed. Roy Torgeson.
   Garden City, NY: Doubleday, 1981, and New York: Zebra
   Books, 1981.

_____. Sabella, Or the Blood Stone. New York: Daw
Books, 1980.

Lichtenberg, Jacqueline. Mahogany Trinrose. Garden City,
   NY: Doubleday, 1981; rpt. New York: Playboy Paperbacks, 1982.

_____. Molt Brother. New York: Playboy Paperbacks,
1982.

_____. "Science Is Magic Spelled Backwards," in Hecate's
Cauldron. Ed. Susan Shwartz. New York: Daw Books,
1982.

_____, and Jean Lorrah. "The Answer," in The Keeper's Price and Other Stories. Ed. Marion Zimmer Bradley. New York: Daw Books, 1980.

Llewellyn, Edward. Prelude to Chaos. New York: Daw Books, 1983.

Lynn, Elizabeth A. The Sardonyx Net. New York: Putnam's, 1981; rpt. New York: Berkley, 1982. (Woman is one of the main characters.)

McAllister, Bruce. "Their Immortal Hearts," in Their Immortal Hearts. Reno, NV: West Coast Poetry Review, 1980.

_____. "When the Fathers Go," in Universe 12. Ed. Terry Carr. Garden City, NY: Doubleday, 1982.

McCaffrey, Anne (Inez). "Cinderella Switch," in Stellar # 6. Ed. Judy-Lynn del Rey. New York: Ballantine Books, 1980.

_____. The Coelura. Columbia, PA: Underwood-Miller, 1983.

_____. Crystal Singer. New York: Ballantine Books, 1982. (This book is based on "Prelude to a Crystal Song," "Killashandra--Crystal Singer," "Milekey Mountain," and "Coda & Finale" in Continuum 1, Continuum 2, Continuum 3, and Continuum 4, respectively. Ed. Roger Elwood. New York: Berkley, 1974, 1974, 1974, and 1975.)

McIntyre, Vonda N. Superluminal. Boston: Houghton Mifflin, 1983.

McQuillin, C. "The Forest," in The Keeper's Price and Other Stories. Ed. Marion Zimmer Bradley. New York: Daw Books, 1980.

Martine-Barnes, Adrienne. "Di Catenas," in Sword of Chaos. Ed. Marion Zimmer Bradley. New York: Daw Books, 1982.

Mathews, Patricia. "Camille," in Sword of Chaos. New York: Daw Books, 1982.

_____. "Paloma Blanca," in The Keeper's Price and

Other Stories. Ed. Marion Zimmer Bradley. New York: Daw Books, 1980.

Maxwell, Ann E. Fire Dancer. New York: The New American Library, 1982. (Two other books in this series, Dancer's Luck, and Dancer's Illusion, are due to be published by The New American Library shortly.)

_____. The Jaws of Menx. New York: The New American Library, 1981.

_____. Name of a Shadow. New York: Avon Books, 1980.

Morris, Janet (E.) Cruiser Dreams. New York: Putnam's, 1981; rpt. New York: Berkley, 1982. (This is book two in the three-part saga of the Kerrion Empire. The woman is one of the main characters.)

_____. Dream Dancer. New York: Putnam's, 1981; rpt. New York: Berkley, 1982. (The woman is one of the main characters.)

_____. Earth Dreams. New York: Putnam's, 1982; rpt. New York: Berkley Books, 1982. (The woman is one of the main characters.)

Niven, Larry (Laurence van Cott Niven). "War Movie," in Stellar #7. Ed. Judy-Lynn del Rey. New York: Ballantine Books, 1981. (Woman is one of the main characters.)

Norton, Andre (Alice). Forerunner. New York: Pinnacle Books, 1981.

_____, and Dorothy Madlee. Star Ka'ats and Winged Warriors. New York: Walker, 1981.

Offutt, Andrew J. Shadow Out of Hell. New York: Berkley, 1980; rpt. New York: Ace Books, 1983. (Woman character is one of the main characters.)

_____. The Lady of the Snowmist. New York: Ace Books, 1983. (Woman character is one of the main characters.)

Paxson, Diana L. "A Gift of Love," in Sword of Chaos. Ed. Marion Zimmer Bradley. New York: Daw Books, 1982.

Reed, Kit (Lillian Craig Reed). "Moon," in Other Stories and The Attack of the Giant Baby. New York: Berkley Books, 1981.

_____. "Pilots of the Purple Twilight," in Other Stories and The Attack of the Giant Baby. New York: Berkley Books, 1981.

Sargent, Pamela. The Alien Upstairs. Garden City, NY: Doubleday, 1983.

_____. Earthseed. New York: Harper & Row, 1983.

Schulman, J. Neil. The Rainbow Cadenza. New York: Simon & Schuster, 1983.

Shwartz, Susan M. "The Fires of Her Vengeance," in The Keeper's Price and Other Stories. Ed. Marion Zimmer Bradley. New York: Daw Books, 1980.

Silverberg, Robert. "Our Lady of the Sauropods," in Omni, Sept. 1980; in The Endless Frontier, Vol. II. Ed. Jerry Pournelle and John F. Carr. New York: Ace Books, 1982.

Tem, Steve Rasnic. "The Sound of Hawkwings Dissolving," in Chrysalis 9. Ed. Roy Torgeson. Garden City, NY: Doubleday, 1981, and New York: Zebra Books, 1981.

Tiptree, James, Jr. (Alice B. Sheldon). "Excursion Fare," in Stellar #7. Ed. Judy-Lynn del Rey. New York: Ballantine Books, 1981.

Van Scyoc, Sydney J(oyce). Darkchild. New York: Berkley, 1982. (Woman is one of two main characters. The two other books in this trilogy, Bluesong and Starsilk, are due to be published shortly.)

_____. Sunwaifs. New York: Berkley, 1981. (One of the two viewpoint characters is female.)

Varley, John (Herbert). "Blue Champagne," in New Voices IV: The Campbell Award Nominees. Ed. George R. R. Martin. New York: Berkley Books, 1981.

Vinge, Joan D. "Fool's Gold," in Galileo, Jan. 1980; incorporated into "Legacy," in Binary Star #4. Ed. James R.

Frenkel. New York: Dell, 1980. (Woman is one of two main characters.)

_____. "Psiren," in New Voices IV: The Campbell Award Nominees. Ed. George R. R. Martin. New York: Berkley Books, 1981. (Not the viewpoint character but a main character nonetheless.)

Ward, Michael. "Delta D and She," in New Dimensions 12. Ed. Marta Randall and Robert Silverberg. New York: Pocket Books, 1981.

Waters, Elisabeth. "The Alton Gift," in The Keeper's Price and Other Stories. Ed. Marion Zimmer Bradley. New York: Daw Books, 1980.

Wilhelm, Kate. Oh, Susannah! Boston: Houghton Mifflin, 1982.

Williams, Kathleen. "Circle of Light," in The Keeper's Price and Other Stories. Ed. Marion Zimmer Bradley. New York: Daw Books, 1980.

Williamson, Jack. The Queen of the Legion. New York: Pocket Books, 1983.

Yermakov, Nicholas. Epiphany. New York: The New American Library, 1982. (This novel is part of a trilogy with Last Communion, New York: The New American Library, 1981. The third book, with a working title to date of Jehad, has no scheduled publication date. A woman is one of the main characters.)

_____. Last Communion. New York: The New American Library, 1981. (This novel is part of a trilogy. See Epiphany above. A woman is one of the main characters.)

_____. Sgt. Knight. (The first in the Time Wars trilogy, having a woman character as one of three main characters. This work is currently being written.)

_____. "Tomorrow Mourning," in Chrysalis 9. Ed. Roy Torgeson. Garden City, NY: Doubleday, 1981, and New York: Zebra Books, 1982.

APPENDIX A:
Collections and Anthologies of Stories
About Women Characters

Kidd, Virginia, ed. Millennial Women. New York: Delacorte Press, 1978. Women writers speculate on futures
for women.

Laurance, Alice, ed. Cassandra Rising. Garden City, NY:
Doubleday, 1978. Women writers writing on women characters.

McIntyre, Vonda N., and Susan Janice Anderson, eds. Aurora: Beyond Equality. Greenwich, CT: Fawcett, 1976.
Women and men write about feminist characters in "non-
sexist futures."

Sargent, Pamela, ed. More Women of Wonder: Novelettes
by Women About Women. New York: Vintage Books,
1976. Collection of novelettes by women writers on women
characters.

_____, ed. The New Women of Wonder: New Science
Fiction Stories by Women About Women. New York:
Vintage Books, 1977. "Recent science fiction stories
by women about women."

_____, ed. Women of Wonder: Science Fiction Stories
by Women About Women. New York: Vintage Books, 1974.
Collection of science fiction stories by women about women.

Scortia, Thomas N., and Chelsea Quinn Yarbro. Two Views
of Wonder. New York: Ballantine Books, 1973. A theme
approach, with one woman and one man writing on each
theme. Four of the twelve stories have women main
characters.

237

The small outgrowth of sf into the erotic--perhaps a more
sophisticated version of the boy's adventure story--continues
with its steady publication of new work. Although the recur-
ring theme in many of these works is women as slaves, the
reader can usually count on there being at least one woman
character in the story merely by definition of the subject matter. The most notable erotic series at present are John Norman's Gor series, Sharon Green's Terrillian series, John
Cleve's Spaceways series, and Dominique Verseau's Yolanda
series.

John Norman's Gor is a planet in our solar system on
which women are quite happiest as slaves. Women definitely
have a place on Gor: as slaves to the men. In Anatomy of
Wonder (2nd ed., New York: R. R. Bowker, 1981) this series is called "soft-core sadomasochistic pornography housed
in SF trappings."

Another author is advertised by Daw Books in this
fashion: "If you like John Norman, you will like Sharon
Green." In Green's Terrillian books, a psychic "operative"
(called "a warrior at heart" on the back cover) is assigned
to a planet on which women--including her--are slaves.

In John Cleve's Spaceways series (PBJ Books, and now
Berkley Books), sex is presented as much more enjoyable to
both partners than in either Norman's or Green's work. The
books follow the adventures--sexual and otherwise--of a variety of characters through space and portray the enjoyment
of sex as normal and healthy for both sexes without the dom-
inance/submission theme prevalent in other erotic sf. "Romps
in Space" might be a good subtitle for the Spaceways series.

Somewhat similar to the Spaceways series in its positive

sex-is-fun approach are Dominique Verseau's Yolanda books:
Yolanda: The Girl from Erosphere (New York: Grove Press,
1975) and Yolanda: Slaves of Space (New York: Grove Press,
1976). These two books, however, are the only two English
translations of these French novels to be published in the
United States, and neither is currently in print.

Another series which might be considered erotic due
to the courtesan main character is Janet Morris's Silistra series: High Couch of Silistra, The Golden Sword, Wind from
the Abyss, and The Carnelian Throne (Bantam Books).

The list below is by no means all-inclusive. In fact, as
there is debate about what actually constitutes an amazon
woman, I have not included here many of the works that have
been annotated or listed elsewhere in this book as sf even
though some researchers consider them to be amazon fantasy.
Among the titles listed elsewhere are the following: J. D.
Beresford, Goslings; Suzy McKee Charnas, Motherlines; Jo
Clayton, Diadem from the Stars, Lamarchos, Irsud, Maeve,
Star Hunters, The Nowhere Hunt, and The Ghosthunt; Mary
E. Bradley Lane, Mizora; Tanith Lee, The Birthgrave; An-
dre Norton, Dread Companion; Doris Piserchia, Star Rider,
Earthchild, and Spaceling; John Varley, Titan; Joan Vinge,
Snow Queen; and Stanley G. Weinbaum, The Red Peri.

Abbey, Lynn. The Black Flame. New York: Ace Books,
1980. The second novel in the saga of Rifkind.

_____. Daughter of the Bright Moon. New York: Ace
Books, 1979. The first novel in the saga of Rifkind.

Baudino, Gael. "Lady of the Forest End," in Amazons II.
Ed. Jessica Amanda Salmonson. New York: Daw Books,
1982.

Belling, Michele. "The Rape Patrol," in Amazons! Ed.
Jessica Amanda Salmonson. New York: Daw Books,
1979.

Bradbury, Ray, and Leigh Brackett. "Lorelei of the Red
Mist," in Planet Stories, Summer 1946; in Isaac Asimov
Presents The Great SF Stories 8 (1946). Ed. Isaac Asi-

mov and Martin H. Greenberg. New York: Daw Books, 1982.

Bradley, Marion Zimmer. The Shattered Chain: A Darkover Novel. New York: Daw Books, 1976; rpt. Boston: Gregg Press, 1979.

Busby, F. M. "For a Daughter," in Amazons II. Ed. Jessica Amanda Salmonson. New York: Daw Books, 1982.

Carl, Lillian Stewart. "The Borders of Sabazel," in Amazons II. Ed. Jessica Amanda Salmonson. New York: Daw Books, 1982.

Cherryh, C. J. (Carolyn Janice Cherry). "The Dreamstone," in Amazons! Ed. Jessica Amanda Salmonson. New York: Daw Books, 1982; novelization The Dreamstone. New York: Daw Books, 1983.

_____. Fires of Azeroth. New York: Daw Books, 1979. The third novel of the Morgaine trilogy.

_____. Gate of Ivrel. New York: Daw Books, 1976. The first novel of the Morgaine trilogy.

_____. Well of Shiuan. New York: Daw Books, 1978. The second novel in the Morgaine trilogy.

Clayton, Jo. "Nightwork," in Amazons II. Ed. Jessica Amanda Salmonson. New York: Daw Books, 1982.

_____. Moongather. New York: Daw Books, 1982. The first in the Duel of Sorcery trilogy.

_____. Moonscatter. New York: Daw Books, 1983. The second in the Duel of Sorcery trilogy.

_____. Changer's Moon. (Proposed title of the final novel in the Duel of Sorcery trilogy, which is still being written.)

Derevanchuk, Gordon. "Zroya's Trizub," in Amazons II. Ed. Jessica Amanda Salmonson. New York: Daw Books, 1982.

Dibell, Ansen. Circle, Crescent, Star. New York: Daw Books, 1981. This second novel in the Kantmorie saga has a woman warrior who is a secondary character.

_____. Pursuit of the Screamer. New York: Daw Books,
1978. This first novel in the Kantmorie saga has a woman
warrior who is a secondary character.

_____. Summerfair. New York: Daw Books, 1982.
This third novel in the Kantmorie saga has a woman warrior who is a secondary character.

Fearn, John Russell. The Amazon Strikes Again. Kingswood,
UK: The World's Work, 1954.

_____. The Amazon's Diamond Quest. Kingswood, UK:
The World's Work, 1953.

_____. Conquest of the Amazon, serialized in the Toronto
Star Weekly, 1949; London: Futura Publications, 1976.

_____. The Golden Amazon. Kingswood, UK: The
World's Work, 1944.

_____. The Golden Amazon Returns, serialized in the
Toronto Star Weekly, 1944; rpt. Kingswood, UK: The
World's Work, 1949; retitled The Deathless Amazon.
Winnipeg: Harlequin, 1955.

_____. The Golden Amazon's Triumph. Kingswood, UK:
The World's Work, 1953.

_____. Twin of the Amazon. Kingswood, UK: The
World's Work, 1954.

Fitzgerald, Gillian. "The Battle Crow's Daughter," in
Amazons II. Ed. Jessica Amanda Salmonson. New York:
Daw Books, 1982.

Fox, Janet. "Morrien's Bitch," in Amazons! Ed. Jessica
Amanda Salmonson. New York: Daw Books, 1979.

Frank, Janrae. "Wolves of Nakesht," in Amazons! Ed.
Jessica Amanda Salmonson. New York: Daw Books,
1979.

Green, Sharon. The Crystals of Mida. New York: Daw
Books, 1982.

Howard, Robert E. "Blades for France," in The Second
Book of Robert E. Howard. New York: Zebra Books,

1976; Sword Woman. New York: Zebra Books, 1977; rpt.
New York: Berkley, 1979.

_____. "Sword Woman," in Sword Woman. New York:
Zebra Books, 1977; rpt. New York: Berkley, 1979.

_____, and Gerald W. Page. "Mistress of Death," in
Witchcraft & Sorcery, Jan./Feb. 1971; in Sword Woman.
New York: Zebra Books, 1977; rpt. New York: Berkley,
1979.

Karr, Phyllis Ann. Frostflower and Thorn. New York:
Berkley, 1980.

_____. Frostflower and Windbourne. New York: Berkley,
1982.

_____. "The Robber Girl," in Amazons II. Ed. Jessica
Amanda Salmonson. New York: Daw Books, 1982.

_____. Wildraith's Last Battle. New York: Ace Books,
1982.

Killough, Lee. "The Soul Slayer," in Amazons II. Ed.
Jessica Amanda Salmonson. New York: Daw Books,
1982.

Lee, Tanith. "Northern Chess," in Amazons! Ed. Jessica
Amanda Salmonson. New York: Daw Books, 1979. See
the following entry for a second story about this character.

_____. "Southern Lights," in Amazons II. Ed. Jessica
Amanda Salmonson. New York: Daw Books, 1982. See
the previous entry for the first story about this character.

Lindholm, Megan. "Bones for Dulath," in Amazons! Ed.
Jessica Amanda Salmonson. New York: Daw Books,
1979. See following entry for a book about this character.

_____. Harpy's Flight. New York: Ace Books, 1983.
See previous entry for a story about this character.

Lynn, Elizabeth. The Northern Girl. New York: Berkley-
Putnam, 1980; rpt. New York: Berkley, 1981.

_____. "The Woman Who Loved the Moon," in Amazons!.
Ed. Jessica Amanda Salmonson. New York: Daw Books,
1979.

Martin, George R. R.   "In the Lost Lands," in Amazons II.
    Ed. Jessica Amanda Salmonson.   New York: Daw Books,
    1982.

Mayhar, Ardath.   "Who Counts a Reluctant Maiden," in
    Amazons II.   Ed. Jessica Amanda Salmonson.   New York:
    Daw Books, 1982.

Moore, C(atherine) L(ucille).   Black God's Shadow.   West
    Kingston, RI: Donald M. Grant, 1977; retitled Jirel of
    Joiry.   New York: Ace Books, 1982.   Contents of these
    two books are identical except for the color plates in the
    Donald M. Grant edition and include five 1930s Jirel of
    Joiry novelettes.

Morgan, T. J.   "Woman of the White Waste," in Amazons!
    Ed. Jessica Amanda Salmonson.   New York: Daw Books,
    1979.

Norton, Andre (Alice).   "Falcon Blood," in Amazons!   Ed.
    Jessica Amanda Salmonson.   New York: Daw Books,
    1979.

_____. Ice Crown.   New York: The Viking Press, 1970;
    rpt. New York: Ace Books, 1981.

_____. Moon of Three Rings.   New York: The Viking
    Press, 1966; rpt. New York: Ace Books, 1981.

_____. Sorceress of the Witch World.   New York: Ace
    Books, 1968; rpt. Boston: Gregg Press, 1977.

_____. Spell of the Witch World.   New York: Daw
    Books, 1972.

_____. Trey of Swords.   New York: Grosset & Dunlap,
    1977; rpt. New York: Ace Books, 1982.

_____. Zarsthor's Bane.   New York: Ace Books, 1978.

Offutt, Andrew J., and Richard K. Lyon.   Demon in the
    Mirror.   New York: Pocket Books, 1978.   This is the
    first novel in the War of the Wizards trilogy.

_____. The Eyes of Sarsis.   New York: Pocket Books,
    1980.   This is the second novel in the War of the Wizards
    trilogy.

_____. Web of the Spider. New York: Pocket Books, 1981. This is the third novel in the War of the Wizards trilogy.

Salmonson, Jessica Amanda. The Golden Naginata. New York: Ace Books, 1982. This is the second novel about Tomoe Gozen. The third and final book in this series, Thousand Shrine Warrior, is not yet completed.

_____. "The Harmonious Battle," in Hecate's Cauldron. Ed. Susan M. Shwartz. New York: Daw Books, 1982.

_____. "The Prodigal Daughter," in Elsewhere. Ed. Terri Windling and Mark Arnold. New York: Ace Books, 1981.

_____. The Swordswoman. New York: Pinnacle Books, 1982.

_____. Tomoe Gozen. New York: Ace Books, 1981. The first book in the Tomoe Gozen Saga.

Saunders, Charles R. "Agbewe's Sword," in Amazons! Ed. Jessica Amanda Salmonson. New York: Daw Books, 1979.

Saxton, Josephine. "Jane Saint's Travails (Part One)," in Amazons! Ed. Jessica Amanda Salmonson. New York: Daw Books, 1979.

Smith, David C., and Richard L. Tierney. Red Sonja #1: The Ring of Ikribu. New York: Ace Books, 1981.

_____, and _____. Red Sonja #2: Demon Night. New York: Ace Books, 1982.

_____, and _____. Red Sonja #3: When Hell Laughs. New York: Ace Books, 1982.

_____, and _____. Red Sonja #4: Endithor's Daughter. New York: Ace Books, 1982.

_____, and _____. Red Sonja #5: Against the Prince of Hell. New York: Ace Books, 1983.

_____, and _____. Red Sonja #6: Star of Doom. New York: Ace Books, 1983.

Wittig, Monique. <u>Les Guérillères</u>. New York: The Viking
    Press, 1971; rpt. New York: Avon Books, 1973. This
    book was originally printed in France in 1969.

BIBLIOGRAPHY

Ash, Brian. The Visual Encyclopedia of Science Fiction.
New York: Crown Publishers, 1977.

Barr, Marlene S., ed. Future Females: A Critical Anthology. Bowling Green, OH: Bowling Green State University Popular Press, 1981.

Barron, Neil, ed. Anatomy of Wonder. New York: Bowker,
1981.

Contento, William. Index to Science Fiction Anthologies and
Collections. Boston: G. K. Hall, 1978.

Cornillon, Susan Koppelman, ed. Images of Women in Fiction: Feminist Perspectives. Bowling Green, OH: Bowling Green University Popular Press, 1972.

Day, Donald B. Index to the Science Fiction Magazines
1926-1950. Portland, OR: Perri Press, 1952; revised,
Boston: G. K. Hall, 1982.

Franklin, H. Bruce. Future Perfect: American Science
Fiction of the Nineteenth Century. New York: Oxford
University Press, 1966.

Lundwall, Sam J. Science Fiction: What It's All About
(English Edition). New York: Ace Books, 1971.

New England Science Fiction Association. Index to the Science Fiction Magazines 1966-1970. Cambridge, MA:
NESFA, 1971. (Other indexes available.)

Nicholls, Peter, ed. The Science Fiction Encyclopedia.
Garden City, NY: Doubleday, 1979.

247

Reginald, R. Science Fiction and Fantasy Literature: A
    Checklist, 1700-1974 (Volumes 1 and 2). Detroit, MI:
    Gale Research, 1979.

Scholes, Robert, and Eric S. Rabkin. Science Fiction: His-
    tory-Science-Vision. New York: Oxford University Press,
    1977.

Searles, Baird; Martin Last; Beth Meacham; and Michael
    Franklin. A Reader's Guide to Science Fiction. New
    York: Avon Books, 1979.

Staircar, Tom, ed. The Feminine Eye. New York: Fred-
    erick Ungar, 1982.

Tuck, Donald H. The Encyclopedia of Science Fiction and
    Fantasy Through 1968. 2 vols. Chicago: Advent, 1974
    and 1978.

Tymn, Marshall B. The Science Fiction Reference Book.
    Mercer Island, WA: Starmont House, 1981.

INDEX OF PHYSICAL AND MENTAL/EMOTIONAL
CHARACTERISTICS OF CHARACTERS
IN THE SYNOPSES

NOTE: The descriptive adjectives in this index reflect as nearly as possible the actual wording within
the works themselves. Therefore, synonymous adjectives can be found throughout this index (e.g., brave
and courageous; ambitious and competitive; fragile and
frail; frigid and inhibited; dedicated and determined;
arrogant and proud; hedonistic and sensuous; hard emotionally and heartless). For that reason, the reader
should scan the adjectives for synonyms prior to deciding that a particular characteristic has only a few
listings.

249

INDEX OF STORY PARTICULARS
OF THE SYNOPSES

NOTE: Societal structure and time setting information
has been omitted from this index if those data were
unclear from a careful reading of the work in question.
Works which were in all probability set at the time
the work was written were listed as present time. All
of the works annotated in this volume have societies
which are male dominated except for those listed under Societal Structure in this index. When two or
more themes have been appropriate for a work, all
relevant themes have been listed.

INDEX OF TITLES AND AUTHORS

An asterisk (*) denotes pages on which titles are main entries and discussed in detail.